Trouble Down the Road

APR 10

Also by Bettye Griffin

A NEW KIND OF BLISS

ONCE UPON A PROJECT

IF THESE WALLS COULD TALK

NOTHING BUT TROUBLE

THE PEOPLE NEXT DOOR

Published by Kensington Publishing Corporation

Trouble Down the Road

BETTYE GRIFFIN

KENSINGTON PUBLISHING CORP.
www.kensingtonbooks.com

DAFINA BOOKS are published by

Kensington Publishing Corp.
119 West 40th Street
New York, NY 10018

All Kensington titles, imprints, and distributed lines are available at special quantity discounts for bulk purchases for sales promotion, premiums, fund-raising, educational, or institutional use.

Special book excerpts or customized printings can also be created to fit specific needs. For details, write or phone the office of the Kensington Special Sales Manager: Attn. Special Sales Department. Kensington Publishing Corp., 119 West 40th Street, New York, NY 10018. Phone: 1-800-221-2647.

ISBN-13: 978-0-7582-3162-8
ISBN-10: 0-7582-3162-8

First Printing: May 2010
10 9 8 7 6 5 4 3 2 1

Printed in the United States of America

In memory of Chet and Micki Morris,
together again,
and
for Harry "Hickey" and Geraldine Pugh,
still together after 57 years

Acknowledgments

Bernard Underwood, Mrs. Eva Mae Griffin. Go, #29!

Elaine English, my wonderful agent.

Kimberly Rowe-Van Allen, my story consultant.

Selena James, my editor. Different editor, same story. I'm late again. (Sigh . . .)

A few very special readers: Louise Brown, Bridgete Georges, Joy Hicks, Tanya Johnson, Darlene Kramer, Dorothy Lites (also my second cousin), Victoria Owens, April Pugh, Charlotte Robinson, Shelrie Smith, Janet Williams. Thank you!

Bessie Taylor, who scooped up copies of everything I've written and insisted on getting a line all to herself. I'll give you *two* lines, Bessie!

A few special book club/reading group presidents/founders: Reneé Booker (and all the ladies in the Cozy Corner of Elegance Book Club as well), Yasmin Coleman, Ella Curry, LaShaunda Hoffman, Radiah Hubbert, Tee C. Royal.

A couple of fellow authors who are Really Nice People: Donna Deloney, Marcia King-Gamble, Shelia Goss, Reon Laudat, Sean D. Young.

Chapter 1

"*Aimeriez-vous une autre bière, monsieur?*"
Suzanne focused a narrowed gaze on her hostess. She didn't want some other woman saying anything to her husband that she didn't understand. She only knew one French phrase, that *voulez-vous* line from a lyric to an old Labelle song. That translated to the rather tacky proposition, "Will you go to bed with me?" Micheline Trent hadn't said *that* to Brad, but judging from that broad smile on her face and the soulful look in her eyes, she might as well have. Suzanne had been in the Trent home for less than thirty minutes, but she already was ready to shove Micheline's face into the cheese dip that sat in a bowl on the table.

When Micheline disappeared, returning moments later with a can of Miller Genuine Draft, Suzanne figured out what she'd said to Brad. Nothing wrong with offering to refill a guest's pilsner, but she frowned with tightened lips when Micheline leaned over to pour the beer, the right side of her tailored white blouse falling away from her chest enough to reveal a glimpse of unspectacular cleavage in a scalloped white bra that nonetheless seemed to capture Brad's attention.

Micheline's demonstration lasted just a few brief seconds, but every muscle in Suzanne's body went on alert. To think she'd actually been happy about coming here to watch the

Super Bowl. When Brad told her they'd been invited to watch the game at the home of one of the guys from the golf club, she'd been thrilled not to have to spend the evening with their neighbors, Lisa and Darrell Canfield. Suzanne had tried to put a good face on it to appease Brad, but since the Canfields ranked among her least favorite people, she figured anyone's company would be better than theirs. It looked like she'd been wrong.

And she needed to get the point across to Micheline that Brad Betancourt was a prize that belonged in *her* box of Cracker Jack.

Suzanne watched as Micheline returned to sit next to her husband, Errol, cozying up to him in an oversized chair that was more like a small love seat; two people could fit on it, provided they didn't carry too many pounds between them. Without even realizing it, Suzanne moved her hand to rest on Brad's thigh, as if staking out her territory . . . or perhaps to try to make up after the words they'd had on the short drive over here.

Her gaze shifted from the uninteresting action playing out on the screen of the large plasma television to her hosts. Micheline's head rested on Errol's shoulder, and his arm was draped around her. The affection between them seemed genuine enough. Suzanne reconsidered. Could she have just imagined Micheline's come-on to Brad? After all, Errol sat right there in the same room, along with five other guests. A person would have to be some kind of idiot to even try to carry on a flirtation with so many witnesses.

Or crafty as hell.

One of the players was running with the football, and everyone in the room either cheered or jeered. Suzanne, who knew nothing about football, took her cue from Brad, who cheered. Out of the corner of her eye she saw Micheline throw her arms around Errol and embrace him. Errol shifted to face her, his hand roaming dangerously high over her thigh, to where the hem of her short denim skirt met her skin. A laughing Micheline playfully smacked it away, with a hiss of, "Later!"

Suzanne began to feel better. Micheline already had a husband who was good-looking, sexy, and successful. She'd probably just wanted to test her French on someone who understood a little of the language. This was Jacksonville, not New York or New Orleans. How many people here spoke French? Even Brad's knowledge of it was limited to a few basic phrases he'd learned for a trip to Paris they took a few years back. Micheline likely knew no more than he did. And as far as the opportunity Brad had to look down Micheline's blouse, she probably just didn't realize it had fallen away from her chest when she bent over. So what if Brad got to peek into her cleavage. It was a natural action. Wouldn't *her* eyes have lingered if she saw an attractive man pulling off his shirt?

Suzanne chided herself for being so paranoid. The last thing she wanted to become was one of those women who felt that every other member of the species was after her man. It probably had to do with the feeling she'd had lately that she couldn't shake—the fear that something wasn't quite right in her marriage. The conversation she and Brad had on the way over here didn't help any.

Once again she glanced at the Trents, sitting so companionably in the oversized chair. What an attractive couple they made. Brad had met Errol when they served together at a traveling clinic that passed through Jacksonville as it moved all about the country to provide medical and dental checkups and minimal treatments for a nominal fee to those without insurance, and he recommended Errol for membership in the golf club he belonged to. Suzanne had been surprised to see how young the Trents were. Memberships at the golf club didn't come cheap, and most of the members were in their forties, fifties, and sixties. But of course, Errol Trent was some kind of dentist—an oral surgeon, Brad had said—and could probably afford it. She put his age in the mid to upper thirties, while Micheline appeared to be about thirty.

Thirty. Suzanne swallowed past a lump in her throat. How nice it would be if she could be that age again. She'd be forty-two this year and was acutely aware of getting older. Her son Bradley was fifteen and way taller than she was. Being around younger women like Micheline gave Suzanne the unwelcome feeling of being past her prime.

Right after the first quarter, Micheline announced she was bringing out the refreshments. Suzanne quickly offered to help, not so much to be of assistance but to maybe get a chance to chat privately with her hostess, get a better feel for her personality. She seemed like a fun type. Maybe they could even get to be friends. Suzanne didn't play golf, but she'd go down to the club and wait for Brad to come off the links if she had a friend there she could have dinner with.

"Everything's so lovely, Micheline. Did you do this all yourself?" she asked as she admired a tray of honey-dipped chicken drumettes Suzanne removed from the oven, where they'd been keeping warm.

"Sure. It was easy."

"I guess it helps that the Super Bowl is on a Sunday, huh? It gives you the whole weekend to prepare." Suzanne watched as Micheline removed a raw vegetable tray from the refrigerator, taking it from her so she could retrieve other foods. "I always liked the idea of having the big game on a Friday night, but I guess that would make preparation difficult for women who aren't stay-at-home moms like me." Suzanne did enjoy informing people that she was a homemaker and had been for years. Many of the wives of Brad's colleagues had high-powered careers, but her status as housewife and stay-at-home mother excused her from having to discuss a professional life.

"Well, I might not be a mom, but I don't work."

Suzanne nearly dropped the tray. A few cherry tomatoes did fall off before she placed it down on the countertop. She swiftly replaced them. "Oh. You don't?" She didn't understand. The Trents had no children. What was Micheline doing staying at home?

She quickly answered her own question. Like herself, Micheline had simply opted to stop working because she didn't have to. It was one thing to practice medicine or law, teach school, or even run your husband's office. But if you had no training to do anything of substance, why go out and punch a clock every day for ten dollars an hour when your husband brought in big bucks?

Suzanne listened intently as Micheline explained she had been ill at the time of her marriage to Errol and that he insisted she stay home to recuperate. Micheline concluded her explanation with a shrug. "One thing just led to another. It's been almost three years, but Errol has never pushed me to go back to work. I think he enjoys having dinner ready when he gets home, or being able to invite guests over for dinner on a weeknight. I won't say I haven't enjoyed taking a break from working, but after all this time I'm starting to get a little restless. I'll probably start job hunting soon."

"I hope you won't have too hard a time. It's a tough job market out there." Suzanne forced herself to sound sympathetic, but she couldn't understand why Micheline would want to shelve books at the library or deal with irate callers on a customer service line somewhere when she could stay at home.

Micheline removed a large glass bowl containing tossed salad from the extra-wide refrigerator. "I don't expect to have that difficult a time. There's a lot of law firms in town."

"Law firms?" Suzanne repeated uncertainly.

"Yes. I'm a bilingual paralegal, English and Spanish. Of course, I speak French, too, but not for work." Then Micheline asked, "What did *you* do before you had your kids, Suzanne?"

"Bilingual, huh? How interesting." So Micheline *wasn't* like her, a high school graduate with no professional work experience. Now that the ball was in Suzanne's court, she scrambled to come up with an answer that wouldn't make her sound insignificant. "Before my son was born I . . . uh, worked with patients at a diagnostic center."

"Oh. X-ray technician?"

Suzanne wanted to say yes, but she couldn't take the chance of exposure if Micheline asked for details of her work that she couldn't supply, or worse, mentioned something about her former "career" to Brad. "Actually, I ran the office." That wasn't true, either, but she couldn't say that she'd merely greeted patients and set up appointments for radiologic screenings and follow-ups, not after Micheline said she was a paralegal. Suzanne wasn't even completely sure what that was other than it had something to do with the law, but it sounded pretty important. Micheline must really know Spanish inside and out if she spoke it on the job. And she knew French, too? Suzanne didn't think she'd ever met anyone who spoke three languages, not even among those in Brad's circle. Micheline had somewhat of an exotic look about her, with those almond-shaped eyes that had a golden tint to them. Suzanne wondered if she was Spanish or French. She looked more Spanish, but her name sounded more French.

"Did you work at Brad's diagnostic center?" Micheline guessed.

"As a matter of fact, yes. That's where we met. He and his first wife were divorcing at the time." That wasn't exactly the truth, either. Brad was very much married when Suzanne was hired for the reception desk.

Suzanne still remembered the jealousy she'd felt toward Lisa Betancourt from the moment she saw her framed photograph on Brad's desk. Lisa was pretty, had reclaimed her figure after giving birth, plus she worked as a pharmacist. Suzanne always had the same thought whenever Lisa stopped by the office to see Brad: *Who is this woman to have so much, while I have next to nothing?* Lisa would flounce in and ask for Brad in a pleasant but impersonal manner that nonetheless made Suzanne feel like, well, the help. Never mind if she *was* an employee. Lisa had a way about her that made Suzanne feel about three feet tall.

Sometimes Lisa would bring their cute toddler daughter, Paige, with her on visits to Brad at the office. Suzanne hated them both. Not only did Lisa have poise and intelligence, but she had style as well. She knew how to pair a tailored blouse and expensive-looking leather flats with jeans in a way that looked downright elegant, and how to add little accessory touches like tying a silk scarf around the strap of her shoulder bag. As for little Paige, she was just too adorable, even then with a strong resemblance to her mother. Suzanne learned from staff gossip that Lisa came from a family in Georgia who had been major players in the civil rights movement of the sixties. Important people had come to their home.

Suzanne, on the other hand, had grown up in Palatka, Florida, the eldest child of teenage parents who married four months before her birth. The marriage almost immediately went on the rocks, but a reconciliation years later resulted in two sons and a brief period of nuclear family life before the marriage busted up for good. Suzanne had only seen her father, Derrick Hall Sr., a few times since. Suzanne's mother, Arlene, later had an affair with a younger man that resulted in an unplanned pregnancy. Arlene's lover was long gone by the time she gave birth, and she gave new her baby daughter the same last name as her other children, Hall.

Theirs had been a hardscrabble childhood, with telephone and electricity often being turned off. They never really went hungry, but they often ate unorthodox meals, like melted cheese sandwiches for breakfast or pancakes for dinner. Their house—not much more than a shack, actually—which Arlene took over after her parents passed away, was always in need of repairs. The roof leaked, the faucets had to be turned gingerly or else they would fall off, and the water heater worked intermittently.

While Lisa had gone to college and then pharmacy school, Suzanne had gotten a job after high school to help her mother pay the bills. It didn't seem like a big deal. Suzanne's intelligence wasn't geared toward books and learning; she was more savvy than smart.

So there she was, looking on enviously as little Paige ran to her father's arms, as Brad laughingly scooped her up and draped an arm around Lisa. Then the attractive family would stroll back into his office, like they didn't have a care in the world.

Even Brad himself had little to say to her back in those early days. Suzanne doubted he even knew her name. But then something happened. Lisa's visits became less frequent and then stopped altogether, and the office scuttlebutt was that the Betancourt marriage had crumbled.

Suzanne engaged in watchful waiting, and the moment Brad removed Lisa's photograph from his desk she tentatively knocked on his office door and asked if he could answer a few questions about medicine for a school paper her little sister was doing. That had been a fabrication, of course, but he had taken the time to answer her questions, which led to him asking about her family, which led to him asking about *her*. . . . Suzanne did her best to be sparkling and enchanting. She recognized that Brad was lonely and uncertain from the breakup of his marriage, and she wanted to be the one who brought laughs and fun back into his life. It seemed only natural for Brad to ask her to join him for dinner, and from that point on neither of them ever looked back.

The only sticky point in their marriage was when, as they prepared to move into their dream house in Jacksonville, they learned that the house under construction next door was being built by none other than Lisa and her second husband, Darrell Canfield. Sometimes Suzanne still couldn't believe that such a crazy thing had happened. Brad decided he wanted to live closer to Jacksonville rather than the remote area where they formerly resided on the outskirts of St. Augustine, well south of the city. He purchased a newly constructed home on a riverfront cul-de-sac from a colleague whose marriage had broken up. He and Suzanne didn't learn that the house under construction next door belonged to Lisa and Darrell until after they closed, when the entire Canfield family pulled up to inspect the progress of the construction. The already existing tension between Suzanne and Lisa had only gotten worse once they became neighbors. In the five years since, they'd managed to make the best of it. Suzanne treated Lisa politely to make Brad happy, and she suspected that Lisa tolerated her at Darrell's insistence.

"Well, *that* was a lucky break," Micheline said now. "I'm sure you were only too glad to offer comfort and a shoulder to cry on to the boss during his time of trouble. And look what ended up happening," she concluded brightly.

It was all Suzanne could do not to pick up the deviled eggs from the tray Micheline had removed from the refrigerator and hurl them at her. Micheline had her figured like a carefully executed chess move. Instinct told Suzanne that Micheline knew all about how she'd schemed to land Brad and was making fun of her.

Suzanne managed to control her temper and get to her point. "Well, it all happened a long time ago. We've been married sixteen years," she said, her voice steady with pride.

"Sixteen years! My, my. How old are your children, Suzanne?"

"Our son is fifteen and our daughter is thirteen."

"Wow. They're almost grown up. When you said you were a stay-at-home mom, I imagined your kids were much younger. It's been what, eight or ten years since they started school?"

Once more Suzanne's hackles were raised. Micheline was getting bolder. She'd practically come out and called her a lazybones for staying home while her children were teenagers. Suzanne straightened her spine, her shoulders back and chest out. *If it's war she wants, it's war she'll get.* "It's true they're older," she said pleasantly, "but there's still plenty to do. My son plays basketball, and my daughter and I go to most of his games in the afternoons. And I like to be there to watch my daughter run track. Besides, with me being home and then knowing I'll be home after they get out of school, there's no hanky-panky with friends of the opposite sex. Teenagers can get into all kinds of trouble when they're not supervised." She smiled and smugly said, "But of course, you have to be a mother to understand that."

"Yes, I suppose so." Micheline clapped her palms against her hips after setting down more dishes from the refrigerator. "That's everything. Can you help me carry these to the table, Suzanne?"

"Sure. That's why I'm here." She sounded as cheerful as she felt.

She'd just put her hostess in her place.

Chapter 2

"**N**ice couple, huh?" Brad remarked as he climbed behind the wheel of the Cadillac SRX he'd downsized to after turning in his massive, gas-guzzling Escalade.

"Charming." Suzanne had to fight to keep the sarcasm she felt out of her voice. All the bad vibes she had initially detected from Micheline Trent came back during their encounter in the kitchen, and this time they were there to stay. No one in attendance was as happy as Suzanne when the game ended and they could leave. As uncomfortable as she felt around Brad's first wife, Lisa Canfield, Suzanne would have preferred to have spent the evening with her and Darrell than with that slinky bitch Micheline. At least Lisa only spoke to Brad in English . . . and she didn't flirt with him at all. "Uh . . . is this your first time meeting Micheline?"

"No, I've met her a couple of times before. She comes to the club and meets Errol for dinner. Sometimes she plays."

Suzanne's acknowledgment came out as a grunt. Another reason for her to dislike Micheline. She played golf, a sport Brad was crazy about that Suzanne had no interest in.

"Errol talks about her all the time," Brad continued. "He's crazy about her. They've only been married a few years. You know how it is."

She looked at him sharply. Was he saying that love diminished after a few years? They'd been married a long time now.

Yes, they'd been under some strain lately, but surely he loved her as much now as he did in those early days . . . didn't he?

Suzanne's annoyance toward Micheline Trent transformed into cold fear for her own future. If Brad got tired of her, what on earth would she do? She was past forty. Brad would soon be fifty, but age didn't matter for men, unless, of course, they were fat, ugly, and poor, none of which applied to him.

Once more she remembered how Micheline bent over Brad and how his gaze lingered on her cleavage. She wasn't sure if Micheline was up to something or not, but she decided to nip it in the bud and send a clear signal that Brad was off-limits.

She was silent for a few moments as she thought of how she could accomplish that. "Brad," she finally said, "I was thinking it might be a nice idea to celebrate your fiftieth birthday with a really nice party. What do you think?"

"Sounds good to me. Are you sure you wouldn't rather take a vacation somewhere, maybe a cruise? Your mother can take care of the kids while we're away."

The thought of romance on the high seas held plenty of appeal and would probably help them strengthen their some-what shaky bond, but she also wanted to get the point across to Micheline Trent that she and Brad had not only a happy marriage, but a strong one, and to tell her to butt out. A party, on the other hand, held at their home with Micheline present, would do the trick. Suzanne would make it the party to end all parties. "No, I think I'd rather do the party," she said after a few moments' thought. "Maybe we can go up to Maine this summer." What she and Brad really needed was time alone, not to be on a cruise ship with hundreds of other people, even if Brad had a tendency to spend much of his time fishing when they were up in New England.

"All right, a party it is," Brad said. "Be sure to invite the Trents."

"I wouldn't dream of overlooking them," she replied sweetly.

Brad grunted. "It's probably just as well we don't ask your mother for any favors, babysitting or otherwise."

Suzanne tensed her shoulders. He'd complained about her mother on the way over. Was he about to start in on her again? She vowed to stay cool and just let him blow off steam. She couldn't really blame him for being frustrated about her mother always being late with her rent, but it was her *mother*. What was she supposed to do?

"It's probably better if don't ask her for any favors if I end up not renewing her lease," he remarked.

She gasped. Venting was one thing. Putting her mother out on the street was something else. "Well, that's a little extreme, don't you think?"

"She's been late with the rent four times in the last six months, Suzanne. The terms of her lease say I don't have to offer her a renewal if she's late more than three times."

Suzanne looked straight ahead at the curving roadway and tried to convince herself that he was bluffing. He wouldn't actually evict her family. This had been a source of contention between her and Brad for months now. She thought if she just rode it out, it would go away, but it seemed to be getting worse. "I'd really like to stay out of this, Brad."

"I'm sorry I even rented to her," he muttered.

"You know, Brad, Mom's been working all the overtime she can get."

"Suzanne, your mother knew how much the rent was when she signed the lease. If it was too much for her, she shouldn't have agreed to take the house. She could have stayed in that apartment she had. It was less money."

He had a point, and she knew it, but to agree would be disloyal to her mother. "That apartment was a dump. You don't realize how hard it is for her, Brad. I think only Matthew is giving her any money for household expenses." Suzanne hoped she could evoke sympathy from him, but his next words told her he remained unmoved.

"That's ridiculous. Your mother has three grown children living under her roof, and they all work. If she declines to accept any money from them, she'll have to make up the shortfall herself and not complain that it's too much."

"Come on, Brad. Kenya only makes a little past minimum wage. And Derrick works for you. You *know* how little he earns."

"Matthew is a medical records clerk, Suzanne. He probably makes only a little more than I pay Derrick to run my Subway franchise. The difference is that Matthew is trying to help your mother out, while Derrick only thinks of Derrick."

"That's not fair, Brad," Suzanne said defensively. "Derrick has a child to support. Matthew doesn't."

"I don't believe for one minute that Derrick is supporting his daughter. Matthew is looking toward the future, but I think Derrick looks upon managing a sandwich shop as a career."

She knew he was probably right. Matthew, who used to be every bit as much of a freeloader as Derrick, had developed ambition, while Derrick had not. But it was her entire family's future that she was worried about. She decided to ask him straight out about his intentions as he turned the corner onto their cul-de-sac. "Brad, are you going to evict my mother?"

He sighed. "I guess that's really not necessary. But the late fees will continue to accumulate every time she's late."

"Doesn't that seem a little heartless, Brad? I mean, she *is* my mother."

"Suzanne, you'll recall how reluctant I was to let her rent the house in the first place. I warned her then that the agent would enforce every term of the lease, and that if she didn't have the full amount of the rent in by the first of the month she'd have to pay a fifty-dollar fine, plus ten more dollars each day until she paid it. She said it would be no problem. *You* said it would be no problem."

Suzanne did remember, but she could hardly admit it. Instead she recalled her mother pleading with her to get Brad to stop the late charges. She'd tried to get her mother to understand that they had a contract with the property managers, and that they were the ones who imposed and pocketed the late fees, not her and Brad. But her mother wasn't having it and insisted that Brad could stop it if he wanted to.

"And now that there's a problem, you want me to forget about having warned her and just look the other way," Brad pointed out as he activated the remote control for the garage door, then brought the truck to a stop next to the sports car parked inside. "This is precisely why you should never rent to family. So maybe you need to talk to her about getting some money out of Derrick and Kenya to help her get the rent paid on time."

Suzanne stared straight ahead. Maybe that's what she did need to do. Not only did she have to get the message across to Micheline Trent to lay off Brad, she also had to get her mother to start paying her rent on the first of every month.

Her nice, easy life was suddenly becoming a lot more complicated.

Chapter 3

Lisa Canfield tore open the printed invitation. She knew her first husband's birthday was coming up, and she knew he'd be fifty. It didn't surprise her to see that he and Suzanne were giving a party to mark the milestone.

"What's that?" her mother-in-law, Esther, asked. "Is someone getting married?"

"No. It looks like a wedding invitation, but it's actually for Brad's fiftieth birthday party."

"Oh, yes. Arlene mentioned it when I ran into her at Walgreens. She said it's going to be the party to end all parties."

Esther, who lived with her only son and his family, and Suzanne's mother, Arlene, who visited Suzanne so often she might as well live with the Betancourts, both had an interest in gardening. Over the years they'd become, if not exactly friends, congenial acquaintances. Lisa had to admit that Arlene Hall did have a green thumb. The Betancourts' house had the nicest landscaping on the block, plentiful without looking like a jungle.

Lisa rolled her eyes. "I guess that means Stevie Wonder will be providing the entertainment. Can you believe it? They actually included admission passes. Who does Suzanne think she is, Oprah?"

"You mean we can't get in without a pass?"

"That's right. They sent four of them. One for Darrell and

me, one for you, and one each for Paige and Devon and their dates." Lisa and Darrell had a remarkably easy time blending their families, as their daughters were just three months apart and loved the idea of becoming sisters. The twin boys they had together, now fourteen years old, completed the unit.

"I'm sure it'll be lovely. But speaking of dates, do you think Paige will invite her new young man?"

"I can't imagine her not inviting him, Ma Canfield."

"Don't you think that'll be a little awkward, under the circumstances?"

"I'm sure it will be," Lisa replied easily. "But they're all adults now. They can handle it."

Esther flashed a knowing smile. "Come on, Lisa. You know this will make Suzanne furious. Aren't you enjoying that thought just a little?"

"I cannot tell a lie," Lisa replied, laughing. "But I'll tell you. I always figured it would happen eventually. I just didn't know if it would involve Paige or Devon. And I can't wait to see the look on Suzanne's face when she sees who Paige shows up with."

Flo Hickman dropped the rest of the day's mail when she saw the Betancourts' return address on the square beige envelope. Not bothering to retrieve the other mail at her feet, she instead tore open the envelope in her hand, holding her breath as she read it.

Oh, my God. An invitation to Suzanne's house.

This had to mean that she and Ernie had truly made a comeback. She couldn't remember the last time they'd been invited to that gorgeous showplace of a house around the corner. She'd tried to talk herself out of wanting to be part of that crowd after Ernie was downsized three years ago. Their financial situation took a dangerous dip that would have been fatal to many, but she and Ernie rolled up their sleeves and tackled the problem. They filled an empty bedroom with a boarder to help pay the mortgage, plus they went into financial counseling to pay off mounds of credit card debt from purchases of big-ticket items they really couldn't afford. She'd taken all the overtime she could at her job doing medical coding, and even with the replacement job Ernie landed, which paid much less than the one he'd lost, he still had to work part-time at a restaurant to meet their substantial monthly obligations.

But Ernie insisted he had to get his bachelor's degree if he didn't want to moonlight in a restaurant kitchen forever. His layoff came after the company he worked for merged with another, leaving two people in each management position. Since he only had an associate's while his counterpart had a full four-year college education, he'd been the one eliminated. Ernie cried racism publicly, but privately he told Flo that without his degree, he'd never get another human resources manager position. Flo couldn't argue with his logic, but she didn't like the stress that put on her. In the end she started moonlighting with a part-time job and Ernie quit his second job and spent his evenings taking night classes. With his new degree plus his experience, he landed a manager position at a newly built hospital in the next county.

The final step back, after Ernie's new job, was refinancing their house. They took all the cash they could out of it, which they used to pay off their creditors and get the financial counseling people off their backs. This step resulted in their having virtually no equity in a home they'd lived in for nearly ten years, but they both felt it was the right thing to do.

They couldn't possibly have foreseen the real estate crash that was just around the corner. It worried Flo that they owed more on their house than it was worth, but Ernie assured her the market would rebound eventually and that they could live like they used to. So she quit her second job and they told their longtime renter—a college student they'd told neighbors was the son of family friends—that he'd have to leave at the end of the semester. Flo missed the check he gave them every month, although it did feel nice to have just themselves and Gregory living in the house with no outsiders.

Flo and Suzanne Betancourt had gotten to be pretty chummy before the bottom fell out for her and Ernie. They would go out to lunch and afterward go shopping, even if Flo ended up taking her expensive purchases back to the store for a refund when Suzanne wasn't looking. Even then, Flo and Ernie had been on the road to financial ruin, but they'd worked hard to project wealth and status to their neighbors and to be recognized as the black couple with an enviable lifestyle. They found it upsetting when the Betancourts bought that expensive new house on the shores of the St. Johns River, just across from downtown Jacksonville. Ernie insisted that Brad and Suzanne didn't have anything they couldn't afford to buy themselves if they wanted, and when Flo told him that was ridiculous, reminding him that Brad was a radiologist, he stubbornly held on to his belief.

They both agreed to befriend the Betancourts and to link alliances, feeling this was their only option, but Flo had been much more successful with Suzanne than Ernie had with Brad. Suzanne opened up to Flo, confiding how unhappy it made her to have Brad's former wife and their daughter living right next door to them.

Flo liked to tell herself that Suzanne dropped her socially because with Ernie's job loss they couldn't keep up financially, but in the back of her mind she knew Ernie probably played a role in it. Flo loved her husband unconditionally, but knew that he could sometimes be a tad overbearing. She feared he'd alienated Brad Betancourt from the start, asking inappropriate questions about financial matters and hinting for an invitation to the Betancourts' cabin up on a Maine lake. Flo had hoped that with their son Gregory dating Suzanne's sister, Kenya, Suzanne would at least invite her and Ernie over for dinner or something, but that hadn't happened.

But at least they'd been invited to the party. She'd have to get a new dress, and a manicure and pedicure as well, so she could wear open-toed shoes. Her eyebrows would have to be waxed. She studied her hairline. Thank God her weave was only six weeks old and still fresh looking.

The Hickmans were about to reenter the Jacksonville version of high society.

Micheline placed the invitation on the refrigerator, holding it in place with a decorative magnet. An invitation to the Betancourts'. The timing couldn't be better.

In the three months since she and Errol had hosted a Super Bowl party, she'd seen Brad a number of times at the golf club. She and Errol often had dinner there, since meals were included in that outrageous annual membership fee he paid. She played the part of beautiful, charming, and cultured wife, hoping to make Brad envious of Errol.

She wondered how Brad stood being married to an airhead like Suzanne. During a boring halftime performance by an over-the-hill rock 'n' roller they'd talked about the latest political happenings, and Suzanne had a look on her face that said she wished they'd change the subject. That girl had just plain lucked out with Brad. She was probably all over him like a cheap plaid suit from the day she'd been hired to work at his place of business. Why else would a cultured, educated man like Brad even notice her?

Micheline thought she'd bust out laughing in the kitchen that day when Suzanne haughtily defended being a stay-at-home mother to teenagers by saying that a woman had to be a mother to understand. Suzanne obviously felt that giving Brad a couple of kids elevated her to demigod status. It had been a dig intended to get her where it was supposed to hurt. Suzanne probably decided that Micheline had no children after three years of marriage because she had difficulty conceiving and wanted to rub salt in the wound. The truth was that Micheline had no desire for motherhood. She'd been tempted to shoot this back at Suzanne, but a wiser head prevailed and she kept her mouth shut. That was a detail about herself that she'd shared with no one, not even Errol. The key here was to listen and learn, not to strike back.

She grinned. When she *did* strike back, Suzanne wouldn't know what had hit her. And neither would Errol.

Married life had turned out to be a real bust. When Errol proposed to her, he said he wanted to be the one to make all her dreams come true. She believed him, but before the first year of their marriage was over she'd become convinced he wasn't the man of her dreams after all. He complained incessantly about the money she spent, which was ridiculous. He could spend thousands to join a golf club, but he squawked if she bought a few outfits or pairs of shoes?

In their newlywed days he'd insisted she not go right back to work after the "trauma" she suffered. Micheline had actually gotten pregnant as the result of a torn condom during a one-night stand with a married man, but she told Errol the pregnancy had resulted from a rape and that she planned to give up the baby for adoption. That part had been true, and it had been a lot easier than Micheline had anticipated. When she informed the man she'd slept with of her pregnancy, he immediately offered to take the baby. It turned out his wife had fertility problems, and the resulting stress on their marriage had been what had led him to sleep with Micheline in the first place. That had been a complication with a happy ending, but the more complex circumstance, the one that haunted Micheline to this day, was that the baby's adoptive mother was a close friend of Micheline's sister, Cécile.

Even Micheline hadn't planned that little twist. She didn't know if Vic Bellamy had ever told his wife that the child they were raising was biologically his, or if he'd convinced her that someone left the baby on their doorstep. The latter scenario was ludicrous, of course, but adoptions had become big business, and women who wanted babies and were unable to have them could be desperate. Vic had made it sound like his wife was about to go off the deep end. Micheline hadn't realized that pregnancy would come as easy to her as it had for Cécile, who had four kids. One thing for sure—she never planned to have another pregnancy. Micheline knew she possessed neither the patience nor the nurturing skills necessary to raise children. Maybe that would change, but she doubted it. She was already thirty.

Cécile just about had a cow when she found out the part Micheline played in the drama. Micheline merely shrugged and went on. Let Cécile and her friends live their boring little lives, lives filled with raising brats and having same-old sex with their husbands.

No, that wasn't true. Norell's husband, Vic, had been a fabulous lover. She thought he might be good because he was so fit and trim, but because he'd been past fifty, it came as a pleasant surprise to find out just *how* good.

That was one bright spot in her marriage to Errol. His sexual appetite was as voracious as hers, and the action in their bedroom was never boring. But in every other way he was all wrong. He'd even suggested to her that she go back to work to take her mind off of her inability to get pregnant.

She chuckled at the irony. That inability was pure fiction. She could probably get knocked up faster than a person could say "nine months." The unexpected pregnancy from one incidence of a torn condom attested to that. She simply made up fertility woes so that Errol, who wanted children, would keep her at home longer.

He'd begun to show a little impatience with the situation lately, though, and she couldn't blame him. She was only thirty, but Errol was thirty-eight. They hadn't been trying for their entire marriage, but for at least half of it. Lately he'd expressed that they should begin a workup to investigate the problem. Errol was a good guy, and Micheline knew she wasn't being fair to him. She reasoned that it would be even less fair for her to have his babies feeling the way she did. If it weren't for the occasional social event at Cécile's that Errol insisted they go to, she would never even see the baby girl she gave birth to three years ago. It satisfied Micheline to know the child, who'd been named Brianna, was being raised by loving parents in a good home.

Micheline knew she wouldn't be able to string Errol along forever. The time had come to find a new husband, one who wouldn't object to a little clothes buying on her part, and one who already had kids—kids who lived with their mother and wouldn't get in the way, of course—and didn't want any more. Her gut told her that the still handsome and sexy Brad Betancourt was a prime candidate.

She smiled dreamily at the invitation. Brad was about to turn fifty himself. Something told her his bedroom skills were every bit as sharp as Vic Bellamy's.

Micheline intended to do everything in her power to find out.

All she had to do was get rid of Suzanne.

Chapter 4

Suzanne surveyed the public areas of the house. Much to her annoyance, her regular housekeeper, Teresita, was off for the week. Not only did Teresita know the house better than anyone, but she did an excellent job. A local agency specializing in housekeepers had sent a temporary replacement, but the woman was slow moving and missed a lot of areas. She'd come in three times this week, and each time Suzanne had to point out to her that the tables were streaked and that there were still spots on the tiled floor. Unfortunately, this same woman would be on duty for tonight's party.

Suzanne sighed wearily at the prospect. She'd offered to pay Teresita double time if she'd come in and work the night of the party, but her longtime housekeeper refused. Of all the lousy luck that Brad's birthday fell on the same weekend as the double celebration Teresita and her husband were hosting for their two children, who had just graduated from high school and college, respectively. They had family members coming in from all over the state to join in the festivities. Suzanne supposed she couldn't blame Teresita for turning her down. Two graduations was a big deal for any family. She just wished they were having their party some other weekend.

At least it looked like Teresita's substitute finally got it right this time, Suzanne thought with satisfaction when she failed to notice anything amiss. Maybe she could relax a bit before starting to dress.

She turned to go to her bedroom, then made a last-minute detour into the kitchen, where her friend Paula Haines was busy with food preparation. "You okay in here?" she asked.

"Fine. I love working in your kitchen, girl. It's a cook's dream."

Paula wore a tank top, sweatpants, and flip-flops. Her long hair was pulled back into a ponytail, and her forehead was covered with a thin sheen of perspiration. Suzanne knew from other events Paula had catered for them that she would slip away after her staff arrived to change and apply makeup. She'd emerge looking like a guest. But it was warm in the kitchen, with numerous pots going on five burners and the oven on as well. The granite countertops were covered with bowls of chopped onion and peppers, spice jars, stoneware, different types of drinking glasses, and cookbooks.

"Good. Um . . . Paula, I'm sorry it didn't work out with Kenya." Paula had offered to pay Suzanne's younger sister to help her with the prep work, but Kenya canceled at the last minute, claiming she didn't feel well.

"No problem. Everything's gotten done."

Suzanne appreciated Paula's cheerfulness, but she still felt bad about her sister's behavior. Kenya would attend the party with her boyfriend in a few hours, showing no signs of illness, and Paula knew it. Sometimes she wondered if anyone was as lazy as her little sister. "Listen, it's five-thirty. I'm going to go chill with Brad for a while. Holler if you need anything."

"Will do." Paula's shoulders and hips swayed to the CD she had playing in a small boom box perched on the kitchen counter.

Suzanne wore a smile as she walked toward the master bedroom. It was pretty funny that she and Paula had become such good friends, considering all the intertwined relationships already in existence. Paula had been previously married to Suzanne's next-door neighbor Darrell Canfield and was the mother of their daughter, Devon. Darrell was now married to Brad's first wife, Lisa, and stepfather to Lisa's daughter with Brad, Paige Betancourt.

Unlike Suzanne, Paula had no issues with Lisa. Lisa had helped Darrell raise Devon, who was just three months younger than Paige. Paula left Devon in the care of her father and stepmother while she embarked on an ultimately unsuccessful second marriage in Texas. She'd never said much about it, but Suzanne sensed that relations between mother and daughter had been strained ever since.

Even more ironic than Suzanne's friendship with Paula was the genuine friendship that formed between Brad and Darrell. It seemed unheard of to Suzanne that two men who'd both been married to the same woman could go out fishing or watch sports on TV together. She wondered if Lisa found it as bizarre as she did.

Suzanne entered the bedroom to find Brad napping in the down-stuffed chair in their bedroom, his feet resting on the matching ottoman, the television tuned in to an NBA semifinal game. Even in repose he looked dashingly handsome, with streaks of gray mixed in the dark brown hair on his head, as well as in his mustache and neatly trimmed goatee.

She bent and gently brushed her lips against his cheek. He didn't stir. She tried again, this time tracing his lips with her tongue.

His eyes slowly opened. "That you, Suzie Q?" he asked sleepily.

"It better be," she replied with feigned indignation.

"What time is it?"

"Going on six."

"Mmm. I really knocked out."

"You don't have to get up yet," she said quickly. "Unless you want to move to the bed. You're going to be fifty in a few hours. I was hoping to get one more chance to make love to you before that happens, just in case you lose it."

He pulled her on top of him. "I'll be just as good at fifty as I am at forty-nine."

"Prove it," she challenged.

Half an hour later they lay sweaty and satiated in bed. "Well, there's no doubt that you've still got it," she said. "Now I can't wait for midnight."

"At midnight we'll have a house full of guests, so you can forget about that. But don't worry. I'm not ready for Viagra yet."

"I'm not worried," Suzanne said confidently. "I'm going to take a catnap and refresh myself before I start getting ready. And, Brad—"

"Hmm?" He was already dozing off.

"I love you," she whispered, so softly that he couldn't hear her.

She truly did.

And no one—*no one*—would take him away from her.

Suzanne frowned as she looked through the peephole. Why did the most boring people always have to be the first to arrive? Even Brad's family members from out of state, all of whom were staying at the same hotel, hadn't gotten here yet. Flo and Ernie Hickman must have gotten in their car at the stroke of eight to drive over. And she'd be stuck entertaining them until someone else arrived and freed her. Brad flatly refused to have anything to do with them. He'd had it with Ernie's endless comments about their possessions, always followed by something along the lines of, "Well, I've been looking for one of those myself. Do you mind if I ask how much you paid?"

The Hickmans lived in Villa St. John, the subdivision around the corner. Suzanne hadn't seen much of them in the last few years. From Kenya, who dated their son Gregory off and on, she'd learned they'd had some hard times, although they tried hard to mask it. Brad encouraged her to leave well enough alone. Ernie could be awfully crude, and they were both nosy. Suzanne had spent a fair amount of time in Flo's company before Flo's spare time suddenly dried up—Suzanne believed she couldn't afford to hang with her anymore. Suzanne had enjoyed Flo's open admiration of their home, furnishings, and cars, and she also found Flo's attempts to keep up with them amusing. The Hickmans didn't want to keep up with the Joneses, they believed they *were* the Joneses and everyone had to scramble to keep up with *them*.

Because of Brad's feelings and the Hickmans' annoying ways, Suzanne had considered not even inviting them, but in the end didn't see how she could make the exclusion. She'd invited friends of Lisa and Darrell's who also lived in Villa St. John, couples whom they saw whenever the Canfields entertained. She hadn't wanted to invite them—both the women were friends of Lisa's, and Suzanne suspected they talked about her behind her back—but Brad asked her to and she had no choice. It wouldn't be right to invite them and not the Hickmans. Then there was Kenya's relationship with Gregory Hickman to consider as well—hardly a boyfriend / girlfriend setup, but a relationship all the same. The sporadic nature of their dating pattern suggested Gregory simply did not share Kenya's devotion, and Suzanne knew from her mother that they were on the outs again. Kenya hadn't even gone to Gregory's recent graduation ceremony from the University of North Florida, but Suzanne felt that regardless, her sister would probably invite him to be her date.

Actually, Suzanne hoped she would, and that he would accept. Brad's daughter Paige, as well as Paige's stepsister and best friend Devon Canfield, were coming tonight. Both girls had crushes on Gregory when they were teenagers. Suzanne and her mother had both been thrilled when Gregory chose her sister over the other two.

The thought of both girls, now completing their junior

year, showing up dateless while Kenya had Gregory at her side brought an unabashed smile to Suzanne's face.

"Ernie, Flo, how nice to see you," she said graciously. "It's been much too long." She gave herself credit for mastering the art of bullshit. Ernie looked fine in a high-collared light gray shirt and dark gray suit, but Flo looked like she was ready for New Year's Eve in a gold sequined dress with a scoop neckline in both the front and back. She must have been wearing every piece of jewelry she owned, including a huge pair of gold earrings that had to be clip-ons; if they were pierced, her earlobes would be sagging like the jowls of a centenarian.

Flo glanced around at the empty family room and the large patio beyond, which connected to each other by the opening of a series of long panel patio doors. The six doors, set on a diagonal angle with three on each side, had been pulled back into the outer walls of the house. This feature made for a transition between the indoor family room and the screened-in patio with its outdoor kitchen, lagoon-style pool, and views of downtown Jacksonville across the St. Johns River that was both seamless and spectacular. "See, Ernie, I *told* you we were too early." To Suzanne she said, "We'll be all right here if you need to finish getting ready, Suzanne."

She considered taking Flo up on her offer, but wanted to hold out until at least one other guest or couple arrived. She knew that if they were left alone, Ernie and Flo would proceed to go through every knickknack and piece of furniture they had, trying to determine what had been added since their last visit and, of course, how much it cost. Brad would have a fit if she left them to snoop around.

"Oh, I'm all ready. It's Brad who's running late. Why don't we sit outside?" Suzanne led the way to the connected family room and patio at the rear of the house, the feature she loved the most and that always got them the most compliments.

Mother Nature had smiled on them tonight. The stars sparkled in the night sky, and the city's skyline looked lovely in the darkness across the river.

"You've got some real fancy touches tonight," Ernie said before they even had a chance to sit down. "I'm glad Flo remembered to bring the ticket, or else we wouldn't have gotten in."

Suzanne wished Flo *had* forgotten. They would have gone home to retrieve the admission pass, which would have given her a few more minutes of peace. She explained, "The man collecting invites has a list to check as a backup in case anyone forgets. He just would have asked for ID." She'd asked Paula to let one of her wait staff man the door; the temporary maid from the agency simply didn't move fast enough to do it efficiently.

"And the valet parking," Ernie continued. "Pretty fancy."

"Yes, well, we're expecting a fair number of people. It seemed easier that way." Suzanne had taken the unusual step of inviting everyone on the block to head off any resentment at having the block crammed with cars, but why was she explaining anything to this oaf?

"Your house looks great, Suzanne," Flo said. "I love the floating candles in the pool."

"Well, thank you."

"And I see you got new patio furniture."

"Yes, we replaced everything last year. We do a lot of entertaining out here." Oops. Wrong thing to say. She'd practically invited Ernie to say something like, *Be sure to invite us.* "Besides, the old stuff was going on five years old, so it was time to replace it," she quickly added, then looked toward the door for the second time in a minute. She was desperate for someone else to show up, but who was silly enough to show up at five minutes after eight? No one would be here for another fifteen or twenty minutes, at least. And she was stuck here with people she'd invited simply to spare their feelings.

Paula, wearing a sleeveless pale green silk sheath, emerged from the kitchen with a bowl of fruit, which she placed strategically on a cloth-covered rectangular table that would eventually hold hot and cold hors d'oeuvres.

"Who's *that?*" Ernie asked loudly, following Paula's moves with his eyes.

Suzanne rolled her eyes. How did Flo stand being married to him?

The next ones to arrive were Frank Nelson, Brad's new partner in the diagnostic center, and his wife Jean. The two business partners socialized fairly often in the three years since Frank bought out Brad's original partner, and Suzanne looked at the Nelsons as a slightly older—they were both in their mid fifties—version of herself and Brad. Suzanne had thought the Nelsons had a perfect marriage when she'd first met them, the model for herself and Brad in the future. She'd been shocked when Brad casually mentioned that Frank had a girlfriend out on the west side of town. Ever since then Suzanne felt a little uncomfortable around Jean because of what she knew. Whenever they had a few minutes alone for girl talk, Jean usually said something about how happy and contented she was with her life. Suzanne would never forget her saying, "You know, Suzanne, all I ever wanted was a husband, children, and a house of my own. And I got all three. Sometimes I think I'm the luckiest woman on earth."

Suzanne didn't see how Jean could possibly be unaware of her husband's multiple indiscretions; she'd heard other wives gossip about it with her own ears. Did an intact family unit and a large house in an exclusive neighborhood mean so much that she could gladly look the other way?

Like Suzanne, Jean didn't work outside the home, and hadn't for years. She and Frank had married while he was still in medical school, and she supported them by working as a secretary. Or, as she liked to put it, an executive assistant. She hadn't worked in probably twenty-five years. Perhaps that was why she tolerated Frank's behavior. If she got fed up and walked out on him, what would she do?

Suzanne liked Jean, but she regarded Jean's attitude toward her husband's cheating as pathetic. If Brad ever stepped out on *her,* she wouldn't do like Jean did and carry on as usual. No way. She'd pack up and leave in a heartbeat. And she certainly wouldn't move in with her mother. No, she'd go to the nicest hotel in town, and she'd charge her stay to him.

No way would she ever put up with infidelity.

Chapter 5

By nine fifteen people were arriving every two or three minutes. The band had set up in a corner of the patio and was playing a mixture of jazz and dance music.

Her mother, sister, and brothers were all here. Both Derrick and Matthew had brought dates, but Kenya was alone. Her sullen and scowling expression made Suzanne consider that perhaps she'd been telling the truth about not feeling well when she begged off from helping Paula with prep work. Then again, maybe it was heartburn of the emotional kind, for Suzanne saw no sign of Gregory Hickman. She knew from her mother that Kenya and Gregory had had some type of spat, but that had been weeks ago. She'd fully expected Gregory to accompany Kenya tonight. If the two of them were still on the outs, that suggested a serious rift between them. That could well be the reason behind Kenya's sour mood.

Suzanne spotted Lisa and Brad when they arrived, accompanied by two couples who were friends of theirs. She had grudgingly complied with Brad's request to add them to the guest list, but now she enjoyed the impressed looks on their faces as they looked around at her showplace of a home, no doubt trying to figure out what had happened to the wall between the end of the house and the start of the patio area. Suzanne smiled triumphantly. As far as she was concerned,

Kim Gillespie and Stacy Prince could talk about her all they wanted. It all stemmed from jealousy, because the looks of wonder on their faces told Suzanne that both women would gladly trade places with her if they could.

The guests smoothly flowed between the two large areas of the family room and patio, mostly sitting in the former and standing in the latter. By now Paula's staff had set up the buffet table, and at least two people circulated through the party area with trays, offering hors d'oeuvres to the guests. Suzanne was delighted to see how easily the house handled the larger than usual number of guests. The list had swelled to nearly a hundred people, nearly twice as many people as the number they usually hosted, because of the special occasion. Suzanne had recruited the teenagers on the block to serve as valets, and also invited all of the adults in the households on both sides of the street. She then obtained permission to use their driveways to park the excess vehicles.

She kept glancing toward the door as she greeted her guests, eagerly anticipating the Trents' arrival. She wanted to see Micheline's reaction when she entered the house. Micheline would leave here tonight convinced that Suzanne and Brad had a relationship that was unbreakable.

She smiled as she heard snippets of conversations about the valet parking plus having to show an admission ticket. She'd read somewhere that the upper crust required this practice to keep uninvited guests or sneaky members of the press from gaining access. With so many people invited, including some she barely knew, Suzanne wanted to make sure some type of crowd control methods were in place, but she also liked the exclusivity factor.

She managed to greet her guests and simultaneously keep an eye on Brad as he greeted Lisa and Darrell. She seethed as he kissed Lisa's cheek and she placed a hand on his upper arm as she leaned toward him. Lisa looked wonderful, wearing a classic yellow sundress that flattered both her complexion and her still-trim figure. Her short curly 'do was combed away from her face for a dressier look. For a woman in her upper forties, she looked pretty damn good.

Suzanne tried to control the jealousy that never failed to flare whenever Brad's first wife appeared. After all, Darrell was standing right there and seemed fine with it. He gave Brad an affectionate hug as they shook hands.

Brad then said something to Lisa, who turned to look toward the door. Suzanne's gaze went in that direction as well. Both Paige and her stepsister and best friend, Devon Canfield, had arrived, each accompanied by a handsome young man, but Suzanne gasped when she recognized Gregory Hickman, Kenya's estranged boyfriend, as the man whose arm was linked through Paige's. They were *together!*

Cold fury filled her as she watched Paige rush up to her father and embrace him. Then Brad shook hands with Gregory and smilingly greeted him. He didn't seem at all surprised to see Gregory accompanying his daughter, which made Suzanne wonder if he'd known about it. And he hadn't mentioned a word about it to her. How dare Paige invite Gregory to escort her, *here,* of all places. How would that make Kenya feel?

Suzanne finally forced herself to look away as Brad moved on to Devon and her date. It wasn't fair. Gregory had chosen Kenya over both Paige and Devon when they were in high school. How could he reverse his decision now?

This was going to break Kenya's heart. She had always been crazy about Gregory, who, in addition to being a very nice young man, had been blessed with the best features of his not particularly attractive parents.

Suzanne hated to see her little sister unhappy, even if she did feel that Kenya could do better than Gregory. Gregory had majored in chemical engineering and would likely do just fine—he already had a job lined up with a leading manufacturer in town, due to begin work in mid-June—but Kenya was pretty enough to land someone from a better family, in terms of both money and finesse. All she had to do was put herself into the right circumstances. Kenya's problem was that she didn't seem willing to take any steps to improve herself. She wasn't likely to meet a bright college student or pro athlete while cashiering at Winn-Dixie. Suzanne privately didn't harbor much hope for longevity in her sister's relationship with Gregory, which had always been on and off more than the kitchen lights.

Suzanne promptly put thoughts of Kenya aside when she spotted Errol and Micheline Trent at the front door. She studied Micheline's expression but was disappointed to see that Micheline showed none of the open admiration demonstrated by Lisa's friends, but at least their arrival got Brad away from Lisa and Paige. He shook Errol's hand, and when Suzanne watched him bend to kiss Micheline's cheek, she hastily excused herself and rushed over. It was time to stand by her man.

Crossing a patio full of people she knew took longer than she expected. Suzanne stopped every few seconds to accept compliments on the ambience she'd created. She smiled at a black-vested waiter who offered guests hors d'oeuvres from a silver tray. Another waiter passed a tray with frothy piña coladas, one of several blended rum-based drinks that would be mixed and served over the course of the evening. An assistant bartender deftly worked at the sink of the outdoor kitchen. Suzanne had wanted all drinks to be served in real glasses, but Paula convinced her that wasn't practical for such a large guest list. Instead she provided high-quality plastic pilsners, wineglasses, and highball glasses, and Suzanne had to admit they worked just as well.

She deliberately took the long way around so she wouldn't have to stop to speak to the Canfields or Paige. When she finally reached Brad, he was still conversing with the Trents.

She possessively linked her arm through his. "Micheline, Errol. Welcome to our home. I'm so happy you could join us tonight," she said warmly. She might not be able to name the current secretary of defense or even the chief justice of the Supreme Court, but she'd match her hostess skills against anyone's.

Errol took her free hand and raised it to his lips. "Thank you, Suzanne. You're looking lovely tonight."

"Thank you, Errol."

"You have a beautiful home," Micheline said politely.

Suzanne wanted to slap her. Not because she'd said anything inappropriate, but because of how fabulous she looked. That white dress with its low neckline in front and daringly low dip at the backside was certain to garner plenty of attention from the men present. Micheline was probably the youngest woman at the party, not counting the barely twenty-one Paige and Devon. Most of the wives of Brad's friends and associates were Suzanne's age, and many of them were older, like Jean Nelson.

Micheline kept her expression impassive, but she was greatly impressed by her surroundings. This had to be one of the most fantastic homes she'd ever been inside of, worthy of being featured in a magazine. It was tough the way the wall had been retracted, essentially making the patio and pool deck area an extension of the main house rather than a separate area. The Betancourts could actually sit in their family room and watch the sun set in the open environment. And to think that silly, useless Suzanne got to live here as mistress of the house.

Micheline had been able to tell from the confused look on Suzanne's face while they were all talking at the Super Bowl party that the woman was about as bright as a forty-year-old penny. But Brad Betancourt, on the other hand, was definitely Micheline's type of man. He had money and believed in spending it to make himself and his family comfortable.

Her in-laws had plenty of money, too, but they lived simply and encouraged her and Errol to do the same.

Once more Micheline took in the open patio and the lush landscaping around the pool, which looked more like a pond in some exotic setting than a pool in a suburban backyard. She didn't want to live simply; she wanted to live like *this*.

It annoyed Micheline that Suzanne had it so good. She didn't like it when *anyone* had it better than she did, and this situation was harder to take than normal, since Suzanne was so utterly undeserving of a prize like Brad Betancourt. If Brad was *her* husband, he'd never get on her case about how much money she spent, nor would he suggest she get a job. Of course, it wasn't as if Suzanne had the qualifications to add anything to the family coffers. *Ran the office, my ass,* Micheline thought. Suzanne had probably been nothing more than a receptionist or file clerk.

A lightbulb went off in her head, and a slight smile formed on her lips. If she wanted to break up this marriage, she first had to make Brad dissatisfied with his wife. She knew where to start.

"Suzanne, did you see that?" Arlene Hall's mouth twisted in an unbecoming manner.

She didn't have to turn around to know her mother referred to Gregory escorting Paige. "I saw when they came in. I didn't know he was seeing her, did you?"

"No. Kenya told me a few weeks ago that she and Gregory were in one of their off periods, but she didn't say he was seeing Paige. I don't think she knew about it until tonight."

"Have you seen her?" It was difficult to pick anyone out in what had become a crowd.

"Dancing with Derrick. She's putting up a good front, but I think she's crushed. Can't you do something, Suzanne?"

She sighed. "I wish there was something I could do, Mom, but I have to be careful. Remember, Paige is Brad's daughter."

Suzanne never thought of Paige as her stepdaughter; that would have implied a warmth to their relationship that they would never have. Instead she was simply *Brad's* daughter, a nuisance she had to tolerate.

"Regardless of that, I think she showed terrible judgment, asking him to come here with her. She knew Kenya would be here. If you ask me, she just wanted to rub it in Kenya's face. She's always been jealous, ever since Gregory chose Kenya over her when they were in high school."

"I don't disagree with you. I'll catch up to Kenya as soon as I can and see how she's handling it."

"Good . . . who's *that?*"

This time Suzanne turned to see who her mother was looking at. She sighed when she saw Micheline mingling. Her back was to them, the daring cut of her dress on full display. The eyes of every man within ten feet of her lingered on her bare back. Suzanne rolled her eyes. "That's the wife of one of Brad's buddies from the golf club. We went to their house to watch the Super Bowl about three months ago."

"Does she play golf?"

"Yes."

"Well, maybe you'd better learn the game yourself. That one looks like a hussy who'll steal your man faster than you can blink. In fact, there she goes now."

Suzanne watched through narrowed eyes as Micheline smoothly slipped away from Errol and approached Brad. Even though other guests surrounded them, it nonetheless made her uncomfortable. Micheline was a crafty one, willing to flirt with Brad right under her husband's nose.

"You'd better get over there fast," Arlene said.

Suzanne did as she was told. Her mother had been blessed with the sharpest of instincts, and she'd taken one look at Micheline Trent and known she was trouble.

She was just a few yards away when Micheline and Brad started to dance a two-step to an old-school song performed by the band's female vocalist. She stopped in her tracks. She couldn't interrupt when they were dancing; that wouldn't look right. She wanted to be as subtle as Micheline, not come off looking like a fishwife.

"Suzanne, want to dance?"

She tried not to show her relief. Ernie Hickman might not be good for much, but he'd never know how he saved her ass just now. She nodded and fell into step with him, pulling back when he initially held her closer than what she felt was appropriate. His cologne was so strong she had to clear her throat to keep from coughing.

"Hey, Brad, look who I'm dancing with," he called out loudly.

Suzanne cringed.

Brad looked over and gave an amused smile. "Just don't step on my wife's toes," he said. Then he turned his attentions back to Micheline.

Suzanne wondered what they were talking about.

"So I was hoping you might be able to put in a good word for me down at the hospital," Micheline said to Brad as they danced. "The opening in their legal department is perfect for me."

"Sure. All you have to do is list my name as a reference on your application. You can list me on your résumé as well," he said.

"Thanks. I'll apply online right away. I've enjoyed staying at home, but I'm really ready to get back to work. I feel so out of touch."

"I can see how you'd feel that way. But Errol will certainly miss your being a homemaker. He raves about your cooking."

Something in Brad's tone hinted that he wished Suzanne had better culinary skills, and Micheline neatly filed that in the back of her mind. "Yes, I think I've done a fair job at being a housewife, but the last thing I want to become is one of those silly women who isn't aware of the world beyond her front door," Micheline continued. "You know, the type who can't carry on a decent conversation because she hasn't a clue about what's going on in the world."

"Uh . . . yes."

"Having a career makes me a more well-rounded person," she continued. "I'm seriously considering enrolling in law school, now that we have one in Jacksonville. I'm still young enough," she added pointedly.

"What type of law would you want to specialize in?"

"Oh, I don't know. Definitely not criminal. I've heard too many horror stories about disgruntled ex-cons going after their attorneys for losing their cases." At that moment the song ended, and she felt satisfied she'd made a good impression, managing to remind him that he was married to a simpleton and that she was both intelligent and young, all in one three-minute conversation. "Thank you, Brad."

"You're welcome. Let me know how you make out."

"I will." With that she sauntered away, hoping Brad followed with his eyes. She also wanted to get away from that loudmouth in the gray suit who'd been dancing with Suzanne before he could trap her on the dance floor. He'd come around, introducing himself as "a good friend of Brad's," which she doubted. No friend of Brad's would be so brazen as to openly stare at her body the way that man—she thought he might have said his name was Ernie—had. He practically addressed her chest rather than her face. Whenever her gaze happened to fall on him while she kept an eye on Brad, he was always flirting with one of the women present, especially with the black ones. He hardly spent any time with his wife, who looked forlorn at having been abandoned, as well as terribly out of place in that sequined dress.

As Micheline walked away she hoped Brad got a good look at the smooth skin of her back. Her backless dress took a dip in the center, exposing the skin of her hips just above the split of her buttocks. She chose this dress carefully, wanting the view from the rear to be just as appealing as that from the front. Errol had whistled when she modeled it for him.

If only he knew.

Chapter 6

Flo watched as Ernie danced with a friend of Suzanne's, a petite brown-skinned woman with a Caribbean accent and a weird name whom she remembered from an earlier party. He really shouldn't be making those suggestive gyrations with his pelvis, she thought. That would be out of place at such an elegant party, even if he was dancing with her, his wife, instead of a woman he barely knew.

The party was lovely, but not as much fun as she thought it would be. She noticed people staring at her dress and felt she'd made a terrible mistake in choosing an outfit. Most of the women wore fabrics like chiffon or silk. She remembered shaking her head at a woman at a Valentine's dance she and Ernie had gone to. The woman clearly thought she was the cutest thing in shoe leather as she strutted her stuff on the dance floor in a red halter dress that made her stomach look like she was expecting a baby—unlikely, given that she was well into middle age. As someone remarked, there was one of them at every affair. Now *she* was the one being gawked at for a fashion faux pas, and she hated the way it made her feel. She would have gone home and changed clothes, but that would be admitting that she'd made a mistake. That would probably cause more attention than her dress.

Ernie was no help. Why did he always act like such a flirt

whenever he was around the Betancourts' friends? She suspected he was making a pest of himself.

Until just a few minutes ago she'd been having a nice conversation with a well-dressed, cultured woman about a decade her senior who said her name was Jean Nelson. Jean seemed to sense Flo's discomfort and made a point out of trying to put her at ease, something Flo appreciated. Things had been going quite well, but then one of the other women asked if Flo had heard about a mutual acquaintance, some doctor who'd apparently run off with a lab technician much younger than his wife. A funny look crossed Jean's face, and she quickly excused herself and disappeared. Flo figured the people being gossiped about were friends of Jean's and she didn't want to play a role in spreading any further rumors. So now she was alone again.

Flo tightened her knit shawl around her shoulders. It wasn't really cool on this May evening, but if her torso was covered, maybe her dress wouldn't stand out so much.

Flo knew she wasn't beautiful. Truth be told, she wasn't even pretty. Her eyes drooped at the outer corners and her nose was too long. She'd learned to play up her good feature, her skin. Smooth and dark, it had a natural glow that required no foundation to cover imperfections, just a touch of rouge for extra color in her cheeks. People complimented her about it all the time. Ernie had even tried to get her featured on a commercial, but Flo doubted that would happen because her face wouldn't look attractive enough in ads.

She had other problems, too. Her legs were more clunky than shapely, and she usually wore Capri pants rather than shorts, and longer skirts than minis, to hide them. Her hair had always been thin and was starting to get thinner. As soon as Ernie got hired to run the hospital's human resources department, she made an appointment to get a weave, not so much for length, but for fullness. Her bob bounced when she walked, and she'd deliberately had it styled so that it was easy for strands in front to fall into her face. Flo wanted people to focus on her skin and hair rather than her nose and eyes. She liked the idea of hiding behind her hair. If it really got in the way, she just casually brushed it away with her hand, a gesture that made her *feel* beautiful.

The one thing that would truly make her feel beautiful would be to have her husband at her side. Flo knew Ernie could come on a bit strong at times, but she loved him tremendously. She was forty-six years old and had been married to Ernie for nearly twenty-five years, more than half her life. He was the man of her dreams, and together they had built a wonderful life, in spite of the hard times of recent years.

Flo broke out into a broad grin as Gregory approached her. Her son was such a good boy, and handsome, too. She and Ernie weren't exactly beautiful people, but Mother Nature had been especially kind to Gregory. He'd just graduated from the University of North Florida, majoring in chemical engineering. Gregory would do well in life, much better than she and Ernie. Not that they'd done badly. They were the first in either of the families to own a home. Originally from Boston, they settled here in Jacksonville after Ernie got out of the Navy because they liked the setting and mild climate.

Flo had been a little upset with her son when he started seeing Paige Betancourt a few weeks ago. Paige was Suzanne's stepdaughter, and Flo knew that Suzanne hated the living reminder of her husband's earlier marriage. It looked like history was going to repeat itself, for just as Lisa, Paige's mother, was better educated and more worldly than Suzanne, Paige had just completed her junior year at the University of North Florida while Kenya was merely a high school graduate, working as a cashier at Winn-Dixie. Of course Paige would be a better choice for Gregory, being a doctor's daughter and all, but Lisa Canfield had never invited Flo and Ernie to her home and barely showed them any civility. Flo sensed that even if Gregory married Paige, nothing would change.

Of course, it was way too early to think about marriage. Gregory was only twenty-two and had just graduated from college a few weeks before. The company he'd interned for last summer had hired him as a junior engineer at an excellent salary, quite a coup in this tough economic time. Even if Kenya's mother, Arlene, only worked for the post office and was a heavy drinker, Kenya claimed a leading radiologist in the area as her brother-in-law, and of course Brad was Paige's father, so no matter which girl Gregory chose, Flo would have a connection to Brad and Suzanne. Forget about Arlene, and forget about Lisa, too. Brad probably had more money and social connections than Lisa and her stockbroker husband combined. Besides, Flo and Suzanne Betancourt had once been good friends. Maybe they could be again. . . .

"Hi, Mama," Gregory said, bending to kiss her cheek.

"Oh, is this your son?" the woman sitting next to Flo said.

"Yes. Isn't he handsome?" she replied proudly.

"Mama," Gregory protested.

The woman laughed before turning her attentions to the person on her other side.

"Are you having a good time?" Gregory asked.

"Oh, yes," she lied. "Suzanne and Brad give such nice parties."

"Where's Daddy?"

"Oh, he's circulating," she said lightly. "You know how your father enjoys being the social butterfly."

"Well, since he's flitting around, how about dancing with your son?"

"I'd love to."

After Flo enjoyed her dance with Gregory, he walked her over to Ernie, who was fixing himself a plate at the beautifully arranged buffet table. "Hey, Daddy, you didn't forget about Mama, did you? She's sitting all by herself."

"Of course not," Ernie said defensively. "I just wanted to

fix a plate, to help coat my stomach. You should always eat when you're drinking alcohol."

"Well, I'd better get back to Paige."

His mother suddenly appeared behind him. "Thanks for the dance, my son," Flo said warmly, giving his hand an affectionate squeeze.

"Anytime, Mama." Gregory raised her hand to his lips and kissed it. "Uh . . . Mama, you could probably do with less rings. One on every finger is a bit much, I think."

She laughed. "My son, the fashion expert. Run along, now, and don't worry about me. I know how to accessorize. I've been doing it since before you were born."

"Flo, you've got to taste this," Ernie said after Gregory went to rejoin Paige. His words were barely intelligible, what with his mouthful of crabmeat-stuffed mushroom. "I don't know which one I like better, these or the ones inside that pastry."

"They're both delicious. I took the caterer's card, even though I'm sure we can't afford her." Flo spoke softly so that no one would overhear her admission.

"Didn't you want to give an anniversary party in September?"

"Yes, but Ernie, this must have cost thousands. I was going to make the food for our party myself."

"You can't do that, not after we've been here and seen all of this. You want to invite Brad and Suzanne, don't you?" At her nod, he said, "Well, how's that gonna look, us serving homemade food when they had their party catered?"

"But we can't afford it, Ernie," she hissed.

"That's why they make credit cards. Don't worry, we can pay it off quickly, in three months or so, four at the most."

"Now, Ernie, you know we promised we'd never get in over our heads again. We're already in enough trouble with the house. Besides, I'm sure there are other caterers."

"The house will recover its value. It might take a while,

but we're not going anywhere. As far as the caterer, we *have* to use Discriminating Taste. I mean, look who's here. The Gillespies, the Princes. They'll be coming to our party as well. We have to measure up."

Flo considered this. She recalled how shocked she'd been when she casually mentioned to Kim Gillespie, her next-door neighbor in the subdivision around the corner, that she and Ernie had been invited to tonight's party. Her mouth had dropped when Kim matter-of-factly replied that she and Michael had been invited as well. If that wasn't bad enough, Flo got another jolt of surprise when Ben and Stacy Prince showed up as here well. She didn't understand it. Had they joined Suzanne and Brad's inner circle while she and Ernie had been outcasts, invited only because of Gregory's relationship with Paige?

Social connections aside, what mattered most was their personal finances. Spending money to try and outdo everyone was what had gotten them into trouble in the first place. They couldn't continue doing that. They'd worked hard and made many sacrifices to recapture their security, but next time they might not be as fortunate. She had to make him understand. "Ernie, I want us to look good as much as you do, but we got into trouble trying to keep up with the Betancourts before. The fact is that Brad is a doctor."

"So what? You and I have two incomes, and Suzanne doesn't work."

She let out an exasperated sigh. "Our two incomes combined probably come to a whole lot less than what Brad makes by himself. I read somewhere that radiologists are among the top-earning fields of medicine, up there with cardiologists and neurosurgeons. He and Suzanne do things that even Lisa and Darrell Canfield probably can't afford. Not that the two of them are doing so badly," she added, "but you don't see their twins going to the Country Day School, and they don't have a second home like Brad and Suzanne do."

"Well, I say that if we can't have a party catered by Discriminating Taste, we shouldn't have one at all."

"Oh, Ernie." He was behaving like a petulant child. How could they let an important occasion like their silver anniversary pass without fanfare? She supposed they could always take a trip somewhere in lieu of a party, but wouldn't a party cost as much as a vacation? A vacation might even cost more. She was tired of going to the Bahamas. Besides, she suspected that Kim and Stacy snickered about her and Ernie always going to the same place. Stacy and Ben were going to Jamaica for a week, and last year Kim and Michael went to Europe. Maybe Ernie was right. If they wanted to reclaim their position, they couldn't skimp.

Discriminating Taste would cater their anniversary party.

This time Micheline hadn't been able to get away fast enough to escape that oaf she'd been avoiding all evening. Part of her suspected he'd been trailing her, waiting for an opportunity to pounce on her like a dog on a bone. She figured she'd dance with him once and that would be it. She politely thanked him when the band played the last chord, but he swiftly grabbed her around her waist and pulled her close as the band slowed down the tempo. She squirmed uneasily. This man was the biggest lout she'd ever seen. How on earth did he get in?

She looked up and saw Brad watching them, his handsome features slightly distorted by a frown. She quickly moved to make the most of the perfect timing, stiffening her posture and giving her dance partner a look so stern she was certain Brad could see it from a dozen yards away. "Look, mister, you don't even know me. The close dancing should be reserved for your wife, don't you think? So how about it, huh? Behave."

"It's just that it's not very often I get to dance with such a pretty lady."

"Your wife is pretty," Micheline lied. His wife, from what she could see, was on the plain side. And someone needed to tell her how to dress. Stevie Wonder could have picked out a more appropriate outfit.

"Well, yes, of course. But we've been married almost twenty-five years. You know how it is."

She felt his fingers probing her bare back and immediately stiffened. "Listen. I warned you once. I don't want to have to make a scene, but if you insist on pawing me, I'll have no choice but to walk off and leave you standing here."

"Oh, all right. I was just being friendly."

Micheline didn't bother to reply, and when the song mercifully ended, she broke away from him as fast as she could. She didn't dare peek at Brad to see if he was watching, but fervently hoped he was.

She headed for the bar. "Chardonnay, please," she told the bartender.

"Micheline?"

She recognized Brad's voice and carefully concealed her elation. She began to wring her left hand with her right, repeating the action in alternating fashion as she waited for the bartender to wash out a glass and pour the wine. "Hi!" she said, as if it surprised her to see Brad standing beside her. "Great party."

"Thanks. I really can't take credit for it, though. Suzanne put it together."

Uh-oh. That was the last thing she wanted to hear. If she could, she'd take back the compliment.

"I saw you dancing with Ernie," he said. At her quizzical look he explained, "He's one of our neighbors from the subdivision around the corner. It looked like he might have been giving you a hard time. Was he?"

She shrugged. "Nothing I couldn't handle."

"You seem upset." He focused on her hands, which she continued to wring.

At that point she looked down, feigned surprise at what she was doing, and stopped. "I guess I did find it a teensy bit disturbing. I didn't expect to encounter a . . . well, a masher at a classy function like this." She tried not to wince at her choice of words. *Masher?* Who the hell used that term in the last sixty years? But it was the first thing that came into her head. She must have been watching too many old movies while cleaning and cooking at home.

"I'm sorry, Micheline. I didn't want to invite him, but Suzanne has a soft spot for them."

I should have known.

"Besides," Brad continued, "Suzanne invited some other couples from Villa St. John, friends of friends, and she felt it would be insulting to them if they weren't included. She was right, of course."

Once more anger coursed through Micheline at Brad's defense of his wife's behavior. "Maybe, but at what cost?" She lowered her voice and spoke in a near whisper. "I was practically assaulted on the dance floor."

He nodded. "I'm afraid you're not the only one. I've noticed him acting inappropriately with a number of our female guests. I'll have to pull him aside and talk to him."

She placed a hand on his forearm in a show of concern. With a note of urgency she said, "I don't want to make any trouble, Brad."

"I know you don't. Don't worry about it."

"Hi!"

Damn, Micheline thought. Weren't there enough people here to keep Suzanne occupied? She was the hostess, after all. When she attempted to join them a little while ago, Micheline spotted her coming out of the corner of her eye and promptly asked Brad to dance with her to keep her away. This time she could do nothing.

"I was just asking Micheline about Ernie," Brad explained. "He's been acting like a real leech, practically trying to feel her up on the dance floor. I won't have him harassing our guests, Suzanne."

Suzanne took a moment to absorb the situation. She didn't like the idea of Brad playing hero to Micheline's damsel in distress. Micheline's husband was here. Why didn't she complain about Ernie's behavior to Errol and leave Brad out of it?

"Calvin already complained to me about Ernie being all over Liloutie," Brad continued. "I've had my eye on him ever since."

That made Suzanne feel better. Brad wasn't merely defending Micheline, but their friend Liloutie Braxton as well. But *she* was his wife, and she'd better get herself on the list of females he was defending. She knew one word from her would automatically put her at the top of the list. "Well, he held *me* closer than he should have when he danced with me," she remarked. "I had to squirm to get out of his grasp."

"That rips it." Brad walked off in search of Ernie.

"Brad, wait!" He'd already started for the outdoor portion of the party area, taking long, purposeful strides, and Suzanne followed, glad to move away from Micheline. "I know he's behaved badly," she said quietly when she caught up to him, "but remember, he's still a guest in our home. You don't want to make a scene. I'd hate for Flo to be embarrassed."

"Is that his wife?"

Suzanne knew the voice belonged to Micheline before she turned and saw her standing there. Damn it, why was she following them? Couldn't she have five seconds for a few words with her own husband without Micheline planting herself in the middle of them? With superhuman effort, she refrained from scowling at her. "Yes, it is."

"Poor thing. When I told him he has a wife to snuggle up to on the dance floor, he said they've been married a long time, intimating he's tired of her."

"Oh, my." Suzanne looked to Brad.

"That's just the type of no-count thing I'd expect him to say." His face softened, and he placed a palm on Suzanne's shoulder. "Don't worry, Suzie Q. I'm not going to make a scene. But Ernie and I are going to have a nice chat about the way he's been acting." He removed his hand and walked away.

"I'm sure everything will work out fine, Suzanne," Micheline said. "Try not to worry."

Suzanne ignored the reassurance and instead said, "Tell me something, Micheline. Did you complain to Brad about Ernie?"

"Not a word," Micheline replied. "He came to me. Remember he said how he'd been keeping an eye on Ernie? He said he'd seen us dancing. I had to push him back and warn him a couple of times about his hands roaming all over my back."

Now Suzanne remembered Brad saying he'd gone on alert after Calvin complained about Ernie, and while it made her feel better to know he wasn't looking out for Micheline personally, she couldn't help having a nasty thought. *If you'd covered up a little, maybe Ernie wouldn't have felt your back was open for exploration.*

Out of the corner of her eye she noticed Kenya coming out of the powder room. "Excuse me, Micheline," she said, glad to have an excuse to leave.

She rushed to her sister. "Kenya, are you all right? You look a little down."

Kenya looked at her through red-rimmed eyes. "Gregory is seeing Paige. Now I know why he dumped me."

"I'm so sorry, Kenya. I think it sucks that she brought him here."

She sniffled. "I want to go home, Suzanne. Can you ask Derrick to drive me?"

"Sure. You go into the guest room, and I'll get him. Don't worry about Gregory, Kenya. He's not the only man in Jacksonville."

Kenya nodded, but she looked like she was about to burst into tears again.

"Go on, now. I'll get Derrick." Suzanne gave her sister a

little push. She didn't want anyone seeing Kenya look so defeated, especially Paige and Lisa. Surely Derrick's date could spare him long enough to take his sister home. The rental house was so close he could be back within fifteen minutes.

Even as Paula posed for pictures with Devon, her practiced eye took in each action of her staff. Everyone seemed to be on their toes, even that lackadaisical maid who was substituting for the efficient Teresita. No wonder Suzanne was at her wit's end with her. And she really should have told her to lose the gum, the way she chomped on it looked so unprofessional. But at least she was doing her job, clearing the drop stations of dirty plates and making sure that plenty of clean ones were available. A heavyset build and shuffling gait made her appear matronly, but Paula took a closer look and could see she was probably in her upper thirties or early forties at the most, not much younger than herself. *There but for the grace of God go I,* Paula thought. That could have been her, wearing a maid's uniform and serving at a party instead of catering it and mingling with the guests. It was true that she'd worked hard, but she'd also been fortunate.

"Paula, smile already," Lisa said with exasperation.

"Oops. Sorry." Paula stopped watching the maid and did a quick survey. The buffet table looked tidy, nothing needed refilling, and a stack of clean white square stoneware plates and folded white cloth napkins awaited anyone wanting to fix a snack. She smiled for the camera, her arm around her daughter.

Paula was so proud of Devon. She'd blossomed into a lovely young woman, as kind and generous as she was beautiful. In Paula's opinion, Devon was much more grounded than her stepsister, the somewhat spoiled Paige. The two girls grew up together, Lisa and Darrell having met when they were preschoolers, but while Darrell was careful not to overindulge Devon, Brad Betancourt had imposed no such restrictions when it came to Paige and had given her just about everything.

They changed places, and Paula tried to ignore the pain in her heart as she focused the camera on Lisa and Darrell flanking Devon and Paige. With Paige looking like Lisa and Devon resembling Darrell, anyone looking at them posing would assume Lisa had given birth to fraternal twin daughters.

Paula knew that Lisa deserved as much credit as Darrell for the fine way Devon had turned out. When she accepted a marketing position in Dallas, all parties involved, including Devon herself, agreed it would be best if Devon continued to live with Darrell, Lisa, and her half brothers. The plan had been for Devon to visit Paula frequently, but then Paula fell in love with Andre Haines, a man seven years her junior. Andre's parents were anxious to have grandchildren, and she allowed him to talk her into telling them and everyone else that she was ten years younger than her actual age to quell any doubts his parents might have about her ability to conceive. Paula went along, and that marked the beginning of the estrangement between Paula and Devon, for Paula, who'd been twenty-two when she had Devon, could not present Devon, then sixteen, as her daughter after claiming to be twenty-eight. Devon resented her mother's denial, and although mother and daughter managed a tentative reconciliation after the situation exploded along with the marriage, Paula's place in Devon's heart had been lost to Lisa, whom she now called "Mom." She doubted she would ever get it back.

Paula had accepted the effect her regrettable behavior had on her relationship with her only child, although it still hurt and always would. She knew she had no one to blame but herself for agreeing to Andre's crazy scheme. Not only did she miscarry her second child, but her second marriage failed. She publicly stated that she was through with marriage, but her secret wish—one that she'd never shared with anyone— was to have a third chance at marriage and a second chance to raise a child.

Fat chance of *that* happening. After her miscarriage, her

doctor informed her it would be difficult for her to carry another child to term, and now she was forty-three.

Darrell wandered off, and the girls flanked Lisa while Paula captured the moment on film.

"I'd be happy to snap a picture so that you can get in it," a deep voice offered.

She turned to see a tall man who appeared younger than most of the ones in attendance, standing beside her. She recognized him as the escort of the woman in the daring white dress, herself young. "That's very kind of you. I think I'll take you up on it." She handed him the camera.

"It only seems right for you to be in the picture with your sisters and . . . aunt, maybe?"

She chuckled. Lisa would certainly not be happy to learn that this man thought they were aunt and niece. "The one on the right is actually my *daughter.*"

"You don't say!"

She nodded, and still smiling, went to stand on Devon's right as Lisa and Paige shifted so that Lisa was on the outside.

Suzanne quickly found Derrick, who agreed to take Kenya home "as soon as I finish my plate." She rolled her eyes. Every time she'd seen her brother this evening he had a plate in his hand. Anyone would think he'd never seen food before.

She next looked for her mother, but found her dancing with an older gentleman, the father of Brad's friend Calvin Braxton, who was visiting his son from somewhere up north.

She'd just have to fill her mother in on what was happening later. In the meantime, she wanted to know how things went between Brad and Ernie. Her eyes scanned the area, first recognizing that Flo danced with Darrell Canfield, then saw Brad talking with Lisa.

Suzanne's jealousy meter soared. She knew Brad and Lisa

retained no romantic feelings for each other, but nevertheless, it annoyed her to see them talking alone. It still stung that Brad seemed to know about Paige and Gregory but had said nothing to her. This latest development only compounded the ever-present feelings of inadequacy Suzanne felt because Lisa was a degreed professional while she'd barely passed high school. Much of the time she found comfort in the fact that she and Brad had a nicer home and more money than Lisa and Darrell, but tonight she experienced no such solace. Being surrounded by Lisa, a pharmacist; Micheline, a multilingual paralegal; and other professional women like Liloutie Braxton, a corporate recruiter, made her feel like nothing more than a girl from the proverbial wrong side of the tracks who through her connection to Paula Haines had metamorphosed into an excellent hostess.

Paula came up beside her and gently tapped her upper arm. "It's ten after twelve. How do you feel about rolling out the cake now?"

"Yes, that's fine."

"I hope Brad's lungs are in good shape. I can't believe you had fifty candles put in it."

Suzanne shrugged. "Well, it's a sheet cake." They shared a laugh. "I'll go over to Brad now and try to hold him in the same spot."

"Perfect. I'll go help light the candles. It'll probably take three of us to get it done quickly."

Suzanne walked over to where Brad stood with his first wife. "Did everything go all right with Ernie?" she asked.

"Yeah, perfectly. I talked to him around the side of the house. He's sulking at the bar." He grunted. "Of course, anyone with any sense would just leave."

Suzanne looked at Lisa, so pretty and elegant. "Did Ernie act inappropriately with you, Lisa?"

"He didn't get a chance to. Every time I saw him coming I moved."

"Smart girl," Brad commented.

Suzanne kept a smile plastered on her face. She hated to be reminded about how smart Lisa was.

Darrell returned, playfully dancing around Lisa, bumping her butt with his. "Dance with me, baby."

They headed toward the center area where people were dancing. Suzanne stayed with Brad and chuckled at Darrell's antics on the dance floor. He'd clearly had enough alcohol to be a little tipsy, and at one point Lisa stopped dancing and merely stared at him incredulously, her hands on her hips and her chin lowered to her chest.

At that moment the music suddenly stopped, and the male lead singer picked up the microphone. "We interrupt the music for an important announcement." He raised his left hand behind him, obviously signaling the band. They began to play the Happy Birthday song as one of the waiters wheeled the large sheet cake, its top flaming with candles inserted around the edges, outside, bringing the cart to a stop in front of Brad. The guests joined the band in singing birthday wishes to Brad, and people immediately began laughing and buzzing about the large number of candles on it.

"At times like this I'm glad I don't smoke," Brad quipped. He took a deep breath, leaned forward, and blew out the candles, not in one breath, but he only needed two.

Suzanne applauded with the others. She spotted Paula looking hungrily at a brawny young waiter. She knew Paula preferred younger men, but this was pushing it, even for her. This young man looked like he was still in his twenties.

Brad impulsively gathered her in a hug, first kissing her lightly on the mouth, then holding her for a prolonged moment. When they finally parted Suzanne couldn't help the way her eyes automatically sought out Micheline, wanting to make sure she'd witnessed the exchange of affection. Standing next to Errol, her hands applauding, it was a cinch she had. She might appear outwardly as happy as everyone else, but Suzanne didn't believe it for a second.

She noticed with dismay that all the men standing within a few yards of Micheline were discreetly checking out her backside, and Suzanne's stomach did a little leap. *She'd al-ways been the one the male guests stole glances at when they thought their wives weren't looking.*

Her looks and sex appeal made up a large portion of what attracted Brad to her in the first place, and what kept him satisfied, but she was getting older. What would happen if she lost them? Would she lose Brad, too?

"Come on, let's get out of here."

Flo looked confused. "I don't get it. What's going on, Ernie? The party is nowhere near over. They're just about to cut the cake."

"They're a bunch of snobs here. I just don't feel like being bothered."

Flo hesitated. It was true that she wasn't enjoying the party as much as she would have liked, and she knew she'd chosen the wrong dress. But Ernie certainly seemed to be having a good time. She didn't understand why he wanted to leave all of a sudden. Didn't he realize this was their chance to get back in with Suzanne and Brad?

"Are you coming?" he asked impatiently, his words punctuated by the smell of alcohol on his breath.

"You want to just leave without saying good night to Suzanne? She's our hostess, Ernie? And what about Gregory?"

"It'll be better if we just slip out. Gregory will just assume we couldn't find him to say good-bye."

"What's this all about, Ernie?"

He sighed. "I'm trying to spare your feelings here, Flo, but if you insist on knowing . . . I overheard a couple of people cracking on your dress. Under the circumstances, I really think it's best we leave, while I'm still able to control my temper. If I hear somebody make another nasty crack, I might forget myself and knock them out."

Flo gasped. It stung to know that people were making fun

of her, but it would be even worse if Ernie got into a shouting match or, worse, came to blows at the home of their hosts. She'd made a terrible mistake in her choice of wardrobe, and the impression had been set in stone. "All right," she said dejectedly. "Let's go."

Chapter 7

Suzanne worked in the kitchen, trimming fat from a thick ribeye steak and placing it in a long shallow dish for marinating, where other steaks already soaked in teriyaki-flavored liquid. Her mother kept her company, perched on a bar stool facing the kitchen, the usual highball glass present in front of her.

"I thought you and Brad would have gone out to dinner, it being his birthday and all," Arlene remarked.

"It didn't seem necessary, since we went out for brunch this morning at the golf club. It was especially nice to have Bradley and Lauren with us." And because there was no sign of Micheline Trent, a thought Suzanne kept to herself. "We both felt a little guilty for banishing the kids to their rooms last night, but the party wasn't for kids." She paused. "Of course, they both pointed out that *Paige* would be there."

Arlene grunted. "I'm sure Brad gave them the line about Paige being a lot older."

"Yes." Suzanne pressed a plastic lid on top of the dish with more force than the chore required. She hated it when her stepdaughter got to do anything her own kids couldn't. Never mind that Bradley and Lauren were mere teenagers to Paige's twenty-one. She still didn't like it.

But she didn't want to concentrate on anything negative. Today belonged to Brad. She wasn't even going to ask him if he'd known about Paige and Gregory. That could wait. "So I didn't feel it was necessary to go out for dinner on top of that," she explained. "I figured some nice boneless ribeye would make Brad happy. It's his favorite cut of steak."

"It was nice of you to invite us . . . even if we didn't get to join you for breakfast."

Suzanne sighed. If her mother had her way, she'd never go anywhere that didn't include her. "Of course we'd invite you to dinner at the house, Mom," she said, choosing to ignore the mild reprimand.

"Derrick and Matthew will probably stop by a little later to pick up plates."

"That's fine, as long as they don't walk off with all the meat." After a party Suzanne and Brad gave a number of years back, her brothers had collected all the meat and seafood leftovers. Brad was the one to discover what they'd done the next day, when he went to get a snack and found that all the leftover containers held nothing but salads and cakes. He'd been furious.

Suzanne loved her family, and she tried to help them as much as she could, but sometimes they took advantage of her generosity, and that had definitely been one of those times.

This seemed to be a good time to bring up a subject that she'd been worried about. "Mom, you do know your rent is due next week. You'll take care of it, won't you?"

Arlene sighed. "I might be a little late."

"Mom!" Suzanne exclaimed in a whine. "I thought you told Derrick and Kenya that they need to contribute. It's not fair. You're paying the utilities, buying all the food . . ."

"It's hard for them, Suzanne. I manage. It's just that I don't get paid until the fifth." She sighed. "That means an extra ninety dollars. Suzanne, why can't you get Brad to stop those late fees?"

"I've told you, Mom. Those fees go to the property manager. It's not like Brad is getting the money."

Arlene took a sip of her drink. "Well, then, can you loan me a couple of hundred, just for two days?"

Now it was Suzanne's turn to sigh. "Mom, you say that every time, but you never pay me back. You always say something came up. I'm sorry, but I can't risk Brad finding out that I was paying your rent, which means that *he's* paying it, since it's his money."

"All right, all right. Well, you won't have to worry about the boys walking off with your leftover meat. Derrick will probably have eaten at work, anyway." Brad had first offered the job of managing his Subway franchise to her youngest brother, Matthew, but he declined, citing that he needed his days free to attend classes at the local college. Instead he found a job at the hospital on the evening shift, using Brad as a reference. Suzanne knew Brad had been reluctant when Derrick volunteered to take the job, but he'd given him a try, at her urging. Suzanne hoped her brother would pursue a career in restaurant management. Derrick was nearly thirty years old and needed to think about his future. Takeout was always popular, even in lean economic times.

"Is Kenya back from the store?"

"Oh, yeah. She wasn't gone long. I think she just ran down to Walgreens. She's probably watching TV with Lauren."

"Good. Lauren felt kind of left out, with Bradley at the movies with his friends."

"She'll be all right. What're you making to go with the steak?"

"Just a salad, some baked potatoes, and I'll put some mushrooms on the grill."

"Mushrooms? Don't you know some of those are poisonous?"

"I didn't pick them up along the side of the road, Mom. I bought them at the supermarket."

"That Paula is certainly giving you grand ideas about food."

"I'm trying to make more foods that Brad likes. But Paula has been a big help, yes." Suzanne's friendship with Paula, her closest in many years, helped her feel more confident about herself, and she was learning new things as well.

Kenya entered the kitchen. "Hi," she said dully.

"Hey," Suzanne replied. "Is the movie over already?"

"No, but I missed the beginning, and it was too hard to keep up with. I promised Lauren I'd watch the next one with her. It comes on in about forty minutes." She climbed up on a stool next to her mother.

"Dinner will probably be ready when it's over." Suzanne looked at her sister quizzically. Kenya seemed so down. It had to be because of Gregory. "Did you buy yourself something nice when you went out? Sometimes when I'm in the doldrums I buy myself something new, and I feel a lot better."

Kenya responded by putting her head down on the granite counter, framed by folded arms, and sobbing.

Suzanne cast a wild look at her mother. "I don't get it. What'd I say that would bring *this* on?"

Arlene returned the look of confusion before standing up so she could embrace Kenya from the side. "Kenya. Don't cry, baby. Whatever it is, it can't be that bad." When Kenya continued to sob she tried again. "It's Gregory, isn't it? Don't cry over him. There are plenty of other fish in the sea."

She lifted her tear-stained face. "None of them will want me. I'm pregnant."

Suzanne, about to prepare the salad, dropped the knife and jerked her hand away to avoid getting cut. "*What?*"

"I just took the test," Kenya said, her face wrinkling. "It came back positive."

Arlene returned to her chair and took a sip of amber-colored liquid. "Is it Gregory's?"

Suzanne found her mother's casual reaction puzzling. Here Kenya was sobbing her heart out, and she acted instead as if Kenya had just announced nothing more significant than plans to go down to South Beach for the weekend.

"Yes. He's been the only one. I don't know what to do, Mom, now that Gregory is with Paige."

"That may be so," Arlene said loftily, "but he has a responsibility to you and your baby now. Isn't that right, Suzanne?"

"Well, yes." Suzanne found Kenya's comment about Gregory being her one and only hard to swallow. She suspected her sister was promiscuous, and she'd spoken to her once about not sleeping with every guy who asked her. Then she realized that Kenya probably meant that Gregory was the only one she'd slept with who could have impregnated her in the last six weeks or so.

"Are you sure you want to go through with this, Kenya? It isn't easy being a single mother, you know. I've never been one, of course, but Mom was single most of our lives, and we all know what a hard time she had."

"This baby is mine, mine and Gregory's, Suzanne. I'm not going to kill it."

"Besides," Arlene added matter-of-factly, "since we all know that single motherhood is difficult, maybe Kenya should be married."

The smile on her mother's face sent a chill through Suzanne. Kenya's eyes widened, as if a lightbulb had gone off inside her head.

"Mom," Suzanne began, "you can't mean—"

"I'm just outraged that something like this happened to my baby girl," Arlene declared fervently. "I don't aspire to have out-of-wedlock grandchildren."

Suzanne tried again to make her point. "Mom, that's a noble thought, but you already have one. Are you forgetting Derrick's daughter?" Nor had her mother been married to Kenya's father, but it would be just plain mean to bring that to the forefront. "Besides, your 'baby girl' is an adult. No one can force Gregory to marry her."

"Besides, he wants to be with Paige," Kenya said morosely.

"Forget about her," Arlene said. "*You're* the one having the baby. He should do the right thing by you." She got off of her bar stool and stood behind her youngest child, hugging her from behind and then affectionately patting her flat belly. "Hard to believe there's a baby in there, is there?"

"Just wait a few months," Suzanne murmured.

Kenya turned to her big sister. "Suzanne, what do *you* think I should do?"

"I think the first thing you need to do is have it confirmed by a doctor. Sometimes home pregnancy tests aren't accurate. Then you need to talk to Gregory. See what *he* says."

"I guess *that* will kill the budding romance between him and Paige," Arlene said nastily.

Suzanne couldn't deny that she found that idea appealing. She bit down on her bottom lip to keep from grinning.

"Of course, Kenya, I would have preferred that you'd been married first, like your sister," Arlene continued. "There's probably plenty of young men out there who will one day be well off after they finish college. There's no reason why you shouldn't snag one of them. But I think Gregory will do just fine."

"He's the only man I ever wanted," Kenya said dreamily.

Suzanne abruptly turned her back under the guise of getting a package of fresh mushrooms from the vegetable bin of the refrigerator. She couldn't understand why Kenya was so stuck on Gregory Hickman.

"And you've seen his parents' house, Mom," Kenya continued. "It's not as nice as this house, of course, but it's really nice. Maybe we'd get to live there if we got married, until Gregory's been working long enough to afford his own place. There's plenty of room for us and the baby, now that the kid boarding with his parents has moved out."

Suzanne, her back still to her mother and sister, rolled her eyes. It was true that Ernie and Flo did have a nice home, but she'd never been impressed with the way they'd decorated it. It was too crowded, for one. All that furniture and wall units crammed with bric-a-brac. The area rugs that lay atop of the wall-to-wall carpeting only served to make the spacious rooms look tiny. And all those horrible painted ceramic dogs. If they loved dogs so much, why didn't they just get a real one?

Still, Kenya was her sister, and she hated the idea of her possibly being disappointed. "Kenya, Mom's just making a suggestion. I really don't think you should start making plans to marry Gregory. You'll feel very bad if things don't work out."

Arlene took another sip of her drink. "Listen, it's as good as done. From what I know about Ernie and Flo, they'd be mortified to have an illegitimate grandbaby."

"I agree, Mom. But it isn't what *they* think, it's what *Gregory* wants."

"Gregory will do whatever they want him to do. He's a nice young man. He's also an only child, which means they probably have a good hold over him."

Suzanne dumped the mushrooms into a colander and let the faucet water rinse them. "Like I said, first things first. Kenya, go down to the women's clinic on Monday." She broke off when Lauren wandered into the kitchen, her careless ambulation and slouched-over posture suggesting boredom.

"Auntie Kenya, you said you'd watch TV with me. I found a different movie that starts in five minutes."

"She'll be with you in a minute, Lauren," Suzanne said. "Go on to your room. We're talking about something private."

"But my water needs ice."

"Go ahead, get it."

Lauren sprinted to the refrigerator, where she removed a pink plastic water bottle. Suzanne and Brad had installed a water purification system, and while Suzanne discouraged the children from eating in their bedrooms, she did allow them to hydrate, as long as they used containers with lids to prevent spillage. Suzanne knew her children were being raised amid privilege, and she wanted to impress upon them a certain degree of thriftiness as well as neatness. She insisted that Bradley and Lauren keep their own rooms clean rather than have Teresita clean them twice a week. She also encouraged them to drink lots of water between meals rather than pop, something they had grown up with. Since the water was purified, she taught them to refresh it with ice rather than dumping the contents into the sink. Suzanne felt it wasteful to continually dump a liter of water into the sink when they had a huge water bill each month due to pool and lawn maintenance.

After Lauren left the kitchen with her refreshed water container, Suzanne said, "Before you go, Kenya, I wanted to tell you not to say anything to anybody. I'm not even going to tell Brad until it's confirmed. If it turns out to be a false alarm, there's no need for anyone other than the three of us to know. So not a word to your brothers or to any of your friends. Got it?"

"I won't say anything, Suzanne." Kenya went to join Lauren, this time moving with a definite pep in her step.

The moment she was gone, Suzanne turned to her mother. "Mom," she said with disappointment, "I wish you hadn't promised Kenya that she's going to be Gregory's wife. If he doesn't want to marry her, he's not going to, and I don't think he does. Now Kenya expects to get married, and when it doesn't happen she'll be heartbroken. Have you forgotten already how mopey she was just a few minutes ago?"

"Oh, it'll be fine," Arlene said dismissively. "It'll be just as I told you. Ernie and Flo will want him to marry Kenya, just to legitimize the baby. They'll tell him he can divorce her after the baby's born. They'll tell Kenya that, too."

"You're forgetting one important detail, Mom. Gregory doesn't love her. I personally believe"—Suzanne lowered her voice to just above a whisper—"that he comes to her between his other relationships, just because she's there. If you ask me, she's a fool to keep taking him back. So what can possibly come from Kenya and Gregory getting married other than a broken heart for Kenya?"

"A wonderful life. All Kenya has to do is make Gregory not want to divorce her."

"Mom, I hate to be a spoilsport, but I just don't see that happening. If Kenya could hold him with sex alone, he wouldn't have gone after Paige." Suzanne didn't even want to think about the loving way Gregory had treated Paige last night, holding her hand, looking at her with love in his eyes. Was her mother blind? "And you know as well as I do that Kenya's housekeeping skills are"—she groped for the right word—"atrocious."

"Well, she'll have to brush up on her housekeeping skills and learn how to cook," Arlene said. "She needs to hold off on a divorce as long as she can. It'll probably be five or six years at least before Gregory starts making any big money. If they have to divorce, I want to make sure Kenya gets a piece of whatever he's got. Then she can get to work on finding a second husband who has even more money than Gregory."

Suzanne had to admire her mother's maneuvering. "You've got it all planned out, don't you?"

"They say you should marry for love the first time, and for financial security with subsequent marriages, no matter how many there may be."

"Tell me, Mom. Did you feel that way about me when I married Brad?"

"Of course not. I could tell you two were madly in love. Brad needed no other reason to marry you other than because he wanted to."

Suzanne beamed, unable to deny how good her mother's statement made her feel, but she still worried about the current situation. She might have requested Brad not be told until after Kenya had her condition confirmed, but she already saw the pickle that put her in. Brad would be upset if he learned about Kenya's pregnancy from Paige, but Suzanne also knew that if she told him as soon as she found out, then *he'd* be sure to tell Paige. It simply wasn't right for Brad's daughter to know about Kenya's pregnancy before Gregory, the father, knew. She had to work it out in her head.

And fast.

Chapter 8

Micheline tried to get comfortable, but it was impossible. She lounged in a shady spot, but the air didn't move. Hell couldn't be as hot as Jacksonville, and it was only May. She'd probably be better off back in the air-conditioned house, but she'd been inside all weekend and was slowly going stir-crazy.

Other people had swimming pools to cool off in, but if cooling off was what she wanted, her only recourse was a cold shower, the beach, or the pool at the golf club.

Suzanne had a pool, she thought bitterly. She was probably sitting in a floating pool chair right now, with a cool drink in the holder and a book in her hand. And if she were there she'd manage to knock that hussy over. By accident, of course . . . in the deep end. It was a cinch that a wuss like Suzanne had never learned to swim.

"Nice party last night, huh?" Errol said as he joined her in the backyard hammock, securely hung between two tall pines.

Micheline slid over to accommodate him. "Yeah."

"We'll have to have a party like that for our twentieth anniversary."

"We'll be ancient by then, Errol."

"You'll never be ancient, baby." He nuzzled her neck. "Did you talk to Brad about that opening at the hospital?"

"Yes. He told me to use him as a reference."

"That job's as good as yours, Michie. They're going to love your qualifications, plus Brad's name on a résumé is going to carry some serious weight." He gave her butt a playful smack. "And you know what? I'll bet you'll be pregnant inside of six months. You've done a great job taking care of me and the house, but I think you need more stimulation."

It annoyed Micheline that Errol had everything all planned out. First the job, then a baby. But she had to say *something* in response to his optimism. "I guess."

"I know you think I'm obsessed with the idea of starting a family, Michie. I'm not obsessed with it, but it's something I want very badly."

Micheline felt her shoulders stiffen. She knew Errol really wanted a child, and she suddenly felt guilty for deceiving him. "We're still young, Errol," she said. "We still have time. It'll happen." *For you and your next wife.*

"Yeah, but maybe not as much time as you think. Technically we're still young, but I've got eight years on you, Micheline. Sometimes I think I'll be forty before I have my first child."

She rested her palm on his midsection and gave it a friendly pat. She could tell he was serious because he'd used her full first name. "Come on, don't go getting morose on me."

"I'll be all right. Hey, Cécile called. They're having some friends over to watch the play-off game and invited us to join them. Want to go?"

Micheline would have considered it if only her sister's family would be present, but it was a cinch that "some friends" would include Vic and Norell Bellamy and their little girl. Vic wore his discomfort the way most people wore their wristwatches when she was around, and she couldn't blame him.

Vic had been nearly as shocked to learn that she and Cécile were sisters as he had to learn that she was pregnant. He'd actually learned about it from Cécile, who'd gone downtown to his bail bonds office and reamed him out when she put two and two together from the vague details Micheline had provided.

"No, I don't think so," she answered, after pretending to have taken some brief time to think it over. "You know Cécile and I don't get along very well, Errol."

"I never really understood why. She's your sister, and she's cool. So is Michael. And the girls all adore you."

"I'm crazy about the kids, too, but Cécile and I are like oil and water. Always have been. If we hadn't promised our parents we'd be sure to see each other at least every few weeks, we probably wouldn't bother even getting together for lunch like we do. But you go on over. I was thinking about going down to the club for a swim. It's so hot."

He hesitated, and she knew he was considering going without her. "I think I know why you avoid going when Cécile and Michael have their friends and their families over, Michie."

Her forehead wrinkled; she hadn't the remotest idea what he was talking about.

"The kids. Well, not the teenagers, but the little ones, especially Regine and Norell's little girl."

Cécile had given birth to her youngest daughter, Regine, just a few months before Micheline had the little girl who had been christened Brianna Bellamy.

Errol's arm tightened around her shoulder. "I know it's hard for you to see mothers with young children. I get an ache in my heart when I'm around kids myself." For a few moments they rocked in silence. "Michie, I've been thinking. Since we haven't had much luck getting pregnant, it's probably time to consult a professional."

Micheline's mouth went dry. Her mind raced to come up with a reason why this wouldn't be a good idea. She certainly couldn't say they hadn't been trying long enough; it had been about eighteen months. "I'm not sure that's covered by insurance, Errol, and isn't that very expensive?" She figured nothing would be more effective than an appeal to his wallet.

"I already checked. They'll cover the initial workup, as well as any corrective surgery that needs to be done. After that, we're on our own. At this point I'm pretty sure there's definitely some kind of problem, but hopefully it's just something minor."

"And if not?"

He shrugged. "We'll have some major decisions to make." He suddenly clutched her upper arm, and she could feel his desperation. "You're still young, Michie, but I'm pushing forty. I want to have kids while I'm still young enough to enjoy them." He released his grip on her arm with the same suddenness, running his fingertips over it absently. "You go on to the club and take a dip. I think I'm going to join Cécile and Michael and their friends for a bit. I'll see you back here for dinner, huh?"

Errol climbed out of the hammock, and Micheline watched him walk away, an ominous feeling spreading throughout her body.

She knew she hadn't heard the last of this.

Micheline sat in her parked car in front of the home of her sister and brother-in-law, Cécile and Michael Rivers. She truly dreaded going in, but she couldn't get the picture of Errol's disappointment out of her head. For someone tight with money, he could be awfully selfless, as he'd been when he insisted she go down to the club to cool off rather than joining him at Cécile's.

She really had planned on going for a dip in the pool, but changed her mind. Her first thought was that with Errol safely occupied at Cécile's, this could make for a golden opportunity with Brad Betancourt. Then it occurred to her that with today being Brad's actual birthday, he likely wouldn't even be present at the club. The day would probably be spent with his family.

Micheline's jaw tightened as she recalled the love Brad had shown Suzanne at the party last night. She'd kept a smile pasted on her face to go with the murmurings of, "Oh, isn't that sweet," and "They're still in love after all these years." For a minute she actually considered that she might have made a mistake in thinking she could replace Suzanne. But Micheline had never been one to give up. Brad Betancourt had everything she ever wanted in a man . . . and if she was able to marry him, she'd have everything else she ever wanted as well.

In the meantime, it was hardly a done deal that Brad would ditch Suzanne to marry her, and she had a husband who needed to be kept happy. Micheline knew that showing up at her sister's gathering would have that effect on Errol. Still, it was difficult for her to be around Vic Bellamy, and he probably didn't like seeing her, either. Not only did she represent a reminder of him being unfaithful to his wife, but little Brianna bore a strong resemblance to both Micheline and Cécile, a similarity that became more noticeable as she got older. Micheline didn't really care if Norell Bellamy found out she was the mother of Brianna—as far as she was concerned, that was Norell's problem—but she didn't want to cause Cécile any trouble. Not only were Cécile and Norell good friends, they were also business partners, owning a third of a successful medical transcription service along with their friend, the recently engaged Dana Covington. Friction between Cécile and Norell could have devastating consequences. It would also back up Cécile's oft-repeated claim that Micheline was a troublemaker . . . and Micheline's determination for her sister not to be proven right outweighed her desire to preserve Cécile's relationship with Norell.

Micheline took a deep breath and vowed to do her best under difficult circumstances. Not only did she and her older sister not particularly get along, but Micheline also had an unpleasant history with both of Cécile's business partners.

Cécile greeted her warmly, as did Michael, and Errol made no secret that he was thrilled at her showing up. Even Norell embraced her. Why shouldn't she, Micheline thought. She had no knowledge of the one-night stand between Micheline and Vic that had produced Brianna.

In contrast, both Vic and Dana offered greetings that at best could be called caution-filled, at worst stiff.

Micheline took a seat in the spacious living room, grateful that the air-conditioning was set low enough to be comfortably cool in the oppressive Florida summer heat. Micheline watched Cécile's friend Dana interact with her future husband, a handsome, if on the short side, green-eyed dude named Gil something or other. Micheline had rented a room in Dana's house when she first moved to Jacksonville from South Florida. Just for fun, Micheline started dating the same man Dana was seeing. She only allowed him to see her on Saturday nights and insisted he take her to the nicest of restaurants. It gave Micheline a satisfied feeling to know she was getting the best the man had to offer, and that there would be little time or funds left for his pursuit of Dana.

Eventually Dana found out, and she'd been furious, as well as embarrassed. She'd confided in Micheline her nervousness about dating again after being widowed in an accident, unaware of Micheline's intimate relationship with the same man. Dana ordered Micheline to move out of her house. Cécile had been equally livid when Dana told her what happened, accusing Micheline of being malicious just for the heck of it.

Micheline knew it had been wrong to deliberately hurt Dana, who'd been nothing but nice to her. Her real source of annoyance came from the man in both of their lives, whom she'd witnessed chatting with Dana at the club before she left. Micheline felt that he should have approached her first. How dare he look around after Dana left to see who else's number he might be able to get before the evening ended? Nobody got away with treating her like a leftover. She decided on the spot to give him a hard way to go, to monopolize his time and money. Dana was just collateral damage.

Or maybe not. Deep down, Micheline knew it irked her to see Dana's life coming together after the financial problems and loneliness she suffered as a result of her husband's untimely death. The medical transcription service Dana began with Cécile and Norell helped solve the first problem, and the man they were sharing took care of the second. Micheline didn't know why it bothered her so much to see other people get what they wanted out of life. She certainly had no interest in the headaches of owning a business, and that man who'd pursued them both could hardly be considered a prime catch. Yet both prospects had brought sunshine to Dana's life.

Just recently, when telling Micheline about Dana's engagement, Cécile gloated in sharing that Dana's relationship with her new fiancé started that same day at the beach when Dana learned of Micheline's duplicity. Now, seeing Dana's obvious happiness, Micheline found herself feeling incensed. No one was supposed to be happy if she still had yet to achieve what she wanted. She liked Dana better when she was struggling to get her business off the ground and wading in the uncertain waters of dating again. Now her business, in which Cécile was a partner, was thriving, and she'd found love again.

The history with Dana aside, by far, Micheline's most dangerous encounter was with Norell and Vic Bellamy. Little Brianna Bellamy was now three years old and just beautiful. Micheline felt no maternal tugs toward the immaculately dressed and coiffed toddler who had yet to become aware of how pretty she was, only admiration for her. Little Brianna Bellamy looked like *she* had as a child. She even had Micheline's eyes.

What she feared most of all was that someone would notice that.

She quickly offered to help in the kitchen, the perfect excuse to avoid the others. Errol, who enjoyed the company of Cécile's husband, Michael, as well as their friends, was fine being left with them to watch the game.

Micheline was cutting some playful celery garnishes for the potato salad when Vic Bellamy, of all people, entered the kitchen, carrying two large bags of ice. "Uh . . . hi, Micheline," he said awkwardly. "I just went out for some ice, and I told Cécile I'd fill the cooler for her."

The large group would be having dinner outside, as soon as the game ended. "Go right ahead. It's right there."

Vic placed the cooler on the counter and lifted out the bags of ice, then began removing six-packs of beer stacked on the floor from the plastic holders and inserting them into the cooler. "So, what do you think of Brianna?"

Micheline shrugged. "I think she's gorgeous. A future cover girl in the making. She looks very happy and well adjusted. You and Norell should be proud."

He stopped his activity and stared at her. "Is that all?"

She put the knife down. "What do you want me to say, Vic? That *I* want her now?"

"Frankly, yes. Even though after three years, it's not likely the courts would let you have her."

Micheline's anger rose like smoke from a chimney. Why was he being so difficult when she was trying to be amiable? "Well, you and your little wifey can relax. I don't plan to make any claims on her." Micheline picked up the knife and calmly sliced a stuffed green olive to make eyes for the face she was applying to the top of the potato salad, conscious of Vic's intense gaze.

"You are really a piece of work, you know that?" he said in a manner both soft and slow. The kitchen was well away from the living room in the front of the house, but they both knew someone could come in at any time. "Cold as these ice cubes. How could you look at the child you gave birth to and not feel any feelings for her? All you can say is, 'She's pretty.' A fucking stranger would say that." He blew out his breath. "I find myself feeling sorry for Errol. He was just telling me how much he wants kids. He seems to think it'll happen any time now, but I think he's in for a tremendous disappointment. You probably have no intention of getting pregnant."

"Who cares what you think?" she challenged, equally softly. "You're not even making any damn sense. You stand there and tell me you expect me to take steps to get Brianna back, and when I tell you that won't happen, you start insulting me." *I ought to ask for her back just to get back at you, you bastard—except I just might be successful, and then what would I do with a three-year-old?*

He studied her and nodded knowingly. "You and I were together just one night, the condom tore, and bam! Nine months later, a baby. You're still young, Micheline. If you got pregnant that easily four years ago, no way would it take you this long to get knocked up now. You must be doing something to prevent it. You're about as maternal as this can of beer." He held up a can of Miller Genuine Draft that he'd just removed from the plastic necking.

Micheline opened her mouth to give a nasty reply, but she froze at the sound of a child's voice just outside the kitchen. She pressed her index finger against her lips and wildly gestured toward the arched entryway.

Vic frowned. "That sounds like . . ." He moved toward the entryway and called, "Brianna?"

Micheline gasped. If Brianna was just a few yards away, Norell couldn't be far behind. She and Vic had been careful to keep their voices down, of course, but the entire episode had been entirely too close for her liking. She turned on the power to the small television on the counter, adjusting the channel to the same one showing the game. This would provide a perfect backdrop and make it impossible for anyone to overhear their words. She heard Vic's voice speaking to someone, probably Norell, and because of the television she could only make out a word here and there.

"All right. I'll be back out as soon as I finish loading the cooler. Cécile said she wants to sit down to dinner right after the game. Hopefully by then it'll be a little cooler outside." Vic bent to scoop up his daughter. "Daddy loves you, Sweetpea."

He returned to the kitchen. "Norell was just bringing Brianna to the bathroom."

"I don't recall the bathroom being so close to the kitchen," she remarked cynically.

"Brianna got away from her and ran this way. It's nothing, Micheline."

She wasn't so sure, and said nothing. A moment later Errol appeared, carrying two more bags of ice. "I think you forgot about these, Vic. I'll give you a hand. Which are you doing, the beer or the pop?"

"I've got the beer." Vic was moving quickly now to empty the packs of beer into the cooler. Then he opened the bags of ice and poured the cubes over the cans. "All right, I'm gonna take this outside." He gave Micheline a quick glance as he left the room, and she allowed herself to glare at him for a few seconds.

"Something wrong, Michie?" Errol asked. "You look kind of funny."

She quickly relaxed her face. "Oh, I'm fine."

"Are you sure? I thought I picked up on some bad karma between you and Vic. Were y'all arguing about something?" He moved to stand behind her, his arms encircling her waist. "I don't have to defend your honor, do I?" he joked.

Micheline cursed herself for not doing a better job of concealing her emotions. At least Errol didn't appear to take it seriously. He'd been blessed with a carefree disposition. "No, of course not," she said with a forced laugh. "We were just talking about that scandal with the football player beating up his girlfriend. Let's just say we have different views about how the NFL should punish him. But Vic and me disagreeing doesn't mean we're not still friends," she added with a reassuring smile. "Now, you probably need to get that pop outside. Isn't the game almost over?"

"Yeah." Errol moved away from her and began to load the soda into the cooler. On his way out with it he stopped behind her and peered over her shoulder. "What's that you're doing?"

"Oh, just a little touch of whimsy. I'm putting garnishes on the salads."

"Smiley faces. Cute. The kids'll get a kick out of that. But I'm not sure how I feel about you working in the kitchen while Cécile is sitting down in the living room with her guests. She's the hostess, and it's her responsibility to prepare the food, not yours."

"It's all right, Errol. Cécile knows I have no interest in basketball. I'm glad to help out." Micheline wiped her brow, which had become damp with perspiration. It had been dangerous for her and Vic to have that conversation here. She still felt all wound up from when Brianna and Norell showed up, terrified that Norell might have overheard Vic say that she was Brianna's mother. And now Errol had picked up on the tension between her and Vic. Fortunately, she covered nicely.

Still, she realized that coming here today had been a mistake.

Chapter 9

The excitement in the Trent bedroom increased with each passing second. Micheline, on her stomach with her hips in the air, moaned uncontrollably as Errol, holding her hips steady, thrust inside her. He felt so deliciously swollen. Her muscles contracted and gripped him.

"Not yet," he said with a grunt. Abruptly he pulled out. "Turn over," he ordered.

Micheline flipped over, her thighs spread invitingly. He pulled her down farther on the bed by her thighs and slid inside her, kneeling upright rather than leaning over her. She squealed in delight as he filled her completely, her palms squeezing her breasts.

Both of them knew they couldn't hold out much longer. Micheline came first, Errol seconds later.

"Hot damn!" he exclaimed as he pulled out of her and fell to the mattress face down, panting heavily. "If that one didn't make twins, I just don't know what to say about it."

Micheline's breath came out in gasps. Errol might complain about how much she spent, but their sex life had never been a problem. He always left her thoroughly satiated and satisfied. Now that the dreadful afternoon at Cécile's was over, she could be glad she'd gone. There'd been a little something extra in Errol's technique tonight, and she suspected it was because of the pleasant time they'd spent together that afternoon.

They lay side by side on their backs in the large bed. Errol put a hand out to stroke the smooth skin of her thigh. "I've been thinking, Michie."

Her shoulders went taut. Whatever was on his mind, it couldn't be good. And she had a feeling she knew what he was leading up to. "Hmm?"

"I know you're not happy about the idea of seeking help from professionals. I admit I find it a little embarrassing myself. Who wants to admit that they're having trouble doing what even teenagers can do?"

Micheline's spirits perked up like a coffeepot. Was he going to suggest they forget about having kids?

"And I wanted to ask you, in case things don't work out for us the natural way, how do you feel about adoption?"

Just as quickly as her spirit had soared, now it crashed and burned. *Adoption?* Was he crazy? Bringing some stranger's child into their home, giving them everything, and then having their ungrateful ass kick them to the curb as soon as they graduated from college? "Gee, I don't know, Errol. It takes a real special person to be able to love someone else's baby as your own. I don't know if I've got what it takes."

"Let me ask you something, Michie. Do you ever think about the baby you gave up?"

"All the time," she lied. "But I know she's in a good, loving home."

"And you have no regrets about giving her up?"

This conversation was giving her the creeps, probably because she'd had a similar discussion with Vic just a few hours ago. "No, Errol, I don't," she said. "You see, every time I would have looked at her, I would be reminded of that terrible thing that happened to me." She shook her head dramatically, closing her eyes for effect. "It wouldn't be a healthy mother/

child relationship, and if you and I had children, she'd sense that I felt differently about them."

"I guess that's fair. I know you don't like to talk much about what happened—"

"That's right," she interrupted. "I don't. And I wish you wouldn't force me to talk about it now."

Errol sighed. He patted her thigh. "Why don't we just get some sleep?"

"Good idea."

Usually they fell asleep locked in each other's arms, but tonight they rolled to opposite sides of the bed.

"This was a birthday I'll never forget, thanks to you, Suzie Q," Brad said softly. "You outdid yourself on the party."

She closed her eyes and savored the moment. Brad was her husband. She was in no danger of losing him, to Micheline Trent or anyone else. After Brad's public display of affection when they rolled out the cake, it was clear to everyone present that Suzanne Betancourt fulfilled her husband's needs . . . *all* of them. "As much as I'd like to take sole credit, Paula contributed quite a bit."

"Yeah, but I don't want to do *this* to Paula." He pulled back just enough to cup her cheeks, then he kissed her, at first sweetly, then with growing ardor.

Half an hour later they lay cuddled in the center of the large bed, the sheet drawn up over their naked bodies. Suzanne closed her eyes dreamily. She truly was a fortunate woman. Her husband was good-looking, sexy, had plenty of money, *and* he was a fabulous lover.

"I noticed how down Kenya looked at dinner," Brad remarked. "I guess the fact that Gregory is dating Paige came as much of a shock to her as it did to me."

"Brad . . . you didn't know?"

"Of course not. If I had I would have told you about it."

"But you didn't seem surprised to see them together," she blurted out.

"I didn't want to give Lisa the satisfaction of being shocked. I guess you were watching my reaction, huh?"

Suzanne hadn't wanted to give him the impression that she'd watched him every minute, but at least he didn't seem angry about it. She decided to just tell him the truth. "I noticed Paige and Gregory when they came in. I don't mind telling you I *was* shocked. Naturally, I waited to see how you would react."

Brad chuckled in amusement. "Personally, I think the reason Lisa didn't mention it to me before the party was because she was feeling a little vindictive."

"Of course she is," Suzanne replied, her lower lip poking out slightly. "It's *my* sister's feelings that were at stake. Lisa wanted to get as much mileage as she could about it, to maximize Kenya's shock, and mine, too."

"I'm sure she felt a little triumphant, given the long history between Gregory and the girls, although she'd never admit it, at least not to me." Brad gently stroked Suzanne's hair. "Suzie Q, I know it hasn't always been easy for you to live next door to my first wife. I want you to know I really do appreciate the effort you've made to get along with Lisa these past five years."

Suzanne put her annoyance at Brad's first wife aside, at least for the moment. Brad had just acknowledged that it had been difficult for her at times to live next door to Lisa and Darrell. Thoughts of Lisa had no place in this bond-strengthening moment between her and her husband.

"Well, you were the one who said that things would be a lot more pleasant if Lisa and I made an effort to be civil to each other," Suzanne said. "I guess it's working." She paused for a moment. "But she still gets on my nerves sometimes."

Brad laughed from deep in his throat, a wonderfully full, rich sound Suzanne never tired of hearing. "C'mon, let's go to sleep."

Five minutes later, still cuddled together, he on his back

and she facing him on her side, Suzanne heard Brad say the words that meant everything to her.

"I love you, Suzanne."

A happy smile formed on her lips that even the sound of his light breathing—he'd drifted off right after speaking—couldn't diffuse. She and Brad were in love now as much as they'd ever been.

And no one, not Micheline or anyone else, would interfere.

Suzanne worked in the kitchen to prepare Brad's breakfast. By the time he emerged from their bedroom, wearing a short-sleeved yellow shirt, a tie, and tan pants, a tan sports coat draped over his arm, she had everything ready.

She enjoyed the children's summer break almost as much as they did. Bradley and Lauren both slept late, allowing her and Brad to have breakfast alone.

"Are you going to the club tonight?" she asked as they enjoyed fresh pineapple. Suzanne savored the naturally sweet taste. Keeping fit meant eating very few of the sweets she loved.

"No, I'll be home after work. Chris gave me the financials for the restaurant. I need to go over them."

"You want to be sure we're still swimming in money, huh?" she asked with a smile.

"Well, I don't know about swimming in it, but the restaurant's numbers seem to have held pretty steady, despite everything going on with the economy."

Suzanne removed their bowls from the table and popped two slices of whole wheat bread into the toaster. When it popped up, she set the microwave above the stove to heat for forty seconds, then buttered the toast. She returned to the table with a plate of beef smoked sausage and scrambled egg substitute, the toast resting on top.

Brad spooned egg and sausage onto his plate, taking a

piece of toast. He was eating as Suzanne fixed her own plate. "This is great, Suzie Q," he said.

"I aim to please," she said, beaming across the breakfast table. She had learned to cook the sausage the way he liked it, sliced lengthwise down the center so it could be cooked flat on both sides.

"The house still looks a little messy from the party," he remarked. "When is Teresita coming in?"

"I asked her to come in today. It's not her regular day, but the family room and the bathrooms need a thorough cleaning."

"Her company's all gone?"

"Yes, they left yesterday."

"Did you give her kids their envelopes?"

"Oh, yes. I gave them to Teresita last Wednesday, the last day she worked."

Brad shook his head. "I can't believe that little Sierra is all finished with high school, and that Ruben graduated from college," he marveled. "It seems like just yesterday that they were sitting in the kitchen doing their homework while Teresita worked."

"It's really something, isn't it? You know, I think Ruben will go down as being Lauren's first crush."

"He's a nice young man. I'm sure he'll do very well for himself." Brad took a forkful of egg and smoked sausage into his mouth. "What're your plans for today?" he asked after he swallowed.

"Oh, nothing unusual," she replied with a shrug. "I'll go to the gym, stop at the supermarket. And Lauren wanted to go riding, so we'll probably drive down to the stables." *As long as we can be back by three p.m.* She couldn't miss her one guilty pleasure, *Facades*. The soap opera had a largely black cast, and she tried to never miss it.

"I was curious about something, Suzie Q."

"What's that?"

"It's just that—since the kids are older now and probably don't need you around as much, have you ever thought about, well, doing something else with your time?"

Suzanne's forehead wrinkled. "I don't get it. Do something like what?" Then she thought she might understand. "You mean, like a *job?*" Had he gone nuts?

"Not necessarily a job. Just some kind of activity. Something that would give you a sense of accomplishment, make your life seem worthwhile."

"I already feel worthy, Brad," she said indignantly. "I take care of my household and my family. That in itself is a full-time job."

"Yeah, I guess you're right. Just forget I even brought it up."

The next day Suzanne heard the words she dreaded from her mother, who called during her lunch break at the post office. "It's official. Kenya's pregnant."

"Oh, God." She'd been praying that the home test results were wrong. "So what happens now?"

"That kind of depends on you, Suzanne. Are you gonna tell Brad about it?"

Suzanne took a deep breath, then made up her mind. "Not until after Kenya's had a chance to tell Gregory. I'm not comfortable with that, but I just don't think it's right for him to know before the father does."

"You know if you do tell him, he'll go right to Paige and tell her that her boyfriend's old girlfriend is pregnant."

"That's a perfectly natural reaction, Mom. I already said I won't tell him. But Kenya has to tell Gregory right away. I don't like keeping this secret from Brad, but it's up to Gregory to tell Paige about Kenya's pregnancy, not her father."

"Hmph. I wish I could be a fly on the wall when Little Miss Paige gets the bad news from Gregory."

Suzanne was silent for a moment. "You really hate Paige, don't you, Mom?"

"No," Arlene said, "but I'm angry that she took Gregory away from Kenya, and I'm glad she's going to find out the hard way that he's going back to Kenya. Are you saying you're not happy to see that snot-nosed stepdaughter of yours get hers?"

"We're not talking about me, Mom," she replied sternly. "What I want to know is, when does Kenya plan on telling Gregory that he's going to be a daddy? I don't care much for the situation I'm in, and I want to get everything out in the open as soon as possible."

"Tonight. She said she already called him to set it up. But there's more involved than just Kenya telling him. They have to decide what they're going to do."

Suzanne rolled her eyes. As far as she understood, Kenya was going to have her baby, and that was that.

"Why don't you and I and Flo get together and have lunch tomorrow?" Arlene suggested. "I have the day off because I'm working Saturday. Let's go someplace really nice, where we can talk undisturbed. Maybe one of those places in San Marco with the hoity-toity chefs. Flo works near there, anyway."

"Mom, I really don't want to get involved in this."

"But I need you, Suzanne! You know Flo better than I do, and it's obvious she admires you. If you take my side she'll be more receptive to the idea of Gregory and Kenya getting married. Without your influence, she might not go for it."

"I don't think I can help you, Mom. This is bound to cause problems between Brad and me." *Even more than we have right now,* she added silently. "It's important that I keep out of it."

"Please, Suzanne. I need your help. I'm trying to secure your sister's future."

She sighed. Kenya did deserve to be happy, and if she could help her sister, she really should. "All right," she finally said. "I'll go with you, but I want to say as little as possible."

"Just don't tell Brad," Arlene continued. "It'll ruin everything if you do. I'm sure Gregory will inform Paige the first chance he gets, and *then* Brad can find out."

Suzanne noticed two things. First, her mother practically came out and said she wanted to go to one of the nicest restaurants in town, which meant she expected Suzanne to foot the bill. That wasn't a big deal; Suzanne knew that the type of place her mother hoped to go to didn't open until dinnertime. But what annoyed her the most was how her mother kept harping on how Suzanne should conceal her knowledge of Kenya's condition from Brad. Suzanne wasn't in the habit of keeping secrets from her husband, and she knew that simply knowing about Kenya's pregnancy put her at risk. There'd already been tension in her marriage in the past over her dislike of Paige and her mother, Lisa. If Brad ever found out that she'd known about it previously, there'd be hell to pay.

It was easy to address the first issue. "Mom, most of the restaurants you're thinking of don't open before four, for the dinner business. They don't serve lunch."

"Oh. I didn't know. That's too bad."

"As far as my keeping Brad in the dark . . . Mom, I'm pretty sure Gregory will want to put off telling Paige about Kenya being pregnant as long as he can. He'll lose her the moment she finds out, and he knows it. So it might be a week before he tells her, even longer than that." She took a deep breath. "I won't deceive Brad that way, and it's wrong for you to ask me to."

"You're forgetting something, Suzanne," Arlene said lightly. "Once Flo tells him that you were at lunch with us while we discussed the situation, he'll think Brad knows already and is waiting for him to do the right thing."

Suzanne's eyes stretched open. She hadn't thought of that. Of course Gregory would think that if she knew about Kenya's condition, Brad did as well, and he'd realize he had no choice but to tell Paige quickly.

"I guarantee he'll give Paige the bad news by Thursday at the latest," Arlene said confidently. "And if Brad finds out you knew, all you have to do is tell him that you wanted to make sure Gregory had a chance to discuss the matter with his parents and decide what to do before he told Paige. Tell him you wanted to give him a chance to do right by Kenya."

Suzanne frowned. "You make it sound like you still expect him to marry her."

"He will," Arlene said, having lost none of her conviction.

Her mother's confidence made Suzanne think about the curious discussion she had with Brad at breakfast yesterday. "Mom, I'm confused about something."

"Something about Brad?"

"Yes. He said something to me yesterday morning that's been bothering me because I can't figure it out."

"What'd he say?" Arlene asked.

"He asked if I'd given any thought to doing something that would make me feel worthwhile, as he put it. As though I don't already have my hands full."

"Have your hands full?" Arlene repeated in an amused tone. "Suzanne, please. I'm your mother, remember? You don't have to put on an act for me."

"I'm not acting."

"No, you're *over*acting. You haven't worked since the day you and Brad announced your engagement. That's been over fifteen years. You don't know the first thing about having your hands full."

"I might not work, but I have a very full life, Mom. I've got the kids, the house, Brad . . ."

"There you go again," Arlene said in an exasperated tone. "Suzanne, Teresita comes in two or three times a week and keeps your house spotless. Bradley and Lauren are almost grown, and Brad certainly doesn't require a lot of care. All he wants is for you to keep yourself looking good and to make him a good dinner." Arlene sighed deeply. "Sometimes I really do think you've lost touch with reality. There are women out there who are struggling every day to find time to do everything they need to do for their families, plus work full-time jobs. And you think that just because you go to the gym and work out most days for half an hour that you've put in a full day's work. It's not the same thing, Suzanne."

"Cooking dinner for my family can often be a real challenge, Mom," Suzanne said defensively. "Lauren is such a picky eater, and Brad has such highbrow tastes."

"Brad can afford to have highbrow taste," Arlene pointed out. "And maybe I shouldn't say this, but for years it seems like you really didn't indulge it. You made box meals from the supermarket."

"The kids like that stuff," she protested.

"Suzanne, it's your *husband* that you really need to make happy. Remember, he's the one who makes it possible for you all to live the way you do. Thank goodness you met Paula and learned to cook the way Brad wants. And now he's giving you a very clear message."

"Yeah, and what's that?"

"He's saying that you need to think about doing something with your life, something that will make you grow as a person. In other words, you have to become more aware that there's a world out there beyond your property line. Look at all those women at his birthday party," Arlene continued. "The great majority of them have kids in high school or college, but they are involved in what's going on in the world. Brad is giving you a hint, and I strongly suggest you take it."

"But, Mom, I'm not like those doctors or teachers or other professional women, and Brad knows that. I'm not trained to do anything, and it's too late to do anything about that now. I'm almost forty-two years old."

"Nobody expects you to go back to school at this point in your life, Suzanne. You don't have to do professional work. There's plenty of things you can do. Why not volunteer at one of the hospitals or social organizations? Remember Weezie Jefferson and her Help Center on *The Jeffersons*?" Arlene said. "And if you don't like the idea of being around sick or needy people, I'm sure that community theater you and Brad sponsor could use your help."

Suzanne wrinkled her nose. "I'm sorry, Mom, but I just don't believe in doing work for free."

"I think you're being a little selfish, Suzanne. It wouldn't hurt you to give of yourself. God's been good to you, and you don't have to work for money. I mean, didn't Brad volunteer when they set up that two-week temporary clinic for the uninsured here in town?"

"That's different, Mom. Brad donated time to the clinic to do what he normally does. Most people have a skill. Look at you and your gardening. But I really don't know how to do anything."

"So take up a hobby, Suzanne. Learn something new. Become more interesting. That's what Brad's suggesting you do. He feels that you aren't growing. Change is a good thing, Suzanne."

Suzanne thought about the conversation long after it ended. Brad had been satisfied with her for sixteen years, longer than that if she included their courtship. Now all of a sudden he was asking her to become more worldly.

Instinct told her Micheline was behind this. What had she said to him the few minutes they spent talking and dancing at the party? Did she flaunt her knowledge? Had she gone out of her way to be captivating and witty?

Sure she had, Suzanne decided. And somewhere along the line, Micheline managed to convince Brad think that she, his wife, was stuck in a time warp.

Her mother was right, she decided. It would be a mistake to forget what Brad said, like he suggested. She had to become interesting somehow. But how?

Volunteering was definitely out. Suzanne leaned forward, pressing her lower palms against her forehead. If she thought hard enough, surely she could come up with some type of hobby or craft. Maybe French lessons?

No, she decided. She still got angry at the thought of Micheline sprouting those foreign words to Brad, but she had to admit that the language sounded beautiful. She envied Micheline for being able to speak it fluently. She'd like nothing better than to best Micheline at something, but in her heart she knew it wouldn't be French. Learning a language was difficult, and besides, she already had enough difficulty with English.

That was something she could do, Suzanne realized. She could improve her vocabulary, one word at a time. Maybe she could understand better when Brad's colleagues used words she wasn't familiar with.

It was a start, at least.

Chapter 10

Flo looked at her only child, her mouth open and her entire upper body feeling like it had been paralyzed. "Gregory! You didn't!"

"Son, I've told you a thousand times, never operate without your gloves," Ernie added. "Now look. You'll be tied to this girl for the next eighteen years, and she probably plans to squeeze you for every one of them."

"Oh, Gregory," Flo repeated.

"I'm sorry, Mom . . . Dad. I know you're disappointed." He hung his head.

"Is she sure she's pregnant?" Ernie asked. "She's not just trying to rook you with a story that she *might* be?"

"No, she's pregnant. She did the home test, and then she went to the doctor for confirmation."

"And you didn't find out about it before tonight?" Flo asked. "She didn't share her suspicions with you?"

"She didn't say a word."

"I see," Flo murmured.

"Does she intend to have the baby?" Ernie asked.

"She says she wants it."

"Wants it, my ass," Ernie snapped. "What she wants is to get her hooks in you, son. And there's not a damn thing anyone can do to stop it. I can just picture it. She'll do things like show up here with the baby whenever you have female company." He grunted.

"A grandchild!" Flo exclaimed. "I never expected to be a grandmother before I was fifty, at least. This is four years early. And out of wedlock. Ernie, what are we going to tell everyone?"

"It wouldn't be a big deal if the child's mother was a young lady of quality, like Paige," Ernie said. "Then they could get married. But that scenario isn't likely. Paige knows how to take care of herself. She'd never let something like this happen."

"It's up to the girl to protect herself," Flo agreed.

Ernie turned to Gregory. "Let this be a lesson to you, son. You should consider yourself lucky that all you got out of this was a baby. I personally think Kenya does a lot of sleeping around. Look at the way she dresses, all those low-cut blouses showing off her tits. Who knows what kind of germs she's carrying."

"That's right, Gregory," Flo chimed in. "You have to make sure you use condoms so you don't pick up any STDs. God forbid you pass on something you caught from Kenya to Paige."

"Paige is through with me anyway, Mom, or she will be when she finds out about Kenya."

"Maybe not, son," Ernie soothed. "She knows enough about Kenya to know what a tramp she is."

Flo shook her head. "No, Ernie. Gregory is right. Paige will have to quit him. It's a matter of pride. Maybe they can find their way back to each other in a few years' time. After all, they're still young."

"So what happens now?" Ernie asked.

Gregory shrugged. "Kenya asked me what I wanted to do."

"I know what *that* means," Flo said with a grunt. "She expects you to marry her."

"I hope you told her you'd like her to get rid of it," Ernie said.

"I suggested that might be the best thing to do. But she said no."

"Well, that's that," Ernie said in a defeated voice. "You can't stop her from having the baby if that's what she wants to do. I'd recommend trying to make a financial settlement with her on your own when the time comes. Make it a legal document. If she brings you to court you'll be paying through your nose."

"For eighteen long years," Flo said dejectedly.

"Oh. Mom, Kenya said that her sister's going to call you tonight."

Flo brightened at the thought of hearing from Suzanne. "Oh?"

"I wonder what she wants," Ernie said thoughtfully.

"I'm sure she'll tell me what a regrettable situation this is, and that we'll have to make the most of it," Flo said. "A pep talk kind of thing."

"I'm not so sure. Remember, Kenya knew about this before she told Gregory. Who knows what kind of scheme she and Arlene and Suzanne have worked out between them."

"Ernie, you're so suspicious."

"I didn't fall off a turnip truck, Flo. I think they're up to something. I'm tempted to call Brad and ask him about it."

Gregory immediately went into a panic. "Don't do that, Dad! He's probably ready to tan my hide. He might have even told Paige about Kenya being pregnant. I'm sure he knows, especially if Miz Betancourt does."

"In that case, I think you should talk to him directly," Flo said. "If you're old enough to have sex, Gregory, you're old enough to deal with the consequences of it."

"I agree with your mother, son," Ernie said. "Call him and ask to have a man-to-man talk. Ask him not to say anything to Paige, because you want to be the one to tell her. He'll respect you for that."

* * *

Flo dressed carefully. She worked as a medical biller, and business casual was the order of the day. She usually wore a simple skirt or Capri pants to work, but today she put on her nicest summer pantsuit, a sleeveless linen in butterscotch and lilac, the top of which buttoned down the back. She wore pearl jewelry: earrings and a double-stranded necklace and bracelet. She had to be careful with her spending, but she still liked to dress nicely. She'd never been to the restaurant Suzanne invited her to, but it was in the San Marco section of the city and had the word "European" in its title, so that told her it was a nice place and she needed to dress accordingly.

She arrived five minutes after the appointed meeting time. As she walked the half block to the restaurant, she saw Suzanne pulling into a just-vacated parking space in the Lexus two-seater she sometimes drove. Flo had ridden in it a couple of times, back when she and Suzanne were buddies. That was before Ernie lost his job and plunged them into financial despair. Flo, too embarrassed to admit that they'd suffered a decline in fortune, chose to retreat rather than to continue her friendship with Suzanne. She was too busy volunteering for desperately needed overtime, and later moonlighting, to try to keep up appearances. To save face, she told everyone she'd been promoted at work to a position of more authority that required more time at the office.

Flo waved jauntily, but when she noticed that both Suzanne and her mother wore Capri pants, she realized she'd committed another fashion faux pas.

Instantly her thoughts went to Brad Betancourt's party last weekend. Ernie had refused to tell her what he'd overheard people saying about her, but it must have been pretty bad if he'd been so anxious to get her and leave.

She nervously brushed her hair back with her right hand, although no strands fell toward her face. She hadn't gotten the weave for length, but for thickness. At her mature age, she didn't need hair streaming down her back. She wore it in a chin-length bob, longer in the front and shorter and curled under in the back.

Suzanne wore a beautiful deep blue-green sleeveless blouse and matching blue and green plaid Capri pants in raw silk. Her mid-heel open-toed strappy sandals were the same color as her blouse, and she carried a medium-sized straw purse. Her long hair was pulled back into a ponytail caught on the crown of her head. She looked casual, yet elegant, like a young matron shopping along Worth Avenue in Palm Beach.

Something was different about Suzanne these days, Flo thought. She carried herself better. She looked like she'd been born to money, not like someone who'd merely married rich. Flo noticed that she wore just three gold bracelets on her right wrist, a simple watch on her left, small gold earrings, and one ring on each hand, her impressive diamond engagement ring and matching wedding band on her left, a coral ring on her right.

Flo glanced at the multiple rings on her own fingers. Maybe Gregory had a point when he said she didn't have to have a ring on each finger. . . .

"Flo, hello!" Suzanne said warmly as she closed the distance between them. "I'm so glad you got here the same time as us and didn't have to wait. Mom was running a little behind." She pressed her cheek lightly to Flo's in an air kiss.

"We got lucky with a parking space," Suzanne said after Flo greeted Arlene. "Did you have to park far away?"

"No, I'm only a block down."

"Good. Well, let's go have some lunch."

They settled at a table at what Flo realized with dismay was nothing more than a deli. She should have dressed the way she normally did.

"I don't know about you ladies," Suzanne said, "but I'd love a glass of wine."

"Sounds wonderful," Arlene said, as Flo expected she would. She rarely saw Suzanne's mother without a drink in her hand.

"Do they serve wine here?" Flo asked uncertainly.

"Yes, and beer, too. I'm surprised you haven't been here before, Flo," Suzanne remarked.

Flo wished she'd done her homework on the restaurant Suzanne had chosen. "Um . . . to tell the truth, I've been so busy at work since I got my promotion that I usually only have time to run out and pick something up from down the street. Unless I'm lunching with a client, of course," Flo hastily added. Dining with her employer's clients was nothing but a dream, but it sounded nice. She could hardly admit that she continued to bring lunch from home, a money-saving habit she'd started during Ernie's period of underemployment that she continued after he landed the hospital job.

The women began talking in earnest once they had their wine. "Well, Flo, it looks like you and I are about to have a grandchild in common," Arlene began. "I take it you were as disappointed as I was to hear about it."

"Well . . . yes." Ernie, convinced Arlene and Suzanne were about to set her up, had warned her to be careful about what she said. She chose her words carefully. "Kenya and Gregory are both so young. I don't think they're ready to be parents. But it's not the first time kids their age got into trouble. I did expect Gregory to be sexually active, but becoming a grandmother . . . It's going to take some getting used to."

"Has Gregory shared his future plans with you and Ernie?" Arlene asked.

Flo looked puzzled. "Plans? Well, I don't think there really are any. Kenya's decided to have the baby, and of course he'll help her raise it. I'm sure he intends to be a hands-on father. Ernie set a wonderful example for him to follow," she added proudly.

Suzanne spoke up. "Flo, does it bother you at all that the baby will be born to unmarried parents?"

It was easy to figure out where this was headed. Ernie had been right, Flo thought. She suddenly had the uncomfortable feeling that she was being backed into a corner. "Well, it's far from an ideal situation, of course, but like I said, it's not the first time something like this has happened, and it won't be the last."

"Well, I find it very disturbing," Arlene declared. "In my day, when young people got into trouble, they got married."

"Married!" Flo exclaimed. "Well, I don't know if that's really necessary in *this* day and age. I mean, I'm sure Gregory plans on giving the baby his last name. Other than that, who really cares?"

"Well, I think he should give Kenya his name as well," Arlene said.

Flo hedged. "It seems to me, Arlene, like there's no longer a stigma in having a baby without benefit of a husband."

"In many cases, yes, but in the Hall family we try to live by certain standards."

"Flo, my mother isn't trying to talk Gregory into a lifetime commitment," Suzanne explained. She flashed her mother a warning look. She must have gone off the deep end with all that talk about family standards. Arlene had given birth to Kenya as a result of a short-term affair with a man who hadn't been seen since, long after her divorce from the father of Suzanne and her brothers. Kenya carried the surname of Hall simply because that had been the name of Arlene and her other children. Derrick had already fathered one child by a woman he hadn't married. What did her mother plan on doing, writing off her grandchild as an oversight? Or tell Gregory that Derrick was dating a woman with a child, leaving out the fact that it was *his* child? "These youthful marriages usually don't last, anyway. Mom just wants to see Kenya married well before her baby comes. They can always get a divorce after the baby's birth. The record will show that the baby's parents were married when he or she was born."

"Who knows," Arlene said, "the child might grow up to run for president or something. I'd prefer my grandchild not have any skeletons lurking in the closet. At least ones not of his or her own making."

Flo shook her head in stunned disbelief. "You make it sound like getting a divorce is no more complicated than registering a new car. I'm sure there's more to it than that, especially with a child involved. And this really sounds like a conversation that should be held between you and my son, Arlene. After all, Gregory is an adult, not a minor."

"Yes, I know," Arlene agreed. "I just thought it wouldn't hurt to get your opinion on the matter."

"Naturally, if it was up to me I'd prefer that my grandchild not be born out of wedlock. . . ."

"My family is a good family, Flo," Arlene said. "We may not have a lot of money, but we're good, hardworking, law-abiding people."

"Oh, Arlene! That's the farthest thing from my mind. I'm not even concerned about that. Ernie and I think Kenya is a fine young lady." Flo exaggerated, but she felt God would forgive her. She could hardly say, *We'd much rather have Gregory be with Paige, who's much better wife material.* "It's just that . . . marriage is a huge step, even if it's only temporary. Gregory just graduated from college a few weeks ago. He's already made it clear that he plans to stay at home while he gets his career off the ground . . . save money for the fu—" She broke off, alerted by Arlene's eager smile that she'd probably said too much.

"Perhaps Kenya and the baby can stay with Gregory at your home while they're married," Arlene suggested. "I'd offer them space in my house, but with my sons both living at home it would be awfully crowded. Isn't it just you, Ernie, and Gregory living in that big house of yours?"

"Well, it's true we do have four bedrooms and a bonus room upstairs. . . ."

"So Gregory wouldn't have to spend additional money to set up a household."

Flo looked taken aback, and Suzanne felt certain she noticed that Arlene hadn't said anything about Kenya spending any of *her* money. She watched Flo's thoughtful expression.

"Tell me this, Arlene," she finally said. "If the marriage is only for the purpose of legitimizing the baby, do they really have to live together at all?"

"Of course they should live together," Arlene said, sounding miffed. "That's what married people do."

Once more Suzanne intervened. "Personally, I don't believe my little sister is ready to be anyone's wife," she said. "And I must say I think the best way for her to learn that lesson is to actually *be* somebody's wife. I think that after a few months of taking care of a husband, she'll be very eager to be single again."

"Well," Flo said, "I'm not going to make any promises, but I will talk to Ernie about it, and we'll decide what to say to Gregory."

"That's fair," Suzanne said.

"I certainly can't ask more than that," Arlene agreed. "Oh, look, here's our sandwiches."

Chapter 11

"What!" Ernie exclaimed. "You've got to be kidding, Flo. Gregory doesn't want to marry that girl. Hell, he's just a kid, trying to get a piece where he could. It's not his fault she gave it up to him. Why should he be tied to her the rest of his life? Bad enough he'll be stuck with her in his life 'til the kid's eighteen. Longer than that, if it goes to college, although with Kenya as the mother I doubt that'll be an issue."

"Well, Arlene was talking about how it's beneath their family standards to have babies born out of wedlock."

"Horseshit. Doesn't Suzanne have a couple of kid brothers? Are you telling me none of them have any babies out there?"

"None that I know of, but I don't see much of them anyway."

"Who is Arlene to talk about this being beneath her standards?" Ernie demanded hotly. "Who does she think she is, the queen of England? If anybody's got low standards, it's that daughter of hers. You know she was up there fucking Gregory in his room whenever you and I weren't home, all the way back to their summer vacations when they were still in high school."

"I figured she was doing something, and chances are she wasn't the only one Gregory's had in his bedroom."

"It's disrespecting our home. Okay, so I understand that Gregory wanted to get some, but Kenya should have known better," Ernie reasoned. "You wouldn't have caught *Paige* doing anything like that. Gregory said they go to a motel."

"That's because Paige has class," Flo said forlornly. "Kenya doesn't. But Arlene said that she wouldn't expect the marriage to last forever. She's hoping Gregory will marry Kenya as soon as possible, but says it's fine with her if they file for divorce right after the baby's born."

"Oh yeah? Did she also say what they're going to live on? Gregory won't be starting his career until next month. He's in no position to support a wife, pay rent, buy food, pay utilities. And that two-bit job Kenya's got—"

Suddenly nervous, Flo chewed her lower lip. "Arlene suggested we might ask them to live here."

"Why am I not surprised?" Ernie said sardonically. "It seems to me like Arlene is making a lot of suggestions about what our son should be doing. Maybe instead of giving out suggestions to Gregory, she should suggest to that daughter of hers that she keep her legs closed."

"Well, she did mention that her house would be awfully crowded with one more adult and a baby, since her sons already live there. It's a small house, Ernie."

He scowled. "Yeah, I know. That poor-but-proud crap. Why do they have to live together at all?"

"I asked the same thing. Arlene said if they're going to be married, even temporarily, they really should live together." Flo hoped Ernie didn't notice how often she was using the words "Arlene said," or "Arlene suggested." She was starting to feel a little like a mouthpiece.

Ernie received her explanation with a grunt. "Just like I told you, it's a damn setup. If I know Arlene, she's probably trying to arrange for them to *stay* married. Not that she can do anything to stop Gregory from divorcing Kenya's ass. That's one devious broad. She's probably thinking about retiring and plans on moving in with her daughter and son-in-law. Gregory had better be careful, or else he'll find himself the main source of support for three people."

"There is one benefit to a marriage between Gregory and Kenya. I mean, besides the obvious, the baby not being illegitimate."

"And what's that?"

Flo took a deep breath and played her trump card. "We'd be related to Suzanne and Brad by marriage. We'd be part of their extended family. And we're right around the corner. Doesn't that mean we'd always be invited over?" Flo had his interest, and she held his gaze. "Maybe we'd even get invited out on their boat. Or up to their place in Maine. Wouldn't *that* be something."

Ernie broke into a slow grin. "It sure would. Hmm. Maybe it's not such a bad idea at that, for Gregory to marry the girl. It won't be forever. And even after the divorce we'll still be linked to Brad and Suzanne. The baby will give us a bond that'll last even after the divorce." He nodded his head thoughtfully, a smile on his face. "I guess I'd better start working on my golf swing, huh? And maybe buy a new fishing rod."

Flo winced at Gregory's stunned expression. For a moment she lost her nerve. How could she and Ernie ask Gregory to take such a step when he clearly didn't want to?

Gregory put down his fork. "You want me to *marry* Kenya?" he said in a disbelieving tone Flo found heartbreaking.

"It's a temporary situation, son," Ernie said calmly. "There's no need for hysterics. Your mother and I, and Kenya's mother as well, want your child born into a marriage. But no one expects you to stay married to her forever. In fact, after the baby is born, you can file for divorce."

"But Daddy, that's . . . You're talking about nine whole months." Gregory shook his head. "It's just not a good time right now."

"Gregory, it's not just about you anymore. You have to think about your unborn child," Flo coaxed. "What if he or she grows up and decides to run for president?" she asked, paraphrasing Arlene's statement from lunch. "This type of thing could be an embarrassment."

"No more than being born seven months after your parents got married. Nothing will change the fact that the damage is already done."

"But that's not the same thing," Flo argued.

"It didn't hurt Obama," Gregory pointed out.

"Gregory, your mother and I would really like you to do this," Ernie said after swallowing a bite of roast beef. Of the three of them, he was the only one who continued to eat. Flo had lost her appetite, and she suspected Gregory had as well. "We truly feel this is the right thing to do," Ernie continued. "It's part of your responsibility for getting Kenya pregnant."

Gregory stared at his mother, then his father. "In case you haven't figured this out, let me lay it out for you. I don't *want* to marry Kenya," he declared. "I've got something good going with Paige, something real. I know y'all think it's just kid stuff, but it's more than that."

Ernie looked at Gregory incredulously for a few seconds before finding his voice. "We can't force you to marry Kenya, Gregory, but stop and think for a minute. You said yourself that Paige won't want to be bothered with you after she learns you've gotten Kenya pregnant. Have you forgotten?"

"No, but I've given it more thought. Paige will believe the truth, that this happened before we started seeing each other."

"It doesn't matter, Gregory," Flo said, as gently as she could. "The timing is bad. Maybe you and Paige can resume your relationship after this is over, but your father and I really think you should do right by Kenya for the sake of the baby."

"It's part of the consequences of having unprotected sex, son," Ernie added. "My mama used to tell my brothers and me, 'Don't sleep with anybody you wouldn't marry.' In other words, if somebody's daddy came to our house with a shotgun looking for one of us, she wasn't going to argue on our behalf."

Gregory stared upward as he thought, but Flo suspected he wasn't even seeing the elegant chandelier of swirling gold and crystal that had cost her and Ernie fourteen hundred dollars. "So . . . just for a few months, huh?" he finally said. "I can end it right after the baby's born?"

"Yes, of course," Flo said. "And Kenya can move in here with us for the duration."

Gregory made a face. "You mean I have to *sleep* with her?"

Flo's heart broke for her son. Right now he looked about six years old, begging her not to make him eat the peas and carrots on his plate. He wasn't six anymore, but nor was he ready for the responsibility of marriage, even to someone he was madly in love with.

"You didn't seem to have a problem with sleeping with her before," Ernie said.

"Uh . . . Daddy. That wasn't really sleeping," Gregory clarified. "Besides, that was before Paige."

"Gregory, dear," Flo began, "I really think you'll have to forget about Paige. I think she's a much more suitable choice for you than Kenya, but she's not the one who's pregnant."

His shoulders drooped in defeat. "When do you want to do this?"

"I'd say as soon as possible. We can have a small ceremony right here at the house. Maybe you two can go away somewhere for a few days, and you'll be back in plenty of time to start work as scheduled."

"Another thing, son," Ernie said. "You'll have to tell Paige about this the first chance you get. You wouldn't want her to hear about it from anyone else . . . like Kenya."

Gregory left the room, looking lower than a thermostat reading in Antarctica.

Suzanne yawned. She'd had quite a workout that afternoon, and it wore her out. She'd probably go to bed early tonight.

Also making her more tired this week was this thing with

Kenya. Gregory Hickman had agreed to go along with the plan to marry her, and she was still keeping it from Brad. She wanted Paige to find out about it first. Surely Gregory planned to tell her. Brad would be angry with her for deliberately not giving him a chance to protect his daughter. Suzanne decided that it would be just plain silly for her to try to convince him that she hadn't known about it. He knew how close she was to her mother and sister. She hoped he'd accept that she felt she was doing the right thing by letting the drama unfold among the main parties involved: Gregory, Kenya, and Paige.

Nevertheless, her uncertainty about his reaction had her sleeping restlessly, tossing and turning in her sleep and waking frequently.

She reached for the ringing phone, answering it on the third ring. "Hello."

"Suzanne, it's Kenya."

Suzanne heard her mother's voice in the background, sounding higher pitched than usual in obvious agitation. "What is it, Kenya? You sound upset, and so does Mom."

"She's trying to calm me down, but it's not working. You won't believe this, Suzanne. I was taking the bus home from work, and Gregory drove past me going in the other direction. He had *Paige* in the car with him."

"Oh."

"He's still seeing her, Suzanne!" Kenya wailed. "I'm carrying his baby, and he's out with her while I'm taking a bus home. He ought to be coming to pick me up. Hell, I shouldn't even be working in my condition."

She sounded so overly dramatic that Suzanne had to hold back the urge to laugh. "Kenya, you need to listen to Mom and calm down," she said. "You're having a baby. That doesn't make you an invalid. There's no reason why you can't work. Millions of women do."

"But what about him being out with her?"

"Maybe he's telling her about the baby."

"He'd better be. Because I'm tempted to call her and tell

her myself. She'd better stay away from him. He'll soon be married to *me*."

"Kenya, didn't I just tell you to calm down? I don't want you to do anything stupid. You're not supposed to tell anyone about either the baby or your marriage plans."

"Paige had no business getting involved with Gregory in the first place," Kenya lamented. "She knew he was mine. It was wrong of her, and she knew it."

"*Friends* aren't supposed to steal another's man, but you and Paige aren't exactly girlfriends," Suzanne said drolly.

"I hate her. She thinks she's so cute."

Eventually Suzanne managed to calm her sister down, and her mother promised that Kenya wouldn't leave the house to confront Paige. Suzanne felt exhausted when she hung up the phone. Fortunately for her, Brad wasn't at home. After dinner he'd taken the kids down to the golf club to practice their tennis game. At least she was able to speak freely to Kenya.

This was all getting to be too much. If only she had someone to talk to, someone who could understand the pickle she was in. . . .

Impulsively she picked up the receiver and dialed Paula's number.

Errol stumbled into the bathroom. He definitely couldn't be called a morning person. It usually took a hot shower to wake him up completely.

He kept later office hours on Thursdays so he could accommodate people who worked during the day. Usually Micheline made him breakfast, but the hospital had called her yesterday to see if she could come in for an interview. She'd just kissed him good-bye as he was getting up.

Errol stepped into the shower, then just as promptly stepped out, holding a bar of soap so thin he knew it would break in two the moment he picked it up. He inserted the bar into Micheline's wash mitt that she kept on a rack spanning the Jacuzzi tub; she swore that pieces of worn-down soap worked every bit as well as expensive liquid soap. Then he squatted in front of the vanity underneath Micheline's sink, where she kept the new bars. As he tore open an individual box he caught sight of something rubbery lying on a paper towel in the rear. Curious, he reached for it. The object was a gold color with a round edge. It looked vaguely familiar.

Errol suddenly dropped it, as if it had burned his fingers. It was a diaphragm. He and Micheline had had sex last night. Apparently she'd washed it after removing it this morning and hidden it in the back of her vanity cabinet to dry so he wouldn't see it.

Cold realization poured over him like a blanket of morning fog. She'd lied to him. The reason she wasn't getting pregnant was because she was using birth control. She'd been guarding against pregnancy ever since they'd been married.

His jaw turned to steel. How could she do this to him? She knew how badly he wanted children, knew he was getting older. All along she'd been pretending to have difficulty conceiving. No wonder she tried to discourage him from getting a fertility workup.

Still numb, Errol took a fresh bar of soap and started the shower. As he scrubbed himself and became more alert, he kept wondering how Micheline could lie to him about something so important to him. Who the hell was he married to, anyway? He felt like he'd been dumped into one of those silly movies on the Lifetime network that Michie watched, where a wife learns she'd been duped.

As the wheels of Errol's mind began to turn, he saw the situation through wiser eyes. Micheline's reluctance to begin an infertility workup . . . her outright refusal to file a lawsuit against the owners of the garage where she'd supposedly been attacked . . . and the friction he thought he'd sensed between her and Vic Bellamy that day at Cécile's.

Then there was the most burning question of all . . . what *else* had she lied to him about?

That lying, scheming bitch.

By the time he dried himself off and dressed, he'd calmed down. He wouldn't confront her, but he'd fix her, all right. He'd be just as pleasant, attentive, and easygoing as he'd always been. He'd bide his time, and when he was ready—or if she should make a slip and give something away, whichever came first—he'd dump her like a tired Christmas spruce on New Year's Day.

Errol pulled his wallet from his hip pocket and rummaged through the business cards inside. He'd felt a real kinship with that woman he'd chatted with at Brad's party.

He sighed with relief when he found the card he was looking for. Fortunately, all was not lost. He could still get in touch with her.

Because as far as he was concerned, he was no longer a married man.

Chapter 12

Inside the restaurant, Micheline reached for her three-year-old niece, who sat in a high chair in the aisle. "Hello, Regine," she cooed.

"Auntie Michie!"

"That's right. I'm your one and only Auntie Michie. Don't you forget it."

The little girl giggled as Micheline tweaked her nose.

Her mother, Micheline's sister Cécile, beamed as she watched them interact. "You really have a way with babies, Michie. When are you going to have . . ." She trailed off.

Micheline sighed. She tried to make the most of these occasional lunches with her sister. Their parents down in South Florida, worried about their two girls living hundreds of miles away, had gotten them to promise they would see each other on a fairly regular basis. Still, Micheline preferred having lunch with Cécile every so often than going to the Rivers home when the Bellamy family was present. She'd have to start making some serious excuses to Errol for not wanting to go to Cécile and Michael's next gathering. That incident with Norell being right outside the kitchen still gave her the creeps. Cécile would be sure to blame her if Norell ever learned the identity of her little girl's biological mother. That would be disastrous, not just awkward, like Cécile asking when she was going to have another baby. *Another* baby.

Micheline knew Cécile was thinking of the baby she'd already given birth to. She hadn't given the broken condom a second thought, and she hadn't discovered her pregnancy until she was in her second trimester—her periods had continued, and she'd thought she just needed to start dieting to control her sudden weight gain.

The pregnancy caused major problems in her courtship with Errol. She tried to hide from him, but when he tracked her down she covered nicely by telling him she'd been raped in a deserted downtown garage and was pregnant by her attacker. She'd cried, saying she couldn't bring herself to tell him the truth, that she feared he wouldn't believe her. Micheline, hoping for marriage, refused to have sex with Errol while they dated, saying she had taken up celibacy after an unhappy love affair. She had a man on the side who fulfilled her regularly, the same man who'd been seeing Dana . . . and then there was that one fateful night she spent with Vic Bellamy.

Her tearful plea had been a success. Errol believed her story. Vic then stepped forward to request that she allow him to bring the baby to his lush of a wife, whose unhappiness over her infertility had her hitting the bottle. Micheline gladly gave him the infant, then managed to convince Errol that she didn't want to sue the owners of the parking lot where the "rape" occurred. She said she feared they would put her on trial and try to dig up dirt on her. She just wanted to put it behind her. Errol kept on her—telling her that it probably wouldn't get to trial, that they would most likely offer a settlement—but she finally screamed at him that she couldn't take it anymore, and he relented.

Shortly after that he asked her to marry him.

"You never even ask about Brianna," Cécile lamented now.

"I don't have to. I know she's being raised by loving parents in a good home. You talk like she's in foster care."

"Well, I've never seen Norell happier."

"She's a fool," Micheline declared. "Didn't she wonder

how Vic managed to suddenly get his hands on a newborn baby just as she was on the verge of a nervous breakdown?"

"I guess I would have been suspicious that it was his baby, too," Cécile admitted. "But I don't know if she ever confronted him about it. She never said anything to me, but then again, that's not the type of thing you want to share with your girl-friends. I wouldn't tell anybody if it were me." She chuckled. "Not that having trouble getting pregnant is a problem I've ever had to deal with, of course. But I do know how unhappy Norell was. She was hitting the bottle hard. She managed to keep up with her work, but poor Vic was being neglected. I can't blame him for feeling frustrated. He's not exactly the most understanding or patient husband—I think it's awful that he left his first wife because she picked up eighty pounds over the years and couldn't get it off—but, given the circum-stances, I don't know if I can really blame him for having an affair."

Micheline's teeth clamped down on a celery stick filled with bleu cheese with a loud crunch.

"You and I know Brianna is Vic's baby," Cécile continued. "And now that she's gotten older, I'm afraid other people might be able to tell as well. She's a composite of your fea-tures and his, but mostly yours. She even has your light brown eyes."

"I know, I know." Micheline readied herself to hear more of Cécile's bitter complaints about the awkwardness of her position. She'd already reported that as little Brianna grew, Norell joked that she looked more like Cécile than Regine did. A pretty sensitive thing to joke about, considering that Brianna was living proof that her husband had slept with an-other woman. Micheline supposed that Norell could laugh about it because at least she knew that Cécile wasn't that woman. But that laughter would turn ferocious if she knew just how close that so-called joke was to the truth.

"She has eyes shaped like yours . . . and like mine, too.

Norell probably won't ever tell me if she ever talked to Vic about where he got Brianna, but I agree, she has to at least suspect something."

"That sounds like a personal problem to me," Micheline replied before picking up the last of her chicken wings.

Cécile sighed and pointedly changed the subject. "You're dressed nice today."

Micheline glanced down at her short-sleeved multicolored summer knit sweater and white skirt. She'd left her suit jacket in the car. "I had an interview this morning at the hospital over by Southpoint. I just e-mailed them my résumé Monday morning. Apparently they're in a rush to fill the position. They called Tuesday and set me up for an interview today."

"I didn't know you were planning on going back to work."

"Errol's been suggesting that I should, and I guess it's time. I haven't worked in three years."

"You don't sound too excited," Cécile observed.

"Oh, I'm fine." At that moment Micheline noticed Suzanne Betancourt being led to a table, along with another woman she recognized from the party.

"Michie?"

"Oh, I'm sorry. I wasn't paying attention. I just saw someone I know."

"Did you want to go over and say hello? I was just telling you that Regine has to go to potty. We'll probably be a few minutes."

"Go ahead. I'll give them a chance to get seated. I'll meet you out front."

On her way out, Micheline stopped at the women's table while Cecile took Regine to the ladies' room. "Hello there, Suzanne." She tried not to burst out laughing at Suzanne's surprised expression. She obviously hadn't expected to see her there. The almost guilty look on her face made Micheline wonder if she had been the topic of her and her companion's conversation.

"Hello, Micheline," she said. "Uh . . . you know Paula Haines of Discriminating Taste Catering. She handled Brad's party. Paula, this is Micheline Trent."

Micheline nodded politely as she said hello. She remembered seeing Errol volunteer to be the cameraman for Paula, but hadn't realized Paula was working the party. Her staff had worn logo-inscribed polo shirts and khaki pants, while Paula was dressed like a guest. Micheline chalked that up to the obvious friendship between the two women. "I was just having lunch with my sister and spotted you, so I wanted to say hello on my way out. How've you been?"

"Good, thanks."

Suzanne spoke politely, but with zero warmth. Micheline felt negative vibes coming from both Suzanne and Paula, so strong it was almost palpable. It was clear they both wished she'd move on. She could understand Suzanne feeling that way, but she didn't even *know* Paula, so how could she want her to get lost?

"Well, if you'll excuse me, I'd better go see how my sister is managing in the ladies' room with my niece. Good seeing you again. Enjoy your lunch." There was no denying the relief on both women's faces. Micheline wondered what they'd been talking about.

"I swear, I don't like that woman," Suzanne said when Micheline was well out of earshot. "You should see how she was falling all over Brad when we were at their place for the Super Bowl."

"I saw that dress she had on at the party," Paula said. "She was clearly trying to get attention. The damn thing was cut down to her crack. She must work near here, huh?"

"She doesn't work."

"No? I spoke with her husband for a little bit at Brad's party. Nice man. They must have young children at home."

Suzanne shook her head. "No, she just stays home and makes like she's Suzy Homemaker." Of course, Suzanne did pretty much the same thing herself, but she told herself that was different. *She* had children who needed her. "Apparently, she milked some type of illness into taking a few years off. But supposedly she's going back to work."

"She might have already started. She's dressed pretty nicely," Paula remarked. "Do you know what type of work she does?"

Suzanne thought for a moment. "She said she's a . . . bilegal paralingual or something."

"A bilegal . . . oh, you mean a bilingual paralegal."

"Whatever," Suzanne said with a shrug. "Who cares? Let's order."

They studied the menu and gave their orders to the waitress. "All right," Suzanne said after they handed their menus back to the waitress. "Back to what we were talking about before Micheline so rudely interrupted us."

"Oh, yes," Paula replied with a nod. "Suzanne, you have to tell Brad about Kenya being pregnant by Paige's new boyfriend right away. Just tell him you feel he shouldn't tell Paige about it, but should give the boy a chance to tell her himself. That's really his responsibility. I'm sure Brad will agree."

"I'm a little troubled that Gregory was out with Paige just yesterday. Kenya saw them drive past while she was riding the bus home. She said it's not fair for Gregory to still be seeing Paige after he's agreed to marry her, and I think she's right. It's humiliating."

"I'm sure she found it very hurtful," Paula said, "but this can cause real problems in your marriage if you don't tell Brad what you know right away. And don't leave anything out, like the fact that he's agreed to marry Kenya to legitimize the baby. I already see a big fight coming out of this, Suzanne. I wish you'd asked me for advice sooner."

"So do I. I guess part of me was angry at Paige for flaunting her relationship with Gregory in front of Kenya at a party at my house."

"Put that aside, Suzanne. The most important thing here is **your relationship** with Brad. Everything else should come second." Paula paused to take a sip of her water. "If there's one thing I learned out of life, it's to be square with people. That's part of the reason my second marriage failed. In hindsight I can see that I married a jerk, but nobody forced me to keep up that lie about my age." That had been a costly lie in regard to her and her daughter, one she would always regret.

"You know, Suzanne," Paula said, "this is a familiar story for me. Darrell and I got married because I got pregnant with Devon. We had never really progressed beyond being fond of each other; it wasn't true love by any means. But neither of our parents wanted the baby born out of wedlock, so we got married. I don't have to tell you how it turned out." She chuckled. "You do realize that this marriage between Kenya and her boyfriend probably won't last 'til death do them part, don't you?"

"Yes, but that's between the two of them." Suzanne saw no need for Paula to know that Kenya's feelings for Gregory were stronger than his for her, or that her mother was plotting for Kenya to be such a good wife to Gregory that he wouldn't want to let her go. That was a familiar plot to Suzanne, who loved reading romance novels, but privately she continued to harbor strong doubts about Kenya's odds for success. This wasn't like the old days, when wives could refuse to give husbands divorces unless the husbands had some dirt on them, like who they were sleeping with. If Gregory wanted to unload Kenya, he didn't need her permission. Divorce laws had become so lax that he probably wouldn't have to give her a reason. Suzanne feared he'd start proceedings right after the baby's birth. Kenya's only recourse would be to try to take him for as much as she could for child support . . . and she had no doubt that her little sister would do just that. She couldn't think of the entire phrase, but she knew it ended with "like a woman scorned."

As their server placed their plates in front of them, Suzanne decided to follow Paula's advice and speak with Brad that evening. Paula was right. It really wasn't fair for her to allow what she felt was her stepdaughter's show of bad taste and her thirst for revenge on behalf of Kenya to come between her and Brad. As Paula suggested, Suzanne would simply ask Brad to consider not saying anything to Paige until Gregory himself had a chance to tell her. She couldn't know how he would react to her request. If he decided to inform Paige of Kenya's pregnancy and her upcoming marriage to Gregory, Suzanne would have to be satisfied with knowing that the news would come as a crushing blow.

Her mother had already asked her to consider holding the ceremony at her home, but Suzanne balked. First of all, Gregory had yet to even propose to Kenya. Second, Suzanne knew Brad wouldn't go for it. How could he consent to hosting Kenya's marriage to Gregory with Paige living right next door?

Arlene immediately began to fuss, saying that the small bungalow she rented from Brad wasn't nearly elegant enough for a wedding, even a small one with just immediate family present. "I'd like it to be as nice as possible for Kenya," she'd said. Suzanne told her that Flo would probably welcome the opportunity to host the ceremony at her place and suggested she speak with her about it . . . *after* it had been established that there would actually be a wedding.

Suzanne understood her mother's eagerness for Kenya to have as nice a wedding ceremony as possible, but she was beginning to feel that Arlene might be going overboard. In the few days since Kenya's pregnancy had been confirmed, her mother seemed almost willing to pursue Kenya's happiness at the cost of Suzanne's.

But everything would be all right. She'd clear the air tonight, present the news of Kenya's pregnancy to Brad and make it sound as if she'd just found out about it herself. There was really no way for him to know she'd known about the situation for the last few days.

*   *   *

On the way home Suzanne stopped at the supermarket to pick up some butter. She browsed the book section to see if they had any new romance novels that interested her. She didn't see anything, so she wandered over to the adjoining magazine display. Her eyes focused on the bridal magazines, and she impulsively put one in her cart. If Flo could convince her son to marry Kenya, surely her mother would ask her for help in planning the ceremony. Of course, there wouldn't be anyone there outside the immediate families, but that didn't mean it couldn't be elegant. She might as well start boning up on the latest trends.

Suzanne skimmed through the magazine while she waited for the pork loin she was preparing for dinner marinated in a Caribbean jerk sauce in the refrigerator. Those glossy pictures of gorgeous dresses, elegant place settings, and mouthwatering cakes would make any girl long to get married.

Even after sixteen years, Suzanne still found it disappointing that she hadn't been able to have the big, splashy wedding she had dreamed of since she was a girl. Unfortunately, there'd been no money in the Hall family budget for frills of that nature. Suzanne couldn't expect Brad to pay for it, so she agreed to a ceremony at City Hall, followed by a luxurious honeymoon at the Sandals Resort in Jamaica.

Her jaw dropped when she turned to a photograph of an ornate cake by a cake designer. Each of the three layers was covered with smooth chocolate icing on the upper part, and white icing with small heart cutouts on the bottom part that looked like a doily. The top layer was garnished with red roses, again made from icing, and these icing flowers also adorned the other layers and the base, more sparsely. A cake like that had to cost over a thousand dollars, but it was truly a work of art. The people who created these cakes probably made big bucks.

The idea hit her like a boxer's left hook. This was something she admired. Why not learn how to do it? Maybe it wasn't rocket science, but it was something she had a genuine interest in, something that she could see results from in the time it took to frost a cake. She could even show off her handiwork whenever she and Brad gave a dinner party. Surely he'd be proud when she received compliments for her creations.

Suddenly excited, she went for the yellow pages and looked under "Cake Decorating."

Chapter 13

Brad didn't know what to say. He genuinely liked Gregory Hickman, in spite of his aversion to the young man's parents. As a man, he understood Gregory's dilemma. He'd just started dating Paige a few weeks ago. That Kenya must have gotten pregnant just before they broke up. It had been extremely unwise for Gregory to sleep with her without wearing a condom, something he knew the boy now profoundly regretted.

"I appreciate you telling me about this, Gregory," he said now, after taking a moment to recover from the shock.

"You didn't know?"

"No."

"I would've thought Mrs. Betancourt would have mentioned it to you."

"That's a perfectly normal assumption," Brad said tightly. "Unfortunately, it's a wrong one."

"I'm sorry, sir," Gregory said apologetically. "I didn't mean to create a problem between you and Mrs. Betancourt."

"Not to worry," Brad said, forcing himself to sound cheerful. His anger at Suzanne was a private matter that this young man had no business knowing about.

"I just wanted you to know how much I regret the situation I've gotten myself into and to assure you that this was something that happened before Paige and I started seeing each other. Unfortunately, Kenya is determined to go ahead and have the baby."

I'll just bet she is, the little slut, Brad thought. *She'll do anything just to spite Paige because she's jealous.*

"I never wanted to father any children out of wedlock, Dr. Betancourt," Gregory continued. Then he shook his head. "This is really hard," he said nervously.

"I think I see where you might be going with this, Gregory. You're trying to tell me that you're planning on marrying Kenya."

"Yes, sir," Gregory said, obviously relieved not to have to put his intentions into words. "And it isn't because I'm in love with Kenya or I want to marry her. I just feel I have to pay the consequences of getting her pregnant. But it's temporary," he added. "I felt that I should talk to you, man-to-man, just to let you know how sorry I am . . . before I talk to Paige."

Brad thought for a moment. "Well, Gregory, man-to-man, I'll tell you that I admire your resolve to do the right thing. For what it's worth, I do understand how certain facets of a relationship can be ill-timed." He gave a wry chuckle, thinking about Lisa's long-held belief that he'd started an affair with Suzanne before their divorce. He'd always felt Suzanne was a pretty woman, but he never even considered asking her out until after he and Lisa separated. Lisa had hit the roof when she learned he was dating his employee, and as a result the two most important women in his life, past and present, had never really gotten along. Lisa might have set the mood, but Suzanne wasn't exactly blameless. Brad knew she resented Lisa's background and education. But at least the two had formed an uneasy truce over the years.

"That said," he continued, "I have to react from my other standpoint, that of Paige's father. I believe my daughter is going to be hurt by this. Maybe just a little, but maybe deeply. You see, I don't know how strong her feelings are for you . . . or how weak."

Gregory winced.

It pleased Brad to see Gregory's discomfort. He'd allowed himself that one little dig, although he suspected that his daughter's feelings ran deep and that she would indeed be hurt. "For that, I have to tell you I'm disappointed and upset myself. I don't want anyone, man, woman, or child, to hurt my daughter."

"I understand, sir."

Brad noted with amusement that if this was the military, Gregory would probably salute him. "But I admire your stoicism; I admire your behavior. I think you did the right thing by coming to me, man-to-man." He managed to smile. "I don't know when exactly you plan on speaking to Paige, but I hope it's soon," he said, his words containing a clear but gentle warning.

"It'll be tonight, sir."

After Gregory left, Brad sat at his desk, his hands clasped behind his head as he leaned back in his chair and tried to sort out the situation. He had the distinct feeling that Gregory hoped he could get back with Paige after what he expected would be a brief marriage. Brad had a lot more respect for the young man he'd always liked for coming to speak with him, but that didn't make him right for his daughter. Marrying a man with children was a serious undertaking. It would be different if Paige was older, but she was only twenty-one and still in college. At that age, she shouldn't have to be concerned with the responsibilities of being a parent to her own child, much less someone else's.

Look at Suzanne. She tried to hide it, but she'd never fully accepted Paige as his daughter. Why else would she not tell him that Kenya was pregnant by Gregory?

What possible excuse could she give for keeping quiet, he wondered. Her reasoning was clear enough. By not telling him what she knew, she all but made certain that the news would come as a huge shock to Paige, with no cushioning from him to soften the blow. The funny thing was, Brad had no intention of informing Paige. That was Gregory's job. He would, of course, be there for Paige if she needed him. He'd speak with Lisa and let her know what was going on after Gregory picked up Paige tonight. As Paige's mother, Lisa needed to be aware that her daughter was about to get her heart broken. He just didn't want to give her the chance to inadvertently give Paige any clues that something was amiss, so he'd wait until Paige left. Lisa had never been any good at keeping a secret.

And, of course, he'd let Suzanne know he knew the deal. He couldn't deny he looked forward to that.

When Brad entered his front door an hour later, his nostrils were greeted with the unmistakable scent of Cajun-spiced boiling shrimp. He gave Suzanne credit—she'd certainly improved her culinary skills since befriending Darrell Canfield's first wife, Paula. She used to cook things like Hamburger and Tuna Helper, which were fine for the kids, but hardly fit in with his idea of a good dinner.

That was a plus, but he personally had little use for Paula Haines. She'd practically abandoned Devon, her only child, not acknowledging her as her daughter during her second marriage, just so she could keep up some elaborate charade. The web of lies ultimately failed, with not only Paula's marriage, but her relationship with her only child on the casualty list.

Devon Canfield outwardly seemed like a happy, well-adjusted young woman, but Brad suspected she was deeply troubled. He hoped she wouldn't marry too quickly and too young in a quest to be a better mother to her own children than Paula had been to her. What could you say about a woman who'd put her child's well-being—Devon had been a teenager at the time—behind that of her husband?

That shrimp Suzanne was making smelled awfully good. Still, she rarely made shrimp on a weekday.

Resentment seethed from his pores. Was she trying to

curry his favor, or even assuage her guilt at her wrongdoing by preparing him a good meal?

He entered the kitchen to find her wearing a short, flouncy striped skirt and a navy tank top, stirring the pot of shrimp.

"Hi!" She greeted him enthusiastically as she slipped her hands into oven mitts and removed the glass pan from the heat. A glass Dutch oven furiously boiled on another burner, and a third pan sat in the center of the stovetop, its lid preventing him from seeing what it contained.

"Shrimp?"

"Yes, scampi. The sauce is done, and the pasta is ready to go. All I have to do is put the biscuits in the oven. I made those cheesy biscuits you like."

Brad did love those drop biscuits with liberal doses of shredded cheddar mixed into the dough and a touch of garlic and oregano, but Suzanne's statement, as with her cooking this meal in the first place, gave him the uncomfortable feeling of being buttered up like a Thanksgiving turkey.

"All right. I'm gonna take a quick swim."

"Mom, can I have another biscuit?"

"Bradley, you've had about four already. Save some for your father."

Brad waved his hand. "I've already had three. I can't eat any more, so go ahead and knock yourself out."

"I'm a growing boy," Bradley said with a grin.

Brad agreed. His only son had shot up in height and at age fifteen stood five feet ten inches tall, a good five inches taller than his mother.

The telephone began to ring. "I'll get it," Lauren said, rising with her plate in hand. A minute later she called out, "Bradley, it's for you. It's Sasha."

Bradley, who'd been buttering his biscuit, grunted, hastily popped the entire piece of bread into his mouth and then grabbed his plate, mumbling something that sounded like, "Can I be excused?"

Brad laughed. Had he been so anxious about girls at that age? "Go ahead. Just don't drop your plate."

"He's a popular boy," Suzanne said with admiration.

"It's only going to get worse." Brad paused a beat. "I saw Gregory Hickman today."

"You did?"

"He came to my office."

"Really? What for?"

"You don't know, Suzanne? You really don't know?" He met her gaze head-on.

Uncertainty reflected in her eyes. "Um . . ."

"All right, let's cut the bullshit. Why didn't you tell me Kenya is pregnant by Gregory?"

She let out a breath. How could this happen? Her plan had been to tell Brad about Kenya and Gregory after the children left the table. She'd never considered the possibility of Gregory going to talk to Brad about it. "I . . . It's . . . such a sticky situation, you know, because of Paige seeing Gregory now and all . . . I thought I should stay out of it."

"So you haven't been involved at all? Is that what you're expecting me to believe?"

"Well . . . I was with my mother when Kenya told her she was pregnant."

"And you had nothing to do with suggesting that Gregory marry Kenya? Because he told me that's what he intends to do."

"My mother suggested that. I told her it wouldn't work, that Kenya isn't mature enough to be a wife."

She sounded indignant enough to be telling the truth. And Lord knew it was just like Arlene to concoct a scheme to marry Kenya off to Gregory. Still, Suzanne had fallen all over her tongue with her explanation for keeping what she knew to herself.

"Will you say something, Brad? You're making me nervous."

She was nervous, all right. He could tell from the unnatu-

rally high pitch to her voice. He deliberately held off on saying anything right away. Instead he sat back in his chair and
looked at her directly across the round dinette table, where
they took most of their informal meals. "I'm going to tell you
what *I* think," he finally said.

"All right." Suzanne toyed with her necklace.

"I think you saw Kenya's getting pregnant by Gregory as a
way for her to triumph over Paige. I know Kenya is jealous of
Paige because Paige is getting her education and will have a
good-paying career, while Kenya is ringing up groceries for
minimum wage."

"Brad—"

He plunged on, ignoring her attempt to speak. "I think
you saw this as a way to pay Paige back for what you per-
ceive as her taking Gregory away from your sister. And I also
think"—he stopped momentarily to hold out his hand palm
out to signal her not to interrupt—"that you chose not to tell
me because you didn't want to risk Paige finding out ahead of
time. You didn't keep quiet because you wanted to stay out of
it, you just wanted to maximize Paige's shock, as you said when
you accused Lisa of doing the exact same thing to Kenya by
not letting on that Gregory was seeing Paige."

"But that's what she did, Brad."

"It doesn't matter. If Lisa wants to keep a secret from me,
that's fine. I'm not married to Lisa, Suzanne. I'm married to
you. And we're not supposed to keep secrets from each other."

His eyes narrowed as hers widened. "I know you've tried
to hide it, but you don't like the fact that Paige is more cultured than Kenya, that she has a wider circle of experience
and knowledge." Suzanne didn't like Lisa for the same reasons, but he knew to say that would be both unnecessary and
cruel. "I know you took Kenya's side over Paige, and I don't
like it. Paige is my daughter. She's more a part of this household than your little sister will ever be. I'm putting a stop to
it right now. Get this, Suzanne. Paige comes before Kenya."

He tossed his crumpled napkin on his plate. "If you'll excuse me, I have an important family matter to attend to."

Suzanne finally found her voice. "Brad, you're not being fair—"

"Not now, Suzanne," he said without looking back.

He went to his bedroom and took a quick shower to get the chlorine off of his skin and hair. Then he dialed the Canfield home from his cell, since he suspected Bradley was still on the house phone. "Lisa, it's Brad," he said when his ex-wife answered. "Don't let on that it's me on the phone. Just answer yes or no to this question. Is Paige home?"

"Yes . . . but not for long."

"Is she going out with Gregory?"

"That's right. How did you know that?"

"He came to see me this afternoon. Lisa, I'm afraid that Paige is going to be upset when she gets home."

"Why? What's wrong?"

He hoped Paige wasn't within earshot. Lisa's suddenly urgent tone was sure to attract attention, but he couldn't blame her for being concerned.

"It's best if I don't give away too much, Lisa, at least not until she leaves." He wasn't sure Lisa could hide her emotions when Gregory called for Paige if she knew the whole story. Best to tell her after Paige was gone. "I'd like to be there for her when she gets home, if that's okay with you. I think she might need us."

"Sure, come over whenever you want."

"I just had dinner. I'm going to go by the club and have a drink first."

Lisa said nothing at first, then asked, "Don't you have liquor in your house?"

"Yes, but I need to get out of here. I'll be over after she and Gregory have left." He knew his statement would raise Lisa's curiosity, but he didn't care. "See you in a few."

* * *

Suzanne was cleaning the kitchen with help from Lauren when Brad stopped in. "I'm going out for a while. I'll see you later."

The look on her face clearly said she wished he wouldn't go. Couldn't she figure out that his eldest daughter was about to get her heart broken? Did she really think he would just let things unfold naturally and not be there for her? If it was Lauren, Suzanne would be singing a different tune. He'd about had it with Suzanne expecting him to favor Bradley and Lauren over his firstborn. He loved all his children. And he had no interest in listening to Suzanne's lame excuses about why she'd said nothing about what she knew.

He was still so upset, he didn't even want to look at her right now, much less be under the same roof.

Brad smelled the tomato sauce and garlic the moment he stepped inside the club. It must be Italian night.

He walked past the dining room, past the bar, greeting familiar faces as he went. The majority of the membership was white, but there were more than a handful of black members. He'd tried to get Darrell Canfield to join, but Darrell was content to golf at the public courses, and as he'd pointed out, "I already have a pool." His friends Calvin and Liloutie Braxton belonged. Liloutie enjoyed golf as much as her husband. And of course there was Errol Trent.

He and Micheline sat at a table for two on the rear terrace, enjoying dinner and a half carafe of red wine. Brad couldn't help noticing how stunning Micheline looked, in a black-and-white sleeveless top with one shoulder bare and her tawny hair pulled back into a short ponytail.

"It's kind of late, even for nine holes, don't you think?" Errol asked.

"Oh, yeah. I just stopped by for a quick drink."

"In that case, join us," Micheline said.

He pulled up a white wicker chair, stopping momentarily

to look at Micheline's legs, which she quickly shifted into a crossed position at the edge of the table just as he was sliding a chair over. He swallowed hard, but quickly remembered himself. It might have just been a coincidence. . . . She might have just happened to move into a position that put her legs on display at the same time his eyes were focused at the corner of the table.

Yeah, right. And that politician from the Bible Belt with the wife, six kids, and a six-figure administrative assistant who couldn't type told the truth when he said he's not having an affair with her. He needed to stop kidding himself. Micheline was definitely sending off signals in his direction. She'd been a little flirtatious the night of the Super Bowl, especially the way she bent in a way that allowed him a clear view of the inside of her blouse; and even at his birthday party Brad had gotten vibes from her. Nothing that would seem out of place to Errol, but enticing just the same. He'd never been in a situation like this before with the wives of any of his friends or associates, and he had to admit that it made him more aroused than uncomfortable.

The question was, what to do about it?

Chapter 14

When Brad returned home, he pulled into his own driveway and walked across the well-tended lawn of the Canfield home. Simple but colorful irises and hyacinths in shades of blue and purple lined the edge of the lawn in front of the contemporary house, which looked deceptively small from the outside but was large enough to comfortably house the seven residents of the blended family.

Lisa opened the door just seconds after he rang the bell, anxiety written across her face.

"She's not home yet, is she?" he asked.

"No. She hasn't been gone an hour yet. What's going on, Brad? Why all the secrecy? When you called it was straight out of *Mission Impossible.*"

He glanced around. "Where's Darrell?"

"He's out on the patio. I think he's trying to keep his distance, in case you wanted privacy, even though I told him I doubted that would be the case."

Brad nodded. Darrell wasn't the type of man to stick his nose into other folks' business, and he also respected Brad's position as Paige's father. It was one of the main reasons Brad thought so highly of the man Lisa chose to be Paige's stepfather. Not one time in all these years had Darrell ever overstepped the sometimes difficult boundaries of being a stepparent.

"There's no reason why he shouldn't hear this. Come on, let's join him."

"You want a drink?"

"Just a beer will do. I already had two cocktails at the club."

"There's beer in the fridge outside."

Brad followed his first wife to the patio, where Darrell Canfield sat at the large square cedar table for eight, the flat-screen television mounted on the outside wall of the house turned to CNN. The table, like the television and refrigerator, sat in an alcove just outside the back door. The roof extended past the alcove, thus protecting the table and its cushioned chairs, as well as the electronics, from water damage. The table was large enough to accommodate the entire Canfield household, which in addition to Lisa, Darrell, and Paige also included Devon, Darrell's daughter from his first marriage to Paula Haines; Esther, Darrell's widowed mother; and Darrell and Lisa's twin boys, Cary and Courtney. Brad knew that the family spent a lot of time on their patio, grilling, eating, and swimming. Brad often saw the entire group dining outside when he took his own family for early evening cruises on his boat, the *Suzie Q*.

Tonight no one was around other than Darrell and Lisa. Brad knew from Darrell that Devon was visiting a friend in Atlanta. He presumed the twins and Esther were in their rooms.

Brad greeted Darrell warmly. He respected Lisa's second husband every bit as much as Darrell respected him, and considered the stockbroker to be one of his closest friends. It was quite a contrast to the often strained relationship between Suzanne and Lisa. Brad knew that many found the circumstances of his friendship with Darrell peculiar, but he saw Darrell as simply a good guy who just happened to be married to his first wife. His marriage to Lisa was so long ago, he hadn't thought of her as his wife for many years.

"Brad said he'd like a beer, Darrell," Lisa said as she took a seat next to him. "Unless you'd prefer wine?" She gestured toward the half-empty bottle of Chardonnay on the table.

"No, beer's fine, thanks."

"Coming right up." Darrell shifted position, turning to the stainless steel refrigerator behind him, from which he removed a twelve-ounce bottle of Icehouse.

"Thanks," Brad said, first giving Darrell's hand a quick shake and then accepting the bottle. He took a seat directly opposite from Darrell and Lisa at the table, which sat two people on each of its four sides.

"Lisa tells me there's something going on with Paige that she doesn't know about," Darrell said.

"Yeah. That's what I wanted to talk to the two of you about." Brad unscrewed the top from his beer and took a quick gulp. "Y'all know that Gregory was involved with Kenya before he and Paige started seeing each other."

Darrell chuckled. "That's been a sore spot with both our girls."

Brad knew what he meant. Both Paige and her stepsister Devon had crushes on the handsome Gregory from the time they moved into the neighborhood when both girls were sixteen.

They all chuckled at Darrell's observation, and then Lisa cautiously said, "Don't tell me Kenya has something to do with this."

Brad's expression changed to reflect the seriousness of the situation. "I'm afraid she does. There's no way to sugarcoat this, so I'll just say it. Kenya's pregnant by him, and Gregory's decided to marry her to legitimize the child."

Lisa gasped, her hand flying up to cover her mouth. Even Darrell's face contorted into a scowl.

"Oh, my God!" Lisa sputtered.

"That little bitch," Darrell said indignantly. "I know she did this shit on purpose. She probably had the whole thing planned."

"I won't dispute that," Brad said, nodding. "Gregory came to my office to talk to me yesterday. He told me what happened and what he felt he has to do."

"That was brave of him," Darrell remarked.

"I thought so. I tried to be understanding, but the bottom line is, I don't know how Paige is going to react to all this. I mean, girls don't usually share these things with their fathers. Lisa?" he prompted.

She made an attempt to speak, but only incoherent sputtering noises came out. "I'm sorry," she said. "I'm . . . just . . . numb. Paige was just getting over the breakup with Jonathan, and now this."

"Do you think she was serious about Gregory?" Darrell asked.

"I don't see how she could be," Lisa replied. "They haven't been seeing each other long enough for that. But I know she likes him very much, and this is going to devastate her." She shook her head. "It might also give her the impression that if you want to hold on to a fellow, stop using birth control."

"I think Paige is too sensible for that, Lisa," Darrell said quietly.

"So do I," Brad said. "And if she's not, the consequences will be *her* responsibility. At any rate, Gregory intends to give Paige the bad news tonight." He looked at his former wife. "Don't be mad at me, Lisa, for not telling you right away. I honestly didn't think you'd be able to conceal what you knew, so I decided to wait until after Paige left with Gregory."

Darrell squeezed Lisa's hand, then directed his comment to Brad. "From the stunned look on her face, I can't argue you did the wrong thing." Then he lightly slapped Lisa's forearm. "Lisa, come on. You've got to pull yourself together."

"I'll be all right," she said unconvincingly. "But excuse me just a moment."

Brad watched as she went inside the house, concern in his eyes.

"She'll be all right, Brad," Darrell said. "She'll go inside, splash some cold water on her face, blow her nose, and then she'll be back." He paused a moment. "You know, I kind of feel sorry for Gregory. Poor kid thought he was getting lucky. He didn't realize that piece was going to come with a high price . . . his freedom."

"I'm sorry for him, too, but I think he handled it pretty well."

Darrell drained his wineglass. "Uh . . . you do realize that after this, Paige may want to transfer again."

"I hadn't thought of it," Brad admitted, "but you're right. I'm going to put my foot down about that. She can't keep running from every failed romance." Paige had returned to Jacksonville to attend college after breaking up with her boyfriend in Gainesville.

"I agree. I don't know about Lisa, though."

"I'll have to convince her. I know it'll be hard for Paige, and I don't put it past that Kenya to flaunt her belly in Paige's face every chance she gets. But still, we can only indulge her so much. It's part of growing up."

"So I presume Gregory shot the guilty load before he and Paige became an item," Darrell said.

"That's what he says, and I believe him."

"Yeah, me too. He seems too crazy about Paige to cheat on her."

Brad glanced inside the house to see if there was any sign of Lisa. Speaking in a low voice, he asked, "Just between us, Darrell, have you ever stepped out on Lisa?"

If Darrell found the question offensive, he didn't show it. "No, and I wouldn't. Not as long as I value my life. She made it very clear how she felt about infidelity before we got married."

"I never cheated on her either, no matter what she may have told you. Nor have I ever cheated on Suzanne."

Darrell looked at him thoughtfully. "Something tells me you're thinking about it now. Or else why the question?"

He shrugged. "Just curious." It probably had been a mistake to even ask in the first place. He knew Darrell didn't swallow his explanation, but he didn't feel it wise to confide his attraction to Micheline Trent, nor did he want to reveal his anger toward Suzanne to Darrell. Darrell and Lisa were quite close—*they* probably had no secrets from each other, Brad thought, his anger at Suzanne building afresh—and telling Darrell about the stress in his marriage would be like telling Lisa as well. Brad knew it wouldn't be right for Lisa to be privy to the stress in his marriage. But he trusted Darrell not to share their exchange about cheating.

"You're a good man, Darrell," Brad remarked, nodding his head.

Darrell grinned. "Why do I get the feeling my name ought to be Charlie Brown?"

"Seriously, man. I mean, how many dudes out there can say they're tight with their first wife's second husband?"

"Craziest thing I ever heard," Darrell agreed. "But if you want to be serious, since you've chosen to confide in me, I can't stress enough that you really need to think about this. My advice to you is not to let a pretty face and curvy body lure you into something you know you shouldn't do."

Brad waited with the Canfields, talking and watching TV, until Paige returned home at ten P.M. "We're out here, honey," Lisa called to her.

But Paige didn't come outside. Instead she opened the back door and spoke from there. "I just wanted you to know I'm home."

Nearly comical surprise showed on Lisa's face, her eyes opened wide, her mouth open. "Uh . . . did you have a good time?"

"No. And I'm sure you know why, or else why would Daddy be here?"

"We wanted to be here if you needed us, Paige," Brad said.

"I appreciate that, all of you. But I don't want to talk about it, at least not now. Good night, Mom, Dad. Good night, Darrell."

"G'night, Paige."

Brad sat back in his chair after she departed. "I'll say this for her. She's handling it with dignity."

"She'll talk to me," Lisa said, her voice ringing with confidence. "Within the next day or two at the most. She *always* talks to me."

"I wish Devon weren't out of town," Darrell remarked. "I'll bet you anything Paige will talk to her first. They're not only stepsisters, they're best friends."

Brad drained the remainder of his second beer of the night. "Well, we tried. Since there's nothing else I can do here, I guess I'll be getting on home."

He sighed as he left the Canfield home. He'd been gone for hours, and part of him wanted to stay out longer. His home was supposed to be his refuge and sanctuary from the outside world, but the truth was that it represented the source of his problem, because Suzanne was there.

Not wanting to go home wasn't a good sign, and he knew it.

Suzanne sat in her beautifully furnished family room, alone except for Buster, the family's beagle, who rested quietly at her feet. She lit a cigarette as she looked out at the skyline of downtown on the other side of the St. Johns River. She'd given up smoking two years before, but the stress she felt had driven her to stop in at the Lil' Champ and buy a pack. Had it really been less than a week ago that she had the patio doors open and the house teemed with people who'd come to join in Brad's birthday celebration? Had it only been then that Brad embraced her when he told her what a beautiful job she'd done, and later, after everyone had gone home and they were in bed together, had squeezed her, told her what a wonderful wife she was and how happy she'd made him?

Listening to her mother had been a terrible mistake. In the nearly sixteen years she'd been married to Brad, she'd never seen him so angry. He wasn't the type to make a lot of noise. His fury traditionally ran cold, like an iceberg.

She wondered how long it would be before he thawed out.

The sound of the front door opening was punctuated by the dual beep of the alarm system going into alert. She jumped up and ran to the front of the house to meet him. His frosty expression stopped her from getting too close.

"How did everything go?" she asked hesitantly.

"Fine," came his crisp reply. "Paige got in a few minutes ago. She said she didn't really care to speak about what happened, that she just wanted to go to bed. It was very quiet and very low-key. No histrionics. Not even any tears."

Suzanne hated herself for the feeling of disappointment that immediately came over her. She'd put her relationship with her husband on the line because she'd been so anxious for Paige to feel raw hurt. In hindsight, it hadn't been worth it.

By Saturday, Brad still behaved distantly toward her, and Suzanne began to panic. She didn't know what to do. She was too embarrassed to admit to Paula that her marriage was in real trouble, and asking her mother's advice was definitely out of the question. Listening to Arlene's pleas that she not tell Brad about Kenya and Gregory had helped create her current unhappy situation.

Brad's attitude seemed softer when the children were present, so after breakfast, as she cleared the table, she said, "Brad, Lauren and I are going to go shopping in a few minutes."

"I'm going to be Auntie Kenya's junior bridesmaid, Daddy," Lauren said shyly.

"And a beautiful bridesmaid you'll make." Brad gave his youngest child a warm smile Suzanne could only envy.

"Lauren, if you're done you can be excused," she said. Bradley had already gulped down two waffles and twice as many sausage links. "Finish getting ready and wait for me. We'll leave in a few minutes."

"Okay, Mom."

When she was alone with Brad, Suzanne slipped into a chair in the nook. "Brad, I hope you don't mind Lauren and I participating in the wedding."

"You too?"

"I'm matron of honor," she said nervously.

"Damn. How many attendants is Kenya having?"

"Just Lauren and I. That's all she needs. There won't be but a dozen people there. I hope you don't mind," she repeated.

"No. Kenya is your sister and Lauren's aunt. When is this going to take place, anyway?"

Suzanne felt a little better. "A week from Saturday. At Flo and Ernie's house."

"Two weeks," Brad repeated. "You do realize I won't be there."

She'd been afraid of that. Under normal circumstances she would try to get him to change his mind, but with the tension between them now she wasn't about to object. "Yes, I can understand why you wouldn't want to." She hesitated before continuing. "Brad . . . I know you're upset with me, and I don't know what to do about it. How can I make things right between us?"

He sighed. "Suzanne, I can't tell you how disappointed I am in you. You did an awful thing. I know you've done a little scheming with your mother in the past, and I didn't like it then, but nothing you did was as serious as this. You deliberately withheld information from me that directly linked to Paige's happiness. I know the only reason you did it was to give your sister a trump card."

God, she couldn't admit to that. "No, Brad, that wasn't it. I just didn't want to get involved—"

"Bullshit!" he said, so forcefully that Suzanne's shoulders

twitched. She quickly turned to see if Bradley or Lauren were within earshot.

"If Lauren was older and she was involved in a triangle," Brad continued, "you'd make sure her interests were protected. The only interests you cared about were Kenya's. Paige got left out in the cold. Admit it, Suzanne, you've always been resentful of my daughter. You hate it when she comes over. You were thrilled when she went to school down in Gainesville, and you didn't like it when she came back to Jacksonville.

"I love all three of my children, Suzanne. I would think you'd be proud to claim some credit for Paige. She's a fine young woman. But you're jealous of her, just like your mother and sister are."

"I'm not jealous of Paige, Brad."

"I'm sorry, Suzanne, but I don't believe that." He held her gaze, and she knew he wouldn't back down from this one.

"You shouldn't keep Lauren waiting," he finally said.

Chapter 15

On Sunday, with dresses already purchased for herself and Lauren to wear to the wedding, Suzanne went shopping with her mother. Normally Arlene visited her, but after the blowup with Brad earlier in the week, she felt it best to keep her family under wraps.

"Just think, in one week my baby girl will be married," Arlene said dreamily.

"I hope you've been working with her, trying to get her ready."

"Absolutely. The first thing I told her to do is get her doctor to put her on disability."

"Why?" Suzanne asked, surprised by the response. "Because she's *pregnant?*"

"It wouldn't be so bad if she had a desk job, but she's on her feet all day. Gregory's going to be making good money. There's no reason for Kenya to spend eight hours a day standing up." Arlene smiled. "I'll be so proud to be able to say that *both* my girls have husbands who provide so well that they don't have to work."

"That's all well and good, Mom, but that wasn't exactly what I meant. I'd hoped you were trying to provide her with some advice on being a good wife."

"Oh, yes. I'm counting on you to help, though. She'll need

ongoing advice after she moves in with him. I did tell her she needs to improve her cooking skills."

"I agree. I'll be glad to help her out. I've learned a lot from Paula." Suzanne glanced in her side view mirror before changing lanes to make an upcoming right turn. "I guess we can start with the wedding. We'll have to serve food afterward to the few people who'll be there."

"We won't be doing that cooking. Flo told me she was going to contact Discriminating Taste, since they did such a good job with Brad's party."

"I don't think Flo realizes how much that'll cost. I don't see why we can't simply prepare a buffet. We're only talking about a dozen people, Mom."

"Hey, if that's what she wants to do, I say let her do it. She's running the show."

"That's just it. She shouldn't be. She's the groom's mother, but you're the mother of the bride. It's technically your responsibility."

Arlene look horrified. "You mean, she gets to order catered food, and I'm supposed to pay for it? Whoever heard of catering a meal for so few people?"

As Suzanne guided the Lexus into the mall parking lot, she wondered if her mother was aware of her abrupt about-face. A minute ago it was fine for Flo to use Discriminating Taste.

Arlene counted off the guests on her fingers. "The bride and groom, myself, Flo and Ernie, Derrick and Matthew, Bradley and Lauren, you and Brad. And the pastor and his wife. That's thirteen people. A baker's dozen. It might not be a lot of people, but it'll probably cost a fortune. I hate the idea of Flo treating me like a charity case."

Suzanne frowned as she pulled into a space. "I don't like it, either." This whole thing was getting out of hand, and Flo was going way overboard. She'd probably contacted Paula rather than one of the many other caterers in town in an effort to prove that she and Ernie could afford the same services Suzanne and Brad could. It was so pointless, and it only served to make her mother look like a poor onlooker who just happened to be the bride's mother. "Tell you what," Suzanne said after a moment's thought. "You get together with Flo and discuss the expenses of the wedding with her, and then take out your checkbook and write her a check for five hundred dollars. Don't worry," she said when Arlene opened her mouth to object. "I'll cover it for you. And, just between you and me, there'll only be twelve for dinner. Don't say anything to Flo about this—I don't want to say anything to her until the very last minute—but I wouldn't count on Brad being there."

They got out of the car and began walking toward the mall entrance. "But it's a family wedding, Suzanne," Arlene said. "He's your husband. How could he expect you to attend all alone?"

"I'm not very happy about it," she admitted.

"Then you should insist he come."

"I can't do that, Mom."

"Why not?"

"Because it wouldn't be right. Brad made it clear to me a few days ago that I'm not to put my sister in front of his daughter. He said that as Paige's stepmother, I have a responsibility to look out for her interests, and that I didn't do that because I withheld knowledge of Kenya being pregnant."

"Well, I like that. What are you supposed to do, feed your sister to the wolves just because Paige's new boyfriend asked Kenya to marry him?"

She made it sound like Gregory had proposed to Kenya because he was madly in love with her, Suzanne noted. "Of course not, Mom, but if Paige's and Kenya's interests conflict, I'm supposed to support Paige. And I will. I'm not going to jeopardize my marriage over Kenya."

Arlene puffed on her cigarette. "Too bad," she said. "I thought it would be a nice touch if he gave the bride away."

"That's not funny, Mom."

* * *

Arlene stood in front of the mirror of the dressing room, hands on hips. "What a rip-off! Dresses like this were everywhere forty years ago, only in primary colors instead of pastels. If all dress designers do is copy old styles, I could've been one and collected a big paycheck."

"I'm sure there's more to dress designing than that, Mom," Susanne said. "You know what they say. Fashion trends come and go. The important thing is that the dress looks wonderful on you. You are, after all, the mother of the bride."

Arlene turned and looked over her shoulder at her reflection from behind. The back of the short-sleeved dress was a solid pink, while the front was done in large blocks of pink, yellow, blue, and white. "It does look nice, doesn't it?"

"Like it was made for you. And the color is perfect. Both Lauren and I are wearing pink."

Arlene looked at the price tag and frowned. "It's awfully expensive, Suzanne."

"Just look on it as an investment. Didn't you say that Calvin Braxton's father said he'd be in touch with you on his next trip to Jacksonville?"

"Yeah, like I'm holding my breath waiting for *that* to happen. This is here and now, Suzanne, and I really can't afford this dress."

A tight feeling stretched across Suzanne's jaws. She was getting a bit weary of her mother's constant hints for money. "I'm sure you'll find the money for it somewhere. You can always ask the boys for it."

"Oh, I hate taking money from them."

"Well, you certainly don't have a problem taking money from *me*. Seriously, Mom, you really depend on me too much. Brad has never been bad with money, but he's likely to start asking questions about everything I've been spending lately."

"Just tell him it was the expense of his birthday party."

"Sorry, Mom. I'm not going to lie to my husband about giving you money. This dress is only seventy-five dollars."

"Only a person with money could say, 'It's *only* seventy-five dollars,'" Arlene snapped.

"I'm sorry, Mom, but I've already committed to giving you five hundred dollars so you can help with the expenses of the wedding and save face. If you want this dress, you'll have to pay for it yourself."

"All right." Arlene sighed. "I do hope I can get the rent paid on time next month, what with this extra expense."

"I really think you should make that a priority, Mom. One of the terms of your lease says that if you're late more than three times in a single twelve-month period, they don't have to renew it."

Arlene drew in her breath. "Are you saying Brad would actually throw us out?"

"I don't like to think so, but I know he hasn't been happy with the situation. It doesn't help when you tell him he shouldn't have you charged a late fee because you're his mother-in-law."

"But I am. We're supposed to be family, Suzanne!"

"That's out of his hands. He never would've agreed to let you move in if he didn't have the management company to handle the business end, because he felt you might try to take advantage of him being your son-in-law."

"Brad has so much. Why shouldn't I ask him to give me a hand?"

"The point is, you said you could afford the rent on the house when he expressed doubts about renting it to you. It's not fair to go back on your word after you've moved in and start asking for favors," Suzanne pointed out. "Mom, you have three grown people living in your house."

"Two. You really can't count Kenya anymore; she'll be gone next week."

"All right, two. But all three of you work full-time. You need to tell the boys to give you more money, and that's that."

Chapter 16

Flo dabbed at the outer corners of her eyes. She hadn't expected to get this emotional. Gregory, her one and only baby, was now a married man.

He looked so handsome in his black suit. Ernie, who served as best man, had suggested they rent tuxes, an idea Flo vetoed. She still remembered the humiliation of being overdressed at Brad's birthday party. This was a small home wedding. Church attire would do nicely.

When she saw Suzanne's simple pale pink sheath, Flo knew she'd made the right decision.

"It's going to be all right, son," she whispered to Gregory, who held on to her like he didn't want to let go. She wished there'd been another way out; already he looked so unhappy.

Flo felt proud to have created an atmosphere both simple and elegant. Paula Haines set up folding chairs outside, and Ernie put up a cedar arbor to serve as an altar, which Flo decorated with flowers from her garden. Gregory and Kenya exchanged vows outdoors by the pool. The sun shone, and the temperature stayed below ninety. With the fans blowing, it wasn't uncomfortable at all. Everything was perfect . . . except Brad Betancourt wasn't there.

She and Ernie had both been startled when they learned this morning that Brad wouldn't be attending. Suzanne had said he didn't feel well, but Ernie said that was bull. Flo thought he was probably right. In hindsight, it made sense that Brad wouldn't care to be present, since Gregory had to put a halt to his budding relationship with his daughter Paige in order to marry Kenya. The most important thing was that he'd been nice to Gregory when Gregory went to his office to explain the situation to him.

Still, she'd been terribly disappointed at the news. Flo had Paula set up two round tables for the thirteen of them rather than one long table, and she made sure she and Ernie were seated at the table with Suzanne and Brad. This was supposed to be the kickoff of what she and Ernie hoped would become a genuine friendship. So what if the marriage between Gregory and Kenya wouldn't last a lifetime? She and Ernie had the opportunity to make a social connection, and she wasn't about to blow it. She and Ernie had poured more money than they should have to make Gregory's wedding—at least his *first* wedding—a stylish affair like this. When Arlene gave her a check to help out with the expenses—a casual act that stunned Flo—instead of pocketing the funds she promptly called Paula Haines and upgraded the menu. But now, with Brad absent, she now regretted having spent all that money.

Arlene also shed a few tears. It had been a lovely ceremony, even if Gregory barely cracked a smile. Kenya looked lovely in a white tea-length lace dress with bolero jacket and floppy hat. She was glad she'd bought the dress she'd tried on at the mall last weekend with Suzanne. It went well with the white slingbacks and purse she already had in her closet.

Best of all, she no longer worried about the money she'd spent. She did pull out her checkbook when she got together with Flo, but the check she wrote was for *four* hundred dollars, not five. When Suzanne gave her the money to cover the check, Arlene simply kept the extra hundred for herself.

* * *

"Good job, Paula," Suzanne said.

"Not bad, considering it was set up at the last minute. I like small events like this. All I need is one person to help me."

Suzanne studied her friend. "You're looking different. Are you seeing somebody new or something?"

"Someone who was of great assistance to me at your party last week."

Suzanne drew in her breath. "That waiter? Paula, he's so young!"

"Shh. It's a hush-hush thing. He's married."

"A married waiter? Girl, you must truly be desperate."

"Listen, I have needs. And unlike some people, *I* don't have a handsome husband to go home to every night. Even if he's an old codger."

Suzanne laughed. Paula often teased her about Brad being eight years her senior. Now she was accustomed to it, but she'd never forget her shock the first time Paula said, "Brad is good-looking and sexy, Suzanne. Too bad he's so old." At the time she wasn't yet familiar with Paula's penchant for younger men.

Suzanne grinned. "Well, just don't get yourself hit with a sexual harassment suit."

Suzanne changed into shorts and a sleeveless blouse the minute she got home. Her feelings were a mixture of relief that it was over, plus both eagerness and apprehension about seeing Brad. Suzanne decided to keep up the pretense that Brad was attending with everyone except her mother and Paula. Not until she arrived at the Hickman home did she casually mention to Flo that a sudden stomach virus had kept Brad at home.

He hadn't even been home. He'd left the house before they did. Before leaving, he praised Lauren's junior bridesmaid dress—Suzanne had picked out something along the lines of Kenya's dress, in pale pink—and asked her to be sure to get her picture taken so he could display it in his office. He'd also slapped the suit-clad Bradley on the back and told him his snazzy tie and matching hanky made him look ready for a *GQ* cover.

When he came into the bedroom to let Suzanne know he was leaving, she was applying makeup in her underwear—a strapless bra and a slip with side slits, both in a peach color that complemented her complexion. The hungry look in his eyes gave her hope that they might make up on the spot, but in the end he left the room without a word.

She was pouring herself a glass of iced tea when Brad walked into the kitchen. She hadn't heard him come in.

"Hi."

"Hi," she said tentatively. God, she hated all this conflict between them.

"How did everything go?" he asked, casually leaning against the granite countertop.

She was careful not to sound too enthusiastic. "Smoothly, with no hitches. They drove up to St. Simons Island for a few days." She didn't dare tell him that the honeymoon trip had been a gift from the two of them. It was something they really needed, and she'd spoken to Flo to make sure she and Ernie hadn't taken care of it. It probably wouldn't sit too well with Brad to know that he'd funded the honeymoon of his daughter's former boyfriend, although if he asked if they'd given Kenya and Gregory a gift she'd tell him the truth. She just doubted he would think to ask about such a thing.

Fortunately, she had a fair amount of cash that she'd saved out of the generous pocket money Brad supplied her with over the years, as well as what she saved from the household expenses, that she kept inside a footstool in Lauren's room. Even Lauren didn't know it was there, and technically it was Suzanne's own money to spend as she pleased.

Instead she said, "I'm afraid Kenya is a lot happier than Gregory is, and it showed."

That seemed to mollify him. "Well, what's done is done. We'll all have to live with it."

She couldn't help asking. "How's Paige taking it?"

"Paige is out of town. She drove over to Pensacola yesterday and met Devon there. She won't be back until late tomorrow. She called Lisa when she arrived, and Lisa said she sounded happy."

For a moment they simply stood looking at each other. Finally Brad spoke, simultaneously holding out his hand. "C'mere, Suzie Q."

The moment Suzanne heard the words she knew the strife between them was over. She happily went into his arms, crying tears of relief. "I'm so sorry, Brad. I didn't handle this well at all." She paused to gather her thoughts, wanting to choose her words carefully. "There's no way I couldn't be involved with the actual wedding ceremony, since I'm Kenya's only sister, but I promise I'm going to stay out of Kenya and Gregory's marriage. I just don't want to know anything."

"It's done now, Suzanne," he pointed out. "It really doesn't matter much anymore."

She lifted her tear-streaked face. "You're not expecting Paige and Gregory to reunite after he and Kenya are divorced?"

"Frankly, no. Paige is still young, barely twenty-one. She and Gregory were just getting to know each other. It's not like she's lost the love of her life. If anything, it hurt her pride to lose him to Kenya. They've always been competitive when it came to Gregory. It may be difficult, but I don't see it as being tragic. She'll have found someone else in a few months' time and can leave Gregory to Kenya, or whoever."

Suzanne listened carefully, both to what he said and to what he didn't say. Of course. Gregory would be a father in another seven months. That made him undesirable in Brad's eyes. He wanted Paige to have children of her own, not be mother to someone else's kids.

She reminded herself not to get involved. Kenya had gotten what she wanted, Gregory Hickman for a husband. And Paige would likely go on with her life, just as Brad predicted. She might bleed, but not for long. And in the long run Paige would see more success out of life than Kenya. Eventually she'd marry someone with as good a job as she would have, while Kenya would find herself a struggling divorcée ringing up groceries for minimum wage.

Suzanne knew that Gregory had no intention of staying married to Kenya, no matter how good a wife she made him. Suzanne wasn't going to break the promise she'd just made to Brad, but that didn't mean she couldn't work with her sister and help her to make something of herself.

But that could wait. At the top of the list was making up with Brad. And a few moments to give thanks that she had her husband back.

Kenya opened her eyes at dawn. Her heart felt full with happiness before she even knew why. Then she looked over at the sleeping Gregory, and it came to her. He was hers now, legal as you please. He was her husband, and she was his wife. This was their honeymoon in a beautiful hotel room overlooking the Gulf.

How wonderful it felt to spend the entire night with him. Sex last night had been dynamite. If that was how it would be, she'd have no trouble holding on to him. She had so much to look forward to. They were going to have a wonderful life together. Another week of this would have him saying, *Paige who?*

He'd thrown off the covers of the king-sized brass bed in his sleep, and she playfully rolled over so she could reach out and trace his nipple with her fingertip.

She gasped when his hand suddenly sailed up and clamped her arm, then moved it off him and closer to her. Almost immediately his breathing returned to the normal rhythm of sleep.

A deflated Kenya laid her head back down on her pillow. It looked like she had her work cut out for her.

Chapter 17

Suzanne held her breath as she turned the cake pan upside down. With her first effort, she tried to remove the cake too soon, and because it was still warm, it fell apart into pieces. Her cake decorating class included whatever she'd be using for decorations, but it did not include the cake to be decorated. She had to provide that herself. Fortunately, she'd purchased more than one box of mix.

Perhaps cake decorating wasn't the most stimulating class she could have chosen—Brad's eyebrows had certainly shot up in a comical manner when she told him—but at least she didn't feel intimidated by it. She'd looked forward to the class offered by one of Jacksonville's few remaining non-supermarket bakeries.

Her family wasn't all that big on sweets, and a cake a week for six weeks would overwhelm anyone, but with Derrick and Matthew living down the road, she didn't have to worry about anything going to waste. She would reserve half for her family and take the rest to her mother's.

After the disaster of her first cake, she was glad she'd gotten started the night before. She really could have found herself in trouble if she'd waited until tomorrow morning. Class started at 10 A.M.

Of course, she probably could have asked Teresita to bake a cake for her, but part of the satisfaction came from knowing that she'd done it herself. Now she looked forward to her first class.

Suzanne was wiping the crumbs off the counter when the telephone rang. She checked the caller ID and broke out into a grin. "Hi, Paula," she said into the cordless kitchen extension.

"Hi. You sound cheerful."

"I just got my cake out of the pan, and it didn't break."

"Your cake! Since when do you bake?"

"Since I enrolled in a cake decorating class at that bakery downtown. I have my first class tomorrow, and I have to bring a cake to decorate."

"Well, good for you. I was calling to see if you wanted to have lunch tomorrow, since I don't have any events scheduled."

"I'd love to. Just tell me where and when. My class is over at noon."

"So," Paula said as she handed her menu back to the server, "how'd the class go?"

"Wonderful!" Suzanne replied. "Today we learned how to make that smooth icing, oh, what's it called again?"

"Fondant."

"Yes, that's it. There are just eight of us in the class, which means we can get personalized attention from the instructor. They only allow a maximum of ten. They're all housewives like me, looking to learn a new skill."

"I didn't know you had an interest in cake decorating, Suzanne."

She sipped her water. "Yes, I just decided to indulge myself in something creative."

"I think that's wonderful, and hey! If you really get good at it, I might be able to throw some work your way."

Suzanne drew in her breath. "Really, Paula?"

"Why not? I don't have a problem with doing business with friends, unless they turn out to be unprofessional."

"That is so exciting, Paula! Now I can't wait to show you some of my handiwork."

"Well, let's not get ahead of ourselves. You just started the course," Paula pointed out. "This is quite a surprise," she said as she leaned back in the booth. "I didn't even know you baked."

"I confess that I did take a shortcut," Suzanne admitted. "I bought some Duncan Hines cake mix. The point is to have a cake to decorate. Where it came from doesn't matter."

Paula shook her head. "You do realize that I'm not able to take that attitude. In my business, I have to use cakes made from scratch using only the best ingredients. For instance, butter, never margarine. I grew up with the feeling of a kid with their nose pressed against the glass of the candy store window. My mother kept supplies in our kitchen that we weren't supposed to touch, brand name everything. I remember," she said with a chuckle, "how my brother used some butter that our mother had bought for her clients on his pancakes, because he knew it tasted better than that vegetable oil spread we were supposed to use. Ooh, did she let him have it."

Suzanne smiled. Paula's mother had operated a successful catering business in her hometown of Charleston, South Carolina, and she'd grown up wanting to do the same type of work. Practicality won out in the end, and she ended up studying marketing in college. It wasn't until she returned to Jacksonville after the collapse of her second marriage that she decided to launch Discriminating Taste.

"No matter how beautifully a cake was decorated, I wouldn't consider using one that hadn't been made from scratch," Paula concluded.

"I guess that's it, then. I've never made a cake from scratch in my life," Suzanne said, her shoulders slumping.

"Give it a try. If you're still as enthusiastic at the end of the course as you are after taking one class, then tackle baking. It'll be another challenge for you."

Suzanne had to agree. Who knew, this might be just the

beginning. Perhaps baking wasn't on the same par as teaching children or treating their coughs and sniffles, but if she advanced to the point where she provided Paula with all of her desserts, Brad would be so proud of her.

Suzanne took a sip of her wine. "Isn't it exciting, Brad?" she said, her voice ringing with exhilaration. "And who knows what it might lead to? Paula says that if things go well, she might consider selling me a piece of the business." She could hardly believe her good fortune. That would sound just great, to be able to tell people she was part owner of a successful catering business. When Liloutie Braxton and the other wives of Brad's colleagues started talking about how busy they were, she could chime right in instead of sitting there quietly with nothing to say.

"I'd be all for that, but just remember, you wouldn't want to move too quickly on such a major decision," Brad cautioned. "It would probably be best if you started by learning the entire business. Everything from the ground up, all that's involved. You want to make sure it's something you like, because if you become a partner it'll be your responsibility to keep the business running smoothly if Paula should become ill or have to go out of town. Before you make that investment, you want to make sure it's a good fit."

"Oh, I agree. But the possibility makes me feel really good. You were right, Brad. I guess I needed to reach outside my comfort zone and see what else is out there, in terms of things I could be doing with my time."

He beamed at her from across the table. "I can see the change in you already, and I'm really excited and happy for you, Suzie Q."

"I know you are, sweetheart. Thank you so much for recognizing what I needed."

Brad lifted his highball glass. "Here's to your new career. May you conquer the city of Jacksonville with your business acumen."

Suzanne had no idea what "acumen" meant, but she was only too happy to tap her wineglass to his. "It means a lot to me that you support what I'm doing," she said.

"Suzanne, I always thought you were bright, from the very beginning. That's why I took such an interest in you when you worked for me. I just didn't know it would eventually get personal."

"And here we are, sixteen years later," she said, nodding.

"It hasn't been a bad sixteen years."

Her grin lit up her entire face. She felt wonderful. It had been too long since she and Brad had a conversation that didn't involve him being critical of her or her family. "You really do love me, don't you, Brad?"

"Of course I do. You're my Suzie Q. I know I've been a little tough on you lately, but you have to put yourself in my shoes. It's discouraging when your wife is always sticking up for her family. You have a family of your own, Suzanne, and we're supposed to come first."

"You do. I'm sorry that you thought otherwise."

A strange voice cut in. "Excuse me."

Suzanne tried not to glare at the nicely dressed, attractive brown-skinned woman who had paused by their table and interrupted the intimate, honest conversation with her husband that had been so long in coming. "Yes?"

"I'm sorry to interrupt, but my husband and I are sitting a few tables away, and you look so familiar to me. I just had to ask . . . Are you by any chance Suzanne Hall? From Palatka?"

In an instant the woman went from being an unwelcome interruption to someone who piqued Suzanne's curiosity. *I know this girl,* she thought. "Wait . . . don't tell me," she said. "I'll get it." Her right hand raised slightly, her index finger wiggling, she searched her memory bank as the woman stood smiling. She tried to picture the pretty face as a child.

Finally her mouth dropped open, and her finger stopped wiggling and pointed. "I remember you," she said. "From Mrs. Brown's second-grade class. I sat next to you."

"What's her name, Suzie Q?" Brad prompted.

His broad grin told her he was enjoying her memory lapse as much as her still-unidentified friend.

"Wait a minute . . . It'll come to me." She lowered her right hand and drummed her fingers on the table top. "It's unusual," Suzanne muttered. Then something clicked in her brain. "Oh! I remember. I thought about you years later, when someone gave me a bottle of perfume with the same name." She grinned triumphantly. "Norell, isn't it?"

"Yes," the woman said, laughing. "You haven't changed a bit," she added as Suzanne stood to embrace her. "I kept staring at you. Finally, my husband said, 'Go over and ask if she is who you think she is.'"

"I remember now," Suzanne replied. "We were inseparable at school, and then your family moved to Jacksonville in the spring, and I had to find a new best friend."

Norell laughed. "Which I'm sure you did within weeks."

"So you still live up this way?"

"Sure do. As a matter of fact, we live fairly close to here."

"That explains why we haven't run into each other. We live in Arlington." Suzanne turned to Brad. "Oh, let me introduce you to my husband, Dr. Brad Betancourt. Brad, this is Norell . . ." She realized she didn't remember her friend's last name.

"It's Bellamy now," Norell supplied with a laugh. She smiled at Brad. "Don't worry about getting up and shaking my hand. I know you're about to start eating. There's my husband over there." She discreetly pointed to a table halfway across the room, and the handsome gray-haired man sitting there waved jauntily when Suzanne turned to look.

"We all have to get together one night," Suzanne remarked. "We can have you and your husband over to our place."

"How lucky it was that we both came here to dinner the same night," Norell marveled.

"Oh, we eat here all the time. We love this restaurant, don't we, Brad?"

He nodded. "A heck of a drive, though."

"From Arlington?" Norell looked puzzled. "That isn't too far, is it?"

"Not the part of Arlington we live in."

"We live on the western end. On the water, across from downtown," Suzanne hastily added. She'd already let Norell know she was married to a doctor when she introduced Brad, but she wanted to leave no room for misunderstanding about the type of neighborhood they lived in. "But we love Barbara Jean's seafood, so we make the drive every so often."

"I know what you mean. Oh, here's your food." Norell reached inside her purse. "I'll let you guys eat, but here's my card. I wrote down my home number on the back. Why don't you give me a call one of these days? I'd love to chat over a meal."

"I'd like that." Suzanne accepted the business card Norell gave her and glanced at it. *CDN Transcription Service*, it said, with the words *Quality Medical Reports* below it in slightly smaller print, and a logo featuring a drawing of a tall stack of paper and the three letters of the company name. On the bottom of the card it was neatly printed, *Norell Bellamy, Co-Owner.*

Well, one day soon *she* might have business cards that said, *Discriminating Taste, Suzanne Betancourt, Co-Owner.*

Chapter 18

"Dr. Betancourt, there's a Mrs. Trent on line two," his office manager informed him through the intercom.

"Thanks, Sarah. I'll take it." He picked up the phone and quickly depressed the blinking line. "Hello, Micheline. How are you?"

Her beautifully cultured voice came over the line. "I'm wonderful, Brad. I just wanted to let you know I was offered the paralegal job in the legal department, and I accepted. I'll start work on Monday."

"Hey, that's great. Congratulations. I'll bet Errol's happy." Micheline's sex appeal came through even over the phone, and mentioning her husband helped Brad to stop thinking about her inappropriately.

"Oh, yes. We're both grateful to you for giving me that reference. I'm sure they asked you about me, and that whatever you said sealed the deal."

"I was happy to do it," he replied sincerely.

"Well, I'd love to be able to thank you personally. Do you have any lunch plans for tomorrow?"

"Um . . . let me check." The invitation caught Brad off guard. He'd expected Micheline to invite him to her home for dinner or something, where both their spouses would be present. He wasn't sure if it was wise to have lunch with Micheline when it would be just the two of them.

He ruffled some papers on his desk to provide sound effects while he measured the pros and cons of making a lunch date with Micheline. Finally he decided that he was being foolish. What harm could come from having lunch with her in broad daylight in what would undoubtedly be a busy atmosphere?

"Yeah, I'm free. The office is traditionally closed between twelve-thirty and two. Where should I meet you?"

"How about that seafood place over by your office, the one on Touchton Road next to the Shell station? I hear their food is pretty good."

"Yes, it is. You really don't have to do this, Micheline."

"I *want* to. It's the least I can do after your recommendation got me the job. I'll meet you there tomorrow at twelve forty, twelve forty-five, huh?"

"Sure. See you then."

Brad frowned. He didn't understand it. If sales were up, why were profits down? Last month there'd been a slip in profits as well, but now it was bigger. He'd meant to dig deeper into it then, but then everything unfolded with Paige and Gregory and that damn Kenya, and that disturbed him so much he didn't get back to the balance sheet until tonight. But now it had happened again. He'd better get with his bookkeeper right away.

The office at the restaurant was so small, two people could barely fit into it. Christine Campbell kept the books for the diagnostic center as well, probably spending ten to fifteen hours there every week. He'd ask her to set aside some time to go over the books with him when she came in on Friday. He knew she'd be only too glad to do it. She'd put a note on last month's statement asking him to look into it, and the Post-it Note she attached to the present statement was laced with more urgency, underlying text, double question marks and exclamation points. He understood her concern. Chris was a meticulous worker. Still, bookkeepers often found themselves at the end of a pointed finger of clients unhappy about diminishing profits, sometimes even accused of "funny money" practices. No doubt Chris had expected him to look into the situation right away and come up with a logical explanation for the smaller profits, not let it continue for a second month.

He put the papers through a three-hole punch, then added them to a pronged portfolio with the rest of the year's financial reports for the restaurant, but left the folder in plain view on his desk. He had planned to go over some patient charts that evening in his home office, but now he didn't feel up to it. His mind was on his restaurant's dwindling profits, wondering how it could have happened. He'd try to get up earlier than usual in the morning. Maybe he'd be able to better concentrate then.

At least things on the home front had calmed down. Paige still hadn't opened up to him or to Lisa about how she felt about this whole fiasco. Brad figured she'd shared her thoughts with her stepsister, Devon. Paige did seem to be adjusting nicely to the abrupt end of her burgeoning relationship with Gregory, going about her everyday activities with no signs of anything amiss. She'd said nothing about transferring colleges again, and for that Brad was grateful. A doting father, he sometimes found it difficult to say no to his children. He knew he tended to overindulge them, but Paige was now an adult and had to accept that sometimes life could be unpleasant.

It felt good to be able to put that crisis behind him. Now all he had to do was figure out what was going on at his Subway franchise.

And keep tomorrow's lunch with Micheline as impersonal as possible.

Brad sighed. He had found himself growing more and more envious of Errol, who often sang his wife's praises when they were out on the links or having a drink afterward. According to Errol, and from what little Brad had seen himself, Micheline was a fabulous housekeeper, an imaginative cook, and a gracious hostess. Of course, Errol was too much of a gentleman to say it—she was his wife, after all—but Brad suspected Micheline performed just as well in the bedroom as she did in every other aspect of their lives together.

He had no problem with Suzanne in that area, either. Their home was always neat and orderly, but that was largely due to Teresita's efforts. And while Suzanne's cooking had undeniably improved since she befriended Paula Haines, her taste still remained extremely simple. Brad had licked his lips when Errol described the dishes Micheline prepared for him—shrimp and crabmeat bisque . . . pecan-crusted catfish, cioppino that Errol swore tasted like it came from one of San Francisco's finest restaurants. Hell, until just a few years ago, Suzanne regularly made Hamburger Helper for dinner and expected him to eat it.

As far as Suzanne's hostess abilities, she'd learned quite a bit about entertaining over the years, but where she invariably fell short was in making conversation with their guests. Suzanne knew remarkably little about world events. He couldn't understand. Suzanne didn't work. She could watch CNN all day if she wanted to, instead of that silly soap opera she never missed. Suzanne usually wore a look of disinterest, even confusion, when the conversation turned to current events. Micheline would never know how closely she nailed it when she commented about housewives who went through life totally uninformed.

Most glaring of all, not once had Errol ever complained about his in-laws, most of whom lived in other parts of the state.

Brad knew it was wrong, because Errol was a friend of his, but he couldn't stop thinking about Micheline in a way he had no business doing. She was everything a man could want: a beautiful face, shapely figure, unrivaled domestic skills, and if that weren't enough, she had a family that didn't get in her husband's way.

Brad had bought this house mainly to get away from his

in-laws, who lived in Palatka and who spent way too much time at his old house in St. Augustine, showing up just about every weekend. He thought he'd be free of them by moving thirty miles north, but instead, the entire Hall family ended up following him and Suzanne here to Jacksonville. He concluded that all of them except Matthew, who had gotten a late start but at least was trying to make something of himself, were hopeless. Kenya believed her best shot in life was to find a man to take care of her. Arlene felt that having a wealthy son-in-law meant *she* would be taken care of. As for Derrick, well, Brad's first thought upon learning about the decreased profits at his Subway franchise was to wonder if his brother-in-law could be involved.

Lisa pulled into a parking space and in one motion, shifted into park and grabbed her keys from the ignition. She hoped they had her lunch order ready. She had a ton of prescriptions to fill at work. Fridays were always so busy, probably because it was payday for so many people. Unfortunately, this was also a popular day to eat out. But this restaurant made the best coconut fried shrimp in town.

There was a line for people picking up take-out orders. She should have known. Surely she wasn't the only one who loved their coconut shrimp.

Lisa forced herself to calm down. She'd get back to work as soon as she could. The consumer warehouse where she worked was just down the road. And she *had* to eat. It wasn't like she would stick around to sit leisurely at a table, she was taking her food back to work for quick consumption. She needed to be well nourished in order to perform effectively on the job. If there was one thing Lisa knew, it was that distractions in her line of work could be career-ending. Errors made by pharmacists could and sometimes did have deadly consequences. So she'd get her food and drive back to work. It would have to take as long as it took.

Bored, she looked around at the patrons as, one by one,

the people in front of her each paid for the meal and carried it out in a sack. Business seemed to be booming. Lisa didn't know how the recession had affected the hospitality industry in other cities, but the restaurant business seemed to be thriving in Jacksonville.

Her gaze passed over a man, then promptly went back to him. That looked like Brad . . . and more interesting, his female companion *didn't* look like Suzanne. It looked like they'd just gotten here; they had no food on their table other than water glasses and a basket of those wonderful herb and cheese biscuits. There was only one person in front of her now. She'd stop by Brad's table on the way out and get a better look.

Out of the corner of her eye, Micheline saw a woman make her way toward them. She initially put the woman's age in her late thirties, but changed it to mid forties as she got closer. Still, she was slim, and her short haircut gave her a youthful look, as did her casual black short-sleeved dress with white trim and white open-toed mules. Micheline knew she'd seen this woman before . . . and the look of recognition in the woman's eyes told her she thought the same.

"Hello, Brad."

"Uh, Lisa. Hi. How are you?"

"I'm good, thanks. Just picking up some lunch."

Micheline noticed that although Lisa's remarks were directed toward Brad, as she spoke her eyes were fixated on *her.* Who was this woman to be so curious? A suspicious friend of Suzanne's who couldn't wait to pass on what she'd seen?

I hope.

Brad quickly made introductions, adding, "You might remember Micheline from my party. She was there with her husband, Errol."

"Yes," Lisa replied with a nod. "That's it. I *thought* you looked familiar."

Micheline smiled politely.

"I gave Micheline a reference for a job in the legal department at the hospital," Brad explained. "She was so happy when they offered it to her, she wanted to thank me by taking me to lunch." He chuckled. "I told her it was her own paralegal experience rather than my reference that got her hired, but she wouldn't hear of it."

He certainly sounded unruffled, Micheline noted, but she nonetheless had the distinct feeling that Brad wanted to make sure Lisa knew this lunch was on the up-and-up.

"Well, congratulations on the new job," Lisa said. "You'll have to excuse me now. I have to hurry and get back to work. Enjoy your lunch. Nice seeing you, Brad."

"You too. I'll probably see you and Darrell this weekend."

"Good," she replied over her shoulder, already moving toward the exit.

"Friend of yours, obviously," Micheline remarked.

"Actually, yes. But it's a little more complicated than that. We used to be married."

"*What?*"

Brad laughed. "It was a long time ago." He paused momentarily as the waiter placed their plates on the table.

Normally the aroma of a steaming lobster pot pie would get Micheline's mouth watering, but she could hardly wait for Brad to resume his story. He moved with such slowness as he reached for the pepper and removed the top bread slice from his crab cake sandwich and sprinkled it, then applied sauce to the top. She wanted to scream at him to hurry up.

He eventually continued, after taking a bite and swallowing it. "Mmm, that's good. Anyway, I had just graduated from medical school, and Lisa was in pharmacy school. What a mess that was. I started my internship right after the honeymoon, and we barely saw each other."

"I didn't know you'd been married before Suzanne." This knowledge had taken Micheline completely by surprise.

"For six years. Or maybe it was seven, I forget. But I know that our daughter is twenty-one."

"You two have a child together?" Micheline knew she sounded dumbstruck, but she couldn't help it. This was astounding.

"Just the one. My other two are with Suzanne."

Those had been the only two that Suzanne had mentioned, but Micheline would have expected that. "And you're obviously friends with Lisa and her new, what? Husband? Boyfriend? You'd said you'd probably see them this weekend."

"Husband. And he's hardly new. Lisa's been married to Darrell nearly as long as I've been married to Suzanne. And we're more than friends. We're next-door neighbors."

"You live next door to your ex-wife? Why? I mean, out of all the places you could live . . ."

"I know, it's freaky," he said with a laugh as he buttered a biscuit and took a bite. "It was a matter of circumstances." He briefly summarized the situation leading to his proximity to Lisa and her second husband.

"That's amazing," Micheline said. "But certainly plausible, since the original builders of your house backed out. It must have come as quite a shock when you all found out."

"Darrell and I always thought it was funny. But our wives weren't laughing, not then and not now . . . and it's been five years."

"I was going to ask you how Suzanne felt about it."

"She wanted to unload the house, which was pretty silly, considering we'd just closed on it and had the movers scheduled."

"Maybe she just didn't understand what a closing means," Micheline suggested.

"No, that's not it. After all, we'd bought a house before, and she was there at both closings."

"Yes, signing her name where she was told to," Micheline replied with a shrug.

"You don't like my wife, do you?"

One look at Brad's suddenly unsmiling face and Micheline instantly knew she'd gone too far. She made herself sound wounded. "I'm surprised you'd say such a thing, Brad."

"Maybe I shouldn't have said that," he said in a gentle manner. "If I hurt your feelings, I'm sorry. But you have to consider how what you just said sounded. Whether you meant to do it or not, you implied that Suzanne is as dumb as a pin. I can't imagine why you would do that unless you dislike her for some reason."

"You're right," she said quickly. "It's ridiculous for me to suggest that Suzanne doesn't know what it means to close on a house. I'm sorry, I didn't mean to be insulting. I certainly have nothing against Suzanne," she lied. "Of course she knows what a closing is. Sometimes . . ." Her mind raced to find a credible alternative. "Sometimes people say things that sound silly when they're faced with a trying situation. That's probably what happened to Suzanne, and why she suggested you sell the house rather than live next door to your first wife and her husband." She watched Brad's reaction carefully, anxious to see if the mood had been broken.

His facial expression softened, and when he spoke he sounded natural. Some people said what they had to say, and that was it. They held no grudges once they made their position clear. Brad was apparently one of those people . . . but Micheline knew she'd never again be able to say anything else critical about Suzanne without incurring his wrath. She hated the way he'd stuck up for her, but that's what she got for pushing too hard.

"Oh, I'm sure she wasn't thinking clearly at the time," he said. "It came as a huge shock to all of us. We'd gone to look at our new house at the same time Lisa and her family were checking the builders' progress. There'd been bad blood between the two of them ever since Suzanne and I got married. Living so close to each other would only exacerbate it."

"Has it gotten any better since?"

He shrugged. "Yeah, but pretty much only on the surface. We manage, though. Darrell and I are actually good friends."

Micheline shook her head as she swallowed a bite of lobster, the flaky, golden brown crust, lobster sauce, and vegetables. "That's certainly a wacky living situation." She sounded enthusiastic and interested, but inside she was swimming in disappointment. It looked like things weren't going to go her way this afternoon. Not only was Lisa unlikely to share the news of Brad lunching with Suzanne if the two weren't particularly friendly, but she'd come dangerously close to antagonizing Brad.

She'd have to move on to Plan B.

Chapter 19

That afternoon, after he'd seen his last patient, Brad sat at the small conference table in a corner of his office with his bookkeeper.

"I'm so glad we're finally sitting down to talk about this, Dr. Betancourt," Chris said.

"It's my fault it took so long," he apologized. "It ended up being an especially busy time for me, and I just didn't get to it. But whatever it is that's happening, it'll keep right on happening unless we identify the problem and do something about it."

"I agree," Chris said. A woman in her mid thirties, she worked for several small businesses around Jacksonville. She was as professional as she was capable, coming in regularly to both the diagnostic center as well as the restaurant, always dressing professionally in business casual for the few hours at a time she spent working in the cramped business office of the restaurant.

"All right, let's see if we can figure out why profits are down even though sales are holding," he said. "Obviously, we had a rise in expenses. We have to identify the problem area and go from there."

"Utilities are about the same," Chris replied. "No spikes in payroll expense, either."

"Well, it has to be coming from somewhere."

"The only thing I noticed . . ."

Brad thought she appeared reluctant. "Was?" he prompted.

"There seems to be this slight spike in the amount of meat purchased."

"That makes sense, doesn't it? A restaurant with higher sales would coincide with purchasing more supplies."

She didn't reply, and instinctively Brad knew there was more to this story, something she wasn't telling him. "Chris, don't hold back. If you know something, tell me what it is."

"I never thought of myself as a tattletale, Dr. Betancourt." At his impatient gesture for her to continue, she went on. "I couldn't help noticing how this man has been coming to see Derrick when I'm there in the afternoons, during that slow period after lunch."

"What goes on between the two of them?" Brad asked.

"The man would come to the restaurant, and then Derrick would go outside and talk to him. At first I thought it was just personal. . . ."

Brad knew Chris was thinking that this man was Derrick's contact for the weed he smoked, and that had been his first thought as well.

". . . but one day I got there at the same time as the man did, and I noticed him getting out of a lunch wagon. You know, a van with lettering on the sides," she concluded. "I wondered if there might be a connection. I'm sure it was silly of me."

Brad's eyes narrowed. He didn't think it was silly at all. It would take a colossal amount of nerve for his brother-in-law to sell meats and cheeses from the restaurant's stock and line his own pockets with the proceeds. And no one could ever accuse Derrick Hall of being short on nerve. Like his mother, Arlene, Derrick believed in living off the fat of the land . . . and they considered *him* to be the fat.

"You say it's the afternoons when this guy comes by?"

Chris thought for a moment. "Of course, I usually come by the restaurant around two-thirty, three, but sometimes it's later than that. And I never see him when I'm there in the early evening."

"I need you to be more observant. Make a notation of when this man shows up. I want days as well as times. Do that for a week, and then report to me."

"Sure," she replied with an uncertain nod.

Brad could tell she was curious about what he planned to do. That was easy. Once he had an idea of the men's schedule, he'd get proof of what they were doing. And so help him, if Derrick was doing what he *thought* he was doing, he'd cut him off. No more job, no more help, no nothing.

He tried to keep the anger he felt under the surface. It would be wrong to accuse Derrick of wrongdoing until he knew exactly what was going on, even though his gut told him that Derrick was guilty.

He'd just about had it with his in-laws.

Brad joined Errol Trent at the bar of the golf club. "Scotch and water," he told the bartender as he sat on the neighboring stool. To Errol he said, "Good to see you. I haven't seen too much of you lately."

"What can I say? I've been busy."

Brad looked at him curiously. "You all right, man? You look a little down."

"Well, *you* look like you're angry enough to murder somebody."

"In-law trouble," Brad admitted. "I hope you realize how fortunate you are that Micheline's brothers live in South Florida. And what about you? You look like you're nursing a serious case of the blues."

"That's because I can't be where I wanna be. I swear, I'm starting to hate Friday nights."

Brad stared at him incredulously. "I think you need your head examined. Who in their right mind hates Fridays?"

"A man who can't come up with a valid excuse not to be home, like office hours."

"Say what?"

"Ah, forget it," Errol said. "Listen, buddy, I feel like getting good and drunk, and the best place to do that is home. So I'm gonna head out." He placed a twenty by his glass, and slid off the stool. "I'll see you next time, huh?"

"Yeah, sure," Brad replied. They shook hands, and Errol left. Brad looked after him. There was nothing about his gait that suggested impairment, so it wasn't necessary for him to intervene and take Errol's car keys. Yet something was clearly troubling him. It didn't take a Ph.D. to figure out that he was having an affair, cheating on Micheline, the seemingly perfect wife.

What the heck was going on with *that?*

Gregory felt invigorated as he drove home. He'd been on his new job for just two weeks and was really getting into it. It felt refreshing to apply what he'd learned in college on the job and to get paid for it.

A group of people from various departments went out for drinks every Friday, and tonight he'd joined them for the first time. He hadn't planned on staying long. Funny how easily a person could lose track of time when they were having fun. The only thing that would make his life perfect would be if he could pick up Paige and go out for some dinner. Instead he had a wife at home, and in six months he'd be a father, just in time for Christmas.

For what must have been the five hundredth time, he cursed himself for not using a condom, for believing Kenya's claims that she was on the pill. Why hadn't he seen it coming? She'd probably thrown her pills away the moment he suggested they consider seeing other people.

He'd been so besotted with Paige Betancourt that it never occurred to him that Kenya would be so sneaky. Paige had transferred to UNF from the University of Florida last semester. He ran into her on campus, and they went for an espresso, and almost immediately Gregory knew everything between them had changed. No longer did Paige seem like just the cute girl from around the corner, a year younger than he, always giggling about something with her equally silly stepsister, Devon. Back then Kenya, his own age, seemed much more worldly—not to mention *experienced*—than the stepsisters. It was a cinch he wouldn't be getting any from either one of them, so he did what any horny seventeen-year-old boy would do and went with Kenya.

In five years both he and Paige had matured, and he felt himself gravitating toward her and succumbing to her considerable intelligence and charms. Kenya, on the other hand, hadn't grown at all as a person in five years. He couldn't talk to her the way he could talk to Paige. She had no interest in politics or economics, only when Keyshia Cole's new CD was going to drop or the fantastic new color she was going to get her nails done in. By the time Kenya informed him of her pregnancy he knew he was in love with Paige, and no matter what Dr. Betancourt said, Gregory had every attention of trying to win her back as soon as his marriage ended.

With a heavy heart, he unlocked the front door and stepped inside. He saw no signs of anyone, which wasn't unusual, considering it was going on eight o'clock. By now his parents had eaten dinner and his mother had cleaned the kitchen. They'd probably retired to their bedroom, even though it was a lovely night to sit outside. Sometimes he felt his parents could have saved all that money they spent installing and maintaining their pool; they never used it. His mother had never even learned how to swim.

The house was designed with a split bedroom arrangement, his parents' suite on one side and the other bedrooms on the other. Gregory headed toward the latter. The door to the room he now shared with Kenya was closed. He knocked as a courtesy, then entered without waiting for an answer. He still couldn't get used to the idea of sharing his room with another person. It felt perfectly natural to sneak Kenya in there when his parents weren't home, but it still felt weird for her to be there openly. Plus, he wasn't used to sleeping with some-one the whole night. It wasn't as bad as he feared it would be. Kenya had a tiny bump in her lower abdomen, and he found it sexy in a crazy sort of way.

Sex was one thing . . . marriage was something else. Gregory's mouth fell open at the sight of his bedroom. Kenya had gotten sloppier and sloppier. The huge pile of unfolded clothes on the bed failed to disguise the fact that it was still unmade at eight o'clock at night. Apparently she'd done laundry and just dumped the clothes fresh out of the dryer onto the surface of the bed. Kenya was nowhere in sight, but Gregory readily understood why she'd seen fit to close the door. He'd be ashamed for his parents to see this mess.

He'd had no idea Kenya was such a slob. Her mother's house always looked immaculate. Kenya worked full-time at the supermarket, but her mother had a full-time job, too, and so did his mother. If Mrs. Hall and his mother could work full-time and still keep clean houses, then he figured Kenya should be able to do it, too. What if they had not just a bedroom and bathroom, but an entire apartment that needed to be kept clean?

Gregory's bladder called out to him urgently, courtesy of the beers he'd drank, and he wrinkled his nose at the state of the bathroom. He left for work before Kenya did, and he left the room neat. She apparently spilled toothpaste in the sink, which had turned into a hardened blue smear. A wet towel lay on the floor outside the shower.

He took care of his business, then sought out his wife. He hoped that whatever she was doing, it involved some type of housework. Maybe she just needed a little rest after dinner and planned to clean up afterward.

But where was she?

She wasn't out by the pool, wasn't out front, and wasn't in the laundry room or anywhere downstairs. That left only one other possibility.

Gregory climbed the stairs to the bonus room, which his parents had turned into a home theater. He heard the surround sound coming from the speakers before he reached the top landing, and as he climbed he could hear Kenya's laughter right along with that of a laugh track.

When he walked in he saw she was watching a sitcom from her perch in the center reclining chair of the first row. His parents had installed a sixty-inch plasma television on the opposite wall of this, the largest room in the house, the same size as the double garage beneath it. For seating, they had a platform built for the second and last row of three attached recliners that raised it fifteen inches above the ground, creating the same stadium seating effect found in theaters.

"So there you are," he said. "I've been looking everywhere for you."

"Hi!" she said. "So you finally remembered you have a wife at home, huh?"

Her ribbing annoyed him, especially in light of what he'd just seen downstairs. "I needed to get out and socialize a bit. It's good for my career. I didn't stay all that long. But I'm surprised to see you up here. I thought you'd be cleaning up. Our room is a mess. I can't even lie down."

"Oh. I wasn't feeling well, Gregory. I've been taking it easy since I got home from work."

Gregory noted that she'd gone from sounding strong and robust to weak and tired, and he knew she was putting on. "You felt well enough to do a couple of loads of laundry," he pointed out. "And it's getting late. I'm sure you don't want to wait until you're ready to go to bed to clean it up. Or do you plan on having us sleep up here?" This was obviously Kenya's favorite room of the house, he thought with annoyance.

"Of course not, Gregory. I'll be down as soon as this show is over and I'll get our room all fixed up. Happy now?"

No, he thought. *I'm not happy. I won't be happy until you're no longer my wife.*

He turned to go down to the kitchen and get something to eat. That was something Kenya should have offered to do for him, the way his mother did for his father, the way Paige would likely do for him, but since Kenya was so reluctant to tear herself away from the television, it looked like he'd have to do it himself. . . .

Chapter 20

"What a lovely home!" Norell Bellamy exclaimed. "Very nice," her husband, Vic, echoed. "And the location is great. You'd probably be spared hurricane damage, for one. And the bridge to downtown is just minutes from here. I work downtown. What I wouldn't give to be home in fifteen minutes instead of forty-five."

"Where do you work, Vic?" Suzanne inquired. She'd been curious about Norell ever since seeing her that night at Barbara Jean's. What type of life did she lead? Did she and Vic have kids, and if so, how old? She found it interesting that they'd both married slightly older men. Had Norell and Vic been married as long as she and Brad?

"I'm down by the courthouse," Vic replied.

"Vic owns Bellamy Bail Bonds," Norell said proudly.

"Good field," Brad said. "I guess business is booming in these hard times, huh?"

Bradley and Lauren came out of their rooms to join them for dinner, grilled pork steaks and chicken quarters that Suzanne served outside, along with grilled corn on the cob, cheesy au gratin potatoes, and a summer salad of spring mix, sliced strawberries and oranges, chopped pecans, and feta cheese. They all marveled at Bradley's ravenous appetite; he put away two chicken quarters plus half a pork steak, as well as two cars of corn. "I guess you have to read a whole lot of X-rays to keep him fed," Vic quipped.

"Are you kidding? I try to schedule at least one surgical procedure every week just to pay his food bill," Brad said with a chuckle. Then he asked the question that had been on Suzanne's mind. "Do you guys have kids?"

"We've got a beautiful little girl, three years old," Norell replied. "Remind me to show you her picture after dinner."

"She's the light of our lives," Vic added. "My kids are grown, and I'm tickled to have another shot at being a daddy. Brianna makes me forget how old I am."

Suzanne noted something else she and Norell had in common: They were both second wives with stepchildren. She wondered how Norell felt about having her daughter share the spotlight with Vic's other children. Then again, if their daughter was only three, chances were that she and Vic hadn't been married all that long. Whenever two people got married who were over thirty-five, chances were that one or even both of them were going to have some baggage.

"It's funny, Suzanne," Norell said. "You and I are the same age, yet your kids are teenagers and mine is a preschooler."

"Brad and I have been married sixteen years."

Norell nodded. "I was past thirty when I met Vic."

"Well, you know what they say. It's not the quantity, it's the quality." Suzanne forced herself to smile. The quality of her marriage probably wasn't anything to brag about these days.

Bradley headed out with some of his friends after dinner, and Lauren's friends from down the street rang the doorbell to see if she wanted to go bike riding with them.

"Go ahead," Brad told her. "You know the rule. Just be in before dark."

"She's so pretty, Suzanne," Norell said. "She reminds me of you when you were little." To Brad she said, "You should have seen her. The cutest thing you ever saw. Long braids, one on each side of her head. And always so well dressed. But she wasn't conceited or anything, just a friendly little girl. She was the type of kid everybody wanted to be friends with because she was so cute."

"Norell was cute herself, Vic," Suzanne said with a laugh. "A chubby little thing, she was."

"Baby fat," Norell corrected.

"And her braids were thicker than mine," Suzanne added.

"But not longer."

"I'll bet y'all were both cute," Vic said. "Of course, when y'all were in grammar school, I'd already graduated from high school."

"I don't think I can quite say that," Brad remarked, "but I was probably in high school." He laughed. "How'd two old guys like us end up with such gorgeous wives?"

"Hey, Brad, how about showing me your boat?"

"Sure. Come on."

"Norell, I'd love to see a picture of your daughter," Suzanne said as the men headed toward the dock.

"Oh! Let me show it to you." Norell reached for her purse and removed a photograph from her wallet. "Here she is, my pride and joy."

"Ooh, how precious," Suzanne said admiringly. She was a beautiful child, dressed in a summer dress of black and white checks with appliqués of fruits on the pockets as well as the oversized white collar. Her dark hair was brushed back into a little Afro puff on top of her head.

"That was taken just last month," Norell said.

Suzanne studied the photo. Her first thought was that the child looked like Vic because of her lighter complexion, and as she looked more closely at the child's features, she kept her original assessment. "I think she looks more like Vic. I'm afraid I don't see you in her at all."

"Yes, she looks like her daddy."

"Something about her eyes," Suzanne said thoughtfully.

"Her eyes don't really look like Vic's, but yet they look familiar."

She was sure she'd seen those eyes before.

"Nice couple," Vic remarked on the way home. "That's a heck of a house, huh?"

"Yes, it sure is."

"I was serious when I said I'd really like to live closer to town, Norell. That drive seems like it's getting longer and longer. And how nice it would be not to have to evacuate if a storm approaches." Vic sighed. "I think I might be getting too old to live at the beach." He took his eyes off the road long enough to glance her way. "How do you feel about possibly moving inland?"

"That's fine with me. I'd be closer to Cécile and Dana. We'd have to find a new babysitter for Brianna."

"That shouldn't be a problem. Cécile's daughters are old enough to watch her if we want to go out." He stopped for a red light and looked at her again. "You want to tell me what's on your mind, Norell? You've been acting a little weird in the last hour or so. What happened?"

"Nothing, Vic. I'm just . . . well, it's pretty incredible that I ran into Suzanne again and that we were able to get caught up. I never expected to see her again. Funny how different our lives have turned out."

"I hope you're not feeling like an also-ran. I may not be a big-shot doctor, but we live pretty comfortably, don't you think? And your career seems a lot more interesting than Suzanne hanging around the house all day."

"Yes, you're right." Norell hummed a tune as the light changed and Vic returned his attention to the road. It wouldn't do to let him know what she was really thinking.

Suzanne didn't know just how lucky she was. There was no question that she'd given birth to young Bradley and Lauren; they shared facial features. She'd clearly married Brad when she was still in her twenties.

Norell was glad that Vic had gone off to look at Brad's boat when she showed Suzanne the picture of Brianna. He might have given something away when Suzanne commented on the lack of resemblance between mother and daughter. Norell didn't want Suzanne to know that Brianna wasn't her biological child . . . but that Vic was her father.

And she wanted no one to know about what she'd feared for the last month. It was so horrible that she could hardly express it to herself, much less to Vic.

She'd been so happy when Vic told her that he'd arranged for a private adoption from a single mother who wanted to place her baby in a loving home. Her inability to conceive had her in the depths of despair, and she'd turned to a vodka bottle to ease her pain—a solution that put further strain on her marriage. Vic didn't care if they had a child or not, but he'd already raised three kids. Norell had always dreamed of being a mother, and with no siblings and both her parents gone, the concept of having a family of her own became more important than ever.

It wasn't until the mother's due date grew closer that Norell became suspicious that Vic might have been personally involved. He'd gotten her thinking with a few unflattering comments he made about the birth mother, whom he wasn't supposed to know. When Norell did the math, she realized that the expected baby had been conceived during a particular low point in their marriage, when the stress on them both became so heavy that they barely spoke to each other. Vic's work as a bail bondsman required him to keep late hours, and at the time she'd been working like crazy from her home office as she and her partners struggled to get their transcription service off the ground. He could have been out there doing anything with anybody.

When she confronted him about the convenience of a baby becoming available when she wanted one desperately, he admitted to having had a one-night stand in which the condom he used tore, allowing his semen to leak out. As apologetic as he was, Norell had recognized a smug undercurrent to his voice, as if he was proud of being able to make a baby without even trying.

They had a terrible fight in the aftermath of his confession, and she considered leaving him, but his heartfelt assurances that the woman meant nothing to him, combined with the bouncing baby girl who was delivered shortly afterward, melted her heart. She also had to consider the part she played in driving Vic into the arms of another woman. At that time she'd barely been functioning, moving between housework, company business, and the bottle with virtually no time for her husband.

Norell told no one that the little girl they adopted was actually Vic's natural child. She gave no thought to the mother, who hadn't been heard from since and who obviously had no interest in the child. That fit in with Vic's description of her as a woman at the center of her very own universe.

From the time Brianna was three months old, Norell noticed that she bore a resemblance to her friend and business partner Cécile Rivers, whose own baby girl looked more like her husband. How many times had she joked about it to Cécile? It seemed so harmless, because Norell knew that her friend wasn't the biological mother of her daughter. Not only because Cécile had been pregnant herself, giving birth just four months before Brianna was born, but because she knew Cécile would never have slept with Vic.

But last month, when Norell stumbled on Vic having a heated conversation in Cécile's kitchen while bringing Brianna to the bathroom, the reason for the resemblance came at her like the proverbial speeding locomotive. Vic had been having the exchange with Cécile's sister, Micheline . . . and Micheline had the same eyes as Cécile.

Norell didn't know Micheline well, but she knew all about the incident in which Micheline deliberately dated Dana's boyfriend while she rented a room in Dana's house. It had been a mean thing to do, devastating to Dana, and it proved that

Micheline fit Vic's description of being heartless enough to have a baby and forget about it.

Norell didn't know what to do with her suspicions. She knew if she asked Vic he would tell her the truth—he'd always been open and honest with her—but part of her dreaded knowing. But she had to find out. It would be terribly embarrassing for her, and almost as much for Cécile, if it became open knowledge that Micheline had a one-night stand with Vic that resulted in Brianna. There'd be no way for Norell to save face. Just a little while ago she had some anxious moments when Suzanne made the comment about Brianna's eyes looking familiar and kept looking at the photograph.

Wait a minute. That might just be her salvation. It proved that a lot of people shared similar facial features.

After all, it was unlikely that Suzanne knew Cécile *or* Micheline.

Chapter 21

Micheline carefully moved the hidden ignition switch that her mechanic had installed under the dashboard into the off position. To make sure it was off, she turned the ignition key. Nothing.

Perfect.

She'd left work early that afternoon with an excuse of having a doctor's appointment, one that had been in place before she accepted her new position. She chuckled. That wasn't too far from the truth. The only thing was, the doctor in question didn't know it yet.

She had to act now, since Errol was in Atlanta at a dentistry class, learning some new technique. It seemed to Micheline that there was still only one way to extract a tooth, but she wasn't complaining. His absence gave her the perfect opening to make a move on Brad. She had to stop being so subtle and make sure he was getting the point, and she had to do it without blundering the way she had the week before last. The only message he seemed to have gotten was that he was married to a nitwit. That was all well and good, but she had to get him to stop looking at her as the wife of a friend, but as a woman he found desirable and sexy. There was no time to lose. She couldn't string Errol along forever. He hadn't mentioned anything more about starting a fertility workup. Maybe he wanted to wait and see if her beginning work would somehow relax her enough so that she could conceive. After a few months with no results, he'd probably start in on her with a vengeance, and she'd be cooked. No way would she be able to convince any reputable doctor to falsify his findings.

Time was running out for her, just like sand through an hourglass.

She cleared her throat as she dialed Brad's office. "Dr. Betancourt, please. Micheline Trent calling."

After he told her he'd be there shortly to see what he could do, she patted the dashboard of the Sebring convertible. "Good girl. You just stay right here and don't start up. Mama's got plenty of shoes, but she needs a new husband."

Brad scratched his head, his brow knit with confusion. "I can't understand it. It won't even respond to a jump."

"Maybe it's the alternator," Micheline suggested. "Those can often be iffy when they need to be replaced, can't they?"

"That's right, they can. Have you had a problem like this before?"

"No, never."

"Well, it's the damnedest thing I ever saw."

"Maybe this is just the beginning of alternator trouble. It's got to start somewhere, I guess." She sighed. "I'd better give the auto club a call. If they can't get it started, I'll just have them tow it to the garage. Of course," she added ruefully, "it might take them a while to get here. It's rush hour." She turned to Brad. "I'm terribly sorry to bother you with this, Brad, but with Errol out of town. . . ."

"It's fine. Errol would have wanted you to call me."

"I probably should have just gotten in the car and gone right home after my doctor appointment, instead of stopping here to shop."

"Micheline, it's okay. Don't worry about it." Brad scratched behind his ear. "Tell you what. Go ahead and call the auto club. Get an idea of how long it will be before they can get a tow truck here. If they say an hour or more, well, there's a Cheesecake Factory right over there. You and I can get some dinner while we wait."

"Oh, you don't have to wait here with me, Brad. The tow truck will be here well before dark, so it's perfectly safe. Suzanne's expecting you, I'm sure."

"Suzanne's working tonight."

"Working?"

She listened as he told her about her foray into cake decorating and the possibility of becoming a partner in Paula Haines's catering business.

"I suggested she spend some time working with Paula to learn the business from the ground up. Paula was raised in the catering business, but Suzanne knows nothing about it. So she's working so she can learn."

"Oh? Some kind of corporate function?"

"No, a wedding. Apparently, people are getting married on Thursday evenings these days."

"How exciting! Did she prepare the wedding cake?" Micheline felt fairly certain that Suzanne, with her course in cake decorating, had hardly graduated to baking complicated multi-layer wedding cakes, but she wanted to hear it from Brad.

He chuckled. "No. She's not quite ready for that. She's just doing some general assisting. She left Bradley money to order pizza for himself and Lauren."

"I must say you don't sound all that happy about it."

"No, I'm fine. It's just a little difficult making the adjustment. It happened awfully fast. I mean, one minute Suzanne's a housewife and the next minute she's gone half the time, often at dinnertime. I guess I thought her activities would be limited to the weekends. I had no idea how busy Paula is Monday through Thursday." Brad was silent for a moment before resuming speaking. "Don't get me wrong. I'm glad Suzanne's doing something that makes her feel fulfilled, but at the same time I guess I'm feeling just a tiny bit left out. For years it was me coming home from work to a hot meal and good company. Now it's just me, the kids, and either leftovers or what the housekeeper made." He shrugged before hastily adding, "But I'm sure I'll get over it."

Micheline suppressed a smile. This was just the opening she'd been looking for. It gave her a perfect opportunity to point out what a dim bulb Suzanne was. "Well, if you're that unhappy, maybe Suzanne should consider getting an office job with set, standard hours."

He shook his head. "That probably wouldn't work. For one thing, she likes to go to all of Bradley's and Lauren's sports events at school. An office job wouldn't give her the freedom to do that. Besides, Suzanne doesn't have the training or experience that you have, Micheline. I'm afraid she'd be severely limited in what she could do. There's nothing about any low-level type of work that would make her feel that she's doing anything with her life. I'm not being critical of her, you understand," he clarified. "That's just the way it is."

"Yes, of course." Micheline hated it when he stuck up for Suzanne, but she supposed she couldn't expect him to say, *She has to do something that's creative because she's short on the smarts.*

She called the auto club and was delighted when they informed her it would be at least sixty to ninety minutes before a truck could get to her. "I was afraid of that," she said in a carefully resigned tone. "Well, since I'm stuck here I'm going to get something to eat, so I hope they don't surprise me by showing up in twenty minutes."

"I'm afraid there's no chance of that happening, ma'am," said the dispatcher on the other end of the phone.

Micheline grinned as she terminated the connection. "It's going to take a while. Again, Brad, you don't have to wait with me."

"It's fine. I'm not in the mood for pizza. Besides, Bradley can devour a whole pizza by himself. Lauren will be lucky to get two slices."

* * *

They walked to the restaurant, were seated in a booth, and spent several minutes perusing the extensive menu. Micheline took a sip of ice water after they placed their order and handed their menus to the server.

"I'm a little confused about something, Brad," she said. "You said Suzanne wasn't qualified to do anything but the most basic office work. But it takes skill to operate an office. She has to pay the bills, handle the money, order the supplies. . . . You look puzzled about something," she remarked at his frown. "Didn't she used to run your office?"

He gave her an incredulous stare. "Wherever did you get *that* idea?"

"From Suzanne," Micheline replied innocently.

"Oh. Well, that was a long time ago. Suzanne hasn't worked since she got pregnant with Bradley—even before that, I think. My current office manager is doing a fine job, and she has no intention of quitting."

Micheline tried to cover her disappointment. She'd hope Brad would expose Suzanne for having told a lie and exaggerating her own importance. Instead, he'd covered for her. Inwardly, Micheline wanted to scream with frustration.

She spent the rest of their time together thoroughly charming Brad and asking him about his work. He seemed surprised that she understood the definition of interventional radiology. Micheline shrugged it off, saying she knew a little about it through her paralegal work, but that wasn't really true. Most of her cases involved orthopedic injuries and medical and surgical malpractice cases. Before beginning her new job, she'd used her time at home during the day to read up about Brad's field so she could speak intelligently about it . . . something she'd bet the ranch Suzanne had never done.

Micheline could tell she'd made an indelible impression upon Brad, just by the look of admiration in his eyes. And she cherished his spoken reaction even more.

"You are an amazing woman, Micheline. And Errol is one lucky man."

Brad insisted on paying the check, and Micheline received a call from the tow truck driver while they waited for the waitress to process his credit card, saying he'd be there in about five minutes.

"Maybe you should try it one more time," Brad suggested as they approached the Sebring. A bright red tow truck was just entering the parking lot on the other side.

"I was just about to say that. I guess great minds really do think alike." Micheline didn't know about great minds, but she did know that she couldn't chance the tow truck driver finding her ignition kill switch in the off position.

She unlocked the door and got behind the wheel. With her left hand carefully out of sight, she reached under the dash and flipped the switch back on. Immediately after, she turned the key in the ignition with her right hand.

The engine hummed to life.

She and Brad stared at each other in astonishment. "Well, what do you know about that?" he said.

Micheline let out an awkward laugh. "Can you believe this?" Leaving the engine running, she quickly got out and ran over to the tow truck, which by now had pulled up behind where her car was parked. "Guess what?" she said happily. "My car just started. So I don't need you after all."

"Micheline, I'm glad you got your car started, but I do think you should get it checked out right away. This might be the start of problems with the alternator, like you said. You definitely don't want to have this problem happen to you again."

"Yes, I'll be sure to do that. Thanks so much for staying with me, Brad."

"I actually had a good time." He smiled at her warmly.

"Since we're both going the same way, I'll stay behind you as you drive home. I want to make sure your engine doesn't conk out on you."

"That's a load off my mind," she said with a dramatic sigh. She reached in the pocket of her purse for her cell phone. "Give me your cell number. You don't have to follow me all the way home. I'll be all right once I turn off the main boulevard, but I'll call you when I'm inside my house. I'll be there even before you get home."

"I guess that'll work." He recited his cell number.

"You're a very nice man, Bradley Betancourt." Micheline moved in to embrace him, and she impulsively planted a warm, moist kiss just under his jaw.

She felt him jerk backward and smiled, her face safely out of his vision. She'd given him an erection, and he'd rushed to move away so she wouldn't feel it.

Brad's hands were damp as he followed Micheline's Chrysler down Southside Boulevard. That friendly good-bye hug she'd given him had transformed from something innocent into something much more than that. If he was a heel, he'd follow her to her door and see her inside, and then let nature run its course.

Too bad he was such a nice guy.

Chapter 22

Flo seasoned the strip steaks on both sides. They were having a quiet Fourth of July, but she'd invited Suzanne and her family to come over. Suzanne hadn't given a definite response, but if they did come she wanted to have plenty of good food. She knew Suzanne had probably heard rumors about the financial problems she and Ernie had, and she wanted to assure her that it was a thing of the past. She'd never lived or worked anywhere where the grapevine was the fastest means of communication. Not only had Kenya figured things out and most likely reported to Suzanne, but Flo had the misfortune to live next door to good friends of Lisa and Darrell Canfield. She doubted Lisa and Suzanne had chats like girlfriends, but Darrell and Brad were pretty good friends. Everyone knew men gossiped just as much as women did. That was all it took for the talk about the student they rented to and their second jobs to get from Villa St. John to the cul-de-sac around the corner.

Flo had deliberately hired Paula Haines to cater Gregory's wedding. She wanted to prove to Suzanne that she and Ernie could afford the same services as they. Unfortunately, she and Ernie were still paying on the bill. At this point she wasn't sure what they'd do for their anniversary in September. They could always go somewhere nearby and tell people they'd gone to their favorite spot on Paradise Island. It wasn't like that weeklong trip to Jamaica Ben and Stacy Prince were about to take, but Flo couldn't chance anyone asking her about a place she'd never been to. If she gave a wrong answer, she'd be exposed.

She'd been shocked when Arlene casually scribbled a check for four hundred dollars and gave it to her. She hadn't thought Arlene had the financial means to write a check of that size on the spot, but it cleared without a hitch. Flo knew she'd have to think twice before giving anyone that sum, not that she'd ever admit that to anyone.

Four-hundred-dollar checks, vacations in Jamaica. Was *everyone* except them rolling in discretionary income?

Finances considered, she was only too happy to tell her coworkers and neighbors that she and her family would be celebrating the Fourth quietly at home. Kim Gillespie, Lisa's good friend who lived next door, offered that Lisa had family visiting, and that she and her husband plus the Princes were headed over there to spend the afternoon.

Flo hadn't been able to resist informing Kim that the Betancourts might be joining them at their low-key celebration. "After all," she'd added loftily, "Suzanne and Brad are part of the family now."

She said nothing to Kim about the *other* part of their family coming, although they, unlike Suzanne, had given a definite acceptance. Arlene told Flo that her younger son, Matthew, was scheduled to work that day at the hospital, covering the medical records department, but both she and her older son, Derrick, would be happy to attend.

When the doorbell rang at a little after three, Flo was thrilled to see the black Cadillac SUV driven by either Brad or Suzanne parked outside. She almost forgot herself and yelled out to Ernie that the Betancourts had come, but then she quickly realized that if Ernie could hear her, so could Suzanne and Brad, and she wisely kept quiet.

The wide grin she wore as she opened the door did a slow

fade. Suzanne stood on the doorstep, and so did her mother, but with them were only Bradley and Lauren.

Flo's eyes darted to the Caddy parked in the street, but it was empty. There was no sign of Brad.

She kept the smile plastered on her face. "Well, hi there! So glad all of you could come." She opened the front door wider. "Please, come in. Ernie's got the grill going, and Gregory and Kenya are outside, too. Go on back."

"I brought you something, Flo," Suzanne said, holding out a brown paper bag as the others headed for the patio.

Flo accepted the bag, her lips forming an automatic response. "Oh, you shouldn't have." She pulled out the long neck of the bottle. "Grey Goose! How nice."

"I remember Ernie saying it's the only vodka he drinks."

Flo felt her face grow warm. Suzanne had been here one of the last times Flo and Ernie entertained before his job loss plunged them into a financial abyss. Ernie had been careful to point out to everyone present that he was serving expensive Grey Goose vodka, "thirty-three dollars for three-quarters of a liter." Suzanne's paraphrasing of Ernie was actually a direct quote; that day he'd informed their guests that he never drank cheaper vodkas. Flo remembered Stacy and Ben Prince exchanging amused glances, and she wished she could disappear into the atmosphere. That had been a prime example of Ernie going overboard in his efforts to impress the neighbors.

Since Arlene and the children had gone outside while Suzanne hung back, Flo decided this would be a good time to ask about Brad, but Suzanne beat her to it.

"I'm so sorry Brad isn't here," Suzanne said. She lowered her voice, although they were alone in the house. "Lisa's brother and his family are here, and so are her parents. They're having a holiday cookout over there, and he felt Paige really shouldn't be the only one of our family to be there. I'm afraid Kenya's marriage to Gregory means our family won't be able to spend the holidays together. You and Ernie will probably have Mom and the boys for Thanksgiving and Christmas."

That hadn't occurred to Flo. Her thoughts went to Gregory and Kenya, outside in the pool. The last time she'd been out there, Gregory had been playfully splashing water on her as she sat in a floating chair on the shallow end. They looked like a happy young couple, and while Flo was proud of Gregory for trying to make the most of it, she also felt disappointment for herself and Ernie. Instead of Gregory's marriage putting them closer to Suzanne and Brad, it had made them social outcasts. First Brad skipped the wedding, and now he'd opted not to stop by on July Fourth. Flo had a sinking feeling he would never make it over to their house. Even if she invited them over to dinner for no special occasion, her gut told her Brad would manage to come up with an excuse to decline.

And she and Ernie would be stuck entertaining Arlene and her sons over the holidays. That certainly made for a depressing scenario.

"As a matter of fact," Suzanne continued, "Bradley and Lauren will be going over to Lisa's later. They usually sit out back and watch the fireworks over the river with Lisa's twins and her brother's kids."

"What about you?" Flo had a hard time believing that Suzanne and Brad would be spending the biggest holiday of the summer separately.

"Oh, I'll probably just pop in for a minute just to say hello, after I take Mom home. I'm not too keen about seeing Lisa's family, but they've been very nice to my kids, and Brad still has a relationship with them. . . . You know how it is."

"I understand," Flo replied, nodding. "I'm sorry Brad couldn't make it, but I'm glad you're here." Her heart felt heavy with disappointment as she realized this was how it would be. If Brad kept his distance from them—and it was obvious to her that he would—there would be no invitation forthcoming to go out on the *Suzie Q,* much less get invited up to the Betancourts' vacation house in Maine. Ernie would likely take the news hard, but they both had to accept it.

Their hopes to draw Suzanne and Brad into their extended family had just gone bust.

Brad remained seated at the Canfields' patio table. Most of the others had moved to the outer edge of the screened-in patio for a better view of the fireworks. Their oohs and aahs drifted across the pool to where Brad sat with Darrell and Lisa.

The door to the house opened, and Paige emerged. "You guys can't see from here, can you?"

"The view is better from out there, but I'm too lazy to get up right now," Darrell said, sipping from his highball glass.

"Well, I'm going over there so I can see."

"Paige, wait a minute," Brad said quickly. "I want to say something to you." At Darrell's questioning glance he held out a hand. "Don't get up, man." Brad glanced at Lisa. "Your mother and I are very proud of the way you handled this whole thing with Gregory. We just wanted you to know that."

"Yes, Paige, we think you're coping beautifully," Lisa added. "Have you met any new young men?"

"No, Mom. Thank you for the compliment, but it's not that big a deal."

"Why's that?" Brad asked.

"Because it'll be over in just a few months, and then Gregory and I will get back together and see if we're truly meant to be or not."

Lisa gasped. Darrell's eyebrows shot up. And Brad was speechless.

"I don't want to miss the fireworks," Paige said. She hurried to join the rest of the family on the other side of the pool.

They all watched her walk away. "My God, was I ever that stupid when I was her age?" Lisa asked softly after Paige had moved out of hearing distance.

"No, because when you were her age you were going with me," Brad said with a smile.

"I'm worried," Lisa said, reaching out for Darrell's hand. "What are we going to do, Brad? I don't want Paige putting her life on hold to wait for Gregory."

"Try not to worry too much, Lisa," Darrell answered. "Kids that age change their minds every other week."

"Darrell's right," Brad said. "I'm sure her enthusiasm will wane as the months pass. She'll eventually meet some unencumbered young man, and that'll be it." He shook his head. "I'll tell you this. I truly do feel sorry for Gregory. He's about to have an albatross around his neck for the next twenty years."

Chapter 23

Suzanne knew something was up when her mother said, "Guess what?" before she even had a chance to sit down at the dining-area table.

"What, Mom?"

"Kenya's not working anymore. Her doctor said that since her job involves standing all day, it's too much."

"I'm surprised he didn't just tell her to cut down to part-time."

"Well, why should she do that?" Arlene asked indignantly. "Gregory's got a good job. Kenya doesn't know how much they pay him, but I'm sure he can afford to keep her at home. It's not as though they even have their own place. Kenya did know that he gives his parents just fifty dollars a week."

"That's not much for room and board for two people."

"It's twice as much as Derrick gives me," Arlene countered.

Suzanne stopped herself from making a weary sigh. "Mom, we've been all through that. I don't want to talk about it anymore."

"What's wrong with you? You get up on the wrong side of the bed or something?"

"I'm sorry," Suzanne apologized. "It's just that Brad seems so distracted lately. Ever since he spent the Fourth over at Lisa's."

Arlene carried two steaming mugs to the table, set them

down, and returned to the adjacent kitchen. When she came back she had a bottle of Smirnoff in her hand. "Maybe you should have stayed longer when you went over there," she said as she sat down and poured a bit of vodka into her mug.

"There really didn't seem to be any reason for me to do that at the time, but I agree that something must have happened after I left. I was tired," she said, knowing she sounded unnecessarily defensive. "I'd already sat at Flo's for about three hours, having Ernie stuff me with food and offer a running commentary. 'This is strip steak . . . These are portabello mushrooms . . . This bread came from the so-and-so bakery,'" she mimicked. "He's . . . insufferable," she said, using a word she'd learned from the Word of the Day Web site on the Internet.

"At least it was a great meal. He and Flo are trying to impress you, Suzanne. Do you really think they'd be serving New York strip if it was just me and the boys? It would be hamburger, honey. So I say enjoy it while it lasts. Because as soon as they figure out that Brad doesn't want to be bothered with them, the gravy train is going to dry up."

"And not a moment too soon. I don't think I could deal with another day like that one. I thought Ernie might have toned down the pushiness and bragging, but if anything, he's gotten worse. Did you hear the way he tried to pin me down to a date for Brad and me to join them for dinner?"

"I don't envy you. He's the type who doesn't want to take no for an answer. You might have to just come out and tell him how Brad feels."

"No, I think Flo will figure it out and tell him to lay off," Suzanne replied after a moment's thought.

"I'm just glad that things are working out well for Kenya," Arlene said, taking a sip of her coffee. "I want Kenya to be just like you, Suzanne." She smiled dreamily. "It feels so nice to know that *both* my girls have made it, found husbands who take care of them. It didn't happen for me, but I'm so happy your lives are easier than mine has been."

"So what's Kenya going to do all day?" Suzanne asked dubiously.

"Oh, the usual, I would imagine. Some housework. Maybe make dinner for the family."

Suzanne could hide her doubts no longer. "Are you kidding, Mom? This is *Kenya* we're talking about. The Kenya who throws her clothes on the floor and never wants to pick them up. The Kenya who will leave your kitchen in shambles just because she tried to make biscuits. She might be able to help Flo with the cooking, because she'll be supervised and won't be able to tear up the kitchen. But do it herself? Puhleeze."

"I've talked to her about that," Arlene said. "I've told her that if she expects to hold on to Gregory, she'd better learn how to keep house."

"I'm sorry, Mom, but I just don't see that happening. Flo and Ernie are fully expecting the kids' marriage to be dissolved after the baby's born, and I'm sure Gregory plans on the same thing."

"And it's Kenya's job to make him change his mind." Arlene snorted. "What's he in such a tearing hurry for, anyway? Does he really think Paige is going to wait for him?"

"I doubt she will."

"What does Brad say?"

Suzanne swallowed past the lump that suddenly formed in her throat. "Brad doesn't say much of anything. He seems to want to keep me out of that part of his life . . . so I don't ask him about it anymore." Whenever she asked how Paige was doing, Brad replied with a quick "fine" and didn't offer any additional information. The breach between them might have healed on the surface, but apparently Brad had decided not to discuss anything regarding Paige with her.

"Oh," Arlene said lightly. "I wouldn't worry too much about that."

"*I* think it's worth worrying about, Mom," Suzanne snapped. "Look at my position. Brad is my husband, and he's shutting me out of a big portion of his life. That's definitely *not* a good thing."

"I'm sure he'll get over it."

Her mother's breezy attitude irritated Suzanne. "You know, Mom, sometimes you need to look at the whole picture, not just a corner of it. I'm very glad things are working out for Kenya, but it's not going to mean anything to me if *my* marriage ends up falling apart."

Brad took a moment to recline in his high-backed leather chair. It had been a particularly grueling week, and today was the worst, with two very difficult cases that presented unique challenges due to multiple medical problems of the patients involved that made treatment options perilous, even life-threatening. He'd been working on these since Monday. He hated trying to explain to families that they were stuck between a medical rock and a hard place, hated the panic and confusion in their eyes as he tried to get them to understand that treating one condition would only exacerbate another. Many people felt that modern medicine could treat any condition, and it was up to him to tell them it wasn't true, and that their loved one would probably die.

He sat there for another half hour, trying to make sure he hadn't overlooked something, a viable alternate to treatment for his two patients. Once he determined that every avenue had been covered, he sat up, reassembled the charts, and left for home.

He felt an eagerness to get there and have dinner with his family. Suzanne had worked with Paula last night to cater a special preview screening the cable company held at a downtown theater. Teresita had made the chicken enchiladas he and the kids loved, but the house felt strangely empty without Suzanne there. It occurred to Brad that he'd become spoiled over the years. Suzanne had always done her outside activities while he was at work, and was there waiting when he got home.

No car sat parked in the brick-paved driveway when he pulled in. Maybe Suzanne had parked in the garage, where the car would be out of the sun.

"Hey!" he called as he walked inside. "Where's everybody?"

"Hi, Daddy!" Lauren said, coming from the kitchen. "I've got the table all set. I just need a few minutes to get the food on the table. Well, maybe a little longer than that. It takes the biscuits almost twenty minutes."

"Are you helping Mommy out?" How cute, Brad thought.

"Mommy's not here."

"She isn't? Where is she?"

"She went to work with Miss Paula."

"She . . ." He couldn't believe it. She'd said nothing to him about working tonight . . . or had she? He'd been so preoccupied with his patients. . . .

He reached for his cell phone and dialed Suzanne's. "It's me," he said when she answered. "What's going on? Lauren just told me you're at work again tonight."

"I told you about that," she said. "Don't you remember? There were two events this week. The screening by Comcast last night, and the fund-raiser at the museum tonight. That guy from A&E is speaking, and they're charging a hundred bucks a ticket."

"Oh. Wait a minute." Brad's memory bank stirred. "It's coming back to me now. You did mention that."

"I cooked a roast this morning, and Lauren is cooking the vegetables and mashed potatoes and heating up the gravy. She's also making the biscuits, so you'll have a good dinner," Suzanne said tentatively.

"Sounds fine. But I miss you, Suzie Q. I missed you yesterday."

"When I get home you can show me just how much, huh?"

"Yeah. I'll see you later."

" 'Bye, baby."

Brad sighed as he disconnected the call. He reminded himself that it had been his idea for Suzanne to learn the catering business from the ground up. He just thought it would involve mostly weekend work. But he couldn't go back on his word now, and especially not since Suzanne enjoyed it so much. He'd have to work off his frustration another way.

"Lauren," he said, "take your time. I'm going to take a quick swim."

Chapter 24

"Oh, it's beautiful!" Lisa exclaimed as Paige held up the colorful chiffon halter dress.

"What a steal it was, Mom. Marked down to twenty-four ninety-nine."

"It's just lovely, and perfect for your friend's wedding. Tell me, um . . . are you bringing a date?"

"No. Devon's bringing Jason, of course, but I don't have a problem going alone. I'll know most of the people there, since I visited Devon so often at Florida State."

Lisa said a prayer that Paige would meet a nice young man at the wedding and forget about Gregory Hickman. Both Brad and Darrell said she'd get over Gregory after Paige's matter-of-fact observation on July Fourth that she and Gregory were just temporarily separated, but Lisa knew her daughter better than anyone, and she wasn't so sure. Paige's remarks had made her uneasy, and her apprehension still existed. She took a deep breath as her mind formulated her next words to Paige. She didn't want to be pushy, but she had to know the answer to her question. "Paige . . . I know you plan to reconcile with Gregory after his divorce. You haven't been seeing him now, while he's married, have you?"

She shook her head vigorously. "No. I'm not going to do that, Mom. He's married, and he's about to be a father. I told him we won't have any contact with each other at all until he's a single man."

The breath Lisa had been holding came out loud enough for Paige to hear, but she didn't care. At least she knew that Paige's brain hadn't gone completely haywire.

Now, if she could just meet someone who made her forget about Gregory Hickman, everything would be fine.

Flo came home to a quiet house Sunday afternoon. She went into her bedroom, where Ernie lay stretched out on the oversized chair, his feet on the matching ottoman, fast asleep in his typical Sunday afternoon nap. Inside the large walk-in closet she carefully hung up her dress and returned her hat to its hatbox, then put on shorts and a knit tank top. Flo was heavier than she wanted to be, but she had great toned arms— she'd had hers long before everyone started raving about Michelle Obama's—and liked to show them off whenever possible. Then she went to fix something to eat.

She noticed a cell phone lying on the coffee table of the living room console table by the door. She picked it up. The red phone belonged to neither Ernie nor Gregory. It had to be Kenya's. Chances were she'd forgotten where she left it.

Flo carried the phone down the hall on the far end of the house, lined with three bedrooms and a bath. The door to Gregory and Kenya's bathroom was closed. She knocked firmly, and when there was no response she opened the door, intending to leave the phone on the dresser.

She gasped at the sight of the unkempt bedroom. The full-sized bed sat unmade, the sheets rumpled and dirty looking, as if they hadn't been changed in weeks. A thick layer of dust made the maple color of the double-wide dresser look gray in the bright afternoon sunlight and, she felt certain, the matching highboy as well. The top of the dresser was littered with dirty drinking glasses and empty bags of potato chips. The carpet practically screamed out for a vacuuming, with pieces of orange potato chips scattered over it, and small pieces of

trash that hadn't quite made it into the trash basket, as if someone had thrown them and missed, lay on the floor near it.

She didn't understand. Kenya no longer worked, and she
rarely worked weekends anyway; she had seniority at the supermarket. Why hadn't she cleaned this bedroom? And what did
Gregory have to say about it? He'd always been so neat.

Flo took one last look at the messy bedroom and retreated.
Gregory's car hadn't been in the driveway when she returned.
At first she'd been glad to see that the newlyweds were out
together, but now she vowed to sit down with both of them.
This business of keeping their bedroom looking like a pigsty
was going to stop right now.

The drama queen inside Flo tried to tell her she'd lost her
appetite after looking at that bedroom, but the growling of
her stomach told her otherwise. She put the picture of the mess
out of her mind and headed for the kitchen.

Flo thought she heard strains of music coming from the
pool area out back, but when she reached the kitchen, for a
few moments she could do nothing but stand there and gape.

Apparently Kenya had cooked breakfast. Gops of dried
pancake batter splattered the granite countertops in the area
around the unwashed electric griddle. A bottle of syrup sat
on the center island, as did a box of pancake mix. Kenya had
thought to fill the mixing bowl with water to prevent the batter
from becoming hard, but the plates had been stacked in the
sink without being rinsed and looked like a sticky mess. That
explained why Ernie slept so soundly upstairs; heavy meals
like pancakes always put him to sleep. She simply stood, her
hands on her hips as she surveyed the mess. No effort had
been made to restore the kitchen to order. Did Kenya actually
think *she* was going to clean this up?

Once Flo recovered from the shock, she became aware of
the music coming from outside. She looked out through the
glass of the door at the edge of the breakfast nook. Kenya,
who couldn't swim, sat in a floating pool chair near the shallow end of the pool, wearing sunglasses, a sun visor, and a

bikini that allowed her belly to spill over. She held a book up to her face as she floated. Flo couldn't make out the title, but it had a picture of a woman wrapped in a floor-length mink draped about her in a way that it was obvious she was naked underneath it.

Great. My kitchen looks like a cyclone hit it, and my daughter-in-law is reading about some gold-digging ho.

She took a deep breath as she pondered her next move. So Kenya *wasn't* out with Gregory. Flo didn't know if she should feel relieved or anxious. She could tell that Gregory was trying awfully hard, but her instinct told her he was miserable being married to Kenya and that his heart still ached for Paige. Kenya's slovenliness only made the situation worse.

Flo wished she knew how Paige felt about Gregory. Would she have an aversion to seeing a married man, or was Gregory out on a rendezvous with Paige right now?

She turned the doorknob and stepped outside. Kenya looked up as she approached, but didn't lower her book. "Hello, Miss Flo. How was church?"

"Uplifting, as usual. How are you feeling today, Kenya?"

"Pretty good, actually. I made breakfast for Gregory and Mr. Ernie. Pancakes," she said proudly. "Mr. Ernie said they were delicious."

"That's fine, Kenya, but you left a bit of a mess in the kitchen. Actually, more than a bit of mess."

"Oh! Well, I'm not used to cleaning up."

"Really? I wasn't aware your mother employed a housekeeper." Even as she covered her distress with sarcasm, Flo had a memory of how Arlene so easily wrote that four-hundred-dollar check before the wedding, and she worried it might be true. Arlene's two sons who lived with her might be giving her enough money that she could afford a housekeeper.

"She doesn't," Kenya replied. "It's just that . . . when it was just me there wasn't such a big mess. There's a lot more to do now that I'm married."

"Yes, but you're not working now. That frees up a lot of time, so there really shouldn't be a problem, should there?"

"It'll get cleaned up, Miss Flo," Kenya said pleasantly.

"When?"

"Gregory said he would do it as soon as he got back from working out."

Flo felt her anger rising like the morning sun. Didn't Gregory do enough without Kenya trying to turn him into Mr. Maid?

"I'm afraid there's more to it than just the kitchen. Kenya, you left your cell phone in the living room. I put it in your bedroom, and I was shocked by the mess I saw in there."

"Yes, well, I haven't been feeling too good lately," Kenya said defensively. "That's why the doctor put me on leave."

"You look like the picture of health to me. I've been pregnant, too, Kenya. Not only did I work right up to the time my labor started, but I kept an immaculate household."

"Every woman is different, I suppose. My back's really been killing me. I was going to ask you—well, my mother doesn't have a housekeeper, but Suzanne does. Do you think you could get her to work for us one day a week? Then there wouldn't be a problem."

A sound she didn't recognize escaped from Flo's throat. Kenya was actually suggesting she hire a *maid?* What was wrong with this child?

"Kenya, Ernie and I can certainly afford a housekeeper," she began, not wanting her daughter-in-law to jump to the wrong conclusion and report back to Suzanne or Arlene, "but I've never needed one. I happen to enjoy keeping my home clean. I'm afraid you'll have to clean not only the kitchen, but your bedroom as well. It's an invitation for ghetto bugs, and I don't mind telling you I've never needed the services of an exterminator, and if all those crumbs and clutter keep growing it's going to attract bugs." She blew out a breath. "Now, I'm going to try to overlook the mess in my kitchen and make a sandwich, and then I'm going to lie down. I do want to make it clear that I'm expecting to see the kitchen restored to order by the time I come back." She returned to the house, not waiting for her daughter-in-law to respond.

She half expected for steam to be escaping from her ears. What was it that Kenya had said? *Gregory said he would do it as soon as he got back from working out.*

So help her, if her son got busy cleaning the kitchen while Kenya sat reading a book while floating in the pool, she'd slap some sense into him . . . and then she'd drag that pool chair Kenya sat in to the deep end and flip it over.

Flo forced herself not to focus on the spots of dried batter on the counter as she made a chicken sandwich, then took it to her bedroom to eat. When she finished she lay down next to Ernie and drifted off to sleep.

It was three o'clock when she opened her eyes. Ernie lay on his back watching television, his arm around her. "Hey, sleepyhead," he said.

Her mouth dropped open when she read the time on the digital bedside clock. Still, instead of sitting up, she laid her head back against the pillow. "I really wiped out, didn't I? It's nearly time to start dinner." Remembering, she frowned. "I just hope I can get in there to cook."

"Why wouldn't you be?"

"The mess Kenya made at breakfast. Ernie, I'm worried about Gregory."

"What about him?"

"I don't think he's happy. Have you noticed how much time he spends away from home?"

"Why do you say that?"

"Because of Kenya. She's lazy, Ernie. Now that she's gotten her doctor to say she shouldn't be on her feet for eight hours a day, she does nothing but lie around and make messes that she doesn't clean up. It's not just the mess she left in the kitchen. You should see their bedroom. I don't know how Gregory can stand it. He's always been so meticulous. Friday morning I saw him ironing a shirt to wear to work. When I asked where Kenya was, he said she was still in bed. Apparently he'd reminded her that he had no more shirts and she promised to iron, but didn't, and she chose to stay in bed rather than get up and do it. She's expecting him to provide her with an easy life, Ernie."

"Well, he married her," he replied matter-of-factly.

"Ernie, that's not fair. We pressured him to marry her." She sighed. "I'm beginning to think we made a terrible mistake." *It certainly was of no benefit to us,* she added silently, thinking of how they hadn't even seen Brad Betancourt since before Gregory married Kenya, much less launched a friendship. "All she does is lie around all day. She knows I'm at work and that I come home and cook for four adults every night. But does she volunteer to lift a finger to help me? And Gregory is so unhappy."

"Come on, Flo. It's not going to go on forever. He'll divorce her as soon as the baby is born. In the meantime, it's a classic case of lying down with dogs and waking up with fleas."

"I've never had fleas in my home, Ernie, and I'd don't intend to start having them now."

"Oh, there you are," Kenya said. She put her book down and began paddling her hands, moving the float toward the pool's edge.

"Wait a minute. Don't get out yet," Gregory said. He held up a camera.

Kenya immediately broke out into a smile and crossed her ankles.

"Do something," he suggested.

"Ooh, is that a video camera?"

"It sure is. I want to have it ready for when the baby comes. I figured if I start using it now, I'll be a pro with it by then."

Kenya hand-paddled toward the edge and climbed out. "I need to start cleaning up the kitchen, and our room, too.

Your mother is a little upset with me. I told her I wasn't feeling good, but I'm better now."

"Good," he said. He was glad she'd waited for him to come home before cleaning up. It had taken him a little time to set the date and time on the video camera.

And he certainly didn't want to miss the opportunity to film how she kept their bedroom, and how she left the kitchen, and how she sat in the pool reading her book instead of cleaning up.

It could only help him when it came time for the divorce . . . just in case she had other plans.

Chapter 25

Brad felt a stabbing feeling in his chest as he entered his franchise. Not the kind that meant he was about to have a heart attack, more from heartburn of the emotional sort. Even though he had his suspicions from the beginning, it still stung that his brother-in-law could have done this to him, after everything he'd done to help him. But photographs didn't lie, and he had the proof in an envelope tucked under his arm.

Derrick looked surprised to see him, as Brad had known he would be. "Hey! What brings you over this way? Did you just land at the airport or something?"

"No," he replied, not offering an explanation. "Can I have a minute?"

"Sure."

If Derrick sensed what was about to happen, he was certainly being cool about it. He smiled at the sandwich artist on duty, who had been watching him converse with his brother-in-law. "Excuse us a minute, Penny. Just holler if it gets busy." To Brad he cocked his head toward the back room, then led the way through the door.

Brad wasted no time. The moment the door was closed he turned to his brother-in-law, scowling. "I'm on to you, Derrick. Why'd you do it?"

Derrick responded precisely the way Brad figured he would. "Do what? I don't know what you mean."

"Come on, Derrick. Cut the B-movie dialogue. You and I both know you've been ripping me off, selling the store supply of meat and cheeses to someone with a lunch wagon and pocketing the profits. Did you really think I wouldn't notice?"

"I swear to God, Brad, I don't know what you're talking—" Derrick broke off when Brad threw the large envelope on the table. "What's this?" he asked apprehensively.

"Go ahead, open it," Brad ordered.

In movements worthy of special effects slow-motion, Derrick reached out, undid the clasp, and poured the contents of the envelope onto the table. Brad watched his movements, and in the midst of this most unpleasant situation, he had to admire the photography skills of the detective he'd hired, capturing Derrick's transactions from a distance of at least two hundred feet.

Amazingly, Derrick retains his claims of innocence. "I still don't know what this is all about."

"Cut the horseshit, Derrick. You know that you've been selling *my* meat, *my* cheese, and *my* bread to your partner in crime. You must think I'm a real chump." Brad got angry just thinking about the situation, but then he managed to smile. "And that was probably your *biggest* mistake. I want you to get your stuff, turn in your keys, and get out right now."

Derrick stared at him, mouth agape. "You're firing me?"

"Damn right. You'll never get another chance to steal from me again." Brad held out his palm, accepted Derrick's keys to the restaurant, and then returned to the dining area and watched as his brother-in-law stormed out.

After that Brad spent a few minutes talking with a bewildered Penny, letting her know that Derrick was through because of wrongdoing. "I want you to just carry on as usual," he said. "And don't worry that what happened to Derrick can happen to you. As long as you do what you're supposed to and don't do what you're *not* supposed to, you'll be fine." He glanced at his watch. "What time does the closer come in?"

"Four o'clock."

Brad's watch showed three forty-five. "He'll probably be here in a few minutes. Tell you what. I'll stick around until he comes in so you won't be alone." Penny looked like a sweet girl, just a year out of high school. Brad knew he wouldn't be comfortable with the idea of Paige or Lauren holding down a consumer business alone, even in the afternoon. He presumed Penny's parents felt the same. He should probably speak with the young man who closed the restaurant anyway, let him know that Derrick was history and that he'd already hired a replacement, who would be starting work tomorrow.

After that he'd go to the club for some golf. He knew it wouldn't take long for Derrick to report his job loss to Arlene, who undoubtedly would notify Suzanne right away.

He glanced at his watch once more, although of course there had been no change in the time. He was simply trying to calculate how long it would be before Suzanne called him to ask what was going on.

He settled on five P.M., an hour and fifteen minutes from now. After all, Derrick had to have time to make up a reason for his firing, since he certainly wouldn't tell his mother the truth.

As was her daily habit, Suzanne relaxed while her daily soap opera, *Facades,* played on TV. She loved to talk back to the characters when they acted foolishly, which was pretty often. "Don't fall for that," she pleaded with one of the main characters, her favorite, whose sister was dead jealous of her, to the point of being downright evil. "It's going to blow up in your face. Can't you see that?" To the character who was taking advantage of her favorite she said, "Now, you know you shouldn't try to be so slick."

When the hour-long show went off with its typical cliff-hanger, Suzanne sat for a few moments as she took it all in and tried to figure where the plot was headed. Then she got up and went into the adjoining kitchen. It was time to start dinner.

She wiped the counter down where Bradley had spilled a little milk while fixing his after-school snack, then took out a thawed package of boneless chicken breasts. She had a pan of olive oil heating up and a bowl of bread crumbs waiting and was beating the eggs for her chicken parmigiana when the phone rang. She checked the caller ID when Bradley didn't answer and saw her mother's name and cell number. When she picked it up, she had to wait several minutes for her mother to stop ranting on the other end.

"I don't get it, Mom," Suzanne said into the receiver. "Why would Brad fire Derrick?"

"Derrick said Brad is unjustly blaming him because profits at the shop are down," Arlene replied, her voice ringing with indignation. "Now, Suzanne, you know that's unfair. People everywhere are cutting back. They're buying cold cuts from Winn-Dixie or Publix instead of going out to eat. So why is that Derrick's fault?" She sniffled, then paused to blow her nose. "I'm glad I go home soon. I'm just too upset to work."

"Well, I don't know, Mom. Brad is not an unreasonable person. And you're describing something totally unreasonable."

"Has he not said anything to you? Did you not know he planned to fire Derrick?"

"He didn't say a word, Mom. That makes me wonder if something came up at the last minute."

"Either that, or he's not confiding in you anymore."

A pain stabbed at Suzanne's gut. She was still very much aware that Brad kept her out of anything having to do with Paige. Paige didn't even come over anymore; Brad and Lauren were always going next door to Lisa's to see *her*. Already Suzanne dreaded the holiday season, which Brad had made clear would be spent with the Canfields before it would be spent with her mother, brothers, and the Hickmans.

That was a prime example of the shift in their relationship.

Brad used to include her in all decision-making, or at least he would discuss with her first what he wanted to do and why before doing it. Well, at least most of the time. When he wanted to buy this house, it hadn't exactly been presented to her as an option. Fortunately, she'd taken one look at the spectacular house and fallen in love with it. Still, in hindsight, Suzanne recalled that back then her relationship with Brad had also been strained. The ironic part was that even then, the source of his aggravation had been her family. Nothing had changed in five years.

"Suzanne?" her mother prompted.

"Brad's not home yet," she said. Her mother's silence spoke volumes. "He always gets home a little late on Wednesdays," she quickly added. "He's finished with his patients by about three, and then he stops at the club to play nine holes. While he's there he has something to eat and a drink or two." She wiped her hands on a dish towel. "Mom, I need a little time to take this all in. It's so unexpected."

Arlene grunted. "As far as I'm concerned, there's nothing to think about. You've got to get Brad to change his mind and take Derrick back."

"Mom, this whole thing sounds fishy to me. Brad wouldn't let Derrick go because people aren't eating out as much. As long as the restaurant is still open, he'll need someone to be in charge."

"Maybe Brad was just looking for an excuse to let him go. But Derrick needs this job, Suzanne. He's got car payments, child support payments . . ."

". . . rent money," Suzanne couldn't resist adding.

"I know he doesn't give me a whole lot, but he doesn't make a whole lot, either," Arlene said haughtily. "I've already lost Kenya. Matthew will be finished with school in December, and then he's sure to move out. All I'll have is Derrick."

Suzanne resisted the temptation to point out that by that time Kenya would probably be back at her mother's as a divorced woman with a baby. Her mother was living in a dream world if she thought that Kenya was gone for good. She'd spoken to Flo a few times, and when she asked how it felt to have the newlyweds living there with her and Ernie, Flo's guarded remark that Kenya had a lot to learn about keeping house told Suzanne that her sister, warnings from their mother aside, had fallen into her old sloppy ways. But Suzanne chose not to share her conversation with Flo with her mother, who would no doubt pull Kenya aside and scream at her to get her act together. She'd promised Brad she would stay out of Kenya and Gregory's marriage, and she meant to keep her word.

"I don't know if I like this about Brad spending Wednesdays at the club," Arlene continued. "Maybe you'd better put down that spatula and get down there and see for yourself what's going on. I'll bet that Micheline is with him, whispering sweet nothings in his ear."

Suzanne's jaws tightened at the insinuation. "For your information, Mom," she replied frostily, "I'm not baking. I'm making dinner for Brad and the kids."

"All right, but does that change the fact that that girl will be all over your husband every chance she gets?"

Suzanne couldn't argue with that.

Brad did head straight for the club after speaking with his night manager at the restaurant. He didn't feel like playing golf, but the thought of a drink after a difficult day appealed to him.

Micheline wasn't at the club, but Errol was. Brad saw Errol approaching, courtesy of the mirror on the wall. He spun his stool around and hopped off. "I'm glad to see you, man," he said as he greeted his friend with a bear hug. "I haven't seen you around a whole lot lately."

"Well, whatever you do, don't mention that to Michie."

Brad looked at him curiously. "You said something the last time I saw you that sounded a little bit like there was trouble in paradise. Want to talk about it?"

Errol didn't answer right away, and Brad could see the pain in his face. "She rooked me, man. That whole perfect wife thing . . . It was all a sham. She made a chump out of me."

"I'm sorry to hear that. You two seemed so well suited for each other."

"We had no problems in the bedroom, if that's what you mean."

Brad couldn't ignore the sense of longing that surged through him. As pained as Errol looked when he spoke about Micheline, he nonetheless admitted that she was great in bed. Brad immediately chided himself for harboring such lusty feelings toward his friend's wife.

Errol continued speaking, unaware of the turmoil he'd set off within Brad with his innocent statement. "I'd prefer not to share the details of what happened, so I'll just tell you, just between us, Brad, that I found out my wife has done something absolutely unforgivable. I haven't let on that I know, and I won't until it's convenient for me. I need to shift some things around, get prepared. But the marriage is over."

Brad's mouth dropped open. This had been the last thing he expected to come out of Errol's mouth. He and Micheline always looked so happy when they were together. Whatever the problem that had intruded on the Trent marriage, he'd fully expected they would work it out. Of course, Errol could always change his mind, but he appeared pretty firm.

"I don't want to let on that I know what she's doing," Errol continued. "When I do make my move, I don't want her to see it coming."

Brad considered that Micheline might not be as oblivious to the situation as Errol seemed to think. Why else would she be coming on to him, even to the point of verbally attacking Suzanne? No woman happy and satisfied in her marriage would behave that way.

That crack she made yesterday about Suzanne being little more than a puppet who followed instructions with no understanding of what she was doing or why still ticked him off. If

Micheline thought that was the way to get him over to her side of the street, she was mistaken. He couldn't deny his attraction to her, but that's all it was, raw magnetism and sexual curiosity. No way would he give up Suzanne for her. As much as Suzanne got on his nerves from time to time, he never worried about her flirting with other men. Micheline's enticing behavior only proved that she couldn't be trusted, even without Errol's mysterious discovery of treachery on her part.

Brad did know he couldn't take much more of Suzanne's devotion to her mother and siblings. He'd been dealing with this shit for sixteen years, and he was tired. Maybe he wouldn't give her up for Micheline, but there were plenty of other women out there who knew how to be loyal to their husbands. What their future held would largely depend on how Suzanne reacted to the news of her brother's firing.

"I don't know what to say, Errol," he said. "I'm awfully sorry to hear that. But I'm glad to hear you're taking your time about it. You can always change your mind."

The younger man shook his head. "No fucking way."

Brad almost guiltily wondered if Micheline's offense had to do with another man. Errol's illicit relationship seemed to have begun after he learned of something Micheline had done.

He shrugged. "Well, just be careful. Try not to give her anything to use against you."

"I will. Thanks for listening, Brad."

Brad wanted to say something like *That's what friends are for,* but the words stuck in his throat. He couldn't tell Errol that.

Because his desire to know firsthand what Micheline was like in bed had just gotten a lot stronger now that he knew Errol was through with her.

Chapter 26

It surprised Brad that he hadn't heard from Suzanne at all since he threw Derrick out of the restaurant. He'd been so certain she would have called to ask for details about what happened.

He considered that Derrick might not have told Arlene yet. Maybe he was still trying to construct a convincing-sounding lie to explain why he lost his job.

Suzanne was in the kitchen when he got home, spraying down the smooth surface of the six-burner cooktop. "Hi, how was dinner?" he said.

"The most tender chicken you've ever had," she said immodestly. "I already packed some in a container for you to take for lunch tomorrow."

"Great."

"You're home early."

"I didn't play today."

"Oh?"

"It was a rather upsetting afternoon. Did your mother or Derrick call you?"

Suzanne moved from the cooktop to the surrounding granite counter. "Actually, Mom did call. She was very upset. She said you fired Derrick this afternoon?"

So she had known. Brad gave her points for not calling him, just as upset as her mother must have been, to pelt him with questions. It was nice that she'd let him go about his Wednesday routine and waited until he got home to discuss the matter. Maybe he'd been wrong to presume that she'd side with her family against him.

"I did. He's been stealing from me, taking the restaurant's stock of cold cuts and selling it to some dude with a lunch wagon and pocketing the profits."

Her shock was genuine. "He's been doing *what?*"

"It's been going on for months. Chris and I have been working to try to figure out why net profits were down if sales were up. She told me about something suspicious she'd seen."

For a moment she simply stared at him. "And you fired my brother based on *that?*"

There was no mistaking the hostility in her tone. He knew where her mind was going, and he looked at her through narrowed eyes. "No, but I had a feeling she was on to something, so I hired a PI to observe. I fired Derrick because of the photographs the PI took showing him accepting money and handing over meats and cheeses."

"Oh," Suzanne said in a small voice, obviously contrite. "Well, I can't imagine what got into him, to do something like that."

"That's not the reason he gave your mother, is it?"

"No," she admitted. "He said profits were down and that you blamed him."

Brad chuckled. "Why am I not surprised?"

Suzanne rinsed the dishcloth she'd been using to wipe down the countertops, wrung it out, and hung it over the divide of the twin stainless-steel sink. "Brad, Mom's so upset, and I'm sure Derrick is sorry. Would you consider giving him another chance?"

Brad leaned forward, pressed his palms into the counter, and bowed his head. He sighed heavily. "You don't mean that. You *can't* mean that."

"Brad, I'm sure Derrick's learned his lesson. And it would make Mom so happy if you'd rehire Derrick."

He was quiet for a moment, wanting to express himself clearly, with no room for misinterpretation. "Suzanne, I want you to listen very carefully," he finally said in a quiet voice. "The only thing your brother is sorry about is that I caught him. Who knows how long this could have gone on if I didn't stay on top of my finances? He's lucky I didn't prosecute him. I could, you know. But I won't. I won't even ask him for my money back. I just want him out. So all things considered, I think he got off pretty damn cheaply.

"And as for your mother being happy, she's about to be a lot more unhappy, because not only will your brother not work for me again, but I don't want him in this house. He's a thief, Suzanne. I don't invite thieves to my home. That's an invitation for things to come up missing."

"Oh, Brad, surely you don't think Derrick would steal from us."

"What the hell do you call what he's been doing for the last two months?" he demanded, his calm exterior replaced by undisguised anger.

"He doesn't think of that as being *us,* he thinks of it as being a restaurant. A thing, not a person. It's the same concept as people who travel on business padding their expense accounts."

A prime example of biting the hand that feeds you, Brad thought. How could Suzanne stand there and defend her brother under these circumstances?

He easily answered his own question. She was operating under Arlene's thumb. Damn it, what did Suzanne's family have to do to them before she would see the light? "I'm not interested in knowing how the mind of a thief works, Suzanne," he said dismissively. "The bottom line, I don't want Derrick in my house, and I don't want him near Bradley and Lauren. He's a lazy son-of-a-gun who'll do anything to avoid an honest day's work."

"I'm sure he's learned his lesson, Brad."

"And *I'm* sure he'd rip us off again the first chance he gets.

That's why I'm not giving him that chance." He straightened his posture, his palms resting against the cool granite, his fingers spread. "So you can tell your mother to forget it."

He enjoyed her surprise as her mouth dropped open. "What makes you think my mother has anything to do with my asking you to give Derrick another chance?"

"Because your mother is always asking you to help out your sister and brothers. And because you always do what she asks. So why should this time be any different?"

Suzanne held his gaze but said nothing.

"Well, let me give you something to think about, Suzanne. I want a wife whose first loyalty is to me and our family. I'm not interested in having a wife who's dominated by her mother." With that he walked away.

He had a big decision to make.

Chapter 27

Norell nervously twirled a lock of hair around her finger as she waited. The law offices looked so luxurious, all mahogany and leather. If she closed her eyes she could probably smell the money.

She'd better make sure she got everything into her half-hour consultation. If she did decide to proceed, it would cost her plenty.

She cautioned herself that it was too early to be making any decisions. She hadn't even talked to Vic about what she suspected.

But eventually she would. She'd thought about it every day for weeks. And when she did bring up the subject, she wanted to know what her rights were.

"Mrs. Bellamy? I'm Fran Parsons."

Norell's hips twitched in her seat. She'd been so deep in thought she hadn't seen this woman approach. She quickly held out her hand. "Very nice to meet you."

"Why don't we go into my office?"

Norell followed the attorney, her short brown hair cut as conservatively as the navy blue suit and navy-and-white striped blouse she wore, down a hall and into a well-appointed office decorated in dusky rose and gray. Soft classical music played on a CD. She took a seat opposite the elegant desk with its curved legs. "I know our consultation only runs half an hour," she said, "so let's get started right away." She cleared her throat. "Nearly five years ago my husband and I had been trying to conceive for a year, and I found out it was because of me. The doctor said I'd likely never get pregnant." She sighed wistfully; even after all this time it was painful to remember. "I took it very hard, and it resulted in a lot of strain between us. He went out and had an affair, his condom tore, and boom! Nine months later the woman had a baby."

"Wow! You weren't kidding when you said you wanted to get right to it," Ms. Parsons said as she furiously scribbled on a yellow legal pad. "Tell me more."

For a crazy moment Norell imagined she was not in an attorney's office, but on a psychiatrist's couch, and it was the doctor requesting more information. The thought brought a smile to her lips, but it quickly faded when she continued speaking. "My husband arranged with the woman for me and him to adopt the baby. We picked her up from the hospital, and all the official papers were filed."

"It sounds as though you had a happy ending."

Norell knew the attorney was trying to figure out how she'd gone from that happy scenario to sitting in this office. "Not exactly. My husband was vague at first, telling me that an infant was about to come available. After a while I got suspicious, and he confessed that he'd had a one-night stand that resulted in a pregnancy."

"But obviously you stayed," Ms. Parsons prompted.

"Yes. I had to consider the part I played in his straying in the first place. I'm afraid I wasn't a very good wife at the time. And then there was the baby." Her eyes took on a faraway look. "I fell in love the moment I laid eyes on her. I saw that I could either walk away or have all my dreams come true. In the end the joy trumped the pain."

"There's obviously a problem now, Mrs. Bellamy, that brought you here today."

"I'd pretty much learned to accept that my husband cheated on me," Norell said. She chuckled. "It's crazy to think that the happiest event of my life came from something so devastating, but I love my daughter." She met the attorney's eyes and took a deep breath for courage. "I'd always noticed that my baby looked a lot like one of my best friends."

"Oh, no."

Norell quickly realized what Ms. Parsons thought. "No, it's not that," she assured her. "My friend had a baby at around the same time my daughter was born. But she's got a sister. Back in June I overheard my husband having a conversation with her at my friend's house. They were together in the kitchen. He sounded so upset. And then it hit me, all of a sudden. *She* was the one my husband had the affair with. *She's* my baby's natural mother."

"Have you asked your husband about that, Mrs. Bellamy?"

"No. In my heart I know it's true." Her voice broke. "It was so much easier when my husband slept with some anonymous woman. But this woman, she's part of my extended social circle. I don't know if I can deal with it. My daughter is looking more and more like her, and eventually people are going to notice. It'll be humiliating for me. I haven't decided what I want to do yet. I figured it would be good if I found out what my rights are if I do decide to leave him."

"Mrs. Bellamy, you have a rather unique situation," Ms. Parsons began. "Your daughter was jointly adopted by you and Mr. Bellamy, but I'm inclined to think that a judge would give your husband the advantage because he's the biological father."

Norell's entire body stiffened. "I was afraid of that."

"Mrs. Bellamy. If I may say so, I think you've handled a difficult—no, make that an *impossible*—situation with great dignity. I have children myself, and I can't imagine my life without them. I get the feeling you've been very happy with your husband and daughter up until the time you figured out the identity of your child's biological mother."

She nodded.

"You were able to forgive him for cheating on you," Ms. Parsons pointed out. "You had everything you wanted. Now, just because you've learned who the mother is, you're seriously considering giving up both your husband and your daughter. I would plead with you not to give up your life just because you're afraid of gossip.. Of course, it's different if your husband habitually cheats on you." Her eyes asked a question.

Norell shook her head. "He doesn't. It was just that one time."

"That's what I thought. Mrs. Bellamy, there's no point in worrying about what people you don't know are saying. And as your friends, if they truly *are* your friends, they'll sympathize with you and be supportive. They won't be scandalmongers, spreading salacious gossip."

Norell shut her eyes tightly in an attempt to hold in the tears. "I've had to deal with so much. I don't know if I can handle any more." She sniffled. The pain had become unbearable. "I just don't know."

Chapter 28

Suzanne instinctively knew that the state of affairs between herself and Brad was much worse now than it had been after his birthday. The tension wasn't as noticeable now as it was then, but it was different. He treated her respectfully, but there was no sharing between them anymore. They had become almost like two strangers who lived together and had sex, but no emotional intimacy. He never called her by the nickname he'd given her years ago during their courtship, Suzie Q, anymore.

She tried talking to him, trying to convince him that he, Bradley, and Lauren came first, pointing out how she had kept her word about staying out of Kenya's marriage to Gregory. All she got out of him was a stony expression and the words, "I'm sorry, Suzanne, but that's not enough. You'll have to prove it to me."

"How am I supposed to do that?" she pleaded.

"By doing what you say you'll do."

"But everything's so quiet. There's nothing going on for me to stick up for us against."

"I'm sure there will be before too long. There always has been."

"But what happens with us in the meantime?" Suzanne hated the urgency and fear in her voice, but she couldn't help it.

Brad had simply shrugged, filling her with dread about what the future might hold.

Brad sat at a table on the veranda of the club that ran across its entire width. He and Errol had just played nine holes. Errol had stopped to speak with an acquaintance, while Brad went ahead to the buffet and helped himself to fried chicken, corn on the cob, potato salad, and buttermilk biscuits.

"Hi, Brad!"

He looked up to see Micheline standing, holding a plate in one hand and a glass of wine in another. "Hello there."

"May I join you?"

"Please. But since Errol is here, maybe we should switch to a larger table." He hastily got up and crossed to a table for four on the opposite side, near the white wooden railing, and pulled out a chair for her, pushing it closer to the table after she was seated.

"Where is Errol, anyway?" he asked as he transferred his own plate and glass to the larger table, taking a seat opposite Micheline.

"He's deep in conversation with a colleague of his. He suggested I go ahead and fix my plate. He mentioned you were out here someplace." She smiled at him. "How are you, Brad?"

"Pretty good. You?"

"Oh, busy."

"I haven't seen you around much lately," he remarked. He found himself wishing Errol would wrap it up and join them. Talking to Micheline and trying to sound as if everything was fine and dandy when he was privy to Errol's feelings about her made him uncomfortable.

"Well, I do have a job now," she replied with a smile. "Errol still expects me to make him dinner. So I don't have a lot of time to play golf. Plus, I'm getting ready to go out of town."

"Oh, really? Errol didn't mention anything." Brad wondered if Errol even knew about his wife's travel plans. It had to be difficult for Errol to live under such stressful conditions. Look at the hard time he was having with Suzanne. Their two situations might be different, but each had involved a betrayal. Maybe it was easier for Errol because he'd already made up his mind to break it off with Micheline, while he was still trying to decide if he could ever recapture the love he'd once felt for Suzanne, an emotion that was slowly seeping out of him like air from a punctured tire.

"That's because he's not going, just me." She sighed. "A family wedding in Boston. My cousin's getting married, and I'm a bridesmaid."

"You don't sound very enthusiastic about it."

"It's not as though she's putting me in a dress with poufy sleeves, but no, I'm not particular. We're actually not all that close, but we're the same age. You know how those family obligations go."

Brad's thoughts automatically went to his wife and in-laws.

"She caught me off guard by asking me to be in the wedding. I couldn't think of an excuse quickly enough." Micheline laughed. "The wedding is next Saturday, and I'm heading out Sunday morning. Since Errol couldn't get away, I'm going to spend a day or two with a girlfriend who lives in town."

"I'm sure you'll have a good time with her," he said politely.

"Yes, I have no doubts about that. But I'm off the entire week." She sighed theatrically. "I wish there was somewhere else I could go while I'm up there, to spend a few days."

That was a hint if he'd ever heard one. Brad thought quickly. Immediately he thought of his cabin in Maine, as well as the vibes he'd been getting from Micheline since their first meeting when she and Errol hosted the Super Bowl party. What was he supposed to do, ignore them? What man in his right mind would do *that*?

It was a cinch that Micheline, too, was thinking about his cabin's proximity to Massachusetts, or else why would she put out that hint? He was faced with a dilemma. He'd never cheated on his wife, neither Lisa nor Suzanne. Besides, Errol was a friend.

Brad reminded himself that Errol would be breaking off with Micheline. If he didn't want her, why shouldn't *he* have a little fun with her? At least he was already armed with the information that she wasn't quite as perfect as she seemed. He'd enjoy it for the fling it was and move on when it was over, his curiosity satisfied. His partner, Frank Nelson, had said that the demands of his various girlfriends over the years had made Jean look better to him than ever. Not that there was any permanence in his feelings, for before too long he always found some other woman to knock boots with.

Frank's observations aside, Brad knew his reasoning was off. The Trents were still together. For all he knew, Errol might have changed his mind. Errol hadn't mentioned anything more about his personal life, and Brad made it a point to not inquire, figuring the less he knew, the better.

The exes of buddies had always been off-limits, and he'd never crossed that line. But damn it, he wanted Micheline. They were two consenting adults, and if they kept the dalliance secret, what harm could it do?

In an instant he made his decision. The idea hadn't even fully formed in his head before he jumped on it. "I'm going to be up in New England myself the week after next," he remarked, even as he tried to figure out how he could clear his calendar to accommodate a sudden absence to his partner and patients. "I have a little cabin up in Cumberland County, Maine. I've been under so much stress lately. I told Suzanne I need to get away for a bit. Just me and a lake full of fish." He chuckled.

"You'll be there a whole week alone? Sounds lonely."

Micheline took a sip of her wine. Her wide eyes met his over the rim in a way that made his pants feel too tight.

Brad tried his best to forget the effect those eyes had on him. "It won't be so bad. I'll fish, golf, do a little reading. It's a nice, quiet environment. Good for thinking." He held his breath, knowing that he'd just provided Micheline with a perfect opening to suggest an assignation. A little wild, non-committal sex was just what he needed right now. He was about to find out if she was serious about those signals she'd been sending him. This was the time to separate the women from the girls.

"Is there something you need to think about?"

Brad realized he'd said too much. He wasn't about to alert Micheline to the turmoil between him and Suzanne. "There are always things to think about. What I'd like to accomplish, the best ways to do it . . . stuff like that."

"You know, I've never been to Maine," she remarked.

Brad knew then that all he had to do was suggest that she stop by for a visit while she was in New England, and that she'd take the bait.

"I still don't understand why you're going for a whole week," Suzanne said. She knew she sounded whiny, but she couldn't help it. She'd tried to talk him out of it ever since he told her of his plans to spend a week at their cabin in Maine. That hadn't worked. She must have made the same comment about not understanding his reasons at least ten times since, and she doubted his answer would be any different this time. Nor did she think it likely that he would suddenly change his mind. His packed bag was in the back of the SUV, and in ten more minutes they'd be at the airport.

Her repeated statements came out of desperation, for she couldn't get over the feeling that something wasn't right.

"Like I told you, Suzanne. I want some time alone."

"To think about us?"

"Maybe," he admitted. "Suzanne, I don't want to torture you. I will tell you not to worry. I think you and I will probably be all right eventually, but right now things aren't good, and I need a break from it all."

"I know," she said sadly, then repeated the words she hadn't been able to forget. "You don't want a wife who's dominated by her mother."

"That's right. Suzanne, you're a grown woman. It's time to cut the apron strings."

"Brad, please try to understand. I'm the eldest. My mother is trying to get all four of us settled. I'm all right, and Matthew will be all right, but Derrick and Kenya need a little help getting on track."

"And the impression you're leaving me with is that you're willing to sacrifice me and the kids for your brother and sister."

Suzanne could hear the anger in his voice, and the thought that he might actually return and tell her he wanted a divorce sent chills through her.

Suzanne placed a salad bowl on the table. "All right, we're just waiting for the biscuits to be done, and I'll call everyone to the table."

"Everything looks lovely, Suzanne," Arlene said with admiration. "But why only four places? Is Bradley not at home?"

"He's here. It's *Brad* who's not here."

"Oh? Where is he?"

"He's up at the cabin in Maine. I drove him to the airport this morning."

"And you didn't go with him?"

"No. First of all, it's not practical, not with Bradley and Lauren back in school."

"I could've come to stay with them for a week." Arlene

looked at Suzanne suspiciously. "There's more to this than what you're letting on. You know I'm always available to stay with the kids. And you never mentioned this before now. Did you two have a fight or something?"

Suzanne sighed. "No, but something's changed between us, Mama." She unconsciously converted to the term she'd used for her mother when she'd been much younger. "It's been going on for weeks now." She decided not to mention the role her mother and brother played in the discord between her and Brad, knowing it would only serve to make Arlene hostile and defensive. The last thing Suzanne wanted to deal with was her mother acting like *she'd* been wronged. She sighed heavily. "I don't know what to do."

"I don't see that there's anything you *can* do, honey," Arlene said. "I wouldn't worry about it. It's probably harmless. Didn't you say that all he does is fish and golf when he's up there?"

"Yes, but still, he'll be gone for a whole week. We've never been apart that long. He practically never goes away by himself, not for leisure travel." Sure, he attended an occasional medical conference, but she usually accompanied him to those . . . unless it was being held in a dull city like Pittsburgh. There'd been times when Brad had actually left for Maine a few days early, but he always took Bradley along, and the two of them would spend their days fishing. But that was different.

And this was a first.

Suzanne hesitated before uncertainly asking, "Do you think I should surprise him and fly up there?"

"No," Arlene said after a moment to think. "I think you should give the man his space. Let him be alone if that's what he wants."

Suzanne voiced the concern she'd kept hidden since learning of Brad's plans. "What if he's not alone?"

"I'm sure he's by himself, Suzanne. He's in Maine, not South Carolina. I mean, Brad doesn't seem to be into white women, and how many black people have you seen up there in that part of the country?"

"Oh. I see what you mean," Suzanne replied with a nod. "I think you might have something there."

She'd probably been worrying for nothing. Brad was doing just what he said, and nothing more.

Chapter 29

Brad's eyes opened to find the living room cloaked in darkness, except for the television. His unfinished beer rested on the coffee table. He'd really wiped out. Stress on the job, stress at home. . . . how much more of this could he take?

At least he was getting plenty of rest while he was here. He had to change planes and arrived too late to do anything other than to stop at the market in town for staples like bread, butter, bacon, eggs, coffee, and a six-pack, plus pick up a take-out meal to take home. He'd hit the tackle shop first thing in the morning.

He'd given up on the idea of Micheline joining him. Errol had finally shown up before she could ask him for details. All she knew was that he'd be at his house somewhere in Cumberland County. That was hardly enough information for her to find him.

He tossed off his disappointment fairly easily. Sometimes things happened in a manner that turned out to be proverbial disguised blessings. Maybe Errol had reconsidered leaving Micheline. Brad certainly wouldn't want to interfere with that. If she continued to flirt with him under those circumstances, he'd just pull her aside and firmly tell her she made him uncomfortable and to cut it out before she lost a good man.

Brad couldn't deny feeling a little let down that the rendezvous with Micheline didn't work out, but he had no regrets about having flown up here to his vacation house. He hadn't felt this refreshed in a long time. His log cabin was situated on a lake, with a sandy beach for a backyard. The rustic surroundings—all maple tables, pinewood floors, and nubby plaid upholstered furniture—actually had all the comforts of home. A plasma television was concealed inside a remote-operated credenza, and a Bose Wave radio provided fabulous acoustics. All Brad had to do was call the property manager, confirm that no one had rented the cabin for the week, and inform them he would be in residence. They had the cleaning service come in and freshen it up, and everything looked warm and inviting on his arrival. He'd never been here alone in all the years he'd owned it. Sometimes he and Bradley flew up for a long father-son weekend, and he and Suzanne spent most Christmases there with the children, enjoying the cold weather that helped define the holidays. The cabin was compact enough that it didn't feel cavernous. Two bedrooms on either side of a bathroom were on the first floor, and a flight of stairs led to a master suite and bath on the upper level.

Brad lazily went to the kitchen and retrieved another beer. No doubt about it, he'd enjoy his time here. Peaceful times like this had been missing from his life in recent weeks. He knew Suzanne was worried, but in his heart he knew he still loved her. He also knew it wasn't a bad thing for her to worry a bit. Eight full days—his return flight was set for a week from tomorrow—was probably more time than he needed, but maybe it would help her understand how disturbing he found her behavior and just how fragile their marriage had become after repeated episodes of Suzanne putting her own family first.

By eight A.M. the next morning he was seated comfortably in his rowboat in his fishing seat installed to the bench, providing him with a cushioned bottom and back. An iPod provided music, and he'd brought along a few frozen bottles of bottled water and a banana for a snack. Plenty of other boaters were out on the lake this sunny August morning, and he waved hello.

He was relaxing, holding his pole and humming along to the music streaming through his earphones, when his cell phone rang. Probably Suzanne calling to check on him, under the guise of wishing him a good morning. He knew from their conversation last night that she was helping Paula put on a wedding, but she might have a few minutes to give him a quick call.

He flipped open the phone without checking caller ID. "Hello."

"Well, hello there," purred a female voice he didn't recognize. Was Suzanne trying to disguise her voice?

"Who's this?" he asked impatiently. He had little tolerance for games.

"It's Micheline. I'm in Boston. My cousin's wedding was yesterday, and I'm just wondering if you'd show me around if I drove my rental car up there."

"Micheline! Um . . . how'd you get my number?"

"Remember the time I had car trouble and you followed me most of the way home? I took your cell number so I could call you when I got in."

"Oh, yes. I remember now." She'd apparently taken the trouble to make sure she retained it. The confusion over, his muscles relaxed. She'd contacted him, and she wanted to come up. His entire outlook had changed in the space of a minute. "Well, this is a surprise. I'd pretty much given up on seeing you. I didn't think you had any way to contact me."

"I'm just full of surprises," she said suggestively. "Now, why don't you give me directions?"

Suzanne worked swiftly to remove the leftover cheese sauce from the chafing dish into the container, and then on to the potatoes, meats, and other dishes. For the first time in her life she understood the satisfaction and joy of a job well done. In the jobs she'd had before she met Brad, even the one at his diagnostic center, she simply performed, having memorized her functions, but there'd been no particular pleasure in it. Doing something she truly enjoyed made all the difference. Now she knew how Lisa Canfield, Liloutie Braxton, and the wives of Brad's other colleagues must feel about their work.

She'd welcomed the work this Sunday morning bridal brunch brought. It took her mind off Brad being so far away.

He'd said he expected they would be all right, but she wasn't convinced. The whole dynamic of their relationship had changed. He'd had very little to say to her for weeks now. When the children were present, like at the dinner table, everything seemed as normal. Brad laughed and was jovial. But when they were alone, he was unnaturally quiet, even borderline sullen.

They still made love on a regular basis, but it had gotten a lot less personal. In the old days they used to cuddle together afterward in the center of their bed and talk. Now Brad just rolled over to the very edge of the bed and went to sleep. It might as well be a one-night stand.

On the night of her forty-second birthday just a few weeks ago she was treated to a glimpse of how it used to be between them. Brad had been affectionate and loving, and she thought they'd finally put their problems behind them, but then after sex that night Brad moved to his side of the bed and fell asleep, telling her the reprieve was over.

A few days later he told her he was going up to Maine for a week of fishing and relaxation.

"You've been awfully quiet," Paula remarked as they prepared to carry out their supplies and load them into her van.

"I'm all right," she hastily replied. She glanced at Paula's assistants, who like them wore black polo shirts with the words Discriminating Taste and the place-setting logo over the breast, plus tan khakis. "Paula, I've been meaning to ask you. In all this time, I haven't seen your friend. The one who worked Brad's party."

"Oh! He's . . . he only worked for me for a brief time. His regular job is construction. He took a job with me while he was laid off."

"You still seeing him?" Suzanne felt she might as well find out about Paula's love life, since her own was in such sorry shape.

"Yes. He's at my place right now, as a matter of fact."

"Doesn't it bother you that he's married?"

"He's going to be getting divorced."

Suzanne grunted. "That's what they all say."

"How about a workout?" Paula suggested. It didn't surprise Suzanne that she'd changed the subject, but it seemed like an offbeat suggestion.

"*Now?*" she asked, not hiding her apprehension.

"Why not? We're close to the beach. The food's on ice. What do you say to walking a couple of miles?"

Suzanne shrugged. "All right, why not? You're sure your friend won't mind? Didn't you say he's waiting for you?"

Paula smiled with a confidence Suzanne envied. "I'm sure."

"In that case, let's go." *If only I could be so sure of Brad. . . .*

Suzanne and Paula strolled barefoot at the shoreline, their khakis rolled up to their calves. At this time of day the beach was crowded with sun and water lovers, and they frequently had to walk around children making sand castles and just plain cavorting in the Florida sunshine, as well as adults playing volleyball. The air was filled with salt and the sounds of various boom boxes. The warm ocean water rolled in and lapped around their feet and ankles before rolling out again.

"Let's speed it up a little," Paula suggested. "I love the extra burn you get in your calf muscles from walking barefoot in the sand. Besides, I feel great!"

"I'll bet you do. You just put on another successful event by Discriminating Taste."

"Yes," Paula happily agreed. "It's always great when things go well. People think it's easy to provide breakfast for sixty-five people, but breakfasts are just as challenging as dinners. And your cake was beautiful." Suzanne's baking wasn't yet up to par, so Paula had baked a light and fluffy three-layer yellow sheet cake with raspberry filling that Suzanne had decorated with white fondant to resemble a large package with a bow tied around it.

"The bride and groom looked real happy, didn't they?"

"Well, I hope so. This is no time to be unhappy." Paula sighed. "Sometimes I envy them, to be young and to have their lives and all their dreams still in front of them."

"You haven't done badly for yourself, Paula. And you can still pass for being in your thirties."

Paula laughed. "My ego and I both thank you. Seriously, though. I'm not sure what's gotten into me, but I've been very reflective lately. Maybe it's because my boyfriend and I have been talking a lot about our lives, sharing all our hopes for the future and our regrets about the past."

"You're getting deep on me, but you're making me curious. What do you regret?"

"Marrying Andre Haines," Paula replied without hesitation. "But my biggest regret by far is Devon."

This revelation shocked Suzanne, and for a moment she was speechless. "But Devon's such a sweet girl," she finally said. "You should be proud of her." Suzanne had no problems with Devon Canfield, who had always treated her politely and with a friendly attitude that she'd never had a reason to doubt.

"I'm *very* proud of her," Paula clarified. "It's just that most of the credit for the wonderful way she turned out has to go to Darrell and Lisa, not to me."

Suzanne's ears perked up. Paula had never said much on her difficult relationship with her only child, and she'd always been curious about it. Only a wish not to pry had kept her from asking Paula how she felt about her daughter's stepmother playing such an important role in her life, possibly even larger than Paula herself. Now that Paula initiated the topic, Suzanne felt free to comment. "It's got to be hard, knowing that another woman raised your child," she said softly.

"It would be a lot harder if they didn't do it right, but Darrell and Lisa did an excellent job, not only on Devon but with Paige as well."

Suzanne wrinkled her nose at the mention of her stepdaughter, and Paula saw it.

"I don't understand why you feel so threatened by Paige, Suzanne," Paula said. "She's a very sweet young lady, and a nice addition to your family. If anything, she'll be a good influence on Lauren."

Suzanne didn't like the sound of that. "As opposed to Kenya being a good influence, you mean?" she asked testily.

Paula shrugged. "I wasn't even thinking about your sister. Their relationship is completely different. Kenya is her aunt, but Paige is her sister."

"*Half* sister," Suzanne corrected.

"Whatever. The bottom line is, what I want more than anything is the opportunity to raise another child, a child who'll be in my custody all the years they're growing up. Not like Devon, in Florida with her father and stepmother while I was in Texas." She gazed at the horizon. "It might have seemed like a good idea at the time, but I've known for a long time now what a terrible mistake it was."

"Don't be too hard on yourself, Paula. Devon turned out fine. And who knows, maybe your dream of raising another child will come true. It sure sounds like you and your boyfriend are getting serious, even though you can't consider getting married until he gets a divorce."

Paula was silent for a moment. "I wish I could explain it, Suzanne," she finally said. "It was intense from the very beginning. I've never experienced anything like it."

"And the age difference doesn't bother either of you?"

"Not at all. It's not all that much."

"Not all that much!" Suzanne exclaimed. "He doesn't look like he's even thirty yet."

Paula looked miffed. "His actual age isn't important. It's how we feel about each other that counts."

Suzanne had doubts about how long Paula would remain so blissfully happy, given her boyfriend's age and marital status, but right now she could only wish she felt that happy, so optimistic about the future.

They walked about two miles when they turned around and headed back. "What's Brad up to this morning, Suzanne?" Paula asked. "I'll bet he hit the links this morning, huh?"

Suzanne took a deep breath. How much could she get away with not telling her friend? "He's fishing." At least *that* was the truth.

"It seems so hot for that. But I guess it's cooler on the river."

After chewing on her lower lip, Suzanne decided to swallow her pride and confide in her friend. Maybe Paula could suggest something that might help.

"Things aren't quite right with Brad and me, Paula. I drove him to the airport yesterday. He *is* fishing this morning, but up at our place in Maine. He won't be back for a week."

The distress in Paula's eyes was genuine. "Suzanne! I had no idea."

"It's been going on for weeks now." She shook her head. "I just don't know what to do."

"Well, what happened to make him stop speaking to you? I sure hope it wasn't the size of my catering bill for the party."

Suzanne told him why Brad had fired Derrick.

Paula listened intently. "Suzanne," she began, "I don't want to sound like I'm being critical, but what were you thinking when you asked Brad to give your brother another chance? I mean, he *stole* from you."

"Oh, I just thought I might be able to convince him that

Derrick had learned his lesson. I talked to Derrick, and he truly was sorry, Paula. He was actually crying."

Paula couldn't keep the incredulity from her voice, but didn't quite succeed. "They're called crocodile tears, Suzanne. Do *you* really think Derrick has learned his lesson? Because all I think he regrets is that he got caught."

"Yes, I believe he has," Suzanne declared. "And I just think it would have been better for everybody if Brad gave him another chance. And it certainly would have made my mother happy," she added.

"Suzanne, I think it is admirable the way you look out for your mother's happiness, but the bottom line is, that shouldn't be your number-one concern. Your mother reacted the way any mother would. She's concerned with her son's well-being. You should be concerned with *your* kids. That money Derrick was taking meant less for Bradley and Lauren," she pointed out. She waited to let that sink in before going on. "I really think you made a bad mistake, Suzanne. Your first allegiance should be to the family you created, not the family you were born into. Most times they're in sync. But if those interests clash, like they did here, the Betancourt family comes before the Halls."

"Hey, Suzanne!"

They both stopped walking and looked in the direction of the voice. "Norell!" Suzanne exclaimed. She rushed forward to greet her old friend, giving a quick hug to Vic as well. "And who do we have here?" she said, squatting down in front of their daughter. "Hello there!"

The child moved to stand partially behind Norell's leg, but she smiled at Suzanne.

"Norell, she's even prettier than her picture."

"Thank you."

"Say hello to Miss Suzanne, Brianna," Vic instructed.

"Huh?"

"Say hello," he repeated. He sighed in exasperation when

the child hid more of herself behind her mother's legs. "Sorry," he said to Suzanne. "She can be a moody little thing."

"That's all right. Oh! Norell, Vic, I'd like you to meet Paula Haines. Paula, this is Norell and Vic Bellamy. Norell and I were friends when we were kids down in Palatka."

The three said hello to each other.

"And what's your name, sweetheart?" Paula asked, directing her question toward Brianna, still standing behind Norell.

The child giggled, then peeked out, only her face visible, staring at Paula curiously, all eyes.

At that moment Suzanne realized who Brianna Bellamy reminded her of.

Micheline.

"We'd better be moving on," Suzanne said a few minutes later.

"Oh, sure," Norell replied. "I'm sorry I haven't called yet to invite you and Brad over to our place for dinner. I've been super busy. The doctors are really swamping us with dictation for our transcription service."

"I know what you mean," Suzanne said easily. "Paula and I just wrapped up the catering of a wedding breakfast. We're taking a quick walk on the beach to unwind."

"I'm so glad you understand. And I'll definitely call you soon," Norell promised.

They all said good-bye, and Suzanne and Paula resumed walking.

"Nice couple," Paula remarked.

"Yes," Suzanne replied tonelessly. She couldn't stop thinking about Brianna Bellamy's resemblance to Micheline Trent. In fact, Suzanne didn't see Norell at all in her daughter, in her features or in her complexion, which was lighter than Norell's rich brown and had obviously come from her father. The whole thing was downright creepy. It was like seeing an embryonic Micheline.

Suzanne decided not to share her observations with Paula. She felt it was bad enough for her to bring Paula into her confidence about the issue between her and Brad. She wasn't about to spill that the pretty, young Micheline both disliked her and seemed interested in Brad. Besides, Micheline had nothing to do with the current problem. Thank heaven for that. Didn't she have enough to cope with?

"You and Norell seem to have one thing in common," Paula remarked. "You're both married to older men. Her husband's a good-looking dude, too."

Suzanne had to laugh. "And this from the girl who never looks at anyone over forty. But I know what you mean. He is awfully handsome, and I think he's even older than Brad." She paused. "Well, now that you know my problem, do you have any recommendations for me? I mean, how can I fix this?"

Paula had been thinking about the situation while Suzanne talked with her friend. "The best thing I can tell you, Suzanne, is to go to him and apologize. Tell him you know you made a mistake by sticking up for Derrick. Better yet, assure him you'll never do it again. But it has to be more than lip service. Something tells me that before too long you'll be in another position where Brad's on one side and your family is on the other. You'd better make sure you side with Brad, because you don't want him to feel that your marriage to him takes a backseat to your mother and your siblings."

Suzanne took a moment to absorb what her friend said. Brad had essentially said the same thing. "So you think if I make a solemn promise to Brad that he and the kids will always come first, I can put an end to all this strain?"

"At this point, I think it's the only thing you can do."

Paula didn't want to tell her friend that it might already be too late.

"I'll do it," Suzanne said. "Not only that, but I'll send him something to cheer him up. A special gift. Something he'll really like. I know he's out in the middle of nowhere, but these days there's nothing that can't be delivered."

"It can't hurt," Paula remarked.

Suzanne began to feel better. Surely she could convince Brad that she knew she'd committed a terrible wrong, but that she would never do that again. Everything would be all right.

She just hoped that Norell hadn't seen the look of distaste cross her face at the moment of realization of who little Brianna reminded her of. It had only lasted for a moment.

But now that Suzanne thought about it, Norell seemed a little uncomfortable herself, especially as she apologized for not having invited her and Brad over. Maybe she felt a little embarrassed, now that she'd been to Suzanne's home, since there was no way hers and Vic's could compare. Normally such a thought would give her a wonderful feeling of superiority, but now she had to consider that there was a chance—perhaps a tiny one, but still a chance—that she might not be living there herself in the coming weeks, depending on what Brad said when he returned home.

Chapter 30

L isa sat on the concrete edge of the pool, her legs submerged in the cool blue water up to her mid-calf. Sometimes she swam laps with Darrell, but that meant either washing her hair or rinsing the chlorine out and then the extra step of rolling it with setting lotion, so most days she simply watched him.

She saw his blurred underwater figure approach her and squealed when he grabbed her ankles. She tried to shake his hands off, but he was too strong. Eventually he surfaced for air. "Don't you *dare* pull me in and get my hair wet," she said in her best I-mean-business tone. "I want to go to the early service at church tomorrow. I'll get in the water with you tomorrow afternoon, because I'll have time to wash my hair tomorrow night."

"You black women and your hair," he scoffed.

"Now that it's short I can't just pull it back anymore. If that's too complicated, you can always get yourself a white woman." She looked at him strangely as he moved to stand between her thighs and put wet arms around her. She felt water seep through her sleeveless polo shirt and against the front of it when he pressed his face and wet hair against her front, between her chest and abdomen. She didn't care about her clothes; she just didn't want him to mess up her hair.

"Why are you so frisky, anyway? You're like a restless little kid this afternoon."

"Oh, I don't know. Maybe I miss Brad," Darrell said with a laugh. He released her and fell backward, falling into a float.

"Is he out of town?"

"Yeah, he left today. Didn't you know? I thought Paige would have mentioned it to you."

Lisa shook her head. "Paige didn't say a word. She's got a date tonight, thank God." Lisa prayed for about the fiftieth time that her daughter would become enamored of this new young man. Then she returned her thoughts to her first husband. "Brad's trip can't be business related, not if he left on a Saturday. Where'd he go, up to see his parents?"

"No, he went up to his place in Maine. Fishing."

"Are you sure they went? I saw Lauren walking Buster this afternoon. Besides, don't she and Bradley have school Monday?"

"*They* didn't go. Brad went by himself."

"Really," she said, more of a statement than a question. "That's probably a first. How long will he be gone?"

"All week. Until next Sunday, I think."

"Sunday! Now, that's interesting. I wonder what's going on?" Darrell grunted.

"What's *that* supposed to mean?" Lisa asked.

"Nothing."

"The hell it doesn't. Darrell Canfield, you're holding out on me."

"Just forget I said anything, will you? Which I didn't."

She leaned over slightly and clamped her hands around his left ankle. "No, Darrell. What's going on?"

He jerked his foot until she had to let go, then quickly righted himself, standing in the chest-deep water. "I guess you're going to nag me to death until I tell you."

"Worse than that. I won't give you any," she said with a devilish smile.

Darrell laughed. "All right. But this is just between you and me, and nobody else is to know. Got it?"

"Yeah. So spill it, already."

"All right." He paused. "I think Brad might be stepping out on Suzanne."

Lisa drew in her breath. "Darrell! What makes you say that?"

"Something he asked me a couple of months ago. I'm not going into details, Lisa, so don't even ask. I've told you too much already."

"Oh, my God! And I'll bet I know who it is. That chick from Brad's party whose dress was cut down to her ass. I saw them having lunch together. Brad tried to say she was just thanking him for getting her a job, but I thought I sensed a little hanky-panky going on."

"Lisa, you look like the proverbial cat who just swallowed the canary," Darrell said. "Just remember, this is between us, so no blabbing to Kim."

"All right." Lisa grew pensive. "You know, in a way I feel bad for Suzanne. I wouldn't wish that on anybody." She placed her right hand on his shoulder. "Darrell, you know I love you, and that I love the life we've built together over the last fifteen years, but I'd be lying if I said I still don't feel hurt by Brad's starting something with Suzanne when he was still married to me. It's not a thing of me carrying a torch for Brad—you know better than that—but it was a huge blow to my ego. We women just don't forget things like that."

Darrell's went around her, his hand settling on her upper arm. "Lisa, during that same conversation, Brad mentioned that he never cheated on you, even though he knows you don't believe him."

"Ycah, yeah," Lisa replied wearily. "He didn't start anything with Suzanne until after we separated."

"I know you and he had this out during your separation, but that's what he says, and personally, I believe him."

She smiled. "I guess the most important thing is that it really doesn't matter at all anymore, does it?"

He pulled her into the water, and Lisa squealed when he deliberately dunked her under. "Darrell! I *told* you not to—"

The rest of her protest was silenced by his kiss, and her arms went up to encircle his neck.

Lisa quietly picked up the kitchen extension. Darrell was in their bedroom watching a comedy special on HBO, and she could hear him laughing all the way out here, but she had to make sure he didn't hear her.

"Kim, it's Lisa," she said when her friend answered the phone. "I know it's kind of late, but I just had to tell you this. You have to promise this won't go any further. If Darrell knew I was telling you this, he'd kill me. He made me promise I wouldn't say a word . . ."

Brad had been nervous when Micheline pulled up to the log cabin. He'd never done this sort of thing before, but instinct told him not to initiate sex right away. For one, it was barely noon. He had plenty of time after dinner.

He greeted Micheline with a warm hug, more friendly than sexual, and invited her inside. He gave her a tour of the cabin, his ears listening carefully for any telling remarks along the lines of, "Oh, this will be *my* room," that suggested she planned to keep her visit platonic.

After showing her the property, at his suggestion, he drove her into town in his rented Jeep, and they had lunch at a little café. As they left the restaurant and prepared to take a walk past the shops and other eateries in the four-block area with its diagonal parking and brick two-story buildings, they ran smack into Hank McGuiness, who owned the house next door, leaving the hardware store.

"Afternoon," he said, his eyes fixated on Micheline as he directed the greeting toward Brad.

"Hey, Hank." Brad hadn't given much thought about how

he'd explain Micheline's presence to his neighbors, all of whom knew Suzanne. He was trying to figure out how to handle the situation when Micheline thoughtfully gave him an out.

"If you don't mind, I'd like to run into that boutique and look at something that caught my eye. Excuse me a moment." She scurried off, leaving him alone with Hank.

Hank watched her move away. "I see there've been a few cast changes in your program since last Christmas," he said with a wink.

"Not necessarily," Brad replied smoothly. In the few seconds Micheline had spoken, he'd come up with an excuse that would probably work. "You see, Hank, Suzanne and I have separated. There's a chance we might reconcile, but in the meantime . . . well, you know how it is."

"I can't say I do, but you're making me wish I did." He patted Brad's upper arm. "But mum's the word."

"I appreciate that, Hank. It's a sensitive situation, as I'm sure you realize. I'm really hoping Suzanne and I will eventually get back together, but I wouldn't want her to find out I had another woman up here during our separation. She's likely to keep harping on it to the point where we break up for good."

"Sure, I understand. You're a lucky man, Brad." Hank held out his hand. "I need to get home with this. That damned toilet is running continuously, and it's driving us all nuts."

"See you later." Brad blew out a breath. How did his friends keep up with all these damn lies?

Satisfied that he'd successfully averted any problem, Brad followed Micheline into the boutique, which featured lingerie.

He found her at the cash register, making a purchase. "You really did want to buy something," he said in surprise.

"Yes, but the timing seemed particularly good."

"I appreciate that, Micheline. This type of thing can be so awkward."

"It was obvious he was curious about me. So what'd you tell him?"

His eyes widened; he hadn't expected her to be so blunt. "I'd rather not say, if you don't mind. The less involved you are in this, the better."

She nodded. "All right."

He couldn't read her tone and wanted to set everything right if she felt miffed. He leaned in and tapped the tissue paper inside the decorative tote-style bag. "So what'd you buy?"

"You be a good boy and maybe you'll get to find out."

Brad looked around at the nightgowns on display throughout the store, and he knew then that this would be no platonic visit.

He could hardly wait for nightfall.

Micheline insisted on making dinner, saying it was no trouble. She made some kind of spicy ground beef baked inside flaky biscuits, which she served with a salad and wine. Brad enjoyed it tremendously.

"Ready for dessert?" she asked.

"Sure. I'm full, but I can always make room for something sweet." He'd noticed that the sun had set outside, this being the weekend before Labor Day, and he thought he'd like to have *her* for dessert. The evening was finally upon him. All afternoon he'd been wondering about what she'd purchased from the lingerie boutique. Did she plan on modeling it for him?

His thoughts were interrupted by the ringing of his cell phone. Of all times for Suzanne to call. He'd tried to reach her this afternoon while Micheline was cooking, but she hadn't answered. Quickly he headed for the storm door and went outside to the deck. "Hi, Suzie Q."

Her gasp reminded him that he hadn't called her that in weeks. "You sound cheerful," she said uncertainly.

"I feel pretty good, yeah. I went fishing this morning, caught two fish, and, um, fried them up for dinner after I took a nice, long nap. I'm feeling pretty refreshed."

"I miss you," she said softly.

"I know. But we really need this time apart."

She grew quiet, and he knew she noticed that he hadn't told her he missed her as well. Brad would only carry hypocrisy so far. He had a beautiful, sexy young woman right here with him, and he hadn't even been thinking about Suzanne.

"Uh, how'd the catering go this morning?" he asked.

"Perfect. My cake was a big hit."

"Did you actually make a tiered cake?"

"No tier. It was a small wedding. Paula made a sheet cake, and I decorated that with white fondant and cream. Brad, there's something I need to tell you," she added, changing the subject.

He listened intently as she assured him that she recognized her error and would never repeat it. He put aside thoughts of Micheline as he listened to his wife try to convince him it wasn't too late for them. She sounded sincere enough. He knew he had to give her a chance, but he also had to keep open the thought that in the end it wouldn't work between them, for he knew he simply couldn't go on this way feeling as though he came second.

"All right, Suzanne," he said when she was through. "It sounds like your feelings are genuine. But this has been going on a long time, and I'm not entirely convinced you can change your behavior just like that. We'll talk about it more when I come home, huh?"

He heard her outpouring of breath through the wire. Had she thought he wouldn't be coming home at all?

"Will you come home before next Sunday?" she asked.

"No," he replied, his thoughts returning to Micheline and what was about to happen. Maybe he should feel guilt, but he felt none. The gray hairs on his mustache and goatee had tripled in the last few weeks because of all this turmoil, and he had more gray hairs on his head as well. "I need an entire week. But I will be back." He forced a yawn. "I'm going to go to bed now."

"But it's so early, just going on eight o'clock."

"I'll be getting up early tomorrow to fish. Why don't you call me in the morning, like you did today?"

"All right. Sweet dreams."

He disconnected the call. In the few minutes he'd been outside it had gotten completely dark. He wondered if that was some kind of omen. He'd just stood and lied to his wife about his activities of the day. Would his time with Micheline actually be worth all his misgivings?

Brad reentered the house and sat on the couch. He was so lost in his thoughts he didn't realize Micheline had been gone for a bit, and she wasn't in the kitchen. "Micheline?" he called out. "You okay?"

He heard the sound of a door opening and figured the answer was yes. Then tapping footsteps on the pine floor made him turn around. His mouth dropped open at the sight of Micheline wearing red open-toe patent leather mules, red thigh-high stockings, and a sheer red corset with cutouts at the nipples and crotch. Those areas were covered with whipped cream.

"I thought I'd offer you a special dish I call Micheline Meringue for dessert," she said in a throaty voice as she walked toward him. Instead of standing before him, she passed the sofa where he sat and gracefully laid down on the six-by-nine furry brown rug in front of the fireplace. "Won't you have some?" she purred from the floor, her folded hands cradling the back of her head and her back arched, raising her hips tantalizingly.

Brad rose to his feet, staring at the enticing sight of her so hard that when he finally moved forward he nearly tripped over the coffee table.

"It's a good thing there's not a fire going, or else I'd be melting right about now," Micheline remarked.

"I'm just, uh, taking a few minutes to savor the sight," he said when he found his voice. "You are . . . breathtaking."

"Thank you," she replied, obviously pleased.

He knelt beside her on the rug. "I've used my sense of sight. Now I'm going to use my other senses, like touch"—he rested his palm on her middle—"smell"—he moved his face close to her hair—"and taste." He began to lick the cream from her nipple.

He'd dreamed of this situation for months, and he was going to enjoy every delicious minute.

Brad's toes curled in pleasure. He rotated his pelvis upward, pushing his fully erect penis into Micheline's wet, tight body. She rode him backward, facing away from him, and he found the way she wiggled her round ass incredibly exciting. She had a pretty back, as he and every other man had noticed the night of his birthday party, but he was most fascinated by the way she stretched and wiggled her butt, as well as the ecstasy on her face he glimpsed when she turned her head, and those little squeals she made.

Pretty. Great body. Damn good cook. Sexually imaginative—they hadn't even gotten off the living room rug yet. No wonder Errol had fallen for her charms . . . and been so crushed by whatever she'd done to betray him.

What a week this would be.

Chapter 31

"I'm back," Norell called out as she carried the grocery bags to the kitchen.

"You need any help?" Vic asked. He sat at the breakfast table, his laptop computer in front of him.

"No, this is all there is. Where's Brianna?"

"Napping," he said as he rose from the console table where he was downloading music onto his laptop computer. He walked over and stood behind her, his arms encircling her waist. "We watched the Cartoon Network for a bit, and she fell asleep on *Underdog*."

"She probably sensed those cartoons are nearly fifty years old. She'd probably still be awake if y'all had watched *Sponge-Bob*." Norell smiled. "So it's been quiet here at the home front, huh?"

"Yeah. I was curious about something, Norell."

"What's that?"

"Why haven't you invited Suzanne and her husband over for dinner? Your transcription workload is under good control. You seemed to be so glad to be back in touch with Suzanne, yet you made an excuse to her this afternoon at the beach. Is there something going on I don't know about?"

Norell placed a bag of fresh green beans on the counter with a sigh. "Funny you should ask me that question. The answer to it happens to be why I haven't invited the Betancourts over. Tell me, Vic. Is there something going on *I* don't know about?"

He frowned at her. "What the heck is going on?"

She met his gaze head-on. "Nothing. I'll start organizing a dinner party. Besides you, me, Suzanne, and Brad, we can have Cécile and Michael, Dana and Gil, and how about Micheline and Errol?" She stared at him defiantly, all but daring him to ask her what she knew.

"Now, why would you want to invite Micheline and—" Vic broke off. "Oh. You know."

He didn't even have the decency to look ashamed, she thought angrily. "Yes. I figured it out, all by myself. I know you wanted to keep me in the dark forever, but Brianna's starting to look just like her." She stared at him in fury, hot tears stinging her eyes now that she finally voiced what she'd been living with all these months. "Just how long were you planning on keeping your dirty little secret, Vic? Ten years? Fifteen? Did you really think that neither I nor anyone else would ever notice the resemblance between Brianna and Micheline, or the friction between you and Micheline? That day you and she were in Cécile's kitchen having words . . . it all came to me then, and I've been wrestling with what to do ever since."

Vic took a deep breath. "I'm sorry, Norell. What can I say? That night, well . . . I had no idea she was Cécile's sister, not even months later, when she told me she was pregnant. I didn't know until Cécile came to my office and started ranting about the difficult position I'd put her in."

Norell gasped. "You mean . . . *Cécile* knows?" Her knees suddenly felt as if they would give out. That possibility had never occurred to her.

"Apparently, Micheline gave her some vague information about me, but since Cécile knows both of us, she was able to put two and two together."

Norell sank onto a conveniently placed stool at the kitchen counter. She could only imagine what Micheline had told her sister. *I had this one-night stand with this older dude, a bail bondsman with a wife who's cracking up because she can't get pregnant, and the SOB knocks* me *up. Is that ironic, or what?* "My God, this is worse than I thought." Another thought occurred to her. "Who else knows about this . . . while you tried to keep me in the dark all these years?"

"No one . . . unless, of course, Cécile mentioned it to Michael. That's only natural. He's her husband."

A sob she could no longer hold in escaped from her throat. Vic quickly moved toward her, but she held up her hand, palm out, silently gesturing for him to stop.

"I need to be alone," she said as she climbed off the stool. "Keep an eye out for Brianna, will you?"

"Of course. She's my child, too."

Norell didn't bother to point out the irony of his statement. Brianna was his child completely, at least where it counted the most—by blood. All the love she'd given, even the fact that to Brianna she was Mama, none of it mattered. According to the lawyer she'd consulted, in a divorce she would lose custody of her little girl to her natural father.

Now that everything was out in the open, Norell simply didn't know if she could get past this. Cécile had known about Brianna all this time, and probably Michael, too. For all Norell knew, Dana knew about it as well. Had her friends been pitying her all this time, clucking their tongues and saying, *Poor Norell, everybody knows where her baby came from except her* when she wasn't around?

She closed the bedroom door behind her and threw herself on the bed face down and cried over all she had to lose. Eventually she fell asleep from sheer exhaustion.

She dreamed she heard Brianna's voice. "Mama. Wake up, Mama!" Norell shifted position, trying to escape. She couldn't bear to think of her little girl thinking she was in bed asleep when she had actually left her alone with her father.

"Wake up, Mama!"

Norell's eyes flew open at the feel of a small hand on her shoulder. This wasn't a dream; Brianna was actually in the room with her!

It only took a moment to see how she'd gotten in the room and up on the high-sitting king-sized bed. A smiling Vic held her up by her armpits.

Instantly alert, Norell sat up and accepted the reaching Brianna from Vic. The child's arms immediately went around her. "Mama! You're up!"

"Yes, sweetheart, I'm awake." She closed her eyes as she savored her child's embrace. However would she survive without her baby girl? How could she even *think* about leaving her?

"Brianna and I have something to say to you, Norell," Vic said.

"Daddy and I have something to say," Brianna parroted.

Norell leaned back against the headboard, moving Brianna to a sitting position onto her lap. "What's that?"

"We want you to know that we realize that sometimes . . . we might do things that get you mad at us, and might even make you wish we weren't around," Vic began.

Norell quickly glanced at Brianna, worried that she shouldn't be hearing this. The child stared wide-eyed at her father, as if knowing she was hearing an important speech, even if she didn't understand it.

"But we want to tell you that we love you very much," Vic continued, sincerity and truth in his eyes.

"We love you," Brianna said, clapping her hands.

Norell blinked furiously to hold back tears that had suddenly formed.

"What's more than that, we need you," Vic said. "And we would never, ever do anything to deliberately hurt you. We want you to be with us always."

She couldn't contain her emotions anymore, and tears rolled down her face.

Brianna stood up, holding on to Norell's arm. "Don't cry, Mama."

"Mama's all right, sweetheart," Norell soothed, even as her shoulders trembled with sobs. Vic bent and kissed away her tears, then quickly kissed her mouth. Desire for him surged through her, the way it always did whenever he touched her. She gave his hand a quick squeeze, and then he reached for Brianna and straightened up, holding their daughter.

"I think we should let Mama clean up, and she'll come out and have dinner with us," he said to Brianna. "Does that sound good?"

"Sounds good."

He smiled at Norell. "Try not to take too long."

"I won't."

After they left the room, Norell got up and went to wash her face with warm water. As the faucet ran she kept hearing the words of the attorney she'd consulted. *Don't throw away your life because of gossip.*

She shut off the water with such force that a piece of the equipment fell off. She'd had her share of hard times in her life. An only child, she'd lost both her parents before she turned thirty. She'd nursed her mother through her illness, returning to full-time work after she died. An emergency appendectomy before her health insurance benefits went into effect resulted in a huge debt. Then, after she met and married Vic and finally thought she'd get her happily ever after, she'd been faced with infertility, and her unhappiness over that almost wrecked her marriage. She would forever find it ironic that Brianna's very existence came from such a low point in her life. And now this. But when she looked at Vic just now, her still-vivid anger had been outranked by a stronger emotion—love.

As she patted her face dry, Norell considered that at the end of the day, that was all that mattered. She couldn't control her feelings; they came naturally. As long as she could feel more love than anything else when she looked at her husband, as long as she felt that he loved her just as much . . . she had to try to find the strength to get past this, to put it to bed forever.

To allow his indiscretion to continue to haunt them would be a terrible mistake, one that would ultimately shatter three lives.

Chapter 32

Micheline stared at the cellophane-covered arrangement the young deliveryman held. She'd never seen such weird-looking flowers.

Then she realized they weren't flowers, they were fruit pieces on sticks that *looked* like flowers, at least at first glance. Red grapes surrounded by green melons, strawberries at the center of round cantaloupe slices. How cute.

She thanked the deliveryman and closed the door with her foot while holding the basket with both hands. Of course they were for Brad, but he was out fishing, and she was eager to see if Suzanne had sent them. It looked very much like a peace offering, an attempt by a wife who sensed she was about to lose her husband. After setting down the large basket on the kitchen counter, she carefully removed the envelope, which was taped to the cellophane. The computer-generated plain white card inside read, *Happy fishing. Miss you much. All my love, Suzie Q.*

Micheline carefully replaced the card, then casually pulled out a stick containing blueberries and pineapple. She ate it while lounging in a recliner opposite the television. "Sorry, Miss Suzie Q.," she said aloud. "I'm afraid you're on your way out, and I'm on my way *in.*"

Part of her wished Brad had hung up his fishing rod and spent the morning with her. She supposed he wanted to be able to truthfully tell Suzanne that he'd spent most of his time fishing during this trip. She'd gone out with him yesterday, wanting to make sure she was in his sight as well as on his mind. It had been a very warm day for late summer in New England, and when Brad took his shirt off, she playfully removed hers as well. Only the fear of being spotted had kept her from removing her bra as well, but she pulled off her shorts, and Brad had gotten so aroused at the sight of her in her sexy peach-colored lingerie that he docked the boat, grabbed her, and they ran into the woods and had daring, energetic sex under a tree, with him sitting up leaning against it and her straddling him.

Micheline was on her third stalk by the time Brad returned. "Hi!"

"Well, hello there. Did you miss me?" she asked in her sexiest voice.

He chuckled. "I thought about what happened yesterday. Only with supreme willpower did I refrain from coming back here to show you just how much I missed you." He looked at the stick she held curiously. "Hey, what's that you've got there? Looks like a giant lollipop."

"I'm too old to be sucking on lollipops," she replied innocently. "Actually, you had a delivery." She pointed with her chin to the arrangement on the counter of the adjacent kitchen.

"Wow, look at that," he said as he walked toward it for closer inspection. "Who could've—" He broke off, obviously realizing the only person who would have sent it.

"It looked so delicious. I hope you don't mind my having helped myself."

"Of course not," he said absently as he read the card. "Fresh fruit like this with no skin on it isn't going to last but for a day or two, anyway."

"So who sent it?"

"Suzanne. Excuse me a minute, Micheline."

She watched, not knowing what to think, as he disappeared into the master bedroom.

* * *

Suzanne checked her watch. Four o'clock. Surely Brad's edible arrangement had been delivered by now. Why hadn't she heard from him? Was the rift between them worse than she thought?

She told herself to stay calm. There could be a dozen reasons why Brad hadn't called. He usually got back from fishing by two or two-thirty. Maybe he stopped in the village to get something to eat. Or maybe he stayed out on the water longer than usual—it wasn't like he had anyone to rush home to—and the basket had been left with a neighbor, or even on the front porch. She should probably just call the merchant and ask if they'd actually delivered it, and if Brad had been there to receive it personally. Best to know the facts rather than torture herself unnecessarily.

She dialed the number. "Mr. Winters, please," she requested to the young-sounding man—a teenager, she guessed—who answered the shop phone.

"I'm sorry. Mr. Winters stepped out. This is his assistant, Brian. Can I help you with something, ma'am?"

"This is Suzanne Betancourt, Brian. I ordered a fruit arrangement for my husband, and I just wanted to make sure they were delivered."

"Oh, I can tell you that. I handle Mr. Winters's deliveries. Betancourt, Betancourt," Brian said, more to himself than to her. "Oh, yes. I remember. Your daughter seemed tickled to get them."

Suzanne chuckled. "My *daughter?* I'm afraid you're getting my order mixed up with someone else's."

"I don't think so. It's on Snowbird Lane, isn't it?"

"Yes." The first dawning of fear descended over Suzanne. She hated for this young nobody to know her business, but he was the only one who could help her. "You say a woman answered the door?"

The silence on the other end of the line spoke volumes, as

if the young man just realized he'd given something away. "I'm sorry, ma'am. I think I might have said too much already."

"I assure you that there's nothing confidential about telling me what you saw at our house," Suzanne said quickly. "You're not breaking any laws, and you won't get in any trouble. This is between you and me. We don't even have to say anything to Mr. Winters. Now, I'm in Florida, so it's impossible for me to know what's going on. I really need your help. Can you . . . can you at least tell me what the woman looked like?" She hated to plead this way, but she had no other choice. She hoped that the door was answered by the housekeeper, who prepared the cabin for vacationers, but even as she had the thought she knew it was unlikely. Laura Poinsette had created a lucrative business, contracting herself out to property managers to clean vacation homes, but she generally only cleaned up after the cabin had been occupied, checking in periodically to dust and vacuum during periods of vacancy. Suzanne held her breath as she waited for Brian to answer her question.

"You're sure I won't get Mr. Winters into trouble?" he asked hesitantly.

"Absolutely sure. And you'll be helping me out."

He took a moment to consider. "Well, as long as you're sure. She was in her twenties, African American . . ."

Suzanne's nasal airway immediately clogged. Laura Poinsette was middle-aged and white. Brian had just described someone else entirely, and she believed she knew just who. She almost didn't have to hear the rest of his description.

". . . light-complexioned, slim, with kind of reddish-blond hair."

Suzanne let out a whimper as her worst fears were confirmed. Embarrassed, she said a hasty "thank you" and hung up.

Her entire body felt numb. Micheline was in Maine with Brad, making love to her husband in the very bed they shared.

Everything she had feared had just come true, and she hadn't the faintest idea of what to do about it. She realized she was in over her head. She had to make some sort of plan, discuss it with someone. And there was only one person she completely trusted.

Suzanne checked her watch, moving for the first time. Her mother wouldn't be home until after five, and the post office frowned on personal calls unless it was during a break. Suzanne could call her mother's cell phone, which would vibrate and alert her someone was trying to reach her, but this was too urgent a situation to rush through in ten minutes. It looked like she had no other recourse but to wait.

"Hi!" her mother greeted her. "I'm just getting in my car. I'll bet you're calling to invite me over for dinner, since Brad's away."

The sound of her mother's voice was more than Suzanne could bear. "Mom." The one syllable came out shaky, as if she were a little girl who'd skinned her knee and wanted Mommy to see her boo-boo.

Arlene jumped on it instantly. "Suzanne! What's wrong?"

"Oh, Mom. It's just awful."

"Suzanne, you're frightening me," Arlene said sternly. "Now, what's wrong? Did something happen to Bradley or Lauren?"

"No, the kids are fine," she replied. "It's Brad, Mama. He's got a woman up there with him in Maine."

Arlene gasped, and Suzanne kept talking. "And not just any woman, Mama. It's Micheline."

"That bitch!" Arlene declared.

"I'm not about to argue with you there. But the fact remains that I'm in danger of losing my husband. I may have lost him already," she wailed.

"Now, don't you go writing off your marriage to Brad. Be real, Suzanne. Do you really think he loves that girl?"

"No," Suzanne said without hesitation. "I believe he loves

me. But the fact that he's sleeping with Micheline tells me he's not happy with me, and that's almost as bad."

"Wait a minute. What makes you so sure it's Micheline who's up there with him? How do you know that anyone's there with him at all?"

Suzanne recounted her ordering and her phone conversation with the delivery boy.

"All right, so you know for sure it's her," Arlene said thoughtfully. Then she fell silent. "I'm going to need some time to think this one over."

"Well, why *don't* you come over for dinner tonight? But remember, we can't say anything in front of Bradley and Lauren."

"That's fine. We'll talk after dinner."

Suzanne and her mother sat on the patio, the television turned to a fairly high volume to prevent them from being overheard.

"Mom, I have to leave him," Suzanne said as bravely as she could. "I just don't see any other way out of this. What's he's done is inexcusable."

"Suzanne, I wouldn't be too hasty if I were you. Men like Brad don't grow on trees, you know. As great as you look, the fact is that there are a lot of girls who look as good as you do . . . and they're younger than you are."

Suzanne winced.

"I'm sorry," Arlene said. "It's not my intention to hurt your feelings. I just want you to take a good look at what you're ready to give up."

"But, Mom, what choice do I have?"

"Well, for one, you can pretend that you don't know anything about it. He's not exactly flaunting it, is he?"

"No. That's why it came as such a shock. But he definitely doesn't want me to find out. He's been covering." *Or maybe he's just waiting to tell me until after he gets home.* Suzanne forced the painful thought out of her head. Hadn't Brad told her he'd be back? Hadn't he said he believed they'd be all right?

"Well, that's in your favor," Arlene said. "You know, Suzanne, sometimes these things just can't be avoided. Brad, just like any other man who's been faithful to his wife all these years, decides he'd like to have a shot at something new and different and exciting. It'll happen, it'll be over, and that's that. When it's all said—I mean, when it's all *done*, he'll come back to you."

"But, Mom, how can you be so sure? Who's to say that he won't want to be married to Micheline, to replace me with her?"

"Suzanne, you've been married for sixteen years. Brad is just a typical man going through a midlife crisis. He just wants to see and touch something new. Of course," Arlene added, "if there's something you're doing that he's not happy about, my advice would be to stop doing it."

"Oh, you can be sure of that." Suzanne found her mother's words ironic. Maybe her mother didn't recognize the irony here, but *she* sure did. "Is that all you have to say, Mom?" she said incredulously. "Just forget about how he betrayed me?"

"What's Brad's partner's wife's name again?"

"Who, Jean?" Suzanne couldn't imagine what Jean Nelson had to do with this.

"Yes, that's the one. She's a smart cookie. Unless she's blind, she's got to know her husband has had girlfriends all over the city."

"Yes," Suzanne said bitterly. "And she looks the other way and talks about how wonderful her life is. Doesn't she know people are laughing at her behind her back?"

"Well, there's a reason why she says that," Arlene replied. "She knows her husband is always going to come back home to her. And she also knows that if she stays with him she'll be taken care of. What kind of life would she have if she had to get out there and support herself?"

"She could work. Secretaries make decent money, and the ones who work for executives make damn good money. That's what she used to do."

"Suzanne, Jean hasn't worked in what, twenty-five years? They barely had computers back then."

"In that case, Frank would have to pay her alimony. The same as Brad would have to do for me. 'To support me in the style to which I have become accustomed,'" Suzanne recited.

"Maybe Frank would have to pay Jean alimony, but she's older than you are, Suzanne," Arlene pointed out. "No judge would require a woman near retirement age to train for a new career. But you're only forty-two. You've got another twenty-five years or more to reach standard retirement age, now that they're pushing it back."

Suzanne seemed less confident as she pondered this, and Arlene jumped on it. "Just remember, you don't want to end up like me, having difficulty paying your rent every month." She sighed. "Of course, things have gotten a little better, now that Kenya's out of the house."

"What about Derrick?" Suzanne asked dully.

"Oh, he can't afford to give me anything. They pay him less at Popeyes than Brad did." She shrugged. "Jobs are hard to find nowadays." Then she studied Suzanne. "Are you still actually entertaining the idea of walking out on Brad?"

"Mama, you're not being fair. Look what he did to me. I don't want people pitying me behind my back, like they do Jean Nelson."

"Suzanne, you're forgetting something. Jean's husband cheats on her openly. Brad, on the other hand, went through considerable trouble to make sure you would never find out. That alone should tell you he doesn't plan on replacing you with Micheline." Arlene paused to let that sink in, knowing Suzanne was listening closely. "It's one thing for a man to cheat. It's another thing for a man to make a fool of his wife in front of an audience. So my advice to you is to act like you don't know anything and to bring out all the good things in yourself that made Brad fall in love with you in the first place."

Suzanne reluctantly admitted that her mother had a point. In her heart, she knew she really had to go along. She'd just learned a hard lesson.

Not to ever say never.

Chapter 33

Brad lay on his back, shouting out his pleasure as Micheline brought him to orgasm with her mouth. He'd never fully understood why men like his partner, Frank Nelson, and others he knew cheated on their wives. He and Suzanne had never had any problems in that area, but it was exciting to be with someone new. He couldn't remember the last time he'd felt so invigorated. All female bodies had the same parts, but he'd long grown accustomed to everything about Suzanne's. Micheline's body, on the other hand, was new and exciting to him. She was pretty down there, too. It amazed him that she'd colored her pubic hair to match the honey blond hair of her head, a startling discovery he'd first made on Sunday as he licked the whipped cream she'd sprayed on herself.

She also knew how to please a man. Still, she was a schemer, and Brad could readily understand why Errol was through with her. Most of the reason for his dissatisfaction with Suzanne stemmed from precisely that type of behavior.

He'd felt more than a little guilty since reading the note Suzanne sent with the fruit arrangement. Just because it hadn't been written in her own hand didn't diminish its meaning. For a few minutes he even considered asking Micheline to leave. He quickly changed his mind, deciding that he deserved this reward after all Suzanne had put him through.

He'd just never tell her about it.

Micheline went into the adjoining bathroom and bent over the sink. He knew she was washing his cream off her face. That had been quite an explosion. Good thing he always worn a condom all the times they had intercourse, or else his children would be having a baby brother or sister . . . and he'd surely find himself out of a wife when Suzanne found out.

Micheline came back and climbed into bed next to him, on her stomach. He rested his palm on her beautifully round butt and gave it a little squeeze. "I've really enjoyed your company this week, Micheline."

"I've had a wonderful time. I'm so glad I came."

"I'm glad you came, too," Brad replied. She rolled over on her side, and he stretched an arm over her shoulder. With a grin, he said, "I'll tell you something, Micheline. I always had a feeling about you, from the first time we met."

"Well, isn't it good that you invited me up here so you could find out for certain," she replied brightly. She looked at him expectantly. "So, what happens now?"

Brad felt a queasiness in his gut and remembered hearing his single colleagues talk about getting that very feeling when the women in their lives started with the where-is-the-relationship-going line of questioning. "Uh . . . you mean, after we get back to Jacksonville?"

"Yes."

Damn. She sounded like she expected the affair to continue. He decided to tailor his response around the deliberate misinterpretation of her question. Patting her shoulder, he said, "I think I know what you're worried about, but it's all right, Micheline. Your secret's safe with me. I have a lot to lose myself if Suzanne finds out. And if both of us keep our mouths shut, there's no reason for either Suzanne or Errol to ever know."

He felt her body stiffen beneath his palm. "That's fine, Brad," she said, "but it doesn't really answer my question, does it? Have you thought about how we'll manage to see each other at home?"

"How we'll see each other?" Brad echoed. "Well, Micheline, I'm flattered, but I never intended for this to continue after we go home, and I didn't think you did, either. It's just too risky."

She sat up abruptly, covering her breasts with the top sheet, and arched a well-shaped eyebrow. "You didn't seem to be too concerned about the risk when you invited me up here to join you."

Brad followed her lead and sat up himself. "It was a spur-of-the-moment idea. Like I said, Micheline, I'd been getting signals from you ever since we were introduced that this is what you wanted. When you said you'd be in Boston . . ." He trailed off. Then he decided to challenge her. "Can you look at me now and deny that you were flirting with me?"

"No. And you obviously thought I was the one-night stand type," she said.

He struggled to fight off his rising panic. He couldn't let her see, or even sense, his fear. Keeping his voice even, he said, "As far as I know, you've been the perfect wife to Errol. And yes, I thought you were just looking for a quick fling. I'm sorry if I misread you."

"Oh, no you don't," she spat out, angrily shaking her head. "You're not going to dismiss *me* with that let's-still-be-friends line. Maybe your other women fell for that, but *I'm* not about to."

Brad discreetly pulled on his pants and stood, hands in his pockets. He felt more authoritative on his feet. "Micheline. You might not believe this, but I'm not in the habit of returning any flirtations. I don't want to sound like an egomaniac, but plenty of women have tried to tempt me. I've been married to Suzanne for sixteen years, and this is the first time I've strayed."

She stared at him incredulously. "And *that's* supposed to make me feel better?" Her voice took on a mimicking quality. "'Gee, baby, as many chances as I've had to cheat on my wife in sixteen years, you're the only one who was actually able to get me to do it.'"

Brad realized belatedly how ridiculous his statement had sounded. He also realized he was sitting on a potential powder keg, and if he didn't handle it exactly the right way, it was going to blow up in his face.

He tried once more. "What exactly is it you want from me, Micheline? I mean, consider my position. I see your husband two or three times every week. Many times we hit the links together."

"Again, Brad, I repeat, you didn't seem too concerned about that when you invited me to come and spend the week with you."

Once again Brad realized his error too late. He could hardly tell Micheline that his being privy to Errol's plans to unload her had heavily influenced his decision to indulge in a quick affair. "All right, then I'll repeat my question. What exactly do you want from me? What is it you expect to happen between us?"

Micheline groped around for her nightgown and, her back to him, pulled it over her head. She got up and gracefully lowered herself into the salon chair, crossing her legs at the ankles in a most ladylike fashion, her arms resting on the arms of the chair. "Brad, from what I've observed of you and Suzanne together, you're not the cheating type, and of course you just said that yourself. But if you're truly happy being married to Suzanne, then *she'd* be the one here with you now, not me. I'm everything she's not. Don't you think I know that?"

He simply stared at her, and she continued. "Sure, maybe you've got a satisfying sex life. But can you actually sit down and have an intelligent conversation with her, like you can with me? And she's no better in bed than I am, I can guarantee you that."

Brad chuckled at that, in spite of his sense of foreboding. Only a woman who'd been around the track for more laps than it took to run the Indy 500 could speak with such authority, although Micheline certainly didn't *look* like she had all that mileage on her. He did see a hard edge to her now that hadn't been apparent before. This was a woman who didn't take losing well. That could definitely mean bad news for him. "Maybe you're right, Micheline," he conceded. "But the fact is, I'm not ready to give up on Suzanne. We've got a lot of years invested in our relationship. Just because there may be a little discord doesn't mean it's time to end it."

"So you're saying you don't want her to find out about us."

She sounded too calm, he thought. He'd better subtly remind her that she had as much to lose as he did—she didn't, of course, but she didn't know about Errol's plans like he did. "No, I don't . . . and I wouldn't want Errol to find out, either."

"We'll just see about that." She rose from the chair and headed for her suitcase in a corner of the room, removed a fresh outfit, and headed for the bathroom. Brad knew she wanted him to stop her, to promise her anything so she'd keep her mouth shut. The little witch thought she could blackmail him. He had to nip that right now.

"I said I wouldn't *want* them to find out, Micheline," he said to her retreating back. "But if they do, they'll have to take their knocks just like anybody else. So don't think for a minute that you can hold the threat of exposure over my head to manipulate me."

She replied by disappearing inside the bathroom and slamming the door behind her. Brad hoped that meant she was leaving. It was already Friday, and after the exchange they'd just had, having her stay on another day and a half would be most unpleasant. He knew he ought to ask her where she was going, to try to show some kind of concern. But he didn't, for two reasons. First, Micheline was a big girl. She knew how to take care of herself.

And secondly, he just didn't care.

Chapter 34

Flo beamed when Gregory praised the meal she made. "Mom, that was a great dinner," he said with admiration. "You'll have to show Kenya how you make your macaroni and cheese. It's still the best I've ever had."

"I'll be happy to," Flo replied. Then she yawned. "Oh, excuse me. I seem to be feeling unnaturally tired today."

"Why don't you go to bed early tonight?" Ernie suggested. "I'm sure Kenya won't mind cleaning the kitchen."

Kenya's eyebrows shot up, her face wearing a *Who, me?* expression. Then she gasped and threw a questioning look at Gregory. Flo wanted to giggle. She suspected her son had kicked his lazy wife under the table before she could make an excuse.

"I think that's a great idea," Gregory said. "In fact, I think it's reasonable for Kenya to clean the kitchen every night after dinner."

"But my doctor wants me to take it easy, Gregory," Kenya said sweetly. "You wouldn't want anything to happen to the baby because I was working too hard, would you?"

"Nobody's asking you to dig a ditch, Kenya," Gregory replied easily. "Loading some plates, glasses, and silverware into the dishwasher will hardly be too much for you. You make it sound as if your doctor doesn't want you to move around at all."

"I have to agree," Ernie contributed. "You do have to take care of yourself, Kenya, but you also need a certain amount of exercise. You don't want to end up like one of those women who blows up like a balloon after having a baby."

"I'll *never* be fat," Kenya declared.

Flo smiled. She, too, had regained her figure within months of giving birth to Gregory. Kenya didn't realize that as she got older her metabolism was going to slow down. If the way she ate was any indication, the minute that happened she'd shoot up to over two hundred pounds.

Of course, by that time Gregory would be long gone.

Flo had put in a load of laundry before she made dinner, and as her last act of the evening she emptied the dryer and folded the clothes. She frowned at an unfamiliar pair of men's boxers—Ernie wore briefs—then realized they had to belong to Gregory. Kenya had probably left the navy boxers behind in the dryer, and they were so dark that Flo hadn't noticed they were there.

She knocked on the door to Gregory's bedroom. "It's Mama."

He opened the door almost immediately. Flo's eyes automatically went to the scene inside. The bed was unmade and rumpled. Clothes were strewn everywhere; she couldn't tell if they were clean or dirty. An ironing board sat in a corner, and Flo guessed it hadn't been collapsed since Kenya took up residence. A pile of dirty clothes covered the carpet.

"Um . . . I was just straightening up, Mama."

"I think you've got enough to do. Cleaning up should be Kenya's job."

Gregory looked so embarrassed that Flo instantly regretted having said anything. "She doesn't do things like you do, Mama."

"No, she doesn't." Flo held out the boxers. "These are yours. They were left in the dryer."

"Oh. Thanks, Mama."

Flo sighed. "I'm so sorry, son. I really applaud you for coping with this as well as you have."

"It's all right. In two more months the baby will be here. I'm going to file right after New Year's."

"Something tells me you're counting the days," she said with a weak smile. "Try not to worry. It will pass quickly."

Flo went back to the laundry room and retrieved her neatly folded laundry, carrying it to her bedroom. She ran a bath in the sculpted oversized tub while she put the clothes away. She'd relax with a book before going to bed.

As she soaked in the tub, she found herself unable to concentrate on her novel. The story was certainly a good one, but Flo's worries about Gregory took precedence over fiction. Her son had paid a terrible price for legitimizing his baby. Thank God it would only last for a few more months.

The next few months would be difficult for her and Ernie as well. Flo dreaded Thanksgiving dinner. That dreadful brother of Kenya's! She'd never seen anyone eat so much as Derrick Hall. On the Fourth of July he must have put away an entire rack of ribs. Flo pictured him wearing a one-shouldered caveman outfit chowing down on brontosaurus meat. If that hadn't been bad enough, he'd washed it down with a third of a bottle of Ernie's good Grey Goose. Ernie had put out the real bottle—not the bottle that he filled with much cheaper Smirnoff—because they both thought Brad Betancourt was coming, and Ernie feared Brad's sophisticated palate would be able to tell the difference. Flo didn't mind putting on a little for Brad and Suzanne, but certainly not for Derrick.

She and Ernie hadn't been in town for Labor Day. They'd decided against hosting a party for their silver anniversary; they both agreed that it would be foolish to spend all that money on catering if Brad wasn't going to come. Besides, with Suzanne now working with Paula Haines, the possibility existed that she might attend as the caterer rather than a guest. Instead of a party, she and Ernie celebrated their anniversary with an extended, romantic weekend up in Charleston. The trip gave them the perfect excuse not to have to entertain the Halls on the holiday, but there'd be no such reprieve for Thanksgiving or Christmas—unless, of course, the baby came a week after Kenya's due date of the seventeenth.

Flo doubted that would happen. Kenya hadn't cooperated with any of them so far. It made little sense to hope anything would change.

Flo frowned as she struggled to free the corner of her blouse caught in her zipper. Thank heavens the ladies' room was empty. A classic R&B act was performing on the stage of the Ritz Theatre. She and Ernie enjoyed coming here. Not only had they admired most of the acts they booked during their youth, but the venue was small enough that the audience could clearly see the faces of the performers, whom they could mingle with after the show. The Ritz had been the center of black Jacksonville entertainment during the time of segregation and had been restored and modernized in recent years.

But what was she going to do if she couldn't get her zipper unstuck? She couldn't pull her blouse out of her pants; it had been tucked in and the bottom of it was all wrinkled. And she certainly couldn't stay in this stall all night. Ernie would start to wonder if she'd been attacked or something. Then again, maybe not. He was sitting with another couple at a table for four in the lounge area near the bar, having a drink and making conversation. Once Ernie got to talking, especially to strangers, he lost track of everything.

Flo heard voices and knew someone else had come in. Good, maybe they could help her get her blouse unstuck. She had her hand on the latch of the stall to unlock the door when she heard laughter and whispers.

"I'm so glad you came in with me," a voice said in a husky whisper.

"Well, you *did* ask me to," said a second voice, equally softly. "I got the feeling you wanted to tell me something away from the guys."

"And you were right. Hold on to your hat, girl. I've got the scoop of the century for you."

"What?"

"It's about Brad and Suzanne."

Flo covered her mouth to hold back her gasp. How many couples named Brad and Suzanne could there be in Jacksonville? She hadn't seen any of their neighbors here tonight, and the whispers disguised the voices.

"What about them?"

"I heard he's messing around on her with that girl from the party."

A snort. "Don't tell me. The one he was dancing with. She had on that backless dress."

"That's the one!"

"I guess her own man isn't good enough for her. I can't imagine why. He's a good-looking devil, and he seemed really nice when Ben and I talked to him."

Flo pressed her palm against her mouth to keep any sound from escaping. "Ben and I" told her the voice belonged to Stacy Prince, one of the residents of Villa St. John.

"If I were fifteen years younger—and didn't have Ben, of course," Stacy continued, "I'd be all over him."

"Same here with Michael."

That told Flo the other voice belonged to Kim Gillespie, her next-door neighbor, who was one of Lisa's closest friends.

"Well, I say good for Brad," Stacey said. "I can't believe he gave up a nice girl like Lisa for that snotty Suzanne. I can't stand her. She acts like we're all a bunch of charity cases or something. Well, Ben and I might not make three hundred K between us like Brad probably does by himself, but we're hardly poverty-stricken. I get mad every time I think of how surprised she acted when I told her Ben and I were going to

Jamaica for a week. 'Oh, you must have family there,' she actually said to me. Hmph. Like *she's* the only one who can afford to stay in a hotel."

"I know what you mean," Kim agreed. "Lisa would never say anything like that. She's never even pointed out that her and Darrell's house is bigger than Suzanne's, even if it doesn't have all those bells and whistles."

"Hmph. I'd expect Suzanne to start adding on if she knew that." The two of them giggled, and then one of them said, "We'd better get back out front. They're going to open the doors to the auditorium at any minute."

It took Flo a few more minutes to finally unhook her blouse. By the time she returned to the lobby, Ernie was waiting for her outside the auditorium doors. "Hurry up," he said. "I've got our jackets holding our seats. They're going to be starting any minute."

She knew then she would have to wait until after the show to tell him about what she'd heard.

But after the show, Ernie wanted to stick around. The lounge area became alive again, becoming clublike with people milling about, standing in groups or sitting at tables. Bartenders scurried to fill drink orders and a deejay spun dance tunes. A table had been set up in one corner from which the performers sold and autographed self-published CDs and posed for pictures with admirers. Flo was grateful that the tables only held four, meaning they were unable to sit with Kim and Stacy and their husbands.

"It was nice seeing Michael and Ben, wasn't it?" Ernie remarked when they were in the car. "I didn't see either of them last week, so I didn't know they planned on being here tonight."

"Yes, it was a nice surprise. Um . . . when did you first see them?"

"They walked past the table before the show on their way

to the bar, so of course I waved to them. I would have said hello, but I was talking to the people sitting with us. I didn't get a chance to talk to them until after the show, though."

"So they didn't know I was in the ladies' room when they arrived."

Ernie looked at her strangely. "That's not exactly the type of thing a person goes around broadcasting, Flo."

"Well, I have a reason for asking. Remember I told you about the zipper trouble I was having?"

"Of course. I remember thinking you must have fallen in. I was about to ask Joanne to go in and make sure you were all right."

"Well, while I was in the stall trying to unhook my blouse, Kim and Stacy came in and started gossiping about Brad and Suzanne."

"Really? What'd they say?"

"They said Brad's having an affair."

"Yeah? Which one of them said that?"

"Kim. She must have gotten it from Lisa."

"So who's Brad sticking it to?" Ernie asked eagerly.

"That young girl from the party. She had on a white dress cut real low in the back."

"Oh, yeah. I remember her. I'll say this much for him. He's got good taste."

Flo let out an annoyed huff. "You know, Ernie, the way you admire all these other women, sometimes I think maybe you ought to be with one of them," she said, her voice trembling a little.

"Come on, Flo. Sure, I may *look,* but that's all I do. I'm married. I ain't dead. Besides, you know you're my queen."

Mollified, she said, "The question is, what do I do about what I know? I hate to think of Kim and Stacy laughing behind Suzanne's back. Stacy made no secret that she doesn't like Suzanne, and of course Kim is in Lisa's camp. They're both jealous of her, you know."

"I don't doubt it. But, Flo, you need to stay out of this."

"How can I do that, Ernie? Suzanne's my friend."

"Trust me. You don't want to get involved. These things have a way of always turning nasty. You're really in a lose-lose situation. If you tell her, she'll be mad. If she finds out you knew about it, she'll be mad, too. So don't let on you know. Chances are she won't find out you do."

Chapter 35

Suzanne laced up her running shoes. She hadn't realized how much she'd missed Flo until Flo called to see if she wanted to go walking. They used to walk all over the neighborhood a couple of times a week before Flo said she couldn't do it anymore because of the responsibilities of her new job. Suzanne knew the real reason. Lisa and Kim had told her at a social gathering at the Canfields' that Ernie had been downsized and both he and Flo appeared to be working two jobs, as well as having taken in a roomer. Lisa and Kim both snickered about the Hickmans' feeble efforts to cover their situation, but Suzanne felt bad for Flo. When she mentioned it to Brad, he advised her to leave it alone and just follow Flo's lead. "She's probably too embarrassed to admit she can't afford to go shopping or have lunch with you anymore."

Suzanne knew Brad shed no tears over the Hickmans' plight. He couldn't stand Ernie and flatly refused to participate in anything that involved Flo and Ernie as a couple. He always cautioned Suzanne against confiding any of their personal business to Flo as well. What was it Brad had said? "They call it comeuppance. After all that bragging they did about how they could afford this and they could afford that, it was bound to happen."

Her heart felt heavy as it occurred to her that now she was getting her own comeuppance. How many times had she attempted to make people envious of her . . . her handsome, successful, generous husband . . . her beautiful home . . . her adorable children . . . the snazzy sports car and the cool Cadillac SUV she alternated driving with Brad?

Suzanne quickly put that thought aside. Instead she told herself it would be good if she and Flo could pick up their friendship. Flo gave her something she really needed, the sense that she would absolutely love to be in Suzanne's shoes, to live the way Suzanne did. Suzanne had never gotten the feeling that Paula envied her material things, just the fact that she had a husband who loved her. Of course, Paula had been a valuable friend in other ways. No way would Flo ever replace Paula, who was Suzanne's closest confidante outside of her mother. Suzanne learned quite a bit from Paula, while Flo simply reinforced how *not* to act.

As had been their habit, Flo drove around the corner to Suzanne's, and they set off on foot, first passing Lisa's house, heading for the streets beyond the cul-de-sac, avoiding Villa St. John by mutual yet silent agreement. For Suzanne, it seemed like old times, but as they were returning to her house, Flo dropped a bombshell.

"Suzanne, there's something I want to tell you," Flo said tentatively. "I'm just not sure how to go about it."

Suzanne couldn't imagine what Flo was getting at. "Well, if you've got something on your mind, of course you can tell me." She smiled at Flo warmly. "We're practically related now."

"It's about Brad."

Her body went rigid. This was supposed to be some embarrassing problem Flo was having, not about *her* husband. "What about Brad?" she asked tightly.

"Well, I heard something. Ernie told me not to say anything, but the more I think about it, the more I just can't keep silent about it. The word going around is that he's having an affair with that girl who was at your party."

Suzanne swallowed hard. She felt as if she'd just been socked in the stomach. How on earth did word of Brad's affair reach Flo? Unless Brad mentioned it to Darrell, who mentioned it to Lisa, whose best friend was Flo's next-door neighbor, Kim Gillespie.

Oh, my God. Everybody and their mama knows Brad cheated on me with Micheline.

She knew she had to save face. She had to act like she wasn't in the least disturbed by this bombshell. Having Flo pity her would be more than she could bear. "That's just gossip, Flo," she said calmly. "I know you must be talking about Kim Gillespie as the one who's doing all the talking. She's Lisa's best friend, and like Lisa, she smiles in my face and talks about me behind my back. Both of them are just jealous because Brad and I live the way we do."

Part of Suzanne did believe that. But what Flo didn't know, and would never know, was the daily battle she'd fought since Brad had come home to act as though she had no knowledge of Brad's shenanigans with Micheline. Her anguish aside, things had actually been pretty good between them since his return. No signs remained of the strain in their relationship. Suzanne had even tried to convince herself that Micheline had somehow turned Brad off that week she spent with him. She knew she'd never be able to forget Brad's cheating on her, but if she tried really hard, eventually she might succeed in putting it away in a compartment of her brain.

"Oh. I didn't think of that possibility," Flo said, looking sheepish. "So everything's okay with you and Brad?"

"Of course. People who can't stand to see other people happy like to read things into other people's actions. Kim and Lisa knew about Brad's fishing trip and automatically assumed he had some slut with him. No one but me knows how hard Brad's been working lately. He's also worried about Paige, you know, because of Gregory marrying Kenya." Suzanne sucked her teeth. "It's a shame that some people don't have anything else to do with their time except spread malicious stories."

"I'm sorry, Suzanne. Now I'm sorry I even repeated it. Not

that I said anything to anyone other than you," Flo quickly added.

"Don't be sorry, Flo. If anything, I'm glad to know what people are saying. I'll be sure to let Brad know how his ex-wife is spreading lies about us. He'll put a stop to it." Her voice rang with confidence, but Suzanne wasn't sure if she should say anything to Brad or keep quiet.

She sought advice from the only person she completely trusted with the knowledge of Brad's affair, her mother. But to her surprise, Arlene was unable to help.

"I'm sorry, Suzanne, but I have a date tonight."

"A date? On a weeknight? Who with?"

"Calvin Braxton's father, Harry. He's back in town for an extended visit. He's a retired judge, you know. He does some freelance work as a mediator. He's here for three weeks this time, and he plans to spend much of the winter here, so I should be seeing him often."

"Oh, how nice."

"He'll be here any minute. I'm so sorry I can't take time to listen to your problem, but I'm not quite ready."

"That's all right, Mom. You go out and have a good time. I'll figure it out."

Suzanne and Brad sat alone at the dinner table after Bradley and Lauren had been excused. Suzanne had finished eating, but she was finishing up her glass of Merlot, and Brad had asked for a second helping of mashed potatoes and another biscuit to have with his meat loaf, the one dish she had always been able to prepare that he truly loved.

When she returned to the table after adding more food to his plate, she sat not in her usual chair opposite him, but in a side chair, which put her closer. He startled her when, in the midst of quiet conversation, he suddenly took her hand and leaned in for a quick kiss. At that moment Suzanne made up her mind. She would follow that old edict: *If it ain't broke, don't fix it.* Confronting Brad about his . . . *cavorting* with Micheline would only turn their relations sour. Flo certainly would have no way of knowing whether she'd spoken to him about the gossip.

The only thing that left a bad taste in Suzanne's mouth was knowing that Lisa, Kim, and probably Stacy Prince all knew Brad had cheated on her. How could she ever live that down? She couldn't all of a sudden refuse to go to any social events that included any of them without explaining why, and she could think of no explanation that would pass muster.

She wondered if Brad had actually told Darrell Canfield that he'd slept with Micheline. It didn't seem like something Brad would say; he was a firm believer in keeping his personal business private. Still, how else would Lisa have known if her husband hadn't told her, and how would Darrell have known if Brad hadn't told *him?* All she could do was put her curiosity aside and hold her head up high when she was around the Canfields. Look at all the women in the spotlight who'd been publicly humiliated by their husbands. If that Kathie Lee Gifford had swallowed her pride and reconciled with her husband after the entire country knew he'd dicked around on her, surely she could do the same thing. Let Lisa and her cronies talk about her. They'd do that anyway.

The bottom line was that unless she was willing to confront Brad, this would always remain a mystery to her. Suzanne had the uneasy feeling that she was about to find out that not knowing could be the worst torture of all.

Arlene had planned on enjoying her day off. She'd spent part of the morning fixing up the house, and she'd washed and set her hair. The afternoon was supposed to be devoted to freshening her manicure and taking a long soak in the tub in preparation for her dinner tonight with Harry. Instead Kenya had shown up unexpectedly, and she listened wearily to her daughter's complaints.

"Mama, it's not fair. Gregory's got me cleaning up the

kitchen every single night. And if that's not bad enough, Miss Flo always shows up as I'm finishing to tell me what I forgot to do. She'll say the sink needs to be cleaned out after I rinse the dishes, that the countertops need to be sprayed down and not just wiped off, and that she can see the stove still has a coating of grease on it."

"Those are all valid points, if you ask me. Kenya, I taught you how to clean a kitchen. Why aren't you doing a thorough job? You know how immaculate Flo keeps her house."

"Mama, I'm six months pregnant," she replied indignantly.

"When I was six months pregnant with you, I worked right up to the day my labor started. Plus I went home and took care of Suzanne, Derrick, and Matthew."

Kenya's pout told her she'd hoped for a different reaction. "I wish we could afford to get our own place."

"And then you'd have even more work to do. Kenya," Arlene said sternly. "I hope this isn't an example of how you've been behaving. This is no way to hold on to Gregory. If you don't keep a clean house, you won't be going anywhere with him. He'll dump you like hazardous waste."

"He won't dump me. I'm having his baby."

Arlene lowered her chin to her chest and gazed at her daughter. "Oh, you don't think so?"

"Of course not. I'm the mother of his child."

"Kenya," Arlene said, not bothering to attempt to conceal her exasperation. "Men leave the mothers of their babies every day. Your own daddy didn't even stick around until *you* were born."

"This is different. I'm not some baby mama. I'm his wife. Gregory already loves the baby. We're a package deal."

Arlene nodded knowingly. "Oh, I get it. You think you can hold the baby over Gregory's head, and deny him visitation. Sweetheart, you might not be a baby mama, but Gregory definitely isn't your typical baby daddy. He'd never stand for that, so don't mix him up with Jojo from the corner. He'll get a lawyer and have you charged with—well, whatever that type of behavior is called. Ignoring a court order, or something."

"But, Mama—"

Arlene stood. "But, Mama, nothing. Kenya, you don't have a whole lot of time left. The baby is due in less than three months. If you've got the strength to walk over here from Flo's house, you should be able to clean that kitchen every night until it sparkles. Now, I'm sorry, I can't listen to any more of your whining. I've got a shot at the big time myself, and I have to get ready."

"You going out with that judge again?"

"Damn right. And I'm not going to blow it, like you seem to be doing."

Chapter 36

Weeks later, when Suzanne looked through her peephole and recognized Micheline's profile, she knew it could only mean bad news. For a moment she considered not answering the door, but she reasoned that Micheline would only come back, and she couldn't hide from her forever.

She took a few moments to relax the muscles of her face, which had suddenly become tense. She didn't want Micheline to see her ruffled. And she certainly couldn't let on that she knew about those days—and nights—Micheline had spent with Brad in Maine.

She unlocked and opened the door wearing a big smile. "Micheline! This is a surprise."

"Hello, Suzanne." Micheline looked uncomfortable. "I hoped you had a few minutes. There's something I need to talk to you about. I hope this isn't a bad time."

"No, of course not." She opened the door fully. "Won't you come in?" Suzanne kept a gracious demeanor, but for a few seconds while her back was turned to Micheline as she closed the front door, she chewed on her bottom lip. Everything had been going beautifully between her and Brad. *What could Micheline possibly want after all this time?*

Suzanne invited Micheline to sit in the formal living room on the left of the entry hall. "Can I offer you a cup of coffee?" she asked in a pleasant tone that belied her frantic worry.

"No, thank you." Micheline took a seat in one of the twin armless chairs, and Suzanne sat in a corner of the plump sofa. "Well, Micheline, you certainly seem upset about something."

"I am. I don't know exactly how to tell you this, Suzanne."

Suzanne's left hand, which had been resting on her knee, suddenly tightened. Micheline's demure posture, her legs crossed at the ankles, was a far cry from the stance she'd likely taken in Maine with Brad. Suzanne's thumb pressed into her flesh at a mental flash of a naked Micheline straddling Brad, or lying spread-eagle beneath him. She let up only when she noticed the skin surrounding the thumb had turned pale.

Micheline seemed to be at a loss for words. "Go on," Suzanne said calmly.

"All right. I guess it's easier if I just come out with it. I was talking with Brad down at the club last month, and I mentioned I was going up to Boston for a family wedding. He said he would be up in New England on a fishing trip at the same time."

"Yes, that's right. He was there about six weeks ago." No way would Suzanne let on that she knew Brad's fishing trip had been hastily arranged *after* he set up a rendezvous with Micheline. "He tries to get up there by himself at least once a year just to unwind." That was a blatant lie, but Micheline had no way of knowing that.

"Well, I'm afraid he had a little more than unwinding on his mind this time, Suzanne." Micheline sighed. "To get straight to the heart of it, he invited me to join him up there."

Suzanne didn't have to fake her distress. Micheline had actually come here to confess her affair with Brad. No longer could Suzanne pretend to be in the dark. Micheline had just forced her hand. She'd have to take action.

But first she had to pretend to be shocked. "He did *what?*"

"I'm afraid it's true. And what's more, I went."

Given the circumstances, incredulity came easily to Suzanne.

"You're sitting here, in *my* house, telling me you slept with my husband?"

"I'm sorry. I know it comes as a terrible shock—"

"A shock you couldn't wait to tell me about, apparently." That wasn't really true—nearly a month and a half had passed since Brad's trip—but in her need to lash out, Suzanne didn't care if she made sense or not.

Fortunately, Micheline didn't seem to notice. "This isn't easy for me, Suzanne."

"I think it's a lot easier than you're letting on." Suzanne jumped to her feet. "What exactly was your point in coming here today, Micheline? You felt I should know what my husband was doing behind my back? You know, you've been flirting with Brad from the very beginning. Do you think I believe it was an accident the way your blouse conveniently fell open when you poured him a beer?" Anger poured into her at the memory of the first time she'd laid eyes on this slimeball. "I knew right then you were a slinky bitch who had the nerve to flirt with another man when her own husband is maybe five feet away."

Micheline, too, stood up. "So I'm a bitch, am I? Well, you must be a piece of work yourself, because your husband sure couldn't wait to get into my panties. If you were keeping him happy, he wouldn't have needed to look elsewhere."

"I want you to get the fuck out of my house, right now." Then Suzanne quickly changed her mind. "No. Let me tell you something first. There's nothing wrong with my marriage. My husband is a flesh-and-blood man, and he did what any red-blooded man would do when a woman practically comes out and says she'll let him fuck her if he wants to. *That's* why you're here, isn't it, Micheline?" Her tone became taunting. "You thought you were going to take Brad away from me. You figured that once he got a taste of you, he was going to forget all about me, put me and my children out to pasture and move you in." Micheline gasped, and Suzanne surmised she'd hit upon the truth. "And when he refused, told you it was a one-time deal, you kept trying. I'll bet you chased after him ever since you've been back, trying to get him to change his mind. And when that didn't work, you decided to pay me a social call and make sure I knew all about it. You're hoping you'll make me so angry that I'll walk out on him, and that you can take over." She stopped to collect her thoughts as well as catch her breath, and she moved to stand face-to-face with Micheline before continuing. "Well, part of your plan worked. Right now I *am* very angry with my husband, but even with that, part of me understands why he did what he did. What would *I* do if a good-looking man kept flirting with me, let it be known that he'd like to get me into bed? I'd probably resist, but women are more emotional. Men don't mind having meaningless sex that they can forget about as soon as they bust a nut."

Micheline's eyes narrowed into slits. "You're going to be sorry you said that."

"I'm sure you're *already* sorry you slept with my husband, now that you know it didn't mean a thing. He's probably forgotten all about it by now, and you, too."

"You'd like to think so, wouldn't you?"

Suzanne didn't like the smug smile on Micheline's face. She looked like someone who had something else up her sleeve.

"Sure," Micheline continued, "I think Brad would be better off with me than with you. You're about as intellectually stimulating as my pinky toe. But if Brad wants to stick with you, that's his problem. I'm glad to hear everything's so hunky dory with the two of you. Maybe you'll even want to raise my baby."

Suzanne's breath caught in her throat, and for a moment she thought her knees might give out. "Baby?" she whispered.

"That's right," Micheline said smugly. "Your husband managed to do in a few days what mine hasn't been able to do in three years . . . knock me up."

Suzanne's eyes flashed. "Who says it isn't Errol's baby?"

"I think the odds are pretty much against that. Like I said, it's been three years. I think my husband's been shooting off a lot of blanks." Micheline flashed a smile. "So you see, Suzanne, I'm not able to just disappear and allow you to forget about my little escapade with your husband. There's going to be a living, breathing reminder of those unforgettable nights in Maine. And I thought that you, as wife of my baby daddy, ought to be among the first to hear the news." She turned and headed for the front door.

"Micheline, wait!" Suzanne followed her to the foyer. "I don't believe you," she said, shaking her head. "All right, so maybe you did have an affair with Brad." She knew there was no point denying it. "But he would have used protection. Are you forgetting he's a doctor? He knows the risks." Suzanne still remembered how, at the onset of their sex life so many years ago, he had insisted they both be tested for STDs before discarding the condoms. If he'd been that careful with her, he never would have had unprotected sex with Micheline. "Not just of pregnancy and having you hold him hostage financially," Suzanne said, "but of catching something from you, since you've obviously *been around*."

"I'm going to let that pass," Micheline said calmly, "simply because I know you're upset at learning all this. Or at least I'd *imagine* that's how you feel. No man has ever cheated on me, not my husband and not my boyfriends before I was married." She sighed lightly. "They knew a good thing when they saw it."

Suzanne grunted. "I guess so. *Everybody's* pussy lips can't blow out the tune to *Let's Get It On*."

Micheline glared at her. "For your information, you were correct. Brad did use protection," she confirmed. "But sometimes it fails, and I'm as fertile as they come. I've already had one pregnancy because of a torn condom. And the father brought home the little bundle of joy for his wife to raise. I'll bet she thinks about me every time she looks at her." She turned and left.

Micheline stepped lightly to her Sebring parked in the driveway. Suzanne would never know how closely she'd hit upon the truth. She *had* contacted Brad several times since they'd returned to Jacksonville to ask if he wanted to resume their affair. She'd become consumed with the need for revenge when he repeatedly refused. She hadn't done all this planning and scheming just for a few rolls in the hay. Finally she decided to make good on her threat to tell Suzanne. Tonight she'd tell Errol about it, too. She hoped he kicked Brad's ass.

She'd leave out the part about being pregnant. That lie came out of her mouth on the spur of the moment. For a minute there it almost looked like Suzanne would get the best of her, but she'd recovered in time to come back with that doozy. Why not? Enough time had passed since her time with Brad for it to be a possibility. And that gave her the perfect reason for waiting so long. Even Brad would fall for that rather than think she'd held off because her continued efforts to get him to give up Suzanne for her had been unsuccessful.

How perfect it would have been if she really *had* gotten pregnant. If she'd thought of it she would've brought some pins and stuck them in Brad's supply of condoms. Then she'd really have something to work with. Surely it would have been the kiss of death for Brad's marriage if he'd gotten her pregnant. Only Norell Bellamy was a big enough fool to raise the baby her husband had while cheating on her.

Oh, well. No point in dreaming. It might not be true, but it would certainly give Suzanne a hell of a lot to worry about.

Suzanne latched the door, then collapsed against it. Tears of remorse ran down her cheeks. It was nearly time for her soap opera, but who needed *Facades*? She was in the midst of her very own drama. This was real . . . and so was her pain.

Chapter 37

Suzanne retired to her bedroom before Brad arrived home. Lauren would get dinner on the table.

In the privacy of her bedroom she allowed herself the luxury of crying, but they weren't long, drawn-out, body-racking sobs. Instead they were slow tears, cold, wet, and steady.

Her thoughts went to Jean Nelson, living in her little pretend world where everything was fine, conveniently looking the other way when it came to her husband's multiple indiscretions. How many times had Suzanne scoffed at Jean for ignoring how Frank made a fool of her? How many times had Suzanne said she'd *never* put up with that?

But now that she was being forced to confront the issue of Brad's infidelity, she wasn't so sure. What would she do without Brad as her husband? She'd have to find another place to live . . . an apartment somewhere. She wasn't making much money working with Paula; it was more like an internship. Nor was it full-time. Even though Brad would have to pay her alimony, it would probably be a supplement, not an actual income. Bradley and Lauren weren't little children anymore; there was no way she could justify continuing to be a stay-at-home mom and let Brad pick up the tab. She'd have to get some kind of a job, probably as a saleswoman or an office clerk.

No doubt about it, her future as a divorced woman looked

pretty dismal, and it would probably last the rest of her life. She was past forty, and available men were scarcer than ever. It was probably even worse for Jean, who was in her mid fifties. Was that why she chose to pretend Frank wasn't cheating on her? Did she prefer spending time with Frank when he wasn't with his girlfriends to being alone for the rest of her life?

Suzanne, lying on her side with her face against the pillow, didn't move when she heard the bedroom door open. She felt the slight downward pressure on the mattress when Brad sat on the edge of the bed, then felt his palm lightly touch her shoulder. His soft words vibrated against her ear, his breath warm and his tone intimate. "Suzie Q? Don't you feel well?"

"No." Her voice came out muffled by the pillow.

"What's wrong?"

She flipped over, noting the shock on his face at the sight of her tear-stained face. "Everything."

"You've been crying. Talk to me, Suzanne. What happened to upset you?"

"Micheline Trent came here this afternoon." She felt his hand on her shoulder turn to stone. "She told me all about how she spent her summer vacation. Of course, you already know that, since you were there."

He sighed. "Suzanne . . . I'm sorry."

"Well, *that* fixes everything, doesn't it?"

"I deserved that," he said, staring at the wall.

"How *could* you, Brad? The whole time—fishing, my ass."

"I did go fishing, Suzanne. Every day."

"I guess you did. That's usually when you called me, when you were out on the lake by yourself. And then you went back to *her*." A sob escaped from her throat. "I don't understand, Brad. We've been so close since you've been back."

He caressed her hand. "Have you considered it's because that time I spent with Micheline made me realize how much I love *you?*"

A furious Suzanne sat up and looked at him through un-forgiving eyes. "So maybe I should go out and spend a week with another man to remind me how much I love *you*, huh, Brad? Is that how it works?"

"No, of course not. But it wasn't all—well, I got to spend a lot of time alone. A fishing boat is a great place to think, and I did a lot of that. One of the things I thought about was my marriage to Lisa. We were young when we got married, and we both had so much on our plates—working, going to school, studying. And the marriage ended because I felt Lisa was unwilling to be a partner. Instead she started making all the household decisions on her own. That wasn't what I wanted marriage to be. We argued about it. Eventually we broke up."

"I knew all that, Brad." The last thing Suzanne wanted to hear about was Brad's marriage to Lisa. That would always be a sore spot for her.

"Yes, you did. But what you don't realize is how much more patient I've been with you, Suzie Q. I stood by while you catered to your mother, your brothers, and your sister. I kept waiting for the day to come when you'd put me first. First you schemed to try to move your family in with us. Then you tried to manipulate me into feeling sorry for your mother when she couldn't pay her rent on time. And don't get me started on this whole thing with Gregory breaking up with Paige because he'd knocked up Kenya, and your involvement that you kept secret from me because you didn't want to give Paige an edge. And the way you stuck up for Derrick after I had proof he was stealing from us . . . I don't know if it's maturity or if I've become a chump in my old age, but the old me never would have stuck around this long. Or maybe it's just that I love you more than I loved Lisa."

Suzanne's breath caught in her throat. He'd never told her that before. She warned herself not to fall for any lines, but that was a sentence she'd always dreamed of hearing from him.

"I'm not in love with Micheline, Suzanne," Brad said softly. "I was unhappy, even unsure if I'd be able to go on with our marriage. She'd always been flirtatious with me, and I decided, why the hell not? I've been through hell with you these past few months. I felt I deserved to simply relax on a no-strings-attached basis."

"But there *are* strings, Brad. Micheline's not some anonymous warm body you picked up," she pointed out bitterly. "Not only are you and Errol Trent friends, but I'm acquainted with Micheline. That made it easy for her to come here and tell me she slept with you. She didn't have to do any research about you; she already knew where you live. There's a personal component to this whole thing that makes it incredibly complicated. Plus that much harder to get over. Maybe impossible," she added, her voice breaking.

"I know. It was a foolish thing to do, and I can't tell you how sorry I am to have put you in that position."

"There's already gossip going around about you and her."

"There is?" He seemed genuinely surprised.

Suzanne told him about what she heard from Flo.

"Damn it!" he exclaimed. "This is Darrell's fault. I asked him something a while back, just after the party. From that little question, he read my mind and figured out what I'd been thinking. He must have said something to Lisa, even though I told him not to."

She frowned. "So you *didn't* actually tell anyone you had an affair?"

"No, this was months ago. I'd noticed that Micheline was coming on to me, and . . . I just asked Darrell a simple question. It was a guy thing, like you and Paula engage in girl talk. I wouldn't tell anyone that I'd actually—you know that's not my style. I wouldn't set out to deliberately embarrass you, Suzie Q."

That meant no one knew anything for certain. A ray of sunshine began to peek through Suzanne's despair. No one had any proof that Brad had cheated on her. It was all gossip and innuendo, a prime example of how the grapevine could spread mere speculation just as quickly as the truth.

But a potentially huge problem existed. "Brad, Micheline told me she's pregnant."

"Not by me, she's not."

His confidence bolstered her. "Are you sure?"

"Suzanne, I may have been careless, even reckless, about some things, but not that. Micheline's got to be lying. She . . . um . . . got pretty angry with me when I told her we wouldn't be seeing each other when we got back home. She seemed to think I was going to tell you I wanted a divorce and take up with her."

Suzanne didn't doubt it.

"I hadn't counted on this," Brad remarked. "I had a lot of anger in me that needed to be set free. The fact that we've been so close since I've been back . . . it's not an act, Suzie Q. I just hope you meant what you said to me that day on the phone."

She knew he meant her promise that he and their family would always come first. "I meant it," she said in a trembling voice.

"I know you're angry at me. I know you're not sure if you want to continue being married to me after what I did," Brad said. "I can't say that I blame you. I had an affair with another woman, and now that you know about it, I'll have to accept whatever you decide. But I do love you, Suzie Q. I hope you'll consider that. I'm going to leave you alone now, let you think on it. You tell me what you want to do, whenever you're ready to talk." He fell silent, and when she didn't reply he said, "Is there something I can get you? Something to eat or drink?"

"No," she mumbled. "Just go."

Chapter 38

Micheline wiped down the built-in shutters of her bedroom. She wondered why she hadn't heard from Brad. Surely Suzanne had told him about her visit. She so enjoyed Suzanne's obvious discomfort when she announced the affair had left her pregnant. There was something unmistakable about the look of a person who learned that something they suspected was actually true. Suzanne might have thought she was covering nicely, but the slight quivering of her lower lip hinted at how she really felt.

Micheline knew she didn't have a chance with Brad; his rejection of a more permanent relationship between them was why she'd spoken to Suzanne in the first place. Still, she thought her actions would have elicited some kind of reaction out of him, especially with her claim of being pregnant. Or was Suzanne playing her bluff?

Micheline smiled slightly as she stretched to reach the top of the shutters. Brad could get away with ignoring the situation now, but once Errol learned of the seduction, she'd like to see Brad try to ignore *Errol's* wrath.

She waited until Errol scooped up the last of his pecan-crusted catfish. "Michie, you're a great cook, but I tell you, this catfish has got to be my absolute favorite." He patted his flat stomach. "I think it's about time for some racquetball to help me keep my shape."

Him and his racquetball. He spent more and more time down at that club pursuing his latest passion. If she didn't know better, she'd think he had someone on the side. He was probably trying to get into shape for the fatherhood he still thought would be coming within a year or so. "Um . . . before you go, Errol, there's something I have to tell you."

"Oh, yeah? Sounds serious."

"It is. I'm afraid I've done something awful."

"Well, *that* sounds ominous," he said, sounding almost cheerful.

A warning bell went off in Micheline's head. Errol was being entirely too cool about the whole thing. She'd noticed that about him lately and attributed it to his anticipation of an imminent pregnancy announcement from her, but now he was carrying it too far. He spoke with an almost flighty air, almost as if he didn't give a damn about what she'd done, or even about *her*. Errol had a naturally easygoing nature, but he could be as emotional as anyone else when circumstances called for it. He'd been so angry on her behalf when she told him about being "raped" and the resulting pregnancy. Her gut told her something wasn't quite right here, that he might not react the way she counted on, but she'd already opened the door. She had no choice but to walk through it. Still, if she was careful, she could probably feel him out a little more before giving him her news.

She hedged. "Oh, it's so hard to say. Maybe I should just forget about it."

"It shouldn't be hard," he said easily. "All you have to do is open your mouth and form the words."

No hint of concern or alarm, she noted. Something *definitely* was off. "I'm afraid I haven't felt very much appreciated lately, Errol," she began. "It started ever since I went back to work. I'm working full-time and still making you the dinners you love, still keeping the house clean, the laundry done, and you've never even commented on my efforts. It's like for you, nothing has changed."

He stuffed a large piece of fish into his mouth. "Believe me, I know things have changed."

It was a strange remark, cryptic almost. Micheline stared at him with uncertainty before continuing. "And, well, sometimes that's the only way a woman has to feel, and when another man comes up to her and compliments her on how she looks, it can be easy to fall into temptation."

He swallowed his fish and reached for his wineglass, and Micheline knew she'd gotten him thinking.

"Is that it?" he finally said, placing his glass down on the table. "You're telling me you had an affair?"

"I'm so sorry, Errol. I've regretted it since the moment it was over." Micheline injected remorse into her tone. "But I couldn't go on deceiving you. I had to confess."

"You must really think I'm stupid, Michie."

Micheline had cast her eyes downward, but her neck jerked as she raised her gaze. "What?"

"You heard me. The only reason you're making this 'painful confession' is because you've got an agenda. You've always had an agenda."

"What are you talking about?" she demanded indignantly, slamming her palms against the table and making the Chardonnay in their glasses slosh higher.

"I'm talking about how I saw your diaphragm. You know how badly I wanted children, and how concerned I was about getting older. All this time you pretended you wanted them, too, but you were making damn sure you *wouldn't* get pregnant. I knew from that moment our marriage was over. There could be no excuse for your deceiving me about something that meant everything to me."

"So why didn't you—"

"Why didn't I make my move before now? Because I saw no need to hurry. I figured obviously you aren't where you want to be, and you probably had a plan in place to leave me.

Why should I spend thousands of dollars to unload your ass if you'd do it first?" He looked at her, the corners of his mouth slightly turned up. "Besides, I had great meals, a clean house, starched shirts, and all the sex I wanted." He made a roaring sound in his throat.

Her nostrils flared in fury. He'd been using her all this time!

"So what happened, Michie?" he taunted. "Are you over-whelmed by guilt at what you've done? Have you decided you can't possibly stay with me? What'd you do, find some-body who won't object to your shopping sprees?"

Micheline averted her eyes from his sardonic stare. She struggled to control her anger at having been found out. She kept her diaphragm very carefully hidden in the cabinet under her sink. How had Errol stumbled across it if he hadn't been snooping?

Aloud she said, "Just because I have a diaphragm, Errol, doesn't mean I've been *using* it. That thing is older than dirt."

"Yeah, I considered that," he replied lazily. "And that's why I kept a close eye on that tube of lubricant you keep next to the case. It's being used regularly. But of course you already know that."

She rested her hands on her hips. "You've got a lot of nerve, spying on me."

"Why, Michie? Because I got wise to you?" He drained the rest of his wine. "I should think you'd be happy that I'm not going to stand in your way. Go on and go wherever it is you plan on going."

"Aren't you interested in knowing who I fell into tempta-tion with?"

He stared at her suspiciously. "I'm a poker player, Michie. I know that look people get when they've got a winning hand. Go ahead, spill it."

"None other than your good, good friend. Dr. Bradley Be-tancourt."

If this information startled him, he disappointed her by

not showing it. His expression didn't change at all. She was at a disadvantage. Errol had discovered her diaphragm months ago. In the time since he'd secretly washed his hands of her completely, but on the surface he continued to play the adoring husband, praising her cooking, making love to her most nights. . . . How could he have been so calculating? Other than his spending a heck of a lot of time playing racquetball and his becoming even more laid back than usual, she hadn't noticed anything really unusual, no hints that his feelings toward her had changed.

All Errol did was calmly nod and say, "That would be about right. He's a radiologist, brings in big bucks, lives in a house deserving of a cover story of *House and Garden*. A little old for you, but it probably helps that he's not short, fat, and bald. Let's see . . . did I leave anything out?"

She wanted to smack that grin off his face. He was laughing at her! "You're a smug bastard, you know that?"

"And you're the worst kind of bitch there is. You play with people's lives like they're pawns in a chess game, but this time you've lost. What happened, Michie?" Errol chuckled. "Did Brad refuse to leave Suzanne for you? Is that the reason for your big conscience-clearing confession? You want to make me so angry that I'll go after him and punch him out? Is that supposed to be his punishment?" He laughed again, and she found it unbearable and threw her cloth napkin at him. It clocked him in the face.

"Go to hell, Errol!"

"*I'm* not going anywhere, but you are."

Micheline swallowed hard. "What's *that* supposed to mean?"

"That means that when I get back from my game, I don't expect to see you here. Pack up your shit and get out." He met her eyes with a gaze of steel. "And don't even think about taking anything that doesn't belong to you."

Brad drove to the club, and he knew the moment he laid eyes on Errol's stormy expression that Micheline hadn't stopped at merely informing Suzanne of their dalliance. She'd told him, as well.

"I need to talk to you," Errol said without preamble.

"Why don't we go out back?" Brad suggested. "We can be out of anyone's range of hearing."

Silently, they went outside to the wraparound deck and then down the stairs, Errol leading the way down. Once on the ground, they walked on the immaculately manicured grass away from the rear of the club. When they were out of earshot, Brad began, "I have a feeling I know what this is about, Errol."

"I'm sure you do," Errol replied tightly. "And I just have one question for you." He paused, staring Brad down with a hostile gaze. "If I hadn't told you I was through with Micheline, would you have made a play for her?"

Brad, mindful of the setting, was determined to stay calm. He knew it would look awful for two of the club's few black members to get into a fistfight. "I think you know the answer to that is no."

"Yeah, well, I think *you* know you crossed the line. She's still my wife, Brad. And you were *supposed* to be a friend. For all you knew, I could have changed my mind and reconciled with her."

At Brad's quizzical expression he clarified, "I haven't. And if you and I were out in the street right now instead of at an upscale, conservative golf club, I'd be kicking your ass right now."

Brad didn't doubt it—at least the part that they would be tussling, not that Errol would win. Errol might be a dozen years younger, but Brad felt he could take him on. Clearly his onetime friend was equally conscious that this wasn't the place for a fight, but Errol's voice was filled with fury despite being low pitched, and Brad knew he'd broken the cardinal rule among males. You don't mess with another man's woman, even a woman he's about to dump. He listened with regret as Errol expressed those very thoughts.

"As a so-called friend of mine, you'd be out of line to take up with Michie even after the divorce, and you're sure out of line by taking up with her when she's still married to me. You and I both know that. You don't see me going after Suzanne, do you, now?" He stuffed his hands in his pockets and waited for Brad to respond.

Brad felt lower than low. He silently cursed Micheline for blabbing what should have been a quick and quiet affair out of spite. "I know that just saying 'I'm sorry' sounds lame," Brad said, "but I truly am. All I can say in my own defense, and you probably won't believe this, Errol, is that Micheline was sending out some very powerful signals my way. I'm afraid that, knowing your plans and all, I wasn't able to resist her charms. It was supposed to be a one-time thing," he continued. "I never had any intentions of continuing it, and when I told her that she got pretty steamed. She came to my house this afternoon when I was at work and told Suzanne about us, and I guess I'm not surprised she told you as well. Maybe that's why I came down here, while Suzanne is deciding whether or not to divorce me over this."

A strange look passed over Errol's face, and Brad could tell this news distressed him.

"I'm starting to learn more and more about the woman I married," Errol said bitterly. "If she doesn't get her way, she doesn't care whose life she ruins."

Brad sighed. "As much as I'd like to put the blame for this fiasco on her, I can't. I didn't really stop to think of the consequences."

They began walking back toward the clubhouse. "I'm not going to dispute the part you played in this, Brad," Errol said. "But I happen to know that this isn't the first time she's done something like this. You know, for a long time, I didn't understand why she and her sister didn't get along. Her sister, Cécile, is the sweetest woman you'd ever want to meet. And before I headed over here to confront you, I stopped by her house, and we had a nice chat about some of the things my wife has done."

They stopped walking when they reached the veranda. "Errol, I know you're pissed at me. Why don't you let me buy you a drink," Brad suggested. "Maybe we can start to put some of this bad blood behind us."

"Sorry, no. Frankly, Brad, I don't see us having drinks together. And right now there's someone I need to see."

Brad nodded, understanding. Had Errol been seeing the same woman all these months, or was this someone new? He didn't offer Errol his hand, and Errol walked off.

Brad went inside and sat on a bar stool, which he suspected would be his home for the next few hours.

Chapter 39

At nine-thirty Brad knew it was time to leave. He felt like a little kid who knew he was in trouble but had to head home.

Would Suzanne really leave him? The venom with which she'd looked at him earlier tonight said yes.

Good Lord, what would he do without her? Suzanne was everything to him, and the kids—including Paige—made up the rest. Nothing else rated nearly as high on the scale of what mattered most. Suzanne's lovely face was the first thing he saw in the morning and the last thing he saw when he closed his eyes at night. On those nights when he got to bed before she did, he'd grab her pillow and hold it close. The pillowcase retained her scent, and it was the next best thing.

How on earth would he get along without her?

He supposed he could fight a divorce. He'd tell her she'd have to be the one to leave the house. He really wouldn't do that, of course. This was not only Suzanne's home, but Bradley's and Lauren's as well. There was no point in his trying to hold on to the children. Suzanne had been home with them since they were born. They'd go wherever she went. But she wouldn't have to go anywhere. He'd be the one to move out if Suzanne decided she didn't want him anymore. It was only fair.

What a mess he'd made of everything. Not only did he

face the very real possibility of his family breaking up, but his friendship with Errol was over.

The house was quiet. Bradley and Lauren likely were still up, but in their rooms. He wondered if Suzanne had emerged from their bedroom at all since he left.

He thought he heard Suzanne speaking to someone as he stood on the other side of the door with his hand on the knob. Maybe Lauren had stopped in to check on her mother. He ruled that out when he heard no voice other than Suzanne's. She was talking on the phone, probably to her mother, but it might be Paula. Brad knew from Calvin Braxton that Arlene had been spending a lot of time with Calvin's father, Harry. Apparently Harry Braxton was quite captivated with her. Brad presumed Arlene was on her best behavior . . . and she was probably giving him some. If he knew Arlene, she thought she was on her way to Easy Street, but he knew it wouldn't be long before Arlene showed her fangs and old Harry would run for his life.

Brad entered the bedroom and quickly realized Suzanne was in the bathtub. It was her favorite way of relaxing, taking a long soak in the sunken Jacuzzi tub with plenty of bubbles, a plastic pillow, and one of those silly romance novels she loved to read. It had been her idea to install an extension in there.

"Mama, I'm sorry, but that's out of the question. Derrick made his bed; he'll have to lie in it. Nobody told him to drive off without paying for gas. And to run away from the police, well, that was *really* stupid."

Brad moved stealthily closer. It sounded like Derrick was in some kind of trouble with the law. That certainly came as no surprise, but Suzanne seemed to be standing up to her mother's pleas for help.

"No, I will *not* pay twenty-five hundred dollars to bail him out, Mom . . . I understand you don't want him sitting in jail . . . No, it's not *my* son sitting in jail. But if Bradley should ever think he can get away with driving off without paying after pumping a full tank of gas, he deserves to sit in jail, and I wouldn't bail him out, either. We taught him better than that . . . No, I don't mean to imply you were a bad mother."

Brad stood still as the night itself, not wanting Suzanne to know he'd entered the room. This was fascinating. So far Suzanne was saying everything he'd want her to say.

"Mama, I've been very good to Derrick. I've even given him a few dollars while he was between jobs so he wouldn't lose his car. But there's a big difference between two hundred dollars and twenty-five hundred. Even if I wanted to help him, and I don't, I couldn't do it without getting an okay from Brad. He doesn't even want Derrick in our house. Do you really think he's going to care if he's locked up? . . . Yes, that's my final answer. Derrick's a grown man. He needs to stop looking upon me as his fairy godmother. I won't help him anymore. He stole from Brad and me, and all that happened was that he lost his job. He stole from Shell Oil, and he's being prosecuted. His attitude is the same. 'They've got money. They can give me a little bit of what they've got.' He didn't learn a damn thing from that episode at Subway. I'm ashamed of myself for asking Brad to rehire him. Brad won't be surprised to hear he's behind bars, that's for sure.

"And there's something else. Remember when you told me that whatever I was doing to upset Brad, to stop doing it? *This* is what Brad doesn't like. You're always asking me to do something to help you, or Kenya, or Derrick. I always did what you asked, even if it meant going behind my husband's back. Well, even if Brad and I break up, I'm not doing it anymore."

Brad could stand it no more, and he rushed into the bathroom.

Startled, Suzanne's hand first flew to her chest, but she quickly relaxed upon seeing it was him. "I have to go now, Mom. Brad's home. I'll talk to you tomorrow . . . Tell him I said he blew it." She hung up. "You're back," she said flatly.

"Yes. And your brother's in jail."

Her eyebrows shot up. "You heard?"

"Everything. I thought you were great."

"Too little, too late," she muttered.

Brad knelt by the tub. "It's not too late, baby."

"Would you excuse me, please? I'd like to finish my bath—Brad! What're you doing?"

He knew his back would hurt him tomorrow, but he scooped her out of the tub. "Stop kicking me," he ordered. "I can't fight you and hold on to you at the same time. Do you want me to drop you?"

"Brad, what the hell do you think you're doing—ouch!" she exclaimed when he dropped her onto the mattress.

He quickly pinned her down before she could get up. "Listen," he said between breaths, "I thought you were great with your mother. You didn't buckle under, you didn't give in."

"What else could I do? Derrick's a slob. He'll never change." She made another effort to free herself, then stared at him meaningfully. "Now, will you let me get up? I'm wet, and I'm cold."

He glanced down at her breasts. "You're also naked."

"I usually am when I bathe. *Brad,*" she said, a warning in her tone.

"All right." He stood up, his eyes taking in her nude body before she rushed back into the bathroom and slammed the door. He'd hoped that if he made like one of the heroes of her romance novels and carried her off, she'd relent. He should have known it wouldn't be easy. He'd committed a serious offense, and the future of his marriage was by no means certain.

He jerked to attention when the bathroom door opened. Suzanne poked her head out. "By the way," she said, "there are several other places in this house where you can sleep. I suggest you find one."

She closed the door.

With a sigh, Brad headed off to sleep in the guest room.

Chapter 40

Cécile took a deep breath when she saw Micheline on the other side of the door. Leave it to her sister to show up unannounced during her work hours. Cécile knew what had brought Micheline to her house, and she was afraid Micheline was about to get the shock of her life.

She opened the door. "Hi," she said.

Micheline moved in for an air kiss. "Hi. I hate to drop in on you unannounced like this."

"Not a problem. Come on in."

They sat at the kitchen table, and Micheline accepted Cécile's offer of a toasted English muffin and coffee. "I'm afraid I'm in a bit of a jam," Micheline said. "You'd probably be bored by the details, but Errol and I have decided to separate. I'm moving out, and he's going to file for divorce. I'll be leaving Jacksonville eventually, but right now I need to stick around until the divorce."

"I'm very sorry to hear that, Michie. Errol is a good man."

"Yes, well, things just didn't work out. I stayed at the Marriott last night, but obviously I can't stay there for the next few months. I was hoping I could bunk with you guys. I'd pay you, of course."

"I'm sorry, Michie, but you'll have to find someplace else."

"*What?*" She practically choked on the word. "You're refusing me?"

"I have to. I can't take you in."

"I don't believe you're saying this to me! What would Mama and Papa say if they could hear you?"

"Don't even try to run that by me. I'm thirty-eight years old, not eight. You don't report me to our parents." Cécile leaned back in her chair and sipped her coffee. "And if you do, I guess I'll just have to tell them a few things about their youngest child."

Micheline stiffened. "Tell them what?"

"About all the trouble you've caused for my friends. You deliberately interfered with Dana at a time when she felt very unsure of herself. You slept with Norell's husband and had a baby by him."

"Dana's on much surer footing now, and as for Norell, well, ignorance is bliss."

"Except she's not ignorant. She knows, Michie."

Micheline's lower lip dropped. "She does?"

"She figured it out. She called me after she confirmed it with Vic." Cécile shivered at the memory. Never before had she heard her friend sound so despairing. "Hell of a spot you put me in. And I'm not going to let it happen again, Michie. Dana is getting married. The last thing I need is for you to come along and seduce her fiancé, for no other reason than because you can. I know you, Michie. When you're not happy— and you seldom are—you do whatever you can to destroy other people's happiness."

Micheline popped the last of her muffin into her mouth. "In that case, I thank you for breakfast, and I guess I'd better be on my way." Her chair legs scraped the floor as she hastily got up.

"Michie, I really am sorry," Cécile said with sincerity. "I wish things had worked out differently."

"It's all right, Cécile. I'll check into the Residence Inn. I'm sure I can work out a weekly rate with them. And at least I'm working. I won't have to use a whole lot of my savings." She smiled weakly. "'Bye."

Chapter 41

Six months later

Kenya sat in the courtroom, conservatively dressed in a tailored white blouse and navy pants, her long hair pulled back into a ponytail at the nape of her neck. The judge had yet to appear, and she tried to tell herself that it would all work out in her favor, that Gregory would never get away with what he was trying to do. She couldn't believe he'd been so sneaky as to actually film their bedroom and bathroom before she cleaned them up, plus the kitchen of Flo and Ernie's home in various states of disarray, and use it against her. He actually wanted custody of little Dillon.

She glanced behind her. Suzanne was in court today to offer moral support, and their mother sat next to her. Kenya wasn't sure why her mother had even bothered to come. She'd been so cranky for months lately. It wasn't fair, Kenya thought. Her mother had only herself and Derrick to blame for her present situation.

After Suzanne flatly refused to cough up Derrick's bail money, Arlene had turned to that judge she'd been dating, asking if he could help her. Apparently she'd made a gross miscalculation of judgment, for right after that her boyfriend was suddenly called back to tend to business in North Carolina, and he hadn't been heard from since. Arlene's dreams of remarrying a well-off man and retiring went out of the window.

With his bail unpaid, Derrick had no other option but to sit in jail until his case was ready to be heard, which took over two months. The presiding judge gave him six months, with credit for time already served, plus three years of probation. He'd just been released a few weeks before, and because he had no job and no prospects, Arlene now found herself supporting him.

The two of them were constantly at odds, with Arlene blaming Derrick for ruining her blossoming relationship with Harry Braxton. Shouting matches and slamming doors had become routine. Kenya envied Matthew, who'd gotten his degree in computer science and started a new job in software design. After just one week on his new job, he moved in with his longtime girlfriend, a nurse he'd met at the hospital, and he'd just presented her with an engagement ring. Matthew had been helping their mother financially, and his departure had given Arlene something else to complain about.

Kenya had found herself back at home when Gregory had her served with divorce papers just after New Year's, when Dillon was just three weeks old. He spoke to her about his plans beforehand, gallantly offering her the opportunity to do the filing. At first she feigned shock, telling him she thought they'd been happy. He retorted that all they'd been doing was just sticking it out until their baby was born, adding that while she might be happy, he was miserable. In less than a minute Kenya went from shocked surprise to sneering sarcasm, accusing him of being anxious to get rid of her so he could replace her with Paige. "You don't care about me, and you don't care about Dillon," she had accused.

"That's not true," Gregory replied calmly. "I love my son. And while I can't say I'm in love with you, Kenya, I do care about what happens to you. I'd like you to have a good and secure future."

His attempt to mollify her only infuriated her more. "Yeah, well, you can tell that to the judge, and that judge will make sure my future is taken care of. I can tell you now, there's not going to be a whole lot left over for you to spend on Paige after you finish taking care of me and our son."

"I have no responsibility to take care of you, Kenya. And as for Dillon, if you're going to have so much financial difficulty taking care of him—" Gregory broke off.

Kenya felt triumphant. It wasn't until a week later that she learned that Gregory's sudden lack of words wasn't due to defeat, but to the idea to sue for custody.

She'd taken the baby with her when she moved back into her mother's house, but she'd had to go back to work. She desperately needed money. For one, her mother was nagging her to death to help out with the rent. Even more important, she had to hire an attorney to represent her. She'd thought she could use Legal Aid, but her mother informed her that she believed that service was for people accused of crimes, not being sued for divorce.

Gregory had been quite generous with Dillon, paying the fees for him to attend an exclusive day-care center, even delivering him there and home again, since Kenya didn't have a car. She'd thought that was nice of him, but Gail Kendrick, her attorney, had told Kenya that would actually help him in his claim for custody.

Thank God for Suzanne. If it wasn't for her, Kenya would be sitting at this table alone. She had paid Gail's retainer, although she informed Kenya it was just a loan and that she'd have to give it back. A thousand dollars was a lot of money for someone who earned as little as she did. At least Suzanne wasn't in a hurry for it. It would probably take her a year.

Along with everyone else in the room, Kenya rose when the judge entered. She'd been overjoyed to see that the judge was a woman, probably a wife and mother herself, but Gail, her attorney, cautioned that didn't mean anything. It was that video Gregory had shot that hurt their case, she added.

Kenya felt Gail was overreacting. Sure, the house looked messy on the film, but Kenya felt certain that the judge understood that she hadn't felt well. She provided the letter from her obstetrician stating that she shouldn't be standing due to her back and hip pain and the swelling in her ankles, to back up her claim. Maybe it would have been better if she'd been reading something other than *Secrets of a Slut* during the footage of her floating in a pool chair, but it had been a good book, and not all that much more racy than the average daytime soap opera.

"Here she comes," Gail said softly as the judge emerged from her chambers. "Let's hope for the best."

"She won't take my baby away from me," Kenya said confidently as she, along with everyone else in the room, stood up. She looked at the other side of the courtroom. Gregory sat with his attorney at the front table, and behind him sat his parents. Just thinking about Flo's testimony yesterday still steamed Kenya. Flo hadn't said anything that technically wasn't true, but it made her look really bad. Fortunately, when Gail put Kenya herself on the stand, she was able to undo some of the damage, recounting how pregnancy hadn't really agreed with her, that she'd gone from the morning sickness in the beginning to painful sciatica as the baby grew inside her. Yes, she'd suggested that her mother-in-law hire a housekeeper, but out of a growing fear that she simply wasn't physically capable of keeping her part of the house up to Flo's high standards. "It's not like I didn't *want* to keep everything spotless; I just couldn't," she explained. "My mother-in-law had an easy time when she was pregnant. She doesn't understand how it was for me."

Judge Carol Jankowski was seated, and the bailiff instructed everyone else to follow suit. The room remained silent while the judge put on her glasses and went over her laptop screen. Finally she cleared her throat.

Her first words were to grant the divorce. It amazed Kenya

how simple it sounded. Just like that, she was no longer married, but a divorcée.

"As for the custody of Dillon Hickman," the judge stated, "I've gone over all the testimony from both sides. I have no doubt that both Mr. Hickman and Mrs. Hickman love their infant. Even though both husband and wife admit that they married only for the legitimacy of their unborn child, I'm rather saddened that the relationship failed. However, Mr. Hickman and Mrs. Hickman are both adults. It's the welfare of the child that I have to be concerned with.

"I have to say I was appalled at the contents of the video of the unkempt, slovenly conditions under which Mrs. Hickman kept the private and shared areas of the house of her parents-in-law. Not only did Mr. Hickman provide absolute proof of the untidiness of the house, he showed simultaneous footage of Mrs. Hickman not lying in bed ill, but lounging in the pool engrossed in a book at the same time. It makes me consider that if Mrs. Hickman had such little interest in housekeeping while she was a stay-at-home mother, the environment will only worsen after her return to full-time work. It's neither safe nor healthy to raise a child in such a disheveled setting, whether it is within the home of in-laws or the home of parents, or even a home of her own." Judge Jankowski paused for a moment and looked at both parties.

"Normally, the custody of a child this young is awarded to the mother. . . ."

Kenya gasped. *Normally?* Was the judge actually going to award custody of Dillon to the care of Gregory? That meant Paige would be seeing him! Jealousy seethed in her chest at the thought of her son developing a relationship with her archenemy. Hell, Gregory would probably have Dillon believing Paige was his mother!

". . . and because of the close proximity of the residences of the senior Mr. and Mrs. Hickman and Dillon Hickman's maternal grandmother, Arlene Hall," Judge Jankowski continued, "and because of the testimony from Mr. Ernest Hickman and Mrs. Florence Hickman to assist their son with Dillon's care, I hereby grant the custody of Dillon Hall Hickman to his father, Gregory Hickman. Kenya Hickman shall have unsupervised visitation rights for one day per week for up to ten hours, plus visitation of up to four hours two additional days per week. Gregory Hickman must continue to live within one mile of Kenya Hickman's current residence. I also order Kenya Hickman to pay Gregory Hickman the sum of thirty-five dollars per week for child support. This matter will be revisited in one year's time, with a possible switch in custody if Mrs. Hickman has shown to my satisfaction that she can provide a healthy and safe environment for what will by then be an active toddler." She banged her gavel. "That's it. We're adjourned."

Kenya held her face in her hands and sobbed, comforted by her attorney. "It's not the end of the world," Gail said. "You'll be able to visit the baby often, and in a year's time you might get shared or even full custody."

Suzanne moved forward and embraced her sister. "I'm so sorry," she told Kenya. "But you'll still have a relationship with Dillon, and maybe next year you'll actually get custody."

"A whole year. Do you know how long that is from now?" Kenya choked out between sobs.

"Oh, sweetheart." Suzanne looked to her mother for help. After Arlene had taken Kenya's hand, Suzanne turned to thank Gail for her services before the attorney left.

"You really should've listened to me, Kenya, and you would still be married, much less not having to worry about losing custody," Arlene said bluntly.

"Mom!" Suzanne exclaimed. "Is that really necessary?"

"It's the truth. I'm sorry if it hurts."

Suzanne rolled her eyes. Her mother was still sulking because she'd scared Harry Braxton off with her request for money.

"Come on, Kenya," Arlene said. She slipped her arm through

that of her daughter. "We'll meet you outside, Suzanne," she said as they headed for the door.

Suzanne felt protocol dictated that she say something to the Hickmans, so she took it upon herself.

"This is difficult," she said without preamble to Gregory and his parents, "but what counts is that Dillon will receive the best of care. And for what it's worth, I never felt that Kenya was emotionally ready to be a mother or a wife. Marriage can be tough." *Don't I know it.*

"Thanks, Suzanne," Flo said.

"No hard feelings," Ernie added.

"I'd really like for things to go smoothly between Kenya and me, Mrs. Betancourt," Gregory said. "Look at how well you and Mrs. Canfield get along. You guys are kind of like role models for me."

Suzanne smiled. Now, *that* was funny.

Micheline ran the tip of her index finger over the official seal on her divorce decree. Her marriage to Errol was officially over, and she had her maiden name of Mehu restored. She'd given her notice at the hospital, and she'd worked her last day. Now that there was nothing to hold her in Jacksonville, she looked forward to getting out.

She'd half expected Errol to look at her with undisguised longing in his eyes that day in court when the divorce was granted. He hadn't done that, and nor had he glared at her in anger. Instead, he barely looked her way at all, and when she sneaked a glance his way, he wore an eager look, as if he was excited about the prospect of legally severing their relationship.

As for Brad Betancourt, Micheline hadn't seen him since she stormed out of his Maine cabin and drove back to Logan Airport, and took the first flight she could get back to Jacksonville. She wondered if he'd patched things up with Suzanne. It would be just like her to be wussy enough to take him back.

But that was *her* problem. Suzanne slipped her divorce papers inside a large goldenrod envelope, then tucked the envelope into the zippered compartment of her suitcase. The rest of her clothes had been shipped to the apartment she'd rented in her new location. All that was left to do was check out of this hotel where she'd been living and drive away.

She'd heard such wonderful things about Atlanta, and she looked forward to getting up there and starting afresh. Micheline Mehu was about to take the town by storm!

After leaving the courthouse, Suzanne met with Paula for business planning. "We've got a slow period coming up," Suzanne remarked. "It might be a good time to take a vacation, before all the weddings start up next month."

"Funny you should mention that. I'm going to need to take a week off," Paula replied. "Do you think you can hold down the fort? I have no events planned for the week I'll be away, but you'd have to take inquiries, maybe even solidify bookings."

"I can handle it," Suzanne said confidently. "So, what are your plans?"

"Um . . ." Paula gave an embarrassed chuckle. "Actually, I'm going on a honeymoon."

Suzanne gasped. "You're getting married! Paula Haines, you've been holding out on me. I had no idea it was so serious between you and the construction guy that used to work for you."

"That's just it, Suzanne. It's not the construction worker."

Suzanne's forehead wrinkled. "Not the construction worker?" she repeated. "But isn't he the one you've been seeing all these months? The one you talked about adopting some kids with?"

"I guess I owe you an apology. You just assumed it was him when I mentioned I had a new man in my life. I was trying to figure out how to tell you, and then when you made that assumption, I decided it would probably be best if I could keep it to myself, so I didn't bother to correct you."

"But I still don't get it, Paula. You said this was some married guy who helped you out at Brad's party. If it's not the waiter, who was it?"

"Errol Trent."

Suzanne's lower lip dropped open. "Errol?" she repeated. "Micheline's ex?"

"Yes. I've been seeing him for a year now. That night of Brad's party. I was posing for pictures with Lisa and the girls. He came up to me and offered to be the cameraman so I could be in the pictures, too. We made a little small talk, I gave him my card, and that was pretty much it.

"But then a couple of weeks later he called me," Paula continued. "He was very honest. He told me he'd just discovered his wife had lied to him about something of great importance to him, and that he was quietly going to get his affairs in order before he filed for divorce, and not let on that anything was wrong. He invited me to lunch." A dreamy smile formed on Paula's lips as she recalled the memory. "He said he would understand perfectly if I chose not to go, since he was a married man. Of course, he stressed that it was only for lunch." She shrugged. "I figured I had nothing to lose. I'd gotten good vibes from him in the brief time I spent with him at your place, but Suzanne . . . by the end of that lunch, I swear, I was falling in love."

"No wonder you didn't want to tell me," Suzanne marveled. "His being married and all."

"Yes. And then, after a few months, it became clear that my keeping quiet would save both you and me a lot of embarrassment."

As realization dawned on her, Suzanne's face burned. "You know, then," she said softly. "About Brad and Micheline."

"Yes. I'm so sorry, Micheline. Errol told me about it the night he confronted Brad at the club. I want you to know, I felt just awful knowing about it and not being able to say anything to try to comfort you. Not that you asked me for advice," she quickly added. "But I couldn't take the chance of it getting back to Micheline that Errol and I were seeing each other. It would have given her something to use against him in the divorce."

Suzanne nodded. "And I wish all the best to you and Errol." She grinned, still taken by the surprise development. "So your dream of having another family is going to come true after all."

"Well, not right away. We agreed to take a year and just enjoy each other, make sure we work as a couple. I'm sure a marriage of at least one year would be a requirement anyway for anyone who wants to adopt a child, but it's also important to us. Let's face it, Suzanne. This will be Errol's second marriage and my third. We don't exactly have the best track record in the world."

"Paula, I'm not trying to be mean or anything, but don't you think you and Errol will be considered too old to adopt a baby?"

"We decided to skip the babies and go straight to older children."

"Children?" Suzanne repeated, surprise in her voice.

"Yes, probably boys. Errol is very concerned about the plight of the black male. You know, that's what destroyed his marriage to Micheline. She was supposed to be trying to get pregnant for the last year and a half, but Errol found her diaphragm hidden under the sink when he was looking for something else."

"That sounds like something she'd do."

"She actually already has a baby. She told Errol she'd been raped, but what really happened was that she had an affair with the husband of her sister's best friend and got pregnant from that."

"Yeah." Suzanne nodded thoughtfully. Norell Bellamy had invited her to little Brianna's fourth birthday party a few weeks ago, and when she saw the little girl again she continued to be struck by the resemblance between her and Micheline. Then she remembered what Micheline had said that awful afternoon when she came to the house and told her she'd spent a week with Brad up in Maine. *I've already had one pregnancy because of a torn condom. And the father brought home the little bundle of joy for his wife to raise.* At that moment she knew the source of Brianna's almond-shaped eyes.

It looked like Suzanne and her old friend had more in common than Norell would ever know.

Flo took a deep breath. Something about the smell of a home improvement store made her wish she could redecorate her entire house. Everywhere she looked, she saw something she'd love to have. All those wonderful faucet fixtures, exotic sinks, and shiny new appliances.

She cast a look of longing over at the imported Brazilian cherrywood. Suzanne and Brad's house had always had tile floors, and Stacy and Ben Prince had just replaced their carpets with wood. That wall-to-wall carpeting she and Ernie had looked terribly outdated. Besides, who needed carpet in Florida?

But she shouldn't be thinking about redoing her floors right now. That wasn't why she and Ernie had come here.

They made their way to the paint section. "Paint would be cheaper," Flo cautioned when Ernie stopped to study a sample of textured wallpaper.

"Come on, Flo. Now that we know Dillon will be staying with us, we both want him to have the best. Wouldn't this look a whole lot nicer than painting his room primary colors?"

"We still have to buy his furniture. Someone in this family has to be the voice of reason, Ernie."

He put his arm around her. "We agreed we'd get furniture that he can continue to use all through his childhood. The only thing we'll have to do is switch out his crib for a bed when he's old enough. None of that nursery stuff that he'll be too old for by the time he's two. Think of how much money we'll be saving."

"Why do I always let you talk me into things?"

He kissed her. "It's going to be a lot of fun having a baby in the house again."

Gregory picked up his son, the tiny person who just four months ago hadn't even existed and who was now the most important person in his life. "Well, Dillon, it's going to be just you and me. Plus Grandma and Grandpa. I want you to love your mommy, but there's someone else I want you to meet. You do your old man proud, huh?" He placed the child into his car seat in the back of the car and secured him inside it. Then he hopped in the driver's seat and took off.

Thinking about being with Paige again had kept him going during those miserable months he spent with Kenya. He was ashamed to admit it, but even during sex, he imagined Paige was his partner, not Kenya. It pained him to know that Paige was dating other guys, but he knew he had no right to object, not when he was sleeping with Kenya.

It only took a few minutes to get to the restaurant. He would have loved to have driven around the corner and picked Paige up, but she'd been right to say they should wait for that. Dr. Betancourt had told him his wish for Paige to fall in love with a guy who didn't have the responsibilities of fatherhood. Neither he nor Mrs. Canfield would be happy about this.

Gregory, on the other hand, was thrilled. He wanted Paige to get to know Dillon, and for Dillon to get to know Paige. He couldn't expect, or even hope, to shut Kenya out, but Paige was the woman for him. He was going to start to convince her of that right away.

She was waiting at a table when he and Dillon went inside. All Gregory could do was stare at her. She looked great. He'd missed her so much.

He bent and kissed her cheek. "Thanks for meeting me here."

"It's good to see you, Gregory. It's been a long time," she said softly. "So you're really a free man, huh?"

"Yes. But things won't be the same, Paige. They can't be. Too much has changed." He looked into the face of his son.

"Let me see him."

He slid into the booth next to her and sat Dillon up. "Dillon, say hello to Paige, a very special friend of your daddy's." Gregory held his breath. All he'd need was for Dillon to start wailing.

"Hello, Dillon," Paige said, smiling.

The baby gurgled, cooed, and finally laughed, displaying a toothless mouth and looking like a gnome.

"Oh, look, he smiled at me!" Paige exclaimed. She immediately leaned in and started making silly little baby noises, accompanied by funny faces.

Gregory knew then that it would be all right. And why wouldn't it be? Paige had been raised with a stepsister. Her parents, though long divorced, had maintained a good relationship over the years. Naturally Paige wouldn't be daunted by the idea of being a stepparent, not when she had grown up with a stepfather.

Her attitude was a great compliment to her parents. Gregory could only hope that maybe one day they would realize that.

Suzanne headed home after her meeting with Paula. She pulled into the driveway and went inside. She had some time to chill before starting dinner; the kids wouldn't be home from school for another two hours.

She heard splashing coming from the pool and went to investigate. She smiled at the sight of Brad swimming laps, moving so gracefully with smooth, even strokes over and under the water. With all the tension surrounding Kenya's divorce, she'd forgotten today was his early day at work.

She watched him through the glass door of the breakfast nook, a bittersweet feeling in her heart. She loved him still, and despite knowing the part she played in his weeklong affair, it nevertheless continued to take great struggle to try to put it out of her mind.

It had been a difficult six months, not just for them, but for their children as well. It hadn't been possible to shield Bradley and Lauren from all the discord between them, and it broke Suzanne's heart that both children feared they would divorce. She wanted her children's lives to be happy and stress free, not full of worry about the future of their family.

Brad was aware of Bradley and Lauren's concerns as well, and one night he got them all together and addressed it. Suzanne stood quietly off to the side as he spoke, having no idea what he was about to say and worried he might give the intimate details. "I know you've noticed some things have changed lately between your mother and me and you're wondering what happened. Well, I'll tell you. . . ."

Suzanne had held her breath, relaxing at his next words.

"One day both of you will find out that when you're married and have children, that in spite of being a family, what goes on between you and your spouse is private from your kids, both the good and the bad. So the reason for the shift in our sleeping arrangements is strictly between your mother and me."

"Can you tell us if you're going to break up?" Bradley had asked.

"Will we have to move?" Lauren echoed, fear in her voice.

"Hold on. You're getting way ahead of yourselves. It's true that your mom is very upset with me, and she has every right to be. I'm trying to get back into her good graces. It'll probably take some time, but I think I'll be able to charm her. So try not to worry that we're going to break up."

Three long months passed before she and Brad resumed living as husband and wife. It happened on Christmas Eve. They normally spent the holiday in Maine, something they both knew was now out of the question. They had driven up to Georgia for Thanksgiving to spend that holiday with Brad's family, with Suzanne and Lauren sleeping in the bedroom portion of their hotel suite and Brad and Bradley in the sitting area. Suzanne knew she would always be grateful that Paige had chosen to remain in Jacksonville with the Canfields.

Suzanne liked to think that what went on behind closed doors was their own family business, and that as far as the neighbors were concerned there were no clues that Brad no longer slept in the master bedroom. As weeks passed with no resolution in sight and the worries of Bradley and Lauren increased, it dawned on Suzanne that perhaps her secret wasn't so secret after all, and from a source she never would have suspected . . . her own children.

Lauren had always idolized her big sister, and Suzanne couldn't shake the uneasy feeling that her daughter had confided in her sister about her fears. It was yet another example of their family dynamic biting Suzanne in the ass. She absolutely hated the idea of Paige running to Lisa with the details about Suzanne's private life with Brad, but yet she didn't feel it would be right for her to instruct Lauren not to share details about her concerns with Paige. Not only had Brad insisted that Paige have all rights and privileges as his other children, but Lauren was approaching that age where she would confide in her sister before Suzanne. Suzanne remembered her own teenage years, and from the standpoint of a parent, she knew it would be a benefit to have her daughter's closest confidante be another member of their family. Paige would come to her and Brad if she learned Lauren was involved in anything they needed to know about, confidence aside.

On Christmas Eve Lauren asked Suzanne if the conflict between her and Brad was almost over, and Suzanne used that opportunity to ask her daughter if she'd spoken about the situation to Paige. She'd been unable to contain her emotions when Lauren admitted she had. The combination of them having to spend Christmas here in Jacksonville instead of the traditional winter wonderland setting of Maine because of the stain left by Brad's affair with Micheline there, along with the knowledge that Lisa and her cronies knew of the dissension in her marriage, had just been too much. When Lauren had been unable to comfort her, she ran for Brad, who held her while she sobbed and eventually managed to calm her down. He'd stayed with her that night and every night since.

For Suzanne it had nevertheless been a miserable holiday. Her mother and brothers were dining with Flo and Ernie, and she imagined everyone would fuss over baby Dillon, just two weeks old on Christmas Day. Brad had accepted Lisa's invitation to join the Canfields. Suzanne didn't know how she could face Lisa under these circumstances. Paige, of course, had no idea why Brad had been banished from their bedroom, but Lisa could easily put two and two together and get four. Suzanne wanted to make an excuse to skip it, but her pride wouldn't let her. Brad's affair becoming public knowledge was one thing. Having it drive her into hiding was something else.

In the end she attended with her head held high, but it had been the hardest thing she'd ever done. Fortunately, Lisa did no gloating. If anything, when the two of them talked, Lisa seemed mostly concerned with Paige. "I'm glad you and Brad and the kids stayed in Jacksonville for Christmas this year," Lisa told Suzanne that afternoon when the two of them were alone. "Paige really needs to have her daddy near her. She's been real antsy lately. I know she's waiting for Gregory to file for divorce."

"I thought she was seeing someone," Suzanne said. She felt a little bolstered by Lisa's intimation that Paige was the reason she and Brad remained in Jacksonville, not his affair.

"She's gone on a number of dates, but nothing stuck. I'm afraid she's convinced herself that Gregory is the only man for her. I don't want her to rush into anything, Suzanne."

"I understand. I'd feel the same if it was Lauren."

In the three months since, Suzanne felt reasonably certain that Brad would never cheat on her again. The stars in her eyes had dulled somewhat and the healing between them continued, but in her heart Suzanne knew she loved Brad more than ever.

She stood there watching him swim the length of the pool for several minutes before finally going outside.

"Hey!" he said when he noticed her approach. He swam over to the side of the pool and climbed out. "How'd it go?"

"The divorce went through. Gregory was awarded custody, at least temporarily. Kenya has visitation rights, and Gregory is required to remain living within a mile of my mother's house so Kenya can get to Dillon easily."

Brad took a moment to absorb the information. "Not a bad ending."

"The judge said she wants to review it in a year's time. Maybe by then Kenya will have more on the ball." She suddenly felt shy. "Brad, I want to thank you for letting me help my sister with an attorney. I promise she'll pay us back."

"It really wouldn't have been fair for her to go into court without representation, or with a bozo from Legal Aid." Brad had clarified for Kenya that the public defender represented those accused of crimes, and Legal Aid worked with civil matters like divorce. "I just hope everything will work out with Paige, now that Gregory's single again. Lisa's worried sick that they might do something rash, like get married."

"Paige and Gregory are adults, Brad," Suzanne pointed out. "All of us probably need to just step back and let them handle their business."

"Have you thought about how ironic it would be if Paige ended up marrying Gregory and raising Kenya's child?" he asked. "Kind of like me and Lisa and Darrell with Paige."

"As long as they don't end up living next door to each other," she said with a smile. "Seriously, the possibility did occur to me. Talk about irony."

"Right now it's still just a possibility."

Suzanne nodded. "But if it does happen, I'll definitely have something to say to Kenya about it."

He frowned at her. "Suzie Q, I thought we agreed not to—"

"I would tell her that it would be a big waste of energy for her to be jealous of Paige," she said. "That she should concentrate on making something of herself. That's a lesson I learned firsthand."

"I'm proud of you, baby." Brad shivered. "It's kind of chilly out here, isn't it?"

"That's because it's barely seventy degrees today. Good thing the pool is heated."

He stood up and toweled off. "I'm going in to warm up in the shower. I'll see you in a few." He got up and gave her a careful kiss, then scurried into the house.

She watched him go, and after he disappeared inside she took a deep breath. In some ways her life was better than it had been a year ago. She had purchased a twenty-five percent interest in Discriminating Taste. Maybe the catering business wasn't rocket science, but she was learning, and that was already a good thing. And her bond with Brad, so tenuous just a few months ago, was well on its way to becoming stronger than ever.

Sometimes she wondered how Norell had coped with knowing Vic cheated on her. Suzanne hated to be judgmental, but she simply couldn't imagine actually raising the proof of her husband's affair. Of course, she didn't know the background story, and she probably never would. Norell hadn't mentioned that Brianna wasn't her natural child, and of course Suzanne would never let on to Norell that she knew about Brianna's parentage. She'd respect Norell's privacy, the way she would want Norell to respect hers if the tables were turned.

That Micheline had left her mark on everyone, Suzanne thought angrily. She'd come close to destroying Suzanne's marriage to Brad, and even though the Bellamy marriage had recovered, it had to have been shaken by the affair and Brianna's birth. And Suzanne's happiness for Paula for having found what looked like true love was dampened by the knowledge that they would never be able to socialize with their men, not with the fractured relationship between Brad and Errol. Micheline was like an inherited disease . . . she just kept on giving.

Suzanne didn't know what happened to Micheline, nor did she care. That woman was a curse on anyone she came into contact with. Suzanne doubted Micheline would ever be happy.

She smiled. In spite of everything she'd been through, if anyone asked her to describe her life in one word, that was precisely what she'd reply. *Happy.*

She had a full life, a rewarding career that gave her plenty of time for her family, and she could and would include Kenya. Her sister would need guidance as she tried to reconstruct her life and find her niche. Suzanne would offer her the opportunity to make some extra money and perhaps learn about the catering business, for she and Paula always needed help. It might be good for Kenya. She was only twenty-three. Matthew had been older than that when he went back to school, and he was doing fine. Suzanne had to do what she could to prevent Kenya from becoming an embittered alcoholic from a lifetime of depending on others to improve her life, like their mother and Derrick.

Suzanne feared for Derrick's future. Would he ever be able to find someone willing to hire him, now that he had a record?

The sound of the phone ringing made her run inside to pick it up. "Hello," she said breathlessly.

"Suzanne, it's me. I was hoping you'd be able to help me out. My rent is due next week, and I'm about two hundred dollars short. My food bills have skyrocketed since Derrick's been out of jail—"

"Sorry, Mom," Suzanne interrupted. "This is where I came in."

"I don't know what's gotten into you lately. Don't you care what happens to us?"

"Mom, you're going to have to make a hard decision about what to do about Derrick. You're going to be retiring in just a few years. Do you really want to be taking care of him the rest of your life? But your most immediate move probably should be to give up the house rental and downsize into an apartment. Get a two-bedroom and let Derrick sleep on the couch if you need to so you can conserve some cash."

Silence. Finally Arlene replied, "I guess I'll look into that, since *you're* no help."

"Gotta go, Mom." She hung up, shaking her head. Whoever said it sure had it right: The more things changed, the more they stayed the same. Her mother would likely keep trying, but Suzanne had finally accepted that she wasn't accountable for the lives of her mother and siblings. She knew where her loyalties and responsibilities lay, and she would do everything she could to see that they were met. If she could be successful in her quest, that was enough.

At least for Suzanne Betancourt of Jacksonville.

TROUBLE DOWN
THE ROAD

BETTYE GRIFFIN

ABOUT THIS GUIDE

The questions and discussion topics that follow
are intended to enhance your group's
reading of this book.

DISCUSSION QUESTIONS

1. How should Suzanne have handled news of Kenya's pregnancy with regard to Brad?

2. Both Brad and Lisa felt Paige was too young (twenty-one) to take up with a man with a child. Do you agree or disagree?

3. Do you think Errol acted too hastily when he discovered Micheline's diaphragm?

4. Should Flo have kept quiet about the gossip she overheard in the restroom, as Ernie suggested? Or did she do the right thing by sharing it with Suzanne?

5. Errol Trent prefers to adopt boys because of his concern over the plight of the black male. Do you feel black boys are at more risk than black girls?

6. Do you think Norell, who already dealt with a major blow in her marriage to Vic, made a wise decision after she learned the rest of the story regarding Brianna's birth?

7. What about Suzanne's decision regarding her marriage to Brad? Do you believe they will heal, and that Brad's affair truly was a one-time thing—or do you see him cheating on her again?

8. What do you think Brad and Suzanne should do with his vacation home in Maine, now that it was the setting of his affair with Micheline?

9. Do you think Micheline will ever truly be happy?

10. Where do you imagine Kenya will be in five years? Arlene? Derrick?